GW00691441

About the author

Martin Morton lives mostly in the Adriatic on a boat.

Visit Martin Morton at www.martinmorton.co.uk

Catch Me

BOOK 5 OF THE CLAUDIA SERIES

Martin Morton

Catch Me

BOOK 5 OF THE CLAUDIA SERIES

Chimera

CHIMERA PAPERBACK

© Copyright 2021
Martin Morton

A CIP catalogue record for this title is
available from the British Library.

ISBN 978 1 903136 72 0

Chimera is an imprint of
Pegasus Elliot MacKenzie Publishers Ltd.
www.pegasuspublishers.com

First Published in 2021

Chimera
Sheraton House Castle Park
Cambridge England

Printed & Bound in Great Britain

Catch Me
The Claudia Series Book 5

Other titles in the series:

The Water's Edge;

The Water's Depth;

Careless Hours;

The Mist in the Valleys

Introduction:

Hi, and welcome.

I very much hope you will enjoy the unfolding story. Catch Me is about a further phase in our characters' lives; yet it is a complete story in itself.

For the new readers, however, I thought an introduction might be helpful.

Peter Dickinson, having disentangled himself from a well-plotted and potentially ruinous divorce, is keen to restructure his corporation.

Claudia Brodie, the chief of his Industry Division, and now his life-partner, is also keen to step back from an active role.

The restructuring creates opportunities for the heads of his three main sectors (Tony King and Henry Gideon on investment funds; Alphonse Newman in properties, and now resorts; and Tania Gunter, stepping up to replace Claudia as head of the industry group) to expand their businesses with the proceeds of Peter's restructuring. They begin to compete for the new resources.

Meanwhile Jack Stephens, Claudia's old lover, has become head of Collins, with which the Dickinson Group has close connections, and interactions, and therefore complexities, are unavoidable.

I hope you find the story absorbing and entertaining,
Martin

Catch Me

Words splash like stars
From the hem of the wizard's cloak,
Bewitching, bedazzling,
Or merely puzzling?
See me run, see me spin,
See me fly.
Catch me!

Glittering feet
Hypnosis of sensuous music,
Effortless posture,
Timelessly fragile.
See me run, see me spin,
See me dance,
Catch me!

Snotty-sleeved rascal,
Old patches on both dirty knees,
Weeping and laughing,
Tormenting, stealing.
See me run, see me spin…
See me stumble.
Catch me!

Chapter 1

The email had come out of the blue:

Dear Jack,

Before you instantly delete, be assured this is not an attempt to resurrect a relationship. I wish, with one narrowly defined exception, to make no reference to things past and I would ask you, if my proposition appeals to you, to observe a similar discipline.

I am inevitably confronted with the outline of your life but have achieved, I assure you, a reasonable detachment from it and have avoided delving into the details that I could easily inspect. So, I have no idea if my proposition will meet any currently unfulfilled needs of yours.

We spent a year or so developing an arrangement that I think we both found ultimately satisfying. At the very least we were able to scratch that big itch that we both felt.

I will comment only on this area of my life and hope and expect that you will similarly restrict yourself. You are aware that I had sought this narrow area of satisfaction unsuccessfully for many years and I was very content with the arrangement we reached, and I think it also filled what had become a gap in your life.

I have made no real attempt to find a similar arrangement since then. My past experiences have taught me that this would be a forlorn and frustrating quest — I leave aside 'undignified' and 'dangerous', because they somehow are part of the experience when it is satisfactory, as it undoubtedly became for me.

So, my question is, and I am feeling brave enough to be very blunt, is our arrangement something you would like to practise again? I envisage using my apartment, so you would leave when you are ready. I envisage the arrangement to be entirely non-verbal (and, from my perspective, non-visual), and non-penetrating. I would supply the implements. And, here my boldness fails me a little, I would also supply the tissues. In other words, I would prefer us both to climax at the end of the session, but would be content to operate as we did before we developed our arrangement that far. (You would be the one with the subsequent and difficult, I always found, car journey home.)

Any instructions you wish to give, e.g. on clothing, posture, situation, implements themselves, should be sent by email prior to the meeting.

Would you have any interest in reviving an arrangement of this sort?

Lavinia.

It took him two weeks and three drafts to reply. In the end it was simple, he needed to respond to a straightforward request. He could, and did, overthink her thoughts and feelings — and dwelt too long on his own scars. He felt ignoble about how he'd left the relationship, she'd taken a big risk to help someone else and he'd allowed that to come between them. But he'd already ruined one other relationship by focusing too narrowly on himself and what suited him, and maybe those scars were even deeper. He still thought about Claudia too often to risk contacting Lavinia again.

But she had contacted him, with a need he could understand.

And a need he shared.

He enjoyed occasional partners and had even drifted into an almost-relationship at one point but neither of two important things had happened: he hadn't felt truly engaged by anyone; and, while a surprisingly large number had enjoyed, even encouraged, some hard slaps when coming, a few had even liked the paddle, but none had wanted to make a real ceremony of it, and he missed that.

And Lavinia clearly missed it. Could he trust her not to try to re-engage emotionally? She was going to some lengths to limit that danger, he should respect that.

So, in agreeing he would doubtless be being selfish, but he finally persuaded himself — guided, he conceded, in large measure by his lower brain — he would be satisfying Lavinia too. It would just be important to get the tone right.

Dear L,

My short answer is yes, and thank you. I agree to all your conditions.

I will expect you to make yourself available at six p.m. on Friday next.

You should find a means of enabling me to access your apartment. I will, of course, be exactly punctual. I expect to find you over the back of the armchair in your living room, wearing a skirt lifted above your waist, a garter belt with stockings, and no underwear.

On the table to the side I expect to find a leather paddle and a thick cane (sixty centimetres long, one centimetre diameter) plus a bottle of water, a glass, and a bottle of Lagavulin twenty-five.

You should expect to receive twenty stokes on each side with the bare hand, thirty in total with the paddle and forty with the cane.

I expect to bring you to a climax in the usual fashion after the spanking and you must then expect to receive me as in our original arrangement.

Yours

J

Next Friday was three days. If he waited longer, he might lose courage.

Chapter 2

Claudia wasn't sure that Tania would even be impressed, let alone convinced, but Peter always loved to choreograph a little drama.

He'd asked Alphonse to move swiftly when the floor three levels above the existing New York office had become available. She never enquired how they managed the property sector so harmoniously, but she was aware that Alphonse always ensured that the lease, which his property division would acquire, could be profitably let to the other Dickinson businesses, and she knew that Peter was always sharp enough, on their behalf, to avoid overpaying — even though it would be, and here she laughed at her own observation, robbing Peter to pay Peter. She wondered, however, whether Will, now CFO of the whole group, would be quite so comfortable when he was informed of the costs of his new home.

But probably he'd be sharing them anyway.

Peter was expecting him to share space and costs with the new Group CEO, but the new Group CEO, now coming up in the elevator, was completely unaware of her impending appointment. Claudia had warned him against expecting a grateful acceptance. She didn't know what to expect, there could even be a complete refusal, and that would leave Claudia spending a good deal of time in this office until they found a suitable candidate.

The office itself was splendid, two walls of glass looking across and down Sixth Avenue, superbly renovated so quickly by the team Alphonse had engaged. But spending half her time in New York was not the life plan she and Peter were aiming for.

After the trials of the divorce, which had challenged his self-esteem for a while, his old ebullient self-confidence was apparently back, "I am expecting a discussion, woman. Good Heavens, if she just said yes straightaway, she'd be the wrong person anyway." Claudia nevertheless thought he was being almost complacent, certainly overconfident. "We're in here," he called, looking down towards the reception area.

Tania came in, looking impressed but slightly disconcerted. She gave Peter a light peck on the cheek, but managed a wholehearted hug for Claudia, "You guys do love your surprises. Do I find out now what all this is about? Have you taken this office on?"

"Please have a seat," said Peter, pointing to the spacious arrangement of sofas and armchairs around the coffee table, "Yes we have taken this on. After the, ah," and he'd taken to pausing in mild embarrassment, every time before he used the word he'd chosen for it, "restructuring last year, we had to recognise that the bulk of our operations are now in the US. That, coupled with the CFO's desire to be New York based, has had us looking for more space here."

She looked around, nodding, clearly impressed, "So this is Will's new home. What do you guys say? The boy done well!"

"Ah, no, his office will be the one in the far corner."

Now she looked puzzled, and then suspicious, "Are you guys coming here?" She looked at each of them in turn.

"Oh, no, no," said Peter, "we're trying, as you know, to pull back a little from direct involvement in operations. I still want to see Peter Dickinson Enterprises expanding, but I want Claudia, Alphonse and I to be a sort of board, more of a supervising committee really, maybe a little more active than a board, but not much. I would stay closest to the hedge funds, Alphonse would remain focused on properties and Claudia would stay in touch with the Group, but more as a chairman."

They both looked expectantly at Tania, "Am I going to like this next piece of news?"

"We very much hope so," said Claudia, "but we realise it's not simple for you."

She was frowning at them, "My mind's racing through a dozen possibilities and I haven't found one I like yet."

"We want you to run the Group, please," said Peter, evidently deciding he'd milked the drama enough.

"You *what*?" Tania almost screeched, "Are you crazy?"

Peter looked stunned, Claudia laughed, and then felt slightly embarrassed, but still found herself smiling broadly, "I warned him not to expect a simple conversation. I would love you to take it on, though."

"Jesus, guys. Well, I'm blown away, obviously, and very flattered, but, wow, there's an awful lot to think about."

"We know that," said Peter, "but we can't make any progress with that until we know how interested you'd be. The blueprint doesn't exist, the CEO has to design it."

"And coming up with a vision for it isn't my strength anyway," said Claudia, "we do want a stronger and simpler P D Enterprises, but that won't happen without the best talent in this position and, no blowing smoke, but you're the best there is."

"Wow," Tania was shaking her head, "give me a moment, wow," they both sat back to let her think for a while. It would be unlike her, Claudia knew, to deliberate too long, she was always rapid, but usually unpredictable. It was that quick, bright mind and the unusual insights that made her so thrilling to work with. "So, what have we got now? Nine tech companies, is it, only seven of which we really control, yes?" Peter nodded, "Two food companies, four consultancies, Sandy's recruitment, and us," she looked at Claudia, who nodded, "Oh," and here she paused, and a wicked smile spread slowly across her face, "and three point nine billion in cash, right?" Peter nodded. Tania looked at each of them in turn, "How much of that are you going to put back into play?"

Claudia turned to Peter and laughed, "I warned you. Be careful what you wish for."

Tania turned back to Claudia, who told her, "This is why I so want you to take this on."

Peter was smiling but, Claudia could tell, was feeling a little uncomfortable. Tania was looking at him intently, "Well," he was unusually hesitant, Claudia thought, as if he were, in some way, a little intimidated by her — *good!* she thought, this is what he wanted, although he didn't really know it, "Well, topping up hedges by a billion would have the dual benefit of attracting more investors in, by showing confidence, and would get us pretty consistent returns…"

"What's a consistent return for you?" Tania was sitting back now, looking relaxed, but concentrating fiercely.

"Well, double digit in every year since the crisis, and even that was stellar by comparison with everyone else, and," he paused to think.

"Thirteen percent a year average over the last five years," Tania said.

He hesitated, "That sounds about right."

"OK, one billion there, that leaves you three. What else?"

"We've earmarked five hundred for Alphonse's resort programme and five hundred for property in general."

"So that would leave me two?"

"Oh, steady," he said quickly, "I'd like to reduce some of the outstanding debt and some securities investments would make the overall portfolio more balanced."

Claudia never quite knew whether Tania's pauses were for thought or for drama; eventually she said, "That sounds to me that, mentally, you've allocated less than a billion to Group expansion."

"Well, there's scope in that. None of these numbers is cast in stone." But Claudia had got the impression from him, in all their discussions, that he was fairly fixed on the allocations he'd described, he'd even talked about topping Group investments at five hundred million.

"When do you want a decision?"

Claudia could not remember an exchange she'd witnessed where Peter was not clearly the master. This morning was a unique event, but Tania had a large logistics company she could go and run and, much as Claudia admired Arthur Gunter, it was already apparent to her that his daughter would do a better job. That was why she'd warned Peter that he had to be prepared to make the Group CEO role enticing. Fortunately, it needed no discussion, Tania took the issue out of their hands.

"Peter, on the basis you've laid out, I have to say I'm flattered, and I'm grateful, but I wouldn't want to accept it as you've described it. I love the Group, even without the Personal Care guys. I can see why it worked so well for you, but that had a lot to do with the chemistry between you and them. And they're a lot of fun, hell, we work inside four of the businesses, so I know them quite well and it's not that aspect that scares me. I just wonder if, as a whole, it's a coherent platform from which to grow much bigger. I don't know whether you could make a big country out of nine little islands."

She stopped and looked at them. She was probably thinking about their feelings now: they'd come to New York again to see her; they'd created an impressive office space from which to run the organisation; and, typically, adorably Tania, she'd come straight to the core of the issue. First truth, then kindness.

But neither Peter nor she wanted kindness. Peter, later, would certainly realise that this was what they'd come for. And Claudia already knew that. They sat there patiently. She knew Tania would have more to say and Peter, she reckoned, would be smart enough to wait for that too.

Tania obviously realised she was expected to continue, "What I would like to do," and she looked expectantly at them. They were smiling back at her. *We must look like proud parents waiting for a child's performance*, thought Claudia, "is take four weeks and work on it with Will. I'd like to come back to you with what I think the Group could be developed into, OK?" They were both nodding, "I'm thinking we might have to lose a little of the cowboy individualism and find a coherent platform for outward growth. That would mean combining some businesses and filling some gaps — and going for some new spaces, maybe, if it makes the entity stronger." Peter was smiling and nodding vigorously, Claudia knew to expect more. "But I will tell you now, half a billion is very unlikely to buy that future. I think I'm going to want you to agree to a lot more than that — but I don't know yet, of course." She waited, she seemed to want to be sure there was no outright rejection. Peter now looked slightly stunned again, but he wasn't shaking his head.

"I'd like us to meet again in four weeks. I will need a lot of Will's time," she looked to Peter, he nodded slowly, "and I might be arguing for you to spend two billion or more. I want your commitment that you'll consider that if I come up with a convincing plan. Do we have an agreement?"

Peter thought for a while. Claudia was willing him to take a positive view. To her, the Group had been fun and the personalities and how they interacted had been a strength, but she'd felt that Tania's points were telling and relevant — they'd spent time on similar discussions themselves, so it hadn't been a total surprise to her.

"OK, we have a deal. I'd not promised the hedgies anything, but I have allowed Alphonse to believe he can access two tranches of half a billion — and I was feeling that debt reduction and more security might be a little more sensible at this time of my life, but if you two guys want adventure, I'll listen. And I will also thank you, Tania, for taking such a positive view."

"Please don't get me wrong. It's a fabulous opportunity, I just believe it will probably need more than you think — and maybe much more than you're prepared for," then she gave him a big, sly smile, "but I don't think

I'm going to recommend anything that a younger Peter Dickinson wouldn't have attacked with gusto."

Finally, he was relaxed enough to laugh.

Chapter 3

He'd been there only twice, and never stayed, he'd only collected her to go somewhere for the evening, they'd always gone to his apartment later.

But it was nevertheless familiar. The small entrance hall — the door had been latched open — a dramatic sea-green wallpaper, black-and-white floor tiles, an art-deco console table and a full-length mirror, that was all. There was a scent of lilies from the oil on the burner on the table. He closed the front door behind him as loudly as he tastefully could. She should know he was there. The double door ahead of him would let him in to the main room. She would be waiting there. He would be, if his memory was accurate and the instructions had been followed, instantly confronted with that particular vision of her. His mind had concocted the picture that had obsessed him in the three days since he'd replied. He'd had no confirmation, until he pushed at the unlatched front door, that she would even be there, and that tension had made the erotic charge of this moment almost overwhelming. He'd been on the verge of cancelling a dozen times as old feelings threatened to overcome him. They had moved on from this, could they go back? But they had done that, the love thing, and they'd come out the other side — well, he was sure he had, he was worried about her — really? Maybe just worried about having to confront her. Now they could just, perhaps, let their sensual natures meet, like they had before, but now without the awkward uncertainties. This would be the erotic experience for her that she had always craved. His hands were shaking slightly as he reached for the door handles, wondering if the scene would match the almost paralysing expectations that had built up over three days.

The drapes were almost closed but there was ample light to see everything clearly. It was like a vision from a very old fantasy, but the voluptuous naked bottom, draped over the chair back, had a strangely familiar aspect. She was a beautiful shape, especially in this perfect pose. His heart was beating fast; impulses to stare, to touch, to slap, to spank competed. There was, curiously, an even stronger urge to speak, even just the punishment-speak of playtimes past. But he was receiving a powerful erotic gift, he should not disturb it. It would be a thrill to fulfil her wishes exactly. Any adjustments to the arrangement would be organised in communications later. Or she could break this off with a safe word whenever she chose.

The stare impulse had won, her bottom looked extraordinarily enticing. Her head, hidden by her hair was on a cushion on the seat. He took the four steps towards her and stroked each cheek lingeringly. She would want time to be taken, drama to be heightened. He stepped to the table, paddle and cane exactly to specification, poured a good measure of the Lagavulin into the glass, it was a new bottle, she would hear the glugs as he poured, and topped up with water from the carafe.

He savoured the unique aroma and held the whisky briefly in his mouth while admiring the beautiful shape before him. She would be excited already. He tried to imagine being in her head, but his appreciation of the bottom's feelings was mostly theoretical, he assumed it in some way mirrored his own, he was using the ritual of pouring, drinking and observing to calm himself. He could see her thighs moving slightly, her hips pushing her pudenda on to the back of the chair. She would want some physical contact now. He stepped towards her and stroked her again, remembering the many occasions he had done that before to that smooth, perfectly textured bottom. He remembered the first time she'd lain across his lap, the sense of heaviness, the awakening thought in him that he could spank very freely and, as he touched her now, a spike of longing seemed to stab him.

He stepped back to the table and placed the glass down with a deliberate motion, she should understand from each sound exactly what was happening. Now he took his position beside her. His memory had not tricked him, the armchair was relatively high-backed, almost the perfect height — for her display and for his movement.

He stroked a few more times, down her cheeks and thighs to the tops of her stockings, it really was a delightful ass. Now he could hear her breathing becoming louder and ragged. Waiting was excruciating.

He assumed for her too. But now it felt right to start.

He slid his left hand to the small of her back, under the waistband of her skirt — had that been permitted? The irony of his indecision flashed through his mind; he was the dom, the top, he should dictate, and he wanted to feel her skin — then he swung twice, quickly, once to each side, the loud noise seemed to reverberate in the stillness, along with the two loud gasps, not so much of pain, it seemed, more of satisfaction.

He looked closely as the satisfying red hand-print outlines emerged. Now was the time to enjoy them, soon the shapes would merge.

But he waited again after the next two to enjoy the emerging shapes again — and to enjoy the minor gyrations of her hips and the slight scissoring of her thighs against each other.

But now he should move to a more consistent rhythm, leaving just enough time for the sharp slap of pain to subside. He could judge this by her movements in response to each pair of strokes, it would take several seconds for her hips and thighs to cease their subtle motions, he read this as her being ready for more.

After ten pairs of strokes he took a longer pause. His hand was stinging badly, he remembered her mock scorn when he had once commented — and remembered too how often they had laughed at this point in their playtimes. The hand spankings were the delightful foreplay to the serious business later. His hand stroked her ass again, his fingers felt drawn to where she was doubtless already wet, but he knew he should follow their precisely agreed choreography.

He resumed the spanking, forcing himself to beat her as hard as before, even though the pain in his hand was inhibiting him. Her gasps were growing louder, but had a sexual edge, her thighs' movements were becoming more pronounced. He was becoming very aware of his own body's response.

The last two he delivered as hard as he possibly could. Here she rolled her hips more violently on the chairback and her gasp had become almost orgasmic — not yet, surely — but she slowly settled into the posture again as he stroked her gently.

Now he could step to the table and take up the whisky, stand back and admire the handiwork. Her bottom was a deep, and satisfying, red all over. He could feel the pressure from his now-standing cock, but he was into the rhythm of the process now.

She seemed to be feeling the same way, but he was missing seeing her smiling face. When they'd been together, they would stand and kiss between hand and paddle. But there was no need to compromise this experience. She had the most perfect bottom for spanking, the full, round and firm buttocks and her seemingly limitless capacity to enjoy what he delivered.

He drank more whisky, put the glass noisily down again, then picked up the paddle. It was leather, but very stiff, almost wooden; that would be painful, he was sure. He had worried before until he learned that she would move almost into a trance as the intensity rose, she seemed to reach a level of deep joy so he knew that, embarrassed as he'd been by the noise the first strokes made in that small apartment, she would have considered that and wanted this anyway. He slapped hard, with long pauses, and her gasps began to sound like sighs as he proceeded. He loved the sight of the response of her flesh to the strokes; those beautiful distortions. Why had he chosen to offer so many, he could come now. But this was for her, he would wait — and enjoy. She was deeply coloured now, the pauses were constant, he would slap, hear her sigh, watch her hips move twice to each side, her thighs scissor three times and then be still again, and she would push her bottom each time slightly higher, it seemed, expectant, provocative.

He lost count! He promised himself he wouldn't, but he'd become so transfixed. He should say nothing. He would wait for the much deeper sigh and the exaggerated hip roll that he knew would tell him he was finished.

And so it was. He thought he still had one more to give, but now she was moving in her special way. He stroked her gently. She remained, as she always seemed to, unresponsive and yet… he knew from their old conversations how much she enjoyed those moments, to feel that sensual contact but not to risk movement — which might bring on premature excitement.

Premature? It would be that. He wanted to savour the cane. It was his favourite. It was her favourite. He poured more whisky and water, but then picked up the cane, not the glass. It was an old one of theirs. It couldn't be, that was still at his place. She must have acquired a replica, the same smooth wood, the same black handle. He swished it twice through the air, enjoying the noise it made, as she would too, he knew.

He drank some whisky, the peak moment for him would come soon, when around six distinct, parallel stripes crossed the already deep red background. That was a visual summit. Beyond that he loved the noise and the feel of cane meeting skin, of her throaty gasps, of her being there at his command. This was their game, this was their bubble, it would be a glorious rainbow-flecked moment, a skin of fleeting, inconsequential happiness enveloping their lives.

He paused after six and touched her tenderly, running fingers along the rising welts — to his eye vicious, but the minimum she demanded. Then, as he moved on, he too found that space she always seemed to get to. It was s thrilling feeling, bringing the cane down, it was a thrilling sight as a new stripe appeared, it was a thrilling sound as she gasped deeply each time. In almost a trance himself, he'd abandoned all thought of counting, he felt his way towards forty and just then, when it seemed right, he heard the very deep sigh and saw the bigger movement. He fell to his knees beside her, wrapped his arm across her lower back and moved his fingers to her wetness, her thighs were spread in readiness, her lips were dripping gloriously, her hole seemed to be enticing his fingers but no, that was not the agreement. He slid on to her clit and almost instantly her violent, bucking movements began. She pushed against him, wanting more and more pressure, but she was groaning loudly already, that beautiful deep-throated growl that he had come to know so well, but tonight it went on and on, he put his face on her hip, put a small kiss on her cheek, and still pressed her clit.

Finally, she began to slow, and then suddenly stopped. This was his moment, that was her signal. He jumped up, unzipped himself, pulled himself out, no time to fiddle with belts and buttons. He held himself, standing over that gorgeous, dazzlingly discoloured bottom and soon the blobs began to fly everywhere, he forced himself to point, he wanted the blobs to drop on the mounds and in the valley. My God, he was coming and coming, this was just as she had been, it was pulsing as if it wouldn't stop, still stiff, still stiff.

But slowly the pressure lessened, now the blobs dropped and no longer flew, but they had merged into pools and began dripping down her skin. He reached for the tissues, wiped himself and stowed his cock away quickly. He would spend more time on her. He wiped her very gently, an absurd contrast, he thought, to what he had just been doing. She remained impassive, although she wriggled away when he tried to wipe too intimately between the mounds.

Now this was the hard part, it struck him. This had been, in its detachment, the most amazing erotic experience of his life. And now he must stand and walk away — and not think that he'd loved this woman once. Stand, Jack, take joy in the fact that you can bring each other joy. He kissed her reddened cheeks, stood up, took a large swig of whisky, and left.

Chapter 4

"I invited Tania this evening, but she was busy," said Will as he poured the champagne on the terrace of their new apartment, twelve floors above the street.

Claudia smiled, "I knew she was that, but I think she was also conscious that this might be the first entertaining you guys have done in your new place. She wanted to let you concentrate on us. Besides, I think she rather overpowered Peter this morning, I don't know if he could have stood that again today."

"Well, it's our first entertaining at all since the wedding," said Martha, "in here it's certainly a first."

"It's a fabulous apartment, Martha, do I get the full tour?" asked Claudia.

Will interjected, "Please let me say cheers, and welcome, we're really thrilled you're here — and that's the closest you'll get to a speech from me when I'm in the presence of His Illustriousness."

Peter beamed modestly, said cheers in return, and with an almost imperceptible nod, seemed to send the ladies away on the apartment tour. So, thought Will, there is business to discuss.

"Claudia's not wrong," began Peter, "I felt I'd been hit by a truck this morning. I'd asked her to come to the new office — thank you for making sure that didn't leak to her, by the way…"

"I haven't even told Martha."

"Ha, well, I imagine you have to have a number of secrets like that."

"We got a lot of practice last year when she was on for Collins on the acquisition. Now her role at the bank's changed, it shouldn't be quite so bad."

Peter looked a little concerned, "You will be really careful, won't you? I'd trust her with my life," he laughed, "but not with my business."

Will smiled, almost from their first conversation, Martha and he had both known about the sensitivities around information and he thought they'd been managing it very well. Well, he knew they had, and she, who had perhaps more to gain from any minor indiscretion, had been extraordinarily punctilious about observing their disciplines.

"Now, the reason for inviting her this morning…"

"Was to offer her the Group CEO job."

Peter looked impressed, then slightly flabbergasted, "I'd only made my mind up last month."

"But I've thought it for a year. Martha told me I was being ridiculous at first, because of Andy, but that seems to have settled down now."

"I hope it has, my boy, but Claudia's still afraid it might rumble on. We're seeing Andy and Jen next week and I'll take him through what we're planning while she talks to Jen, and I absolutely must stop addressing you as my boy. I do apologise," Will chuckled, "You're the finance head of a forty-billion-dollar conglomerate, even its head doesn't have the right to call you my boy," he paused, "my boy," and then laughed uproariously at his own joke. That was one of his few foibles. Will smiled. He loved the man and was very aware of the almost father-and-son bond that had grown between them.

"Anyway, given what comes next, it's a good job you have a healthy respect for her. She's come up with a major burden of work for you for the next four weeks."

"She'll only take the Group on if you invest in it?"

It was Peter's evening for being surprised, "How did you know…"

"I'm not going to say I'm guessing. When we've bumped into each other in the office, we've talked about what you might do when Personal Care had gone, and if you and Claudia really were to pull back from operations. We both think you run it wonderfully, but it's a personality matrix that makes it work…"

"Ha, I like the way you've put that. I know there's something in it. I've always looked at the person first, and how she or he would fit, and only then did I look at the business — and Claudia's a very empathetic person anyway, so it was easy for her to carry on in that style. But personality matrix, yes, that's been it…"

"I don't know which one of us came up with it, so it was probably Tania," and he smiled modestly, even though the phrase was his, he was happy to ascribe it to her — he wanted her arguments to stack up when she went back to Peter with their plans and the higher her standing with him, the better the chance of having the plans accepted. "I know she thinks…"

"Woah, please let me stop you," but he was smiling, "I'm still feeling battered from this morning. Please let me feel you'll be a moderating influence — and watch my money. As you know, I was thinking about a billion for that area…"

"I think you and I had talked about half of that…"

"You see! She'd already doubled my stake money, but she won't take the job unless I listen to her plans, and it didn't sound like she'd come back with a plan that would take less than two, and she's obviously got the figure of four in her head."

"Well, I'm in favour of investment, but also of well-diversified returns."

Peter relaxed and smiled, "I'm very pleased to hear it, my…" he hesitated.

"Boy!" and Will laughed. Peter looked shame-faced, but smiled, nonetheless. "But that money did sit in the Group until last autumn, and we thought the sectors were balanced then."

Peter clutched his heart, "So you've gone over to the dark side already."

Will laughed, "No, it won't get past me if it's not coherent and sensible. You know I'm boring like that."

"That's the last thing you are, young man. Anyway…" and they drifted into a conversation about the new apartment for a few minutes until Peter looked over his shoulder, "Ah, the ladies…"

Claudia was smiling effusively, "It's absolutely gorgeous, darling, you should have a tour later."

Peter nodded and said, "Yes, later," quietly, but he was looking at Martha.

"So," and she put her arm through Will's and pulled him to her, "I gather you have an intense month with Ms Gunter ahead of you."

Will hadn't seen that look on her face before.

But it disappeared quickly, and she led them all into the dining area where the little team they'd hired was waiting and the conversation over dinner moved on to other things, as it always did with Peter.

Chapter 5

Dear J

It would be ridiculous to pretend that I experienced last Friday solely as an event in itself. Part of what made it perfect was that we understand each other's need so well, and that we tune in to each other's rising excitements. So, I will confess that a lot of memories were triggered.

But I do want to reassure you that I am viewing it and treating it as an event in itself. And I'm hoping it was an experience you will be prepared to repeat.

I have no idea, in my case, where these peculiar impulses come from and it took years as you know, some very difficult years, to refine them to a point where I understood my own desires fully.

I can now admit that last Friday's experience was perfect for me and my strange psyche. I hope it met your desires too and that the next occasion is not too far away.

L

If it was as simple for her as she seemed to be saying, then it had hit him rather differently.

As the scene played through his mind throughout the weekend — he'd cancelled a dinner date on Saturday, with no great reluctance, he admitted to himself — the intense memories of the experience itself became mingled with many other memories and feelings.

He thought back a lot to Martha, trying to reassure himself that he had found the blueprint there to enjoy a relationship like the one Lavinia was suggesting. But, at the close of each event, Martha had seemed almost to take a delight in detaching herself and reinserting herself into normal life.

But each time with Lavinia when they'd become a couple, they would go to bed. The orgasm was not the afterthought, the sex was the main meal, the spanking the hors d'oeuvre. Or had it been? Perhaps not. There were many times when they'd come very quickly as their bodies met in bed, perhaps the orgasms were the mere sugar rushes of dessert after the main course of pain, inflicted and suffered. What he was missing now was the long, slow drift into sleep of two entwined and naked bodies.

That's how it had been with Claudia too.

And Martha? She was now married, presumably she'd also been missing the long, slow drift. All the time they'd been meeting, he wondered if their playtimes were all she wanted. Perhaps, but the secret then was that he had been with Claudia — and Martha had never challenged that. They had both had that mechanism for managing their kink with detachment.

He had misgivings about how and whether he could manage that with Lavinia, especially with Claudia's memories still so vivid.

But he did keep returning to the experience itself,

and how could that ever be better than being, as she'd said, shared by two people who understood each other's need, and each other's bodies, so well.

Dear L,

As an experience of our mutual kink, I can think of nothing that would exceed or improve upon last Friday and I am delighted you found it so too. I even reached, during that third phase, that disembodied state of grace you sometimes spoke of, where you would surprise me by only wanting more of something I was already thinking of as excessive. So, for me, it was the perfect top's experience — and it is one I should very much like to repeat sometime.

Your first email did, however, broach the very important issue of discipline around this arrangement, and I apologise for that unintended pun, I think what you specify is absolutely necessary and that should define this relationship for us both.

J

He'd agonised about whether to say that he had problems with his memories. It seemed callous to leave it out.

But including it would have been cruel, he decided.

Chapter 6

The catamaran was anchored above a sandy seabed at the edge of Butterfly Bay. Alphonse sat on the bottom step at the stern with his feet in the warm, clear water. Small pieces of bread suddenly dropped near his knees. He turned to see Bree standing behind him with half a loaf.

"Don't worry, they won't bite," she said, smiling.

He turned back to look at the fish gathering quickly to nibble, they swam nonchalantly past his feet and calves, seeming untroubled by any contact. There were dozens quickly around him. She threw the bread even closer to him.

"You can stroke them."

He'd got used to their sociability on his snorkelling swim. It had been captivating to hang motionless on the water's surface, looking down into the reef, and the longer he stayed still, the more the different populations would swim closely by in their shoals, appearing briefly curious about their alien intruder but utterly untroubled by him.

Now one group of his new friends were brushing past him, brilliant blue creatures with dazzling yellow dorsal fins and yes, they let him stroke their backs as they eased slowly past, more concerned with their bready lunch. It was enchanting.

Technically, he thought, this was business, but it was important to appreciate what the consumer experience would be. The Malaysian resort at Teluk that had so attracted him eighteen months before was already a successful element of his Property Group, its sister resort at Morkuda would be opening next week, and he would soon be travelling there for that event. But where to establish the next project was his current challenge, and how to build quickly enough to profit from the rapidly expanding Chinese vacation spending.

Australia had always appealed since his six months of back-packing more than twenty years before. His preliminary thoughts from his exploratory trip eighteen months ago had driven him to focus on the area he was now in.

Even as a student all those years back he'd caught a whiff of the big southern cities' snobbery about Queensland in general, and Brisbane in particular. When he'd finally travelled north, however, he found himself captivated by the islands, the coral reefs and the rain forests. and he began to sympathise with the locals' 'fuck you' detachment from the rest of Australia.

It was an attitude that Tony shared, but he didn't allow it to appear when talking, during each of his two 'Oz months' every year, to the Sydney and Melbourne money men about investing in his funds. And Alphonse, having spoken so warmly about his time in Tony's home town, was treated as complicit in the pungent observations Tony would sometimes make subsequently about some of his southern countrymen.

It was Alphonse's memories of the coastline, and of the more consistent climate, which sparked the thought that this would be the best place for the next projects and, coming out of a casual conversation six weeks before, he found himself on the boat of a friend of Tony's, having another look at the Whitsunday Islands, but now through the eyes of an affluent tourist. They would be the people needed to make his resort venture profitable, not the impecunious fellow-students of Alphonse's distant memories.

He'd brought Raymond with him. Raymond was a smiley Malaysian whom Alphonse had appointed as CEO Resorts when the project had started. He'd proved to be, in Alphonse's view, very effective, but the next phase was critical. He was envisioning two or three projects here and, thinking ahead, he had picked Raymond in part because of the years he had spent studying and working in Australia. These had left him with the quite common incongruity in these parts of a perfectly Asian appearance coupled with a pronounced Australian accent.

Jerry, the boat's owner, was nominally skippering for the week, but Alphonse felt more comfortable when Sue, his wife, was on the helm for docking or anchoring. She was a tall, athletic woman, with glorious pale blue eyes set in a tanned and well-lined face. She seemed utterly incapable of fear, or tact. And Jerry, altogether smaller, had a breezy self-regard which enabled him to deal with her 'leave it to me, Jerry, you're fucking useless' observations with a good-natured smile and a 'fuck off yourself' response. Having to hand the control over to her after three failures to anchor that morning didn't seem to faze him in any way. And their disputes in general were conducted with such evidently cheery hostility that their four guests were only ever amused by the altercations.

And Alphonse felt like a guest, although he knew the twenty thousand Aussie dollars for the boat charter would go through his business account without any contribution from Tony.

Tony at least picked up the hotel and dinner bills for the nights they spent ashore on Hamilton and Hayman. Alphonse was keen to leave his name in as few places as possible until he and Raymond had decided on their target locations. Being a boat tourist for a few days gave them some anonymity and a necessary customer perspective.

And he loved it! The Bommie restaurant, high above the Hamilton marina, served menus it would be hard to emulate anywhere, and nowhere on the island had better views, so the meal they had on the first night was intensely pleasurable but set a demanding benchmark for what they would have to aspire to.

Once he'd registered the business elements of being in the place, Alphonse felt free to give himself to what rapidly became a boisterous party. It had been kick-started by the two bottles of champagne they'd enjoyed on the back deck of the cat soon after they'd arrived. That had been their introduction to the Jerry and Sue show. Raymond was disconcerted at first until he saw Alphonse relaxing at what was obviously, to him, a comedy routine they loved to put on for guests. If Alphonse had harboured any doubts, they were soon extinguished by Tony and Bree's reactions to the tirades. It wasn't just how their relationship worked, Alphonse decided, it was their way of entertaining people.

Sue leaned across to him after the first course, putting her hand on his knee, and, in what should have been a whisper, asked, "We're not upsetting you, are we? I thought you were fun back there on the boat but, Jeez, you've gone all quiet now."

He smiled at her and, checking the waiter had disappeared, leaned towards her and whispered, "I've just been checking this place out. You know why we're here. This is seriously good. We'd have to be brilliant to make a project work here."

"Oh," she said, patting his knee, "but that wouldn't trouble you, Alphonse, Tony says you are brilliant."

Tony's ears pricked up, so Alphonse responded, "Oh, you know Tony, Sue, if it's not bullshit, it's hyperbole." There was laughter around the table, "Fortunately Raymond's the brilliant one, so I think we've got some good prospects," Raymond smiled, but looked embarrassed. Now Alphonse moved closer to her again and said quietly, "but it's not a topic we want to discuss in the open."

"Well, he also says you're gay. Can we talk about that in the open?"

Her eyes were sparkling, she obviously loved provocation, Alphonse had realised that already, and fun, so he addressed the table, which had been silenced and made nervous by her question, "Well, of course we can talk about that, but what's to discuss? It must surely have been obvious to you all anyway. Look," he pointed to Jerry, "your husband is a well-turned-out man, Sue," he turned to look directly at her, and said in a stage whisper, "I assume you buy all his clothes," then he stood up, spread his arms wide and rotated for the table, "but I don't think anyone with an iota of fashion sense could possibly think he could qualify as one of us, whereas..." and he turned again.

Sue stroked his arse of his yellow trousers slowly as it passed her, "You fill yours better, too, Alphonse," she was laughing, "I take your point."

If that were to be the end of it, they would have an enjoyable few days together, he thought. He didn't get the impression there were any difficult attitudes, but she may have just cleverly cleared the air for all of them.

He looked at Breeana, who was quiet, but now smiled sideways at him. She was a lovely woman, who may have had her own amusements during Tony's long absences, but at least he would now no longer have to worry about avoiding her would-be seductive glances. They had been evident on their plane and in the early encounters on the boat.

If Tony had told her of Alphonse's preferences, she plainly hadn't believed him.

"That said," *because*, he thought, *one had to keep things socially stimulating*, "I'm more interested in beauty than gender," and he allowed himself a cheeky smile at Bree.

The second courses were served, and Alphonse was finally forced to confront a bug, "Now when I spoke of Tony being guilty of hyperbole…"

"You said bullshit and hyperbole before…"

"Sue, darling, you and I, the intellectual sector of the table, are well aware they are essentially synonyms, but I was striving for both accuracy and a more inclusive vocabulary, hence the rather wasteful tautology. Anyway, on no topic on which he has ever engaged me, has he soared to such extremes of eulogy as on the subject of his beloved bugs. I mean, heavens, if you want people to love them, please give them a more attractive name."

Jerry, who'd probably, thought Alphonse, had a lot more than one sixth of the alcohol the group had consumed, decided to weigh in, "We don't want to let anyone else in on the secret, they'd all disappear to fucking China. We've banned exports."

The waiters were distracting the others by serving the dishes, Sue leaned towards him and reassured him the course would be spectacular, then got closer and whispered, "Thanks for reacting so well just now, I reckoned it would help some people round the table be a little less confused this week," and she looked towards Bree before turning back to him.

He wasn't so keen on his thigh being so persistently fondled but her somewhat crinkly smile was so dazzling as her eyes lit up that he decided he would definitely enjoy the week. She plainly had both sense and insight, as well as a wicked sense of humour. He smiled and looked down as his dish was served, then nodded and, turning back again slightly, said, "Thank you," so she clearly knew that was meant for her.

Now he confronted the fat little lobstery body, with the exposed meat facing up to him from the opened shell, just graced by a little sauce. The legs and claws had been left to adorn the plate, but there was no complicated cutlery implying that anything should be done with them.

The first mouthful was a revelation. This, of course, was how lobster should really taste; tender, succulent, sweet and flavourful — the sauce was barely needed. He closed his eyes to savour it, moaned in a low murmur, and then looked up to find them all waiting expectantly for him. "That was disgraceful," he said, "a major disappointment," he enjoyed their concerned faces, even Raymond's — he'd looked the most shocked, "for the first time since I've known you Tony, you have utterly failed to exaggerate!" There were howls around the table, "I would go further," now he had their full attention, "you have utterly failed to even remotely describe it accurately," he smiled, cutting a second portion, "you have not come within a mile — that's about one and a

half kilometres to you apostates — of doing it justice."
He set his knife down and raised his glass, "But your
glorious wines, fortunately, are able adequately, almost,
to salute the celestial bug, which has been so signally
traduced by your piffling inarticulacy. Ladies, gentlemen
and dear, dear departed bugs, I salute you. Cheers!"

And all of them, grinning broadly, toasted with him.

* * *

Sue sent him with Breeana to the bakery the following
morning — 'we've provisioned everything else, but fresh
bread's nice'. He'd been aware, as the evening
progressed, that the women were switching to water as
the men were ordering more wine. He'd tried a
disapproving glance at Raymond when he, too, began to
get loud. Raymond had looked embarrassed, clearly
understanding the mild reproof, but then continued to
drink at the same pace as Tony and Jerry.

Alphonse, having excused himself when they
returned, late enough, back to the boat — 'still managing
the jet lag' — was relieved to note that there were only
two glasses beside the nearly empty whisky bottle when
he, first up, went for a morning run around the island. So,
Raymond had shown some judgement.

The bakery wasn't far from where the main pontoon
met the promenade, but Bree put her hand in his and
asked, "Could we go for a little walk? I don't think the
boys will be up very early."

He looked down at her and smiled, she had the prettiest green eyes, "Of course. I wanted to get a feel for the place. I ran round it all this morning, but you can take more in when you're pleasantly dawdling."

"Is this all business for you?"

She was looking firmly ahead now. He squeezed her hand, "Nothing's ever all business," and they sauntered wordlessly along. If she felt unselfconscious about holding hands, he thought, then so should he — and it was almost two years since he'd been able to enjoy a woman's company like this. But as the memories of Claudia began to intrude, he brought his thoughts back sharply to the present.

"You were thinking about something," she said, looked up at him and smiled, "but I'm not going to ask what. I've never found it a productive question anyway. If I ever catch Tony with that faraway look, I just tell myself he's been fucking someone and there's no point in asking." She said it without bitterness, almost philosophically.

"And it works for you?"

She shrugged but didn't look at him, "It works, I suppose," she squeezed his hand a little tighter, then laughed, this time with an edge, "it certainly works for him."

Now he laughed with her and they walked on in silence, hardly troubled by the golf buggies that were the only motorised transport available to visitors on the island.

After they'd bought the loaves and croissants on their way back to the boat, she took his hand again, not releasing it until they were halfway along the pontoon. Sue was waiting on the back deck with an indulgent smile.

"How are you on boats, Alphonse?"

"I know my way around, I think. Why, do you want sober help when you're moving off?"

"Too right. We've got an east wind blowing this morning, but it dies in the afternoon. I'd like to get up to Hayman under sail, this thing's wonderful with the wind on the beam, and I hate listening to a motor droning when I'm on a sailboat, so I don't really want to wait for those drunken layabouts to emerge."

He looked quickly around the boat and up at the mast, "No worries, mate," and he smiled at her, "all the lines on slips already, an easy breeze to get out on and all-round electric winches when we want to put the sails up. Will you take me on as crew?"

She put a half smile on, "Well, you talk a good game, mate, but I think you've just illustrated the difference between bullshit and hyperbole. What you just said was the former." They smiled at each other, "Let's the three of us eat breakfast and then we'll get going." She turned to Breeana, "Do you mind putting stuff out? Then I can show him what we're doing."

"No worries," said Breeana and hopped off to the galley.

"It's easiest from the bridge," and she led him up the

steps. The satnav display was already on and she used it to show him the layout of the islands and the route she would take. It would be a simple sail north. "No tacks or gybes today, too easy. I think they'll be glad of a quiet day. Hayman will be simple when we get there, they've always got one or two people in the marina waiting to help. And as you said, it should be easy getting out." She looked around, feeling the wind; it was gentle, coming on to starboard, "You'll do bow, then port stern and I'll start her moving when you ease that starboard stern line. OK?"

"Too easy," he said, smiling.

"Watch it!" she said, plainly enjoying his cheek with the accent. Then she spoke more quietly, "We're good about last night, aren't we? I was trying to warn her about you, you handsome bastard, but I did no good at all, looks like."

He took her hand, kissed her cheek and said, "We're all good," he paused, "and Skipper, you're in charge. I'm just following orders."

She laughed and went below to the back deck.

Raymond emerged while the three of them were still eating. "Am I the last?" He looked sleepy, rather than rough or fragile.

"No, mate," said Sue cheerily, "Jerry will be ages yet. Don't know about Tony but he usually sleeps well on board." Bree, munching a croissant, merely nodded.

"I left when they got the whisky out," he said sheepishly.

"Anyway, here's breakfast. It's all on the table. Eat

what you want and then clear up, OK? We're moving out as soon as you finish eating."

Raymond, unused, at home, to assertive Amazons, nodded meekly and sat down. He turned to Alphonse, "Will we have a chance to walk round here when we get back?"

Alphonse looked to Sue, hoping the plans had been made clear to her. He'd dealt with Jerry in preparing the trip, but it was obvious that the decisions were made elsewhere.

"We're back in here the day before you fly out, is the plan, and we're in Qualia that night. You've got the rest of that day and the following morning. Is that right? If you need to change it, let me know. The weather looks good, so that shouldn't interfere."

"That'll be perfect," said Alphonse, "thank you."

The marina exit was straightforward, and they were out in the channel by the time he'd stowed the lines and fenders. He went up to Sue on the wheel. "Nice work," she said, "you've got the job. Do you want to helm while I do sails?"

"Do you mind if I try sails?"

"No, mate, delighted, but we'll just get out between Dent and Henning before we muck about with that. But you can open the sailbag on the main now, if you like."

He eyed her suspiciously, "It's an in-boom furler, there's no bag."

She laughed uproariously, "Just testing you. You're good. D'you like sailing?"

"I love it, but I'll admit I spend most of my sea-time on big motor-boats," and he thought about the eighty-eight he'd organised for Claudia and Peter last year. It was beautiful, he'd gone over budget — for the first time ever — on furnishings and fittings, and she'd been very obviously thrilled but, so far, he'd resisted spending time on it with them. They were always too curious about who he might bring. But, in fleeting moments, when he was more honest with himself, he knew that he was happier just knowing she was happy with Peter, rather than having to witness it. "I don't think anything compares with the serenity of moving under full sails."

When they'd cleared Dent Island, she pointed the boat east to let him get the main up, "All the way," she called, "it's a perfect wind," and as she then eased the boat to the north again, the genoa ran out easily down the port side.

He got back beside her just as she'd turned the engines off, "Oh, I wanted to do that," he smiled at her, "I love that moment when the sails take over completely." She laughed. There was only a half metre of sea, calm enough for the boat to move smoothly forward, and enough wind to push it up to nearly eight knots. They kept to the west of the channel to get the smoothest wind and it felt, he thought, utterly glorious.

He'd kept the job when they left Hayman. Sue was getting almost possessive about him. She'd juggled the places at dinner to keep him beside her, and away from Bree, which had amused him a little, but irritated him more. But it was a boisterous evening again, without the alcohol consumption reaching the previous evening's dizzying levels. They'd arrived in plenty time for him to have a good walk round the Interconti with Raymond and make close observations of all the facilities, and the clientele; not as many Chinese as Alphonse had been expecting 'it's not well-promoted up there yet', Raymond had said. He'd asked Tony to book each kind of room; classic, executive, and suite so they could look closely at each style 'I'm a fucking client', Jerry had said at dinner, 'and he's put us in a shitty little room'. Alphonse, having seen the space they enjoyed and the gorgeous lagoon view, was not inclined to sympathise.

Breakfasting in the hotel gave them a chance to try a second restaurant. It was leisurely, "It's only a couple of miles to Butterfly," Sue had said, "and I'm not even going to make you put sails up this morning. We'll anchor there for some snorkelling," and her hand was, once again, stroking his leg.

So, there he was, with Breeana now sitting down beside him to help feed the fish. The others were on the foredeck, sunbathing. The bottom step was wide, but she sat near enough for her leg to be touching his and her shoulder was gently leaning into him. He didn't lean away but was a little relieved when he heard Sue behind them, "We're going to be heading out soon, could you manage the anchor Alphonse? It's his boat, I know, but I trust him less and less."

Breeana moved away from contact only slowly and

Sue stared at her as she went up the steps. Alphonse didn't know if that was censure, or possessiveness. He was beginning to think the latter. "I'll show you what we're going to do first, before we get moving," and he followed her up to the bridge platform again. "We'll head east to Hook Point here, but wait with the sails until we're ready to turn south, OK?"

He nodded.

"It's still easterly so we should get a great run down to Chalkies Beach here and we'll anchor for the night. You can dinghy over in the morning for a walk on the sands," she pointed at the long white line of Whitehaven on the chart, "I'm sure you'll have some offers of company," she was squinting at him now, "be careful."

He nodded, "Yes, Skipper."

The sails went up again easily at the Hook Point turn, where they had to bounce through a little rough water, but they soon settled on to one seven zero, "just take it out west a bit to avoid the wind shadow when we go round Border," she said, pointing at the one big island ahead of them, "I'm just going to make some snacks for lunch."

The course was set on autopilot, but she had trapped him at the helm. Her scheme, if that is what it was, backfired quickly as Bree was soon on the bench near him, but Raymond and Tony followed not long after, Jerry obviously having been retained for servant duties.

"Is it winning you over?" asked Tony.

"Emotionally I was there already, and there's one

property on Hamilton that would meet our criteria, I think. We'll have a closer look at that tomorrow, then we get two days up the coast for two more candidates, they're the ones near Cairns. We'll see which measures up best, that's where Raymond has to put numbers together."

"Well, you can go faster, you know, some of the fund guys you met in Malaysia want to expand their property interests as well. They liked what you were saying." He chuckled, "I tell 'em, just put it in my funds, but they want diversification and they like the leisure/property combination."

Alphonse smiled and shook his head, "Peter hasn't really been a constraint on how fast we can expand."

Tony looked unconvinced, "Raymond here thinks opportunities are going begging."

Raymond looked embarrassed, "We talked about Malaysia Three the other night."

Alphonse smiled indulgently, "That would have been after the ninth bottle, I think?" Tony laughed but Raymond looked crestfallen. "Don't worry, buddy, I love your ambition, but that's a chunky project. I like your scheme, you know that, but it's probably bigger than Peter would want to deal with."

"That's my point," Tony jumped in, "I know there are other people who'd like to help."

"Going outside Dickinson for funding?" he was shaking his head, "Not sure I'm ready."

Now it was Tony's turn to shake his head, "It's

business, mate, not fucking treason."

"Has this divorce thing slowed him down?" asked Bree.

Alphonse was pleased to see Jerry coming up the steps with a tray of food, which was an opportunity to get off that subject — and he could tell Tony was very grateful. He doubted whether Bree was fully aware of Tony's minor input to that process; he'd have been only one of at least a dozen of Yvonne's sex partners.

"Sorry, guys," said Jerry, "I lost the debate on drinks. No beers till we're anchored."

"No bloody way," said Sue, following Jerry with sodas and water, "we run this ship properly. Now, ETA Chalkies, Mr Mate?"

"Sixteen hundred hours, Skipper," said Alphonse.

Sue seemed to consider, "I wouldn't want to be later, but the wind's supposed to hold. But if she drops below six knots, you'd better put the engines on."

"Aye, aye, sir, ma'am," said Alphonse, smiling. He liked her easy authority.

Sue looked directly at him, but spoke to Tony, "Your mate's a cheeky bastard, Tone."

Tony pursed his lips and eyed Alphonse, "Not cheeky enough, maybe."

Alphonse looked to Raymond, "We'll go over Malaysia Three next week, I promise. If you can convince me, we'll take it to Peter."

Raymond nodded eagerly, but Tony added, "I was just saying, mate, I wasn't talking open insurrection.

Think about it if you want to go faster."

The wind held well, and they stayed ahead of schedule at above seven knots, so Alphonse took the boat further west to give everyone a better view of the sands as they sailed past. The dazzling white five-mile strip curved gently down the east of the main island. Even he was impressed, having always dismissed the stunning pictures he'd seen as products of the photographers' artifice.

They were nearing Chalkies, opposite the southern end of the sands, and he'd been on the helm for over three hours. Sue had made a couple of offers to replace him, but he'd waved her away politely, "I'm only watching the autopilot. This is just bliss."

Now she came again, "You want to do the anchoring?"

He pointed at the display, he was already focused on Chalkies, and smiled at her, "It doesn't look like there's much room between the reef and the beach. I'd rather leave it to the expert, if you don't mind."

"Come on then," she smiled at him, "let's get these sails down first. Jerry!" she bellowed suddenly, "give this man a hand with the sails, you lazy bastard."

She got them in first time. Alphonse was impressed, there truly was only a narrow strip she could aim for, and she spent the following fifteen minutes looking a little tense as she checked the anchor was holding, "The electronics'll tell me if we move too much, but by the time that alarm goes I could be dragging some coral. I like to be sure myself. Do you think we're steady?"

He'd checked his key points, "I think we're good," he said, and felt almost flattered that she'd clearly valued the second opinion. She was a very good sailor.

There was time for a swim while Jerry prepared the back-deck barbeque, and revealed, by the time they sat down to eat, a remarkable talent for it. He kept it simple, offered the rib-eye steaks in small, perfectly cooked portions and served them only after the skewers of jumbo prawns — *no surf and turf abominations here*, thought Alphonse. Accompanying that was a choice of perfectly grilled vegetable skewers or a colourful variety of salads that Raymond had prepared — a reminder of his background in hospitality.

It was a muted gathering after the excesses of the two previous evenings, although the brandy came out after everything had been cleared away. Alphonse's attempts to help were dismissed by Sue, "You've had all day at the helm, let these lazy bastards do something."

He'd walked out to the front deck to look up at the staggering golden band of the Milky Way. He lay down on the webbing to stare up at it and tried to let his mind empty. Twenty years before, that last time he'd seen the night sky's real majesty, he may have been moved to philosophical musings, he could no longer remember, only this image had stayed with him. Now all he could do was open himself up and revel in the great and pointless immensity of it all.

But he wasn't alone, he sensed. He looked up and

saw Bree, midships, by the guardrail.

"I didn't want to disturb you," she said, "you looked so lost in thought."

He sat up and smiled, "I think it's thought I was trying to avoid."

"And did you succeed?"

"Nearly, but now I must stop being anti-social." He was already guessing what might happen, Sue had already drawn conclusions about them, he didn't want the men to do the same.

He went astern, sat down with them and poured himself a small brandy.

"Don't be too long guys," said Sue as she headed to her cabin, "we want to get Alphonse back to Hamilton by lunch tomorrow and some of you will want a walk on the sands before we leave." It was a comment with no conviction, but he guessed the guys' stamina was ebbing anyway — and even doing nothing but walking around on a moving sailboat would prepare them well for a night's sleep.

But he was sleeping fitfully, occasionally waking to feel he wasn't sleeping at all, but it was a shock to turn and find her next to him. He'd not heard her come in. "What time is it?" he whispered.

She snuggled in and kissed him, her breasts against his chest, "It's not twelve but they're all sound asleep. Well, Tony is, he won't stir before seven. Kiss me!"

His mouth went tenderly to her lips, their tongues teased each other's. He felt his cock stiffening embarrassingly quickly against her belly.

"Do you have condoms?"

"Somewhere hidden at the bottom of my bag. Emergencies only, I wasn't expecting to need them."

She kissed him again, "Doesn't matter, let me make you come. I want to taste you. If you'd like to lick me later, I'd be thrilled."

He let his hand slide down over her hip, across her naked belly, and he slid a finger on to her clitoris. She was very wet, "Please, not yet. I know I'm nearly ready but let me take you first, just lie back." He angled himself across the wide bed to leave her room to kneel between his legs. He pulled two pillows under his head so he could look at her. She was holding his shaft in both hands and looking up at him. There was only enough light to catch a glint from her eyes, he'd been trying to avoid their green magic since their encounter on the stern steps. But her smile was there, just before the head of his cock was taken gently between her lips. She looked up again, "Please go slowly, I've been planning this for three days, I want to enjoy it," but now she took him deeply into her mouth.

"I won't be able to if you do that," he said, and already the nervousness about who might hear or notice had left him. The cabins, fore and aft in each pod, were well separated anyway.

She seemed to tune in exactly to him. She would stroke his balls gently, but then ease back as his breathing quickened.

After a while one hand left him, followed, a moment later, by a moist finger tickling his anus, she must be using her own juices for lube. Her mouth came briefly off his cock, "Do you like that?" she whispered.

He looked down at her, smiling, "I love it, of course."

He got a wicked smile from her and then she pushed her finger in quickly and deep. He gasped. "You OK?"

"Yes, it's gorgeous, but I'm glad you're well lubed."

"Oh, you wait till you get there, I am so, so wet."

"I want to do that soon, sweetheart, make me come now."

"My pleasure," she said, and went down very deeply on him.

Wow, he was right in the back of her throat, he'd rarely been taken that deep. So deep he felt tense. But she sensed that and pulled back, looked up at him wickedly again, and said, "More of that next time. But now you can come." And she took half of him in and licked and sucked and played with her finger and they both knew he was soon coming. And oh, did he come, and come, and come. And she stayed there sucking and sucking and he realised slowly that she would stay to take every last dribble. He was almost soft by the time she slid up beside him and kissed him very full on the mouth, letting him taste the last pieces of himself. They wrapped their limbs tightly round each other. "Give me a moment like this," she said, "I'm going to be so quick when your tongue touches me, I want to enjoy your body a while."

"I'm enjoying your body very much, it's very beautiful, but we can cuddle again when I've kissed you."

"No, no," she chuckled, "you'd probably fall asleep, and I'm certain I would, so I'll warn you now, as soon as I've come, I'm off quicker than Cinderella at midnight."

"Can you leave a shoe? I think the Prince will want to come and find you."

She snuggled in even tighter, "Oh, Alphonse, you're adorable, unfortunately, but we know this stops being a fairy tale in the morning," then she gave a quiet dirty laugh, "Now get down there and eat my cunt!"

He laughed quietly too and slid down between her legs. She was very ready and pushed her wet lips at him, but he enjoyed this; 'not so fast' he thought. He pulled a pillow down and pushed it under her arse, she lifted her hips to make it easy for him. He wrapped his arms around her thighs to pull her wide open — and to control her pushing herself on to his mouth. He loved the sensuality of this, and the feel of her reactions. He let his tongue tip caress her clit very gently and sensed from her movements and her breathing just how close she was. He eased lower and let himself enjoy licking the juices from her lips. But he heard her panting, "No, no, please, let me come now."

"Not until you promise I can see Cinderella again."

"You think I won't want this again. Are you crazy, now eat me, you bastard."

And he pushed his tongue, flat and wide, firmly down on her clit and began to enjoy her violent motions

— and the guttural animal noises that were her way of trying to stay as quiet as possible. It worked, but they went on and on. He loved the feeling of her coming and coming, and he found new nuances as he moved his tongue as she slid slowly down the slope beyond her orgasm. Then, just as her final movements were subsiding, she said, "Oh, please stand up and hold me. I must feel your body again but we daren't lie down."

He stood, helped her up and pulled her to him and felt a few of her tears drip on to his chest. She sniffed, looked up at him, kissed him, smiled wickedly again and said, "I'll see you at breakfast. I'm using your bathroom, don't worry, no water noises, I've brought wipes. Condoms next time, please," and she was gone.

Moments later she was out, tee shirt and pants on, waving cheekily to him, and then she left the cabin quietly.

He lay back, briefly considered how strange it all was, and fell deeply asleep.

He slept until light crept in, but when he opened his eyes, he was shaken by the sight of Sue in the chair nearby. He frowned at her, but she smiled, stood up and moved towards him. She stretched herself out across the bottom of the bed. "Your secret's safe with me," she whispered, paused, held his gaze, "but I need a little favour from you."

He sat up slightly, feeling puzzled about what would come next. She grabbed his duvet, pulled it down and reached for his cock before his hands could cover himself. "Don't worry. I know he's been busy, so I'm not making any demands on him. But you can lie down on your back again." She stood up and slipped her shorts down very quickly, "I need you to pay my lady place a little attention."

He raised his eyebrows and smiled. She had a lithe shape for an older woman and was fastidiously waxed. He liked her. This would be interesting. He slid down the bed, "You'd better come and sit on me then."

She quickly straddled him, but he held her hips to make her lower herself slowly on to his mouth. It was a pretty pussy revealed beneath the smooth skin of the well-shaped arse, although the dim light hid any blemishes. Then he pulled her on to him and found her wet already, as he'd expected. This intrigued him, he'd known he'd felt a troubling affection for Breeana, but this was different, a friend wanted to borrow his body. And she had a tasty cunt. She didn't push hard down on him, she let his tongue find her clit and let him find her rhythm. He pulled her down further and tickled her anus a little and she wiggled in enjoyment, "That's a little new," she whispered, "but when we've more time, maybe."

Oh, no, he thought, *this must be a one-off, surely*, and he moved back to focus on her clit. But now she was holding his cock and he was surprised to find it rising. He tried to ignore that and focus on her. Her hips were moving faster now, and she was pushing her clit on to his tongue, but she seemed to be adding to her excitement by taking him in her mouth. He felt quite stiff now, but perhaps she would leave him when he'd made her come. He pushed his face into her and began to lick rapidly, he could feel her breathing harder, she was near coming, but she was taking him deeper into her throat. But now he could hear her gasping and shaking as her loins moved wildly. This was it for her. She'd got what she came for and her belly relaxed on to his chest.

But her mouth stayed on his cock, did she want that too? She had a lovely mouth.

And a nice arse, his hands stroked her cheeks. This seemed to make her take him deeper. He was too deep, really, he thought, but she seemed to want to take all of him. My God, this was extraordinary now. He normally liked to come with just his cockhead being sucked, but that was now deep in her throat and he could feel his excitement rising. Wow, he thought, if that's what the lady wants, and he found himself gasping. He was going to come again, very deep in her throat. It was weird - and glorious.

When he'd almost finished, she pulled back, licked him quickly, leapt off him, jumped into her shorts, bent over and kissed his lips, patted his cheek, said, "You were lovely, sailor man," and was gone.

He plumped the pillows, leaned back on them and watched his softening dick dribble on to his thigh. She'd meant that to be an event without consequences, he assumed. He found himself smiling. Since a delightful affair after the original Malaysia resort meeting, easily concluded by the convenience of geography when the man began to get boring, he'd done little dating. But now twice in one night, and both of them women!

Sue, he thought, had scratched an itch for herself, but Breeana might have taken a little poison into her system. He would need to draw that painlessly. At least Sue, bless her, had made sure that he wasn't too preoccupied with dreamy memories of the night's first encounter.

Could that have been on her mind too? He was beginning to find her unique, if not extraordinary.

And the cheery back deck greeting was as though nothing had happened, "Good morning, sailor, can you drop the dinghy down off the davits? You could check the pressure, it should be OK, but give the motor a turn, will you? It hasn't been run for a month."

"OK for fuel?"

"Should be, but you could check." All said matter-of-factly.

That gave him a job, and an enhanced sense of 'no consequences'.

Bree was a little different. When she appeared, there was a little look of longing — and he found himself responding with an involuntary warm smile. He was glad Sue was busy in the galley.

In the end, just he and Raymond took the dinghy. Breakfast was dawdling on and his gambit of 'we have to check this out' worked — it made a business trip of the enterprise and that discouraged other company, which is what he'd wished for. He did, after all, want to feel this as a tourist.

He ran the dinghy up the sand, cutting the outboard and lifting it with fairly precise timing. OK, maybe Raymond's shorts got a little wet as he jumped off the bow with the painter. "Sorry, buddy, didn't want to get you damp," he said, as he stepped into shallow water after Raymond had managed the first tug up the beach. He looked to Alphonse to help him give the painter another pull. Alphonse smiled, "Tide's going out, buddy, that'll just make it harder work pushing her in when we come back. She's good where she is."

They were both shoeless. He knew that, in the morning, the sand would be cool, and they could walk anyway in the little waves lapping the edge of the beach. Raymond stayed island side of him, having been spooked by how close the manta ray had come to them, its eerie camouflage concealing it from him until it was almost at his feet in the ankle-deep water. Alphonse had laughed when he'd jumped with a shriek, "It's relatively small and it's harmless." Raymond looked sceptical, Alphonse laughed again, "But I do agree it looks scary."

"So, what do you think?" he asked after they'd walked along the empty beach for a few minutes. Alphonse had to admit to himself that he was giving too much time to thoughts of the previous night. He jolted himself, he needed to engage Raymond.

"I've been here before, I thought it was stunning then. But can I tell you I'm worried. I shouldn't have talked about Malaysia Three when I was drinking."

Alphonse patted his back, "That's fine, really it is. I

admit it's given me a problem," Raymond looked at him, obviously concerned, "oh, don't worry about that. No, it's a good problem. You and I have debated before about whether your team's capacities or my ability to finance would be the bottleneck, and I have to admit, now," he paused to make sure he had Raymond's attention, "this is a compliment alert. I'm worried that their rarity might induce another manta ray reaction in you, but you might actually be right." Raymond smiled, but looked expectant. "I'm impressed by your team. I thought the Morkuda opening next week was massively aggressive timing, but it sounds like you have it all in place."

Raymond shook his head a little, "I'm nervous, can I admit that?"

Alphonse laughed, "I think I'd fire you if you weren't. But come on, what about this place?"

"Oh, I think we go ahead. You made a good point about few Chinese on Hayman. But you think about how many we pull into Teluk. Our marketing's good. We'll get them here. I'm not sure we're being ambitious enough with the scale of the projects here."

Alphonse mulled that over, enjoying the warm little waves lapping his feet as he walked on the firm sand, "I take your point; bookings for Morkuda have pleasantly surprised me, and ninety-two percent occupancy in Teluk is remarkable."

Raymond smiled, not truly modestly, Alphonse thought, "It's ninety-three, and we're underspending on discounts."

"Ha, but you've spent the savings on promo."

Raymond looked a little hurt, "I can beat profit plan if you want."

Alphonse laughed, "You know that's not what I want. I want profit plan and extra growth, more Chinese tourists. I'm just proving to you that I read your monthly accounts in detail. Now don't go all gay on me. We're not doing hurt feelings."

Now Raymond laughed very loud.

The cat was all ready to leave when they got back. Jerry let the blocks down from the davits to let them haul up the dinghy and with that quickly in place, they were off. It seemed a subdued mood on the boat. Sue stayed on the helm to lift the anchor and then take the boat south through the gap in the islands and made no move to get him to take over. He felt a perverse need to talk to Tony but felt awkward. Fortunately, Tony came to him, "Have you two made any decisions?"

There was a fleeting moment of terror before Alphonse realised Tony was referring to Raymond and him, "I think you've emboldened my CEO to push to go bigger and faster."

A smile spread on Tony's face, "You said it yourself a while ago, you can get more done out here. People believe in growth and business, they don't want to spend all their time in debates and discussions. You'll think about what I said?"

"I will, of course, but it could lead to tensions. I hope you won't take this the wrong way, but why are you pushing?"

"Nah, that's OK. Big money out here deals in relationships. They see Henry and me as just a bunch of funds; introducing your properties and resorts to them has made us a package, potentially. Peter might lose a little control, but he could pull a lot more investment in. They loved him, they'd like to work with him," his smile got a little bigger, "of course, they think you're a bit queer," and he laughed loud at his joke.

Raymond tittered, embarrassed, but that grew into a laugh when he saw Alphonse smiling. He liked Tony, he was a friend, there was no point in being all middle-class about being in bed with the man's wife. An odd thought flashed through his mind — he couldn't think of a woman he'd been to bed with who hadn't been married.

They talked more about the scale of the projects; what could be done with Peter's probable investment budget; how much faster they could go with more funds. Finally, after they'd rounded the north of Hamilton and were heading for the marina, Alphonse closed the discussion, "I know you'll talk to Peter, Tony, obviously I'm comfortable with that, but my official position is that I'm committed to working within the boundaries of his funding, OK? You need to understand that too, Raymond."

Raymond nodded as Tony said, "I get it mate, but it does sound like we've opened your mind a bit. That's all I wanted to do."

When they'd docked, he and Raymond rented a

buggy to have a closer look at all the hotel properties; the one being marketed for sale, and others whose locations appealed more, who might be susceptible to offers. All the while the conviction was growing that they would want to build, or rebuild, here.

They'd booked into Qualia's Long Pavilion for dinner. This would be the competition. Tony had booked them rooms again and Alphonse and Raymond managed a detailed inspection of each and agreed that the challenge of emulation would be considerable, even Teluk didn't match these standards, he would find out next week if Morkuda did. But this was their market, and they were going to have fun in it.

He'd managed to brief the party before they left the boat that the resort topic could not be discussed when they were there and, although Jerry threatened the odd comment at dinner, Sue kept a close eye on him — and wine consumption was much more modest now, anyway. He slept well and was amused when he woke, first light, to see the unopened condom packet where he'd left it on the bedside table. His expectations had been very low, but he thought he should at least be prepared. Now he found himself curiously sorry that she hadn't come but didn't give it too much thought before preparing for a run. She did find a way, later, of standing beside him at the breakfast buffet, "I'm sorry, I desperately wanted to come but…"

"I was hoping you would," *and it was funny*, he thought, *I mean it*.

"Can we stay in touch?"

"I'd love to."

And that was all. When he packed, late that morning, for the flight to Cairns, he realised there was going to be a strange feeling of regret when he left.

Chapter 7

This is a crazy project, thought Tania, glad she had detailed knowledge of some of the tech businesses, but not yet agreeing to take the CEO role on meant that she couldn't talk to the others.

And Molloy loomed out there. Peter had assured her he'd had a productive and positive conversation in Boston, but she'd felt like saying 'bullshit'. It wouldn't have helped, but it was what she'd felt. She would have to talk to Andy anyway.

"Will you stay over?" he'd asked when she called to fix a time to see him.

"No," *just keep it simple*, she thought, and was relieved he didn't argue. Maybe he was being a big boy about it. She'd heard nothing from Claudia about their conversations up there. Surely, she would have called if there had been anything Tania should know.

But later that day Claudia rang. "How are you getting on?"

"Jeez, I thought I was working hard before — and I do still have a day job. But I have to go to Boston next Tuesday."

"That's why I've called."

"How are they doing?"

"Well, I thought they'd been doing better. I need to be careful here though, any couple is going to go through rough patches. They seem to be having more than their share. I've also got the problem that, although I'm quite close to Jen, she knows about you and Andy. You have to admire them for talking to each other, but she knows I'm much closer to you."

"But it's eighteen months now."

"Are you nervous about meeting up?"

"A little," there was a pause, Claudia said nothing, "OK, quite a lot, I admit. Look, I'm having a lot of fun at the moment, in those tiny windows of time my life used to give me before this project, but I did have more feelings there than I'd realised. And now I'd be his boss, sort of."

"I never used to look at it that way when I was running the Group — well, I still am until we can get you to take it on — but I always felt more like a partner to them."

"I do get that. That's how it works for me with you as a boss, but my early thoughts on the way ahead are to make a bigger group with tighter links between the elements. It would be more focused, more coherent, and the CEO is more clearly a leader, I think, not so much a partner anymore."

"What does Will think?"

"We're on the same wavelength. I hope you'll be impressed when we talk to you."

"I can't think of anything you've done where I

wasn't. But how are you getting on with Will?"

"It's brilliant, he's so bright and knowledgeable, and he doesn't get upset about me challenging his ideas."

"Yes, we think he's wonderful, too. So, the relationship's good?"

Tania paused, there must be something on Claudia's mind, "What is it? You know we're good. He's the brother I never had. Oh, no, you're not thinking about that?"

"I'm not, but Martha is. It just took a mere mention of your name on the project to ignite that little fire of jealousy. She's going to feel very vulnerable."

"But they're married," Claudia didn't respond, "OK, I guess that was a pretty stupid comment wasn't it?"

"No, it wasn't stupid. It was quite touching, really. I'm just telling you though because he'll come under pressure. She'll be feeling vulnerable, especially now she's married. You'll have to cut him some slack if he can't put in the late nights."

"Nice one, boss, Will goes home to jealous wifey, but Tania can do the sixteen-hour days."

"Cutting back already, are you?" and they both laughed, "but no, your problem's Andy."

"I got that feeling when he asked if I'd stay over."

"I thought he might. You'll be careful, won't you? You're my main concern in all this."

"I know, boss, and I love you too," and they both knew that was true. "Oh, wait, wait, I have one other topic, also sensitive."

"I do love you, you know," and she laughed lightly, "but what's this one now?"

"Well, I need someone to help pull all this together, it was getting hard with just Brodie Gunter Jeavons."

"Are you going to suggest who I think you're going to suggest?"

"You'd be disappointed if I didn't," and they laughed again, "it's over a year since she and Jack were together."

"You don't know that." Claudia suddenly seemed to have gone a little frosty.

"I do, we talk sometimes. Come on, you know she's good, you said so yourself, and we kind of owe her something."

"I gave her Jack," she said sharply.

Tania hesitated, "Wow, that's not like you."

"No, you're right, it's not." Now Claudia was hesitating, "I'm sorry, that was pretty ungracious of me. I'm telling you about Martha's jealousies and I dredge that up out of the past. I'm sorry. No, I'm sure she'd be excellent. Would she want it?"

"Me, or Uncle Rod, that's her choice."

Claudia laughed again, she'd plainly got over her little issue, "I take your point. Have a talk to her," she paused, "with my full blessing, in case she asks. Christ, she saved us a fortune, now fuck off and leave me to my own embarrassment, I'm a little ashamed of my reaction now. But Tania…"

"Yes, you're going to say be careful with Andy."

"Ha, why do I bother?"

* * *

She had a full day with Will the next day. He had no qualms about occupying his new office and it made a very pleasant place to work. She avoided 'hers', it felt like tempting fate, and she'd been happy with the stance she'd taken with Peter and Claudia. She knew Will supported her in principle, but one of his great strengths was an ability to evaluate everything unemotionally and to avoid committing too early to a particular course. They agreed on their initial thoughts, the Group couldn't be run on the basis of the CEO, like Peter and Claudia, just being the glue. It had to be run on a platform of interconnecting businesses, technologies and skills. But she was aware that, if they couldn't put a coherent plan together, Will would opt for some different arrangement — he had, after all, to think about the overall group picture. He could recommend putting the money into the funds or property, or even safe securities. But she never doubted his commitment to examining the full range of the Group's opportunities. It meant that they spent a lot of time on a number of options and, even with his new team, sworn to secrecy, helping to gather data, they were always there well into the evening.

Apart from the four group companies she worked with directly, Will's team could provide her with everything she needed to know on the others. That made it easy to assess the strengths and weaknesses, and the gaps and overlaps of their current businesses. But it was harder to identify areas where a future Group Corporation could focus, and to assess what else they would need to acquire to make any new grouping powerful and impregnable.

"Will, it's nine, it's Friday."

"You have a date?"

"No, but you have a wife."

"She's all right, she understands how this works."

"I would understand it too, but I wouldn't accept it."

"Ha, have you been talking to Claudia?"

She laughed, "Yes, but when you're hearing us in stereo, you should listen. We've got three more weeks of this. Martha will get pissed at you."

He seemed to consider, "OK, a little break from this might be good to clear our heads. Will you take some time off over the weekend?"

"I have plans for tomorrow, but I'll be reading more stuff on Sunday, I think. Let's wrap up."

"I feel we ought to go for a drink."

"That would be a great idea, but I'll only do that when Martha joins us. I'm far too beautiful to be allowed to spend time with someone's husband."

He laughed, "That's true, it's also a good idea about Martha. Would you want her to bring along a rich banker?"

She smiled, "I don't get time to enjoy the offers I get. But thank you — and I would like the three of us to get together."

"I'll sort it out." *Not, 'I'll ask her'*, Tania thought,

but 'I'll sort it out' — and on the very few times they'd had together, she'd been intrigued by how deferential Martha was to her young husband. She'd originally thought it was like a mother pandering to a precocious son but, knowing a little of Martha's tastes, there must be something in her that wanted that almost callous domination that Will could briefly exhibit. And that wasn't his normal way either. She parked the thought, she had her own life to think about. Lately she'd been starting to wonder if there should be a little more structure to that. And maybe that was emerging, but she doubted whether the lunches at Noah's every six weeks or so could be a regular feature of her future life. She watched Will pack and leave, calling, "See you Monday," without looking back.

But tomorrow was a lunch with just Robert, he'd actually said, 'just the two of us', and it hadn't been her 'I can do vanilla' remark a few weeks before that prompted it, she was sure, but she knew too much about his overall life to take him seriously — and he'd seen her enjoying the groups Noah had organised for her, so this was staying friends with benefits, surely.

He hadn't been at the last one. That was a little joke of Noah's, there had been a narrow racial selection of the group that day, just four black men, quite a thrill for a little white southern girl. But they'd all been curiously polite. The previous time had been the best, although that got weirdly confusing when Robert had tried to intervene when he thought two guys were being too rough. She'd called 'no' and they'd stopped, but she'd only been trying to stop Robert interfering. It had rather spoiled the moment. She'd worried then about whether he was getting too affectionate, and now with tomorrow's lunch being 'just the two of us' maybe that was a worry. Still, he hadn't said he wouldn't bring some friends for the afternoon. *Time to pack up, Tania,* it would be wonderful if Debs was at home alone.

She wasn't. She was working, of course, Tania remembered as soon as she got to the apartment. But it meant she could catch up on domestic chores. She was still busy when Debs got in at eleven but after a hug, they were both too tired to talk.

Tania managed her longer run in the morning, it was a gorgeous spring day in the park, the trees in full blossom and the air still morning-crisp, sounds of the city coming to life were all around her, a chance to take a different perspective on the project — and on her life and what came next. Her response to Peter and Claudia had been spontaneous, but as the week evolved, she'd grown happier with the position she'd taken. In its new and smaller form, the group was a bunch of interesting companies with not many clear links. It worked as a group because of the personality of Peter, but she was not Peter. She might make a passable job of administering it but that wouldn't be an interesting challenge. It wouldn't teach her much about herself or business.

If she were to go back to Atlanta and run Giddings, she would make changes there. They'd made progress since Claudia's project, but that had only made the place work better — and be happier too, she thought — but Dad was not taking the business forward, with technology, with geography, with interconnections. It would be interesting and, if he let her take over soon enough, it could almost be exciting. But that was a big if.

And it was Atlanta. Running around the big reservoir with the backdrop of the Manhattan skyline all around her, leaving New York would be hard right now.

Dickinson was a project she could shape, but just managing it in its current form would not be enough.

She and Will had found enough ways forward for it, although the thoughts were still ill-formed and confused, but several possible groupings could make sense, each with some chunky acquisitions, however, to give the groupings the right focus and shape. She would need help, she had to call Lavinia. OK, it was too early, really, but that was a gamble Lavinia might take, and someone that discreet, that calm, and so effective at pulling information out of all available sources would be invaluable.

After a shower, she was on the phone.

"Tania, hi honey, how are things?" They didn't speak often, and Tania was sure most people would find Lavinia cool and formal, but that way of hers helped Tania get calm and think at a different pace. And Tania knew they had the bond of having outfoxed Uncle Rod. Outfoxed? She sometimes thought; that man walked away with twenty million dollars, instead of a ruined business. But she'd ended up with a perverse respect for the way he'd managed himself. It was like she'd sometimes felt playing tennis against a tough opponent when she'd just won a tight game, especially when the opponent had been cheating.

And he'd kept Lavinia on, in spite of his obvious suspicions about the role she'd played. But Tania knew that she wasn't especially happy, so, "Things are great and could be exciting, maybe, but I need help. Would you come and work with me in New York?"

It developed, of course, into a long conversation, Lavinia's methodical questions about everything to do with the project and then what her role might be just confirmed to Tania how much she could bring if the everything went ahead.

But if it didn't? "I can't promise you we'll find a coherent plan, or that Peter would fund it if it's aggressive enough to be interesting, but just talking it all through with you now makes me realise how much you could help us. I've taken an hour of your time and it's already helped me get lots of my ideas straight, but I can't make you a firm offer until I've got Peter to agree."

There was a long pause. *That's probably a good sign*, thought Tania, *it's best to just shut up and wait.*

"Why don't I spend a week with you, the week after next, say? Then I can work alongside you, maybe gather a bit more information, and help you start to pull it together for the following week. Then we have a better idea of what my job might be — and whether we find each other insufferable."

Tania laughed very loud, the woman was so calm and dry that a joke like that, *Oh God, I hope it was a joke,* was as sharp as a stiletto stab. But Lavinia was laughing too. This could be so good, Tania thought. And Lavinia had clearly already made the first big step of opening her mind to the idea.

"That would be really wonderful if you could. I'll get everything booked for you."

"Woah, no you don't, you concentrate on the project. Leave the rest to me. I'll see you in the office at nine o'clock on Monday morning in nine days' time."

"I can't thank you enough," said Tania, already feeling a weight being lifted. Someone would share the burden.

"Oh, I should be thanking you. I *am* thanking you, in fact. I'm already hoping it comes off, but that, of course, would not interfere with our objective evaluation of the right way forward."

And Tania could feel the woman smiling at the other end of the phone, "Of course not," but Tania was laughing as she said it, and she heard Lavinia chuckling. It wouldn't interfere, of course it wouldn't, but a little humorous self-awareness was very welcome. "See you Monday week."

* * *

"You're looking pleased with yourself," said Robert, after he'd risen to kiss her at the table.

"I've had a very good morning, I think. I'll tell you about it when you've explained today to me."

"What's to explain? We've had lunch before."

"Once, and since then we've always been — how shall I put this — in company," she smiled at him. She was teasing, but she was intrigued.

He tried to look offended, but a smile was never far away, "I'm just having lunch with a beautiful woman, does it have to be more than that?"

"It doesn't have to be, but it usually is. I was relieved to see it's a table for two. It's been a heavy week," she narrowed her eyes at him, "we're not expecting company later, are we?"

He laughed, "If that's what you want, we can be, but I was hoping my charm would suffice."

"That and a bottle of La Scolca," by now the waiter was beside them and overheard.

Robert smiled and nodded, "But two prosecco first." The waiter bowed, handed the menus to them and left. "You look effervescent today."

"You and Noah do come up with some questionable terms. I remember radiant."

"We feel compelled to avoid the bland and obvious."

She chuckled, "The vanilla too."

"The vanilla certainly, but let me not get lost in your diversions, I just wanted to see you, OK?"

She eyed him suspiciously, but put her hand on his,

"And just seeing you is good too," and she blew him a kiss. Then they got lost in conversation. He was setting up a gallery on the west side, mostly funded by Noah, but some of the money was his, and there was lots of work getting ready for the opening. It wasn't near the gallery he worked with and he would focus anyway on different things, 'Noah' would be more contemporary, edgier, riskier. But he wasn't so self-absorbed that he didn't have lots of questions about her project and what that might lead to — so they agreed on an afternoon tour of his gallery space and her new office. By the time they got there however, she had some misgivings: was she already too committed to the idea of the project? Those feelings were enhanced by his reaction to the space.

"Wow, serious C-suite!"

Now she was hesitating, "I have to say yes yet. They have to put up the investments or I won't agree."

"OK, but when you've said yes to them, can I come and fuck you on the sofa here?"

"Of course, but shall we go to your apartment now?"

He smiled, "Of course," and took her hand.

She leaned up and kissed his cheek, "This is lovely," she said, "it's almost like a date."

"It is a date," he said, and kissed her lingeringly on the lips, "so now I want to show you my apartment."

They held hands in the cab going over Brooklyn Bridge. Tania knew they were about to have sex, but this was no teenage, tear-the-clothes-off coming together. It was intriguing, though, as she looked at him, they'd fucked half a dozen times, maybe, but never just the two of them.

"You're thinking 'why just the two of us', aren't you?"

"I was, but it's not that big a thing for me. I'm happy to go with it." He smiled and looked out at the East River. "Are we going far?"

He pointed to a group of buildings to the left of the bridge, near the waterfront. "The tallest one there, the dark red one. I get the Manhattan views, you have to live there."

It could be a chip on the shoulder, she thought, or maybe it was a really cool place to live; whatever, she wanted the sensations of a one-on-one fuck. She'd loved the parties, but the dwindling population of acceptable friends of Deb's friends, coupled with the increasing workload, meant that these experiences were becoming rare. And it wouldn't do to take a cargo of frustration to Boston next Tuesday. It reminded her that Andy had been good. And might have been even better if she'd opened herself up the way she did nowadays. At least she knew, smiling to herself as the cab turned off the bridge road, she would have no inhibitions that would get in the way of her enjoying the rest of today.

It was a stunning apartment, a huge window opened on to the river with its Manhattan backdrop.

"Wow, but I really think you should fuck me first and then tell me about this place later. I was almost tempted by the sofa in the office, please don't make me wait any longer."

* * *

They were naked and lying across his bed, still breathing heavily, and she reached for his cock, very wet but still stiff, "Are you going to let me deal with him now?"

"No. You can hold him like that if you're gentle, but he still has a lot of work to do."

"Ah," she smiled, still wanking him gently, "so you want to do this all on your own, with no reinforcements."

"Oh, I wouldn't say that; I have a drawer full of electric helpers beside the bed here. I thought I could risk you coming quickly…"

"I couldn't wait."

"That was gratifyingly obvious," he smiled, "but you do have the capacity for a few more of those whereas my little friend here might have to stop after two." She bent down towards his cock and took its head in her mouth. "That is, of course, extraordinarily pleasant, but it won't help the afternoon's programme."

She looked up at him, smiling, "No scope for spontaneity?"

"Plenty scope for spontaneity, but I think it suits both of us if we keep him standing, don't you?"

"Well, if you can have more fun than letting me suck your dick dry now, then it could be an interesting afternoon."

"I think, for once, you can let someone else set the agenda. We all love fucking you, especially those two guys I thought were almost raping you at Noah's, but I've come to realise that we're essentially following your instructions. You are now going to follow mine for the rest of the day. I'm hoping you'll have even more fun that way. And I can…" he took his cock from her hand and held its head against her clit, she closed her eyes, it felt so good again already, "I can promise you, he and I will too."

He pulled away slightly, "Now you have to move around a little," he reached into the lower drawer of the bedside unit and pulled out a thick white sheet. He nudged her gently to the foot of the bed and spread the sheet across it, then put two pillows in the middle of it. "Now lie across here with your belly on those."

She did as she'd been told and it struck her that, even with Andy, she'd been dictating what happened, and Robert was right, even the gangbangs at Noah's had effectively been choreographed by her. But she was happy now to lie across his pillows and feel him sit down on the back of her legs. He was moving strangely but when she heard a drawer open and articles being removed, it was time to relax.

She smelt the vanilla just before the oil landed between her shoulder blades, "You wanted vanilla sex," he said, "I've taken you at your word. I've not used this one before," now his hands were spreading it slowly across her shoulders and down her back, "I don't know if the perfume will linger, I hope it won't interfere with any other plans you may have for later this evening."

She felt his hands grip the top of her shoulders and

his thumbs began to massage her neck. It was quite blissful, "I'm not thinking remotely beyond this." A professional would have been pressing firmer, this was little more than sensual stroking, and that was exactly what she wanted. She stretched her arms out and let her hands dangle over the sides of the bed, it could almost become soporific, she thought, but for her awareness of his cock, still stiff, rubbing between her buttocks. Now, as he moved his hands to her lower back, pushing firmer now, she felt it lodge between her thighs, but, moments later, his hands left her, and he was clearly preparing something else. Then his cock was pushed into her pussy, that opened her eyes, she was curious, but then she saw the empty condom packet by her elbow. Now his hands moved to her rib-cage and his cock pushed further. She was very ready again, she pushed her ass up slightly to welcome him deeper.

"But I hope you're not going to come before my massage is finished."

"I plan not to do that, but he has reinforcements if I weaken," he pushed even deeper but seemed to be maintaining a steady rhythm, "besides, I think he wants to enjoy your new favourite."

"That's embarrassing," she said, "have I made it that obvious?"

"Oh, I wouldn't say that," he was speaking slowly, matching his words to his movements, "but we know that whoever comes behind you doesn't have that long to enjoy himself, and you were very loud, I remember when

Ezra was there."

"I'm afraid you may be right. Perhaps if it's just you, I can focus on that and see how much I really like it."

He slapped her ass playfully, "because I'm so much smaller than him?"

"No, stupid, you know very well I was sitting on you when I had Ezra like that. My God, what am I saying? Oh, and will you slap my ass harder later? We really should find out what they see in it."

"My dear Miss Gunter, we know your capacity seems almost limitless, but I have enough ideas, I hope, to entertain you today, and I need to think about what I can manage. If you want more after you've exhausted me, you can tell me who you'd like me to call."

"That's fair. Obviously, it's a little boring with just you, but we'll see how I feel when I've worn you out." *It's getting very difficult*, she thought, *not to start enjoying this too much. It's just Robert, for fuck's sake, Tania!*

Now she felt his hands massaging her ass cheeks. He was obviously spreading her to look at her, to admire her, even, she thought, and she'd been surprised at how much all of that, the touch, the licking, the lubing, had turned her on, my God, she'd even enjoyed Noah watching, that made her pussy relax even more. She'd let Andy begin to play with her ass, but that all fell apart when his feelings, for her and for Jen, got too confused and entangled, and she'd felt she had to detach herself. But at the parties here... well, her inhibitions had evaporated completely and only her curiosity, and her awakening sensuality, were engaged.

And this is mere sensuality, she thought, as Robert's tongue began to tease her anus. *It's sensuality and it's only Robert. Relax, and enjoy.* He pulled one more pillow toward her without moving his face from between her cheeks. She pushed her ass higher and pushed it on to the pile under her belly. Nice! Now his tongue was making her tingle, now he was pushing it into her. She was wriggling, but her pussy was starting to feel greedy and empty. Suddenly he was moving again, and she felt a small device being clipped on her vulva. It began buzzing. Oh, that was thrilling.

"Have you tried one of these?"

"No, it's nice, I've just been a straight rabbit girl up to now."

"Oh, we'll have those later."

"Those?"

"Oh, yes. I think maybe you coped a little easily with Ezra. Those loud screams didn't fool me. That was pure pleasure. But I thought I'd provide a little light entertainment for your pussy while we found out how much of an ass girl you are. It's new, isn't it?"

"Yes, it's very new, and it surprised me, but when you let yourself go with these things…" the buzzing noise was getting louder and her clitoris was tingling, "Robert, you can't, I'll come just like that," and he was easing off already, letting the buzz fade to a murmur and the vibration to a gentle tickle, which was perfect.

Now she felt the lube being squirted and massaged around and into her anus. That was the new thrill, and the first finger, that was easy, but he pushed slowly in and out, it was gorgeous, but she wanted more. Even two, when they came together, were very pleasurable.

"I think my friend's waited long enough," he said, and she felt another drop of lube drop on her. His thighs squeezed hers together, she felt one hand holding her cheeks apart and then his cock was pushing at her hole. "Oh," she heard him moan as she felt him slide deeply into her, then his hands were on her shoulders. She had a feeling of voluptuous fullness when he pushed down. The distant tingle on her clit just kept her on an edge, her orgasm hovering somewhere in the middle distance.

He was managing his quite well, it seemed, but then his movements began to get rougher.

She loved that, "Go on," she urged, "stick it all the way up my ass!"

But he pulled out suddenly. She felt his chest on her back, he was kissing her ear, her cheek, the edge of her mouth. She could feel his cock, very hard, squeezed between his belly and her ass — he hadn't come yet, thank God, she wanted to feel that.

"I will come soon, sweetheart, but it's a gentleman's rule: ladies first."

The device was still buzzing on her clit, she was thrilled by the feel of his body all along her back and legs, "So a gentleman is a person who pins a young lady down on his bed, attaches dubious electronics to her vagina, and sticks all of his cock up her ass. My God, I know I'm with the Yankees."

He rose a little and slapped her ass lightly again, "We'll see if our little southern lady can enjoy something a little larger than Ezra."

"What are you doing?" she tried to turn. He kept her pinned down.

"Don't look, just feel, just enjoy big Ezra."

Why not relax? He'd judged everything perfectly so far, but an even larger dollop of lube on her ass made her wonder how this would go. He slid down to sit on the back of her knees. One hand went to the small of her back to pin her down firmly.

"Now pull you ass cheeks apart, as wide as you can."

That made her nervous, and did she enjoy listening to instructions? Commands? He wound up the clit vibrations slightly, this was no time to be shy, but it felt weird, she reached back and pulled herself open, "Be careful!"

"Of course. This will be very slow. We'll give you plenty time to take everything."

Was this about sensuality, or curiosity? For him, or for her? Oh, he'd played lots of games, with lots of people, she was certain of that. Now she would just relax and see what she could enjoy. So yes, let him push her and see where her boundaries were. "Just one thing."

"Yes?"

"Can I have that controller."

He laughed, "Definitely not, Miss Gunter. I know

your little tricks, but I want you to learn to hand over control. Trust me."

She laughed very loud, "Trust you?" she almost shrieked but, when he handed her the last pillow and told her to put it over her head. She meekly did.

"You know you want the boys to do what they want to with you. Big Ezra wants yo' ass, missy. Now let's take our time and see what you really enjoy."

But taking his time meant pushing his cock into her again first, "Maybe it's not something a southern gentleman would say but you sure do have a beautiful asshole, and when my friend here has made you scream, I'll be coming back for some more," and he slowly withdrew — and quickly replaced himself — but with something much bigger.

He let it vibrate slightly, "That should help you a little. Give yourself time."

He pushed, and the vibrations were helping as he moved it very slowly into her. It was feeling very uncomfortable now. Ezra was uncomfortable, but that had been a moment of screaming passion anyway. This was curiosity and challenge. "Much more?"

"A little, you OK?"

"Give it to me," said this strange guttural voice, "stay slow, but fucking give it to me!" There was a ring of searing pain, but it quickly passed. Oh, she felt so joyously full, but he still continued to push even further. But not too far. Then he stopped pushing and began to turn up the intensity of the vibrator. Oh, she could feel a massive wave coming. It hit her suddenly and everything spun around like falling of a surfboard in a huge breaker: you knew you would eventually right yourself but there would be a breathless few moments, of absolute, incomprehensible, turmoil. She had no idea of how loud she was screaming, or for how long. It was so massively intense. She felt a sharp tug of pain as she began to slow and grow quiet. He'd pulled the thing free, but then she felt him sliding into her. "Oh, Rob, come inside me, let me feel you. That was so fabulous, but I want to feel you coming."

"Oh, you will feel me coming," and he was pushing harder and harder, she took him easily, even when he pushed deeper, pushing roughly, almost violently, but that was what she wanted to feel, and she felt him and heard him climaxing loudly into her.

Then he slumped on to her, making less effort now to support his weight but somehow that felt more intimate, more together, now all her senses were feeling all of him again, not just his softening presence behind her, but his chest on her back, his legs entwined with hers, his mouth nibbling her ear.

He moved his arms to ease some weight off her but kept his chest touching her back, his belly still on her ass until, just as she came down into that green valley of contentment, he rolled off her but wrapped her in his arms. She pushed all the pillows away and kissed him deeply, leaned away, smiled at him, then kissed him again, their tongues dancing around each other's while their lips touched tenderly, gently. When she pulled away again, she said, "I'm afraid I'm still enjoying it, but maybe the little vibrator could take a rest."

He chuckled and reached for the controller, but she pulled it out anyway to examine it, "Wow," she said as he stilled it, "such a little thing, giving so much pleasure."

He laughed, "A lot of the ladies say that about me," but it was a self-confident laugh.

"Well, you wouldn't want to be the monster, would you, surely? Where is he?"

"You sure?"

"Of course, this is my education along with my ecstasy." He pulled up the Red Rabbit from behind him, "Wow, hello big Ezra." And it did look huge, maybe just not quite as big as Andy.

* * *

"I'm not going to want you there again for a while," she was on his sofa, dressed only in his bath robe, looking out at the deepening red sun dropping into Manhattan.

"So, I should call the guys and tell them not to bother coming?" Over in the kitchen area he was putting things from the fridge on a large plate, "Just as well, I don't have enough food for them. I'm just putting out cold meats and cheese, do you want wine or beer?"

"Red wine, please," she paused, "why am I here?"

"For the sex, I assumed," he said, quite coldly, "not for my company, surely." And he moved towards her and put a tray on the coffee table in front of her, "It's certainly not for my catering."

"This is perfect," she said to his retreating back as he went to fetch glasses and wine. She could admire, briefly, the tall, athletic body in the grey shorts and tee shirt. "Hey, it was a genuine question. If you start to get prickly with me, I shall think I've managed to offend you. I'm having a wonderful day, thank you, and I actually wouldn't mind another one like this some time. OK? That's my position on it."

He was looking at her from behind the kitchen worktop, opening a bottle, "Well, that's good. We're usually pretty clear on what Tania's position is, but it's nice to have it confirmed."

She was surprised, "Robert! You are getting prickly. I am having a wonderful day. I didn't know how it was going to turn out, but I've been thrilled," she fidgeted with her position, "although I think I'm going to have reminders for days." She did get a slight smile from him just before he tasted the wine, "I'd like to feel you'd had a good time too. Like I said, more please, some other time. Now how are you feeling. Or are you going to be a man and not tell me?"

It was almost a laugh from him this time as he brought the bottle and two glasses over and sat down beside her, "I also am having a wonderful day, thank you," he began pouring, she waited, he was probably going to say more, "and I would like to do this again some time."

He seemed to be waiting for her to say something, "But this isn't going to affect the rest of our lives…"

"Is that a question? Or are you telling me?"

He was being unusually tentative. She'd seen him as the boisterous party boy — on her way to lunch that day she'd tried to count the number of women she'd seen him having sex with but had stopped at double figures — but, talking about his work and Noah's paintings, she'd seen a different side. But this was new. "Can I make this easy for you, without being bossy, controlling Tania?"

He nodded, "I hope so."

Now she was feeling perplexed, she wasn't looking for a boy with needs — well, except sexual ones — "I was very much looking forward to today. I liked the sex, and I loved the conversation, although," and she lifted her glass, they clinked and drank, "it seems to be straying into peculiar territory. Cheers, by the way."

"Cheers," and he was looking somehow expectant.

Best continue, she thought, "I'm not doing dating. I've done a few parties, as you know, and sometimes my sister and I entertain friends of hers, but today was the first real date, can I call it that?"

He nodded, "I'd be glad if you would."

"Well, it's the first real date in a long while," she leaned across and kissed him lightly on the cheek, "and I'd like another one sometime, please. That's pretty simple, isn't it?"

"That's pretty simple, yes," and he put his glass down, took hers and put that down, then pulled her horizontal on the sofa and kissed her tenderly, "and that's where I'd like to start."

She looked at him somewhat sceptically, "I don't know if I'm reading this right, but I'm not usually scared of looking stupid. I think you're saying that we'll be doing dates occasionally, right?"

"No," now she was a little shocked, "I'm not saying, I'm asking." He smiled at her, "You're saying, but that's what you do."

"Really?" Now there were a few things to think about, *but focus on the priorities, Tania.*

"Really, but it is one of the things I love about you. We all know what you want us to do, but you get us doing things we love doing." It was a surprising perspective for her but, she supposed, it wasn't wrong. "Well, I'd just like a little bit of that to myself now and again. Is that too much?"

She kissed his lips and sat up again, picking up her glass. "No, I'd love to date now and again. Cheers!" and he sat up and raised his glass to her, "I didn't have you as the dating sort. You'll have to forgive me for not taking that too seriously. You're just a party boy, but one I like very much and find…"

"Oh, please don't say interesting."

She laughed, "Oh, no, that would be going too far."

"You're starting to make me see the attractions of spanking."

"I hope we can agree that my ass has had far too much attention for one day." He smiled. "You're a dangerous man, of course, so I'm not going to take it too seriously, but more dates, yes please, and does this mean I can ask you out, too?"

"I hope you'll feel free to do so," but he looked a little dubious.

"It's just, with my folks in town next week…" and she laughed at his horror-struck face, "Gotcha Master Robert! I think I've correctly judged the depth of your commitment. Occasional dating partners it is!"

* * *

She had a pleasant turmoil of feelings in the cab going back across the Brooklyn Bridge. She could still taste him, and her pussy was still warm and wet from their languorous sixty-nine. And in her handbag, she had the small clit-clip. He'd kept the controller, he would bring it to their next lunch date — *next week!* — where she would be wearing the clip. She smiled again at the thought, *just don't take it seriously, girl.*

Chapter 8

"I know it's a little cold out here, but it's a bit thrilling for me to have breakfast on a Manhattan terrace," Will said, "and, given how much you paid to have this, I do feel we should use it."

Martha sat down, having just fetched a thick cardigan for herself, "It's sweet of you to put it that way, but we paid for it, not just me. Half of your London apartment's mine if you leave me."

He thought for a moment, "A studio in docklands against three with a terrace on the East side. I didn't want the pre-nup, but..." he laughed gently.

"Well, I felt a little ridiculous. I was only doing it to reassure Ed, because I knew he'd ask, and I never told him the full story about Peter's little problem." They smirked at each other, as they usually did when glossing over that topic, "Oh, we have to have dinner with them some time, he's asked me for dates."

"I'm free any time."

"Tania would have to release you one evening. Shall I pour you some more coffee?"

He nodded and smiled at her, she always tried to sound open and friendly when she brought Tania into the conversation but, he thought, she does keep bringing

Tania into the conversation. So, it was obviously troubling her, but it would go away soon, he would see much less of Tania after they'd put their plan together. It was slightly touching that Martha was showing a sensitivity, a fragility even, about the topic. She was a woman, normally, of immense and well-justified self-confidence, but, apart from her surprising devotion to the kinky games they played, where she liked him to be so dominant, this was another unexpected aspect of her, this sensitivity to him being around younger women. He supposed it must be quite natural, even if it was a little irritating. Best to ignore it, he thought, "She wanted you to come and meet us for a drink after work yesterday, but I wanted to get home and I didn't know how you'd feel about it anyway."

"I wonder if you'll always be so disarmingly tactful." She eyed him suspiciously, "I would like to meet up some time, but drinks after work doesn't feel quite right."

"I know, and we'll get to a point in the fourth week when I'd like you to look over what we're doing, if you wouldn't mind. Can I set something up? You could come and see the office, we'll go through the stuff and then go for dinner with her afterwards."

"Sounds like a good idea. When were you thinking?"

"Peter and Claudia are back on the Friday in three weeks. If you could do the Wednesday, that would be perfect, it would give us a day to reshape, because you're bound to see something — if you don't torpedo the whole thing. You could get there by six, couldn't you?"

"I'm hardly going to torpedo it, you two guys are very good indeed, but I'd love to think I could help. If I'm at the bank that day, of course, I can definitely make it, my life's much more civilised now. Not that you see what time I get home, you're never here," but it seemed a good-natured comment, "seriously though, does she have a life? She's a very attractive young woman, but she doesn't seem to give herself much time."

He thought for a moment, "Well, when we talked about you coming for a drink, I asked if she'd want you to bring a rich banker — not that she'd need money with the family business behind her — but she said she didn't have time for the offers she already gets. I'd just assumed she does all right for company."

"Wasn't there something with Andy Molloy?"

"You know there was," he smiled again, "you just love a bit of gossip, don't you? Peter mentioned there'd been something, and she's going up to Boston on Tuesday. She said it was going to be a tricky conversation and I just said, 'I know' so she didn't have to go into details for me."

"Is the plan coming together?"

"Well, a few different plans are taking shape. I think she's right that the group should be reformed into something more coherent, so the businesses can use each other's strengths. But I'm worried I'll get too enthusiastic about the plans for this, when we could make good use of the money elsewhere. So, if you could do that

Wednesday, it would be brilliant, if I'm losing perspective, you'll be able to tell us."

"And she'd be happy with my input?"

"She's pretty good at keeping an open mind. They're tough skills to combine, aren't they? If I see people who have a clear vision of what they want, they're not always the most receptive to alternative thoughts, but she seems extremely good like that — although I've really only had this week of working closely with her, Hey, we're talking too much about work."

He got a slightly mischievous smile from her, "I wasn't talking about work, I was talking about Tania Gunter."

Yes, I knew you were, he thought.

Chapter 9

Andy's new PA showed Tania into the office. He came towards her to greet her with his arms open.

She smiled but put her hand on his chest, "Andy, it was harder to get out of the 'us' thing than I thought, I admit it. I'd like to try to pretend it didn't happen. Can you go along with that?"

He seemed to mull it over, "Would you compromise and agree to at least talk about it later?"

She paused a while, then leaned forward and kissed him quickly on the cheek, "If we're not fighting about the important stuff and we've still got time, then yes, but I am enjoying my life at the moment, I have to tell you that. Well, I was until they dropped this on me…"

"Come on, sit down," he gestured to the armchairs, "I gather congratulations are in order, boss." He was squinting at her, more sceptical than hostile, she thought. It reminded her, he was one of that rare few who could actually laugh at themselves.

"Andy, this will always be your business. You built it, it's got your name on it, and it's brilliant. I just want to see if there are ways of making the Group stronger, but I'll say right up front that yours is the most standalone of them all. So, I'm certainly not threatening your autonomy and I'm hoping you can give me the most detached view of some ideas Will and I have been working on."

"Was that your prepared speech?"

She looked straight back at him, "Yup, pretty good, wasn't it?" and she smiled at him.

"Fuck you, Tania Gunter," but he was smiling back at her, and shaking his head.

She pulled two reports from her bag and handed one to him, "Paper for you, old man, I know computers frighten you."

"Are you trying to make sure we argue about all this stuff?"

"We'll see where your interests lie, if you can agree on these plans, I won't even mind talking about us." She stopped, looked at him and smiled again, "No, seriously, you can flip around easier through the pages on paper. I think it makes it easier for discussion."

"I know, I was just yanking your chain — like you were doing with me. OK, what's on your mind?"

Then he let her review all the businesses briefly, and then she spent more time on how they interacted and supported each other.

"Or don't," he said, and then talked about areas where he could see changes being beneficial, "but you do have one or two Hanks out there."

"Hank?"

"He was my COO before Eddie, my oldest and best friend, but Claudia made me get rid of him. Ruthless bitch," but he was almost laughing, "she was dead right, of course, as she almost always is. The business had outgrown him. You have a couple of CEOs out there who are in the same position."

"Wanna tell me who?"

"From what you've been saying, I think you know one of them, and it sounds like Will knows the other. But tell me more about that network idea of yours."

"I'll have to give it another name. I couldn't steal that one from Rod. Well, his is a kind of sinister concept anyway, the way he exploits it, but it does usefully describe the idea."

"I agree, I could even see that working for us. We're better since you guys got involved but we're still not exploiting what we could do with data, or a better service network."

And she talked at greater length about distribution, service and field support all being more clearly linked, "And if we just replace and not repair, we can deskill the service jobs — or let the guys out there service all of our businesses, not just the ones they currently specialise in. The IT support for it all is a lot like Giddings does already. Dad has a much better team than he realises. I'd like to set them up as an independent unit, fifty-fifty Giddings and Dickinson but I suspect he's a little old-fashioned for that. But there are one or two people out there starting to offer the full package, some even experimenting with AI, we could buy one of them."

"You have a preference?"

"I like the thought of us developing the new skills,

especially in using AI, but we'd go quicker if we buy someone, especially Radius…"

"Those are the guys on the west coast?"

"Yes, they have the best technology, it looks like, but they don't really have a nationwide network."

"You could do both, buy them and set up ourselves, all in one bigger business. We've almost got complementary skill sets, if I've understood you right."

"And you'd support that?"

"Sure I would; ultimately I get a more responsive support network, even if I'm sharing it. And I think you're on to something with replace and not repair, you take some of the skills away and the job gets done on the day, we have some jobs not completed until more parts are ordered. That's a delay for the customer and a double visit for us — the second of which isn't billable."

"Will's guys have worked out, across the Group, that ninety percent of repairs in the field cost more than replacements, that's without the costs of the double visits you just mentioned."

"Have they looked at my data in that?" He raised his eyebrows.

She nodded, "It's a little over ninety for you."

He pursed his lips and nodded, "Son of a bitch, I never knew it was that high."

"Eddie knew. He's been working on ideas to change things before he talks to you. I haven't talked to him about this yet, we've only been working on it a week, but I'm pretty sure it would help him."

Andy seemed to be weighing this over, "I like your thinking. I could see it working."

"So you'll support it? I can tell Peter and Claudia?"

"I'll tell them myself. I'm not sure about the other areas you want to buy into, but they don't affect me. But this could be a big idea, you shouldn't sit around and wait. You offer this as a platform and you could reverse your way into other businesses that fit us, if you like them."

This had gone much better than she'd imagined. She was getting the best of Andy; the imaginative, the positive, the dynamic, the inspiring — even the Japanese had warmed to him. She had lost sight of that when she'd got wrapped up in the man — and he'd got wrapped up in his own relationship issues.

"Can I admit that this has gone much better than I'd thought?"

"Me too. I think we both deserve a pat on the back for ignoring the elephant in the room."

Their eyes met, "We do, and thank you."

He leaned back in his chair, a dangerous sign that he thought that part of the discussion was over. And it was, she thought, she'd got a much more supportive Andy than she'd expected. But what was coming now?

"You want to do this? The whole Group CEO thing?"

Well, at least that wasn't a relationship question, "I haven't really thought it through from the personal angle. I've just thrown myself into it to see if there's something we can put together that makes more strategic sense than Peter's personality matrix."

"What the fuck is that?"

"It's Will's term for describing how Peter put the Group together. He believed in people who could run their own businesses but who would want to interact with and profit from like-minded souls doing similar but different things. You can't argue it didn't work, but you couldn't carry on like that without someone like Peter keeping it together — and, in a funny way, Claudia is a lot like Peter."

Andy laughed, "Well, they like similar things."

Tania felt, unusually, slightly embarrassed, then said. "Does that mean we've concluded the business part of the discussion?" somewhat frostily.

"Don't go all schoolmarm on me. We're talking about two people we love and respect, they can stand a bit of irreverence. Nobody needs to be taken seriously all the time, that's the path to madness."

Were they going to stray into the relationship area? If the business discussion was concluded — and she'd got all the support she came for — there was an hour before she needed to leave for her fight. "Is that where we'd got to?"

He seemed to ponder again. Perhaps he hadn't meant to stray into that area, he was spending a long time mulling it over. She began putting papers away. Then suddenly he said, "I miss you. So, a little part of me will be glad if this comes off. You'll have to come and talk to me about my business and I do love working with you. I'll get used to the other part of it not being there…" he stopped, then raised his eyes to hers — he'd been talking to his feet, or the table — she'd been pretending to be paying attention to some stupid papers. "You OK talking about it now?"

"Not really, but I can't go on avoiding it, can I, not if we're going to work together."

"It was good, wasn't it?"

She nodded, "I hadn't expected it to go that far, with feelings and things, neither had you, had you?" Now she shook her head, normally she'd take control of a situation like this, but she ought to let him get this out.

"It did affect me, and Jen saw that, and I thought, at the time, that she was getting too deep with someone else anyway," he laughed to himself, "you tell yourself it doesn't matter so much if your wife's with another woman, but it did. I hadn't had feelings of jealousy for a long time and neither, it turned out, had she. But now I wonder what you're doing, and I try to be noble and hope you're happy."

"I'm happy," she said, "but not in the way you're worrying about."

He looked a little irritated, "That's not really fair. I do want you happy."

"I believe you. But you were becoming the big relationship in my life, and that was starting to fuck things up for both of us. I'm not looking for another one of those. I seem to be doing quite well without it. I'd just like you to tell me that you're feeling settled now."

"I can't really say that, no. We've tried to re-establish what we had, but we watch each other more, irritate each other more."

"You still have other partners?"

Now the silence fell again. He looked uncomfortable.

"Can I make it easier for you? I have other partners, but I did even when we were seeing each other. I hope you're doing something. I'd hate to think of him going to waste," she regretted that as soon as she'd said it. Humour wasn't yet appropriate. He was smiling only wanly. "I'm sorry. I'm not really ready for jokes yet either. That was silly of me, but I've said it now. So, I can tell you there are things about him that I don't miss," now she got a slightly bigger smile out of him, "and, just to get a little irreverent, I think Claudia had the right idea, try him once, just for the experience, then leave him alone." Now he was actually chuckling, "But you're not telling me he's been inactive. I wouldn't believe you."

Now he was looking straight at her, "No, I'm not telling you that. He's had one or two outings. But, since we're speaking frankly, his most common partner is my right hand, and I'm thinking about you when I'm doing that."

She sat forward in the chair, getting ready to leave, "Look, it was lovely, and you were a wonderful fuck, but I was spending too much time thinking about you, worrying about how you were with her — and I really didn't want to fuck that up. I've no idea what the right answer was, but feeling shitty because you're fucking someone's life up, and because you're missing them, didn't seem the right thing to be doing. And you seemed to be pushing me away for something that wasn't really making you happy." She was aware she was getting animated.

He was still sat back in his chair, looking surprisingly relaxed, "Was that your other prepared speech?" and he smiled at her, that wretched Andy smile, she thought.

Now she sat back again, sighed, but smiled, "No, that was improv." She thought a moment, "I actually think it was better than my prepared effort earlier," she waited for him to smile and nod, "I've had a great morning. I'd forgotten how good you were with these things. I'd missed all that as well. I would love us to work together again. If only you didn't have such a gorgeous cock!" Now she stood up quickly.

He stood up now, "Well, he's still available. My right hand doesn't get jealous."

"Your wife still does. And I don't want all that feelings shit again."

He was nodding pensively, "That feelings shit — I think I'll treasure that as an abiding romantic memory," now he smiled again and opened his arms. "This is a hug. It's entirely appropriate. I will open the door first if you require witnesses to ensure its innocence."

She put her bag down and opened her arms to embrace him. God, it was good to hold him again.

Chapter 10

"I know you're going to say this is gorgeous, my love, but I think he's put us in the presidential villa to soften us up."

"Very well," said Claudia, smiling at him, "I shall ask him to put you in a normal room so you can evaluate the full range of the facilities from a mortal perspective."

He looked sheepish, "No need for that. A detailed tour will tell me all I need to know. My God, you look disturbingly fresh considering that journey," but he continued to walk around the rooms, opening every drawer, turning all the taps on and off, but turning his back on the bath, "That control panel spooks me. You'll have to work it out."

She was coming to realise that the most majestically capable man she'd ever met, for that was how she'd originally seen him, was decidedly more majestic than he was capable. With Andreas and Hannes missing, almost everything devolved on to her. That was easy, to a point, she'd always organised everything; at home, where Dave had always been useless; and at work, where there was usually a vacuum to be filled — but once you'd established that you would fill it, so much got delegated to you that you slowly became indispensable, and then, over time, you became the one deferred to. Once she'd established her own business, she was always careful to make sure everything was fixed at the appropriate level. It meant a lot of delegation, but no abdication.

Was Peter abdicating? She smiled to herself; no, not really. She'd also grown used to having Pat and Penelope organise everything for her. It meant that this brief hiatus, until Raymond and Alphonse took over the management of their time for the next few days, caught them slightly unprepared. That was a situation she could cope with much more easily than Peter.

Soon enough there was a gentle bell sound at the door. Peter was out exploring their veranda. She let Alphonse and Raymond in, Alphonse looking cool and relaxed in his tropic cream ensemble, Raymond, whom she was meeting for only the second time, looked slightly dishevelled and even more harassed than on the first occasion.

Alphonse pulled her to him and kissed her lightly on the lips, then said, "I don't know how you can travel this far and still look so perfectly wonderful," he got a smile, but a raised eyebrow with it, "You've met Raymond before haven't you?"

"Of course, I met him at Teluk, last year," she turned to him, "hello again Raymond, and I have to say extremely well done. First impressions here are amazing, and this is all your work, isn't it? Not something we've bought and converted."

Raymond had started to look relaxed but had now

moved on to bashful, "I thank you very much, but the overall concept comes from this man here... and the money, of course, comes from you."

"Well, the money comes from this man here," she pointed to the large double doors which opened out on to the patio, Peter was coming back in.

"Someone's trodden on a plant at the edge of the veranda! Only perfection in paradise, please." Raymond rushed towards the doors, "Where are you going, man?"

"I need to see, I need to sort this straightaway."

"Raymond, my dear chap, I think you might let me greet you first," and Peter held out his hand and put on, belatedly, the big smile. Raymond hovered a moment but then stepped back into the room, bowing slightly on his way to shaking hands. Peter then turned to Alphonse, "First impressions are good. Would you like to give us an hour before you take us all around the place?"

"We'll fit in with whatever suits you. It's a long journey..."

"It is a long journey, it was nearly four hours from the airport. That's too long."

"It would have been less than thirty minutes in the helicopter, that's the VIP package. I told you how long the car journey would be." Alphonse had such a calm and neutral way of presenting facts, they never appeared as admonishments, although they clearly, and effectively, were. It was a skill that few possessed, and one she wished she could emulate. He had told Peter how long it would take and what the alternative was. He was being

118

as patient as a parent — or as a parent would like to be.

"I wanted to experience it for myself. It's not that nice a journey, either. Anyway, what have you got planned for us?" *He was seldom testy like this,* thought Claudia.

Alphonse looked quickly at her, as if wondering if the same mood was afflicting her. She smiled at him and raised her eyebrows slightly. "We have planned a familiarisation tour this afternoon and, at some point in the three days we have you, we need a serious discussion about the next phase. But I need you in a better mood for that."

She could see Raymond flinch, and even she wondered whether Alphonse had overreached himself. Peter certainly hesitated, but then a broad grin spread across his face, "Am I being that grumpy?"

Now Alphonse smiled and nodded, "No more than any other mature gentleman who's been travelling for eighteen hours would be. That's why I'd like you to take tomorrow to just relax here, try some of the spa treatments, see the beach and pools as a resort guest."

Peter was nodding, he turned to Raymond, "And I don't want us given any special treatment, we're just normal guests, OK?"

Raymond was recovering his self-possession, "Well, in this suite you would normally have a butler on duty, so you're already on a reduced package — in line with your instructions."

"Who issued those?" he asked sharply. Claudia and

Alphonse smiled at each other and then looked at him, "I did?" he looked surprised at himself.

"You did, my love, and before you terrorise poor Raymond any more, we'll ask them to return in one hour to take us round, by which time we'll have located the persona of the charming English gentleman, which is obviously still in your suitcase, and we'd like you to wear that for the tour and the meal." She turned to Raymond, "I know the clock tells me that will be dinner, but my stomach won't let me call it that. Anyway, we'll see you in an hour."

* * *

The tour took two hours. Claudia found it thrilling to walk along the white sand and see the well-spaced villas and cottages in the shadows of the palms. They looked round two of them, she reflecting how delighted she would be with any, Peter taking a very detached but detailed view. When he started stripping beds back, Raymond told him gently that all linen and mattresses were identical to the ones in his suite, unless the guest had requested something different.

"So, if I want a softer mattress?"

"It would be changed within the hour — even during the night if you can't sleep well," said Raymond. Claudia smiled and nodded to him as Peter, with a barely detectable shrug, made his way into the bathroom.

The main building was, for her, enchanting. It

appeared to have no walls at all around the reception area, or on either side of the large dining room.

"Storms?" asked Peter.

"The glass panels, hidden in those thick wooden columns, will slide shut within ninety seconds. Would you like a demonstration?"

"I'll wait for the storm, but if we've had nothing by Monday, I would like to see them then. You're in an area that's new to me, gentlemen, as you well know, I'm afraid you'll have to forgive my intrusive questioning. Well, that's an interesting figure of speech, isn't it? You don't have to forgive it at all, of course, but you do have to put up with it."

The other men both smiled, but Claudia wondered what was troubling him. Maybe it had been the journey, but on last year's trip to the first resort at Teluk he'd been his charming, phlegmatic self. But the length of the tour meant there was little time to talk to him before dinner, but she showered quickly and changed again — keeping everywhere open meant being a prey to humidity — in order to make a little time. He was waiting when she emerged, "We're almost late."

"I'd like you to sit down for ten minutes and talk to me."

"We told them seven-thirty."

"We'll do less damage by being ten minutes late than we could do if your mood continues as it was this afternoon. Something's bothering you, what is it?"

His brow furrowed, he breathed deeply twice, then

shrugged, smiled and opened his arms, "If I promise not to crease that gorgeous silk dress, could I possibly have a gentle cuddle?"

"Of, course, my darling, as long as you understand me being a little careful about smudging make-up on that beautiful shirt," they embraced silently for a minute or two, then she looked up and kissed him, "at least you haven't complained about all your clothes being ironed, that is part of the standard VIP package, I know, and I haven't had treatment like that since the weekend on Yvonne. Now, what's up?"

He hesitated, but he was clearly going to talk, "There is something troubling me. I can't even accuse you of excessive sensitivity for noticing it. I have been a bit shitty, haven't I?" She just smiled and nodded, "We need to talk about it tomorrow, it's just a business thing, but let's just have a charming, best-behaviour dinner this evening and try to get some sleep, OK?"

"OK, but best behaviour, promise?"

And it almost worked.

He was very complimentary about the development: 'I love the designs, better than the mock-ups you showed me'; the standards, 'only one little crushed plant, but by my veranda', he was smiling now; and how wonderful all the food was — he just tried small samples of most things; and the excellent business results from Teluk, 'even I know that's astonishing occupancy'. The atmosphere had become very relaxed and friendly, although the wine consumption had been modest, but then, as they were finishing dessert, Peter asked Raymond about the next stage of expansion. She wondered later if Peter had waited with that question — he had drunk unusually little; Raymond, after days, if not weeks of tension, had not been quite so careful, "Well, that depends on whether we can interest you in the chain." Peter's face was very still, she may have seen an eyelid flicker, but she knew this apparent passivity from the critical phases of the divorce proceedings, he was struggling to control a submerged fury.

She looked across to Alphonse, whose face gave even less away, but he stepped in quickly, "It's just one of the thoughts, very blue-sky thinking, we've got plenty time on Monday to go over all the options."

"I'm happy to wait however long you want to discuss plans," this was calm but with no animation, not like his normal expressive, smiley calm, "but I have no patience about discussing treachery," he was looking very fixedly at Alphonse, who turned slowly to look at him.

"I can't imagine anything that's happening that could be described by that word, Peter, I really can't, but I'm happy to talk about anything, any time," here he looked to Claudia, as if looking for support, then back to Peter, "but I really would plead for a night's sleep before we discuss any plans."

Peter stood up, "I will grant you that I don't entirely trust myself in my current frame of mind, but nine in the morning is the latest I'll wait. Goodnight." And he turned and left. She'd never seen him do that before. Part of her wanted to find out what was troubling him, but she would understand that better, she thought, if she spoke to Alphonse first.

Raymond hadn't moved. He looked shocked. Alphonse smiled, reached out and patted him on the shoulder, "Don't worry," he said, "I don't know what the misunderstanding is. We'll be fine in the morning."

"I don't know what this is about," said Claudia, looking at Raymond, "I know we've had a long day travelling and he didn't sleep well on the plane. But I've had a wonderful day, I think this place is beyond what I could ever have imagined. You've done a fabulous job. But I think you should get some sleep. I'd just like a few minutes with Alphonse, but I'm sure we'll calm Peter down in the morning."

"Thank you, and I'm very…"

"Don't," said Alphonse quickly, "there's nothing to worry about, honestly. Claudia's right, you should get some rest."

Raymond was standing up, still looking shaken. "I'm so…"

"There's absolutely nothing you should feel sorry about. We'll talk in the morning, main meeting room, nine o'clock, OK? Sorry if we've messed up your Sunday, apologise to your wife for me," he turned to Claudia, smiling, "his wife and son are here for the opening. It's been a godsend, we've needed every pair of hands," he smiled again, "and we have absolutely no scruples about using child labour."

Raymond managed a wan smile, turned to Claudia, "Thank you for your very kind words. Will I see you in the morning?"

"Oh, she'll be there," said Alphonse firmly. That seemed to relax him, "See you at nine."

Alphonse made sure Raymond had left the dining area before he turned back to Claudia, "Treachery, eh? More than a little strong, I would have thought. I can only think of one thing. Have you got a little time?"

"The more I know the better, if I'm going to help."

He took her hand in both of his, "I do appreciate that."

"What do you think is behind it?"

He kept one hand on hers, "I'll tell you what I think the trigger might be, but even if I'm right, this feels like a major overreaction. I can't think I've ever seen him like this before in the fifteen years I've known him."

"Well, I've known him much less than that, but he has surprised me since we got here. So, what do you think has set him off?"

"I'm making a leap, because it's not something that should have happened. When we were out here eighteen months ago," he paused, "you weren't here that time, were you? I'd just persuaded him to buy Teluk. We flew a lot of guys in who were managing the big new money out here, it was mostly to bring more into Tony and Henry's funds, and Peter is obviously a major ambassador for that, but a number of them were also interested in property propositions, including what we were starting up…"

"I gather it was interesting socially too," she smiled at him.

He squeezed her hand and smiled back, "There was an interesting development for a while, but it didn't last long. That's where geography helps when you get bored with someone. Anyway, a couple of the guys who are putting money in with Tony are also interested in the resort programme. Tony's kept the conversation live, although I've told him we like our autonomy in this area, so I've discouraged it. I actually asked him to be very careful when talking to Peter about it, and to stress that I was against it — which I was, at the time. But there's a resort chain coming on to the market, the properties are not so high-class, but the locations are excellent, from what I can see. Raymond knows them and he's excited, but I wanted to broach it carefully. It's more money than we have, and I've been reluctant to contemplate joint ventures. But it sounds a little like Tony may have been encouraging Peter to open his mind a little, and these days, I'm finding, I need to be a little more careful around him. It's your fault, of course, you know that don't you?"

She was shocked, he'd posed the question too seriously for her to think it a jest, it would have been bad taste anyway — that was not his style. He was looking at her kindly. She was shaking her head, "You can't just say that to me. You're not joking, are you?"

"I'm not, and I shouldn't be so glib. It's not a throwaway line. We may have two big issues here and

I'm worried because he's either gone straight to sleep, or he's walking around the main room down there wondering what you're still doing with your erstwhile lover. I do mean erstwhile physical lover," he squeezed her hand again and smiled, "emotionally I'm still committed, but now I'm worrying about both of you. So, I won't keep you."

"But you have to tell me why you said what you've just said."

"Of course, and very quickly. I suspect Tony's pushing him to open things up, I expect he has investors who want to work with us on resorts, and there's a major opportunity out there, and they will be people who would put more money into his funds as part of a package but, taken all together, we might be compromising our autonomy and Peter has always cherished his independence." Now he moved a little closer, "The other point is actually a bigger one, and I do mean it very kindly to both of you…"

Now she was puzzled and very apprehensive.

"When he was married, he was never really in love. I think he always had enough judgement to recognise the eros phase for what it was, something soon over, and he'd always seen the potential his wives had to promote interesting social events, if I can call them that," he smiled at her warmly.

"OK, I get that."

"But it's different now, he's very much in love with you, and it's making him feel terribly vulnerable in a way he hasn't felt since…"

"Anne?"

"Yes, he has told you then?"

"Yes, it was a kind of breakthrough moment. But I'm not Anne, for heaven's sake."

"My darling, you have slept with his best friend, well, I don't think I'm that really, but I'd say we were close. Yet he's been different with me since the two of you have been together, I'm only surmising, but I am putting things together that I've been noticing. Make of it what you will, and I'm sure you'll be very tactful when you talk to him. I'll get hold of Tony overnight, I'm not sure where he is, but it will help to know exactly what's been said. I am seriously pissed off with him, we agreed that I should broach the subject, not him, but maybe he thought I'd be too cowardly, and he's worried about missing an opportunity. And on the bigger topic, your relationship, those are just my views, I'll let you handle it. Come on, you'd better get back to him."

He stood up and held out his hands to her. She stood and kissed him for longer than she should have done. She still thought he was adorable. "Thank you, lots to think about. I guess I'll see you at nine, we'll have breakfast in the villa, he and I obviously need to talk."

He was asleep when she got there. He always managed that quickly. When stressed, not often, she thought, he would wake in the middle of the night and read or work, leaving her to wake up next to a cold, empty space.

She undressed and climbed naked into bed, touching him carefully with leg and hand. If he did wake early, he could, she hoped, ponder her nakedness. She smiled to herself as she closed her eyes, she mostly wanted to talk, but if other things happened, that was OK too.

* * *

It was still quite dark when she woke but there was a hint of light outside, the view from their large window faced west into a silver sky. She was startled to see him in a chair, looking at her. "You've been awake ages, I assume. I was hoping you'd wake me."

"Ah, using your naked body as bait, now I understand."

"I can't see your face in this light, but if that was anything other than a joke, you and I have a major problem."

"Don't I have enough of those?"

"I don't know whether you have the problems you think you do — and one thing I am sure of, not one of them is helped by you sitting over there in that chair. Come here this minute, Peter Dickinson, and put your arms around my body!" Slowly he eased himself up and moved to the bed. "No, you don't. You're not getting into bed with those things on. You may find it hard to believe but I want to feel that hairy chest on my breasts."

He slipped out of the pale blue pyjamas. She had never seen any other colour, it was as if he had a romantic attachment to the memories of their first real night together. He slid naked into the bed and wrapped his arms tight around her, "Am I being very stupid?" he asked, his voice cracking with emotion.

She kissed his lips gently, "I very much doubt that, but there are obviously things I don't understand. But I'm not sure you understand how much I love you. Now hold me for a while."

She liked his body. It was older, true, and had maybe never been lean, but he was tall and broad and altogether substantial. And he would normally be responsive, but that was not happening yet. That was a small relief. She would be happy to take him, but she knew she could make him much happier when she really wanted him. Right now, he seemed happy to hold her.

"When it gets a little lighter, could we take a walk along the sands?"

He answered slowly, "It's a lovely idea, although we may find the romance disturbed by an army of Malays restoring the beach to pristine perfection before the guests go down." At least there was now a little laughter in his voice.

She reached for his cock gently, "If we stay here now, I shall be pressing him into service. I think it's best we take a walk first and clear your upper brain."

He started to move, that was a relief. She slipped out of bed and pulled bikini, shorts and top on in the time it took him to find his shorts.

"Ready, already?" he nodded appreciatively.

"You're with a working girl now, PD, not one of your decorative sirens."

"I was feeling a siren call just now."

"I have plans for our siesta, later, let's get the morning sorted first. Come on," and they walked, hand in hand, through the living area and out on to the veranda. "Not locking up?"

"No, everything valuable's in the safe and I'm keen to see if there are any attempted intrusions. Although I think Raymond's good on security too. He seems to be very good all round."

"He won't think that's what you think."

"After last night, you mean?" and he looked pensive. They reached the sand quickly. At the far end of the property, in the dim light, she could make out movement and noise, the team were obviously getting ready to prepare the beach for the day, but they would have the shoreline to themselves, so they plodded through the soft, dimpled sand to the smooth, firm surface left by the lapping little waves. "Did Alphonse say anything after I left? I suppose he did. I know you two are close."

"Ha," she stopped, turned towards him and took his other hand, went on tiptoes and kissed him. She was with the most impressive man she'd ever met and here she was, deploying almost two decades' worth of parenting skills, "You're right, we are very close, and we both love you very much in our different ways. We do love each other a little bit, too, but neither of us wants to revisit what we had before you and I got together. So, stop that, please. You and I don't like to admit it's troubling you, and maybe I've said too much, but I don't want you distracted by a non-issue." He looked down at the sand, obviously not yet convinced. But she'd at least made the point, and it had been almost true. "But he did say he's worried there is another issue, a business issue, and that's on your mind, maybe."

They started walking along the water's edge, "What's he said?"

"Oh no you don't. You're not catching me like that. I might find myself in a nine o'clock meeting with two issues to discuss," she was smiling up at him as they walked. He was looking ahead but began to smile and nod. "I have been learning from you, you know."

He chuckled, "Oh, I think you went past me some time ago."

"But come on, you used the word treachery last night. That was a bit heavy, wasn't it?"

"It was melodramatic, I admit that, but it describes how I felt."

Now she chuckled, "Yes, you made that very obvious. I think we revived Raymond after you left, but I was fearing for his health. I hadn't seen you like that either."

"I may have gone too far."

"Only may?" she wasn't enquiring accusingly.

He seemed to mull it over again as they walked along, "I'm sticking with may," he said, after a while. They walked further, he was plainly formulating some thoughts. After a while, he said, "Keeping the right level of control over this sprawling monster has always needed careful judgement," he looked to her and waited to see her nodding. "In the Group I've tended to go for forty percent in the early phases, so the guys know that, overall, what they're running is still their own business, but they're not allowed to ignore me. With the two early ones, where I made my first fortunes, it's a much smaller percentage than that now. I'm just an ordinary major shareholder and it's been a few years since I've needed or wanted to say something. They're major businesses in their own right now and don't really need my advice or guidance.

"With funds it's different, of course. I was their first big backer. At the start I was over sixty percent, and the rest was mostly from friends of mine who trusted my judgement, but now I'm only about ten percent, although my dollar stake is much bigger, that's how much they've grown, but the understanding we have," he kept walking for a while and then stopped, "maybe I have to say had," now he was walking again, "anyway, the arrangement is that I remain always their biggest investor, and my share is set to sustain that. I just feel that gives me the level of input into what they're doing that I want to have, and it helps me remain their biggest ambassador.

"On properties my stake is, proportionately, much greater. It's really just me and the bank. And it's only when things go a little crazy, like last year, that the bank feels the need to get involved. What's up?"

133

She'd been smiling, almost chortling, "I'm sorry, I mustn't distract you. When you mentioned the bank, I just had some thoughts about Martha and Will. Absolutely not relevant at the moment."

"Go on, distract me for a while, I'm getting too serious."

"You're not, you're coming on to talk about property and, I suspect, resorts, we're at the core of the issue."

"The core of the issue is control, and you were thinking about Martha and Will."

"Yes, do you think that plays a part in their sex life?"

"Control?" he asked. She pursed her lips, and looked doubtful, "Discipline?" now she smiled, "I'm pretty sure it does. It was after I told him she had unusual tastes that he seemed to get keener to meet her again."

She gasped, "You set him up!" but she found it funny, then she laughed again after a while.

"What is it now?" but he seemed intrigued more than irritated and maybe it wasn't a bad idea to distract him a little.

"Well, Martha's all prickly about Will working closely with Tania, but she'll have more to worry about when Lavinia gets there, if that's what Will's truly interested in. Funny, isn't it? I wouldn't have guessed he was one of those."

"One of those what?"

"Spankers."

"Is that how you see me?"

"I hope so, my lovely man. Don't let me down at

siesta time. I want everything. But first I want to get to the bottom of this problem, absolutely no pun intended. Tell me about property control."

"It's more about resort control. Alphonse has a vision about establishing a major global brand of exclusive resorts. The demographics and spending patterns say he's right, there are more and more wealthy people wanting exclusive experiences and that's what he wants Psamathe to stand for."

"I thought that was just the name of the first place he bought."

"No, that was the name he gave it. It's the Greek god of the sea shore, apparently. It's a weird enough name, probably unpronounceable in every language on the planet, but at least it's distinctive," and he chuckled to himself. "I know he wants to go faster, but I'd like the concept proved first and it's early days yet," he grew pensive, "but I couldn't support a fast roll-out financially anyway, and he knows that. But it seems he's also been listening to Tony's moneymen, who see us, in total, as an attractive package they want to latch on to," now he looked to be getting a little animated again. "It seems they've both gone much further with those discussions than I gave them permission to, so we have a mess to deal with, because it will make our disagreements obvious and we'll look like we don't know what we're doing, and that I have a team I can't trust." He spat the last words out.

She just held his hand and carried on walking slowly. They were way past the end of their beach now and approaching another property. "Time to turn back? I'd like to shower before breakfast."

"Yes, time to turn back. Thank you. I should really have talked to your earlier."

They stopped. She could ask why he didn't, she was puzzled about when he could have spoken to Tony, but that might just create another problem. He left her enough freedom with the Group and she hadn't been looking for more issues to involve herself in. They turned back towards their resort, feeling the sun now on their faces as it rose above the palms. "I think I'll like it here very much if we can calm things down this morning."

He looked doubtful.

They managed to talk about other topics over breakfast and got to the meeting room, as almost always, punctually. Alphonse was there alone. "Raymond not joining us?" asked Peter.

"He will when I call him, but you and I should clear the air about the 't' word first."

He let that hang in the air.

Peter stayed stiffly formal, "You thought it inappropriate?"

"Of course I thought it inappropriate, but if the man I admire above anyone else in the world uses it, then I have to take it seriously and work out what the problem really is."

"The problem is that you appear to have been having negotiations with other parties that we'd already discussed and ruled out. You both know I am against them. I thought I'd been very clear about that."

"You had been clear about what you were outlawing, and it's your money and it's your business, ultimately."

"What does ultimately mean?" he snapped.

Alphonse looked slightly tense, but he was managing his emotions better than Peter. "Ultimately means I expect to get your approval for any big decision, but I do expect a lot of scope to formulate proposals for you."

"But if I know those proposals go far beyond what I'm prepared to accede to, then what's the point of pursuing them? You waste a lot of time and money and make us look uncoordinated, if not ridiculous."

"I can't tell you what these proposals will cost without some further conversations…"

"Tony had a very clear number in his head, and a clear idea about where he wanted the money to come from."

"I have Tony ready to join us on speaker phone, but I'd rather you and I settled our differences first."

Peter still looked prickly, "Do you want Claudia to stay for this discussion?" He looked at each of them in turn. It felt like a trick question.

"I'm staying anyway," she said defiantly. They both looked a little surprised, "You normally talk these things through so calmly. It doesn't feel like you've got the emotion out of the discussion yet. I'm going to referee that for you."

"This isn't a tournament," Peter said sharply,

looking betrayed, "It's about my corporation."

"Which has thrived because you choose people who are prepared to challenge you and bring you new ideas."

"But we work the big things out together, we don't go outside first."

"I'd like to understand this transgression a little better before I can comment on whether it deserved the word treachery," she said. Peter breathed deeply and shook his head. Alphonse remained studiously unemotional. "You say Tony had a clear number. What was it Alphonse?"

"I don't know, but I don't want to talk about Tony's numbers and conversations anyway without him being a party to this discussion."

"That's fair," she said, determined to hang on to the initiative, "but what about the guidelines for investment in your programmes?"

Alphonse looked at Peter, "My understanding was that you would earmark five hundred for property and five hundred for resort programme expansion…"

"When the profitable basis had been clearly proven. We're a long way from that yet."

"Teluk is beating all its numbers and we're ahead on bookings here."

"Teluk is not beating all its numbers. You're only on plan for profit."

"Because Raymond has increased his promotional spend to get even higher occupancy. We'd always agreed we would control to profit."

"So you can't say it's beating all its numbers."

Claudia could see this was unreasonable, but just pointing that out was not going to make him change his mind, so she asked him, "What's your timescale for going to new resorts?"

"I thought we'd be doing one at a time, maybe at eighteen-month intervals, which wouldn't overstretch the team." He turned to Alphonse, "I thought you were ready to make a decision on Australia."

"I was, I am, but this opportunity has come up and I was starting to explore whether we had a way of capitalising on it."

"What does 'starting to explore' mean?"

"There have been conversations with the chain's bank, they're the ones trying to set up the sale, and with Tony's new investors out here, but I'd rather bring Tony into the conversation if we're going any further."

"You'd better get him anyway so I can explain to you all how we run this business."

Alphonse called reception from the speaker unit in the centre of the table, "Could you get hold of Mr King please, and patch him through."

"Do you want Raymond to hear this?" asked Peter, slightly overbearingly.

"No," said Alphonse curtly, "I'd rather we got clarity amongst ourselves first."

The silence was awkward. Claudia couldn't see a way of easing the tension. Peter was leaning forward on the table, drumming his fingers. Alphonse was slumped in his chair, looking thin-lipped and a little aggressive, she thought, very unlike him.

"Good morning guys," suddenly the Aussie voice crackled through.

"Tony, old chap, where are you?" asked Peter, with a fairly good impersonation of his usual bonhomie.

"Still in Oz, I'm flying to New York tonight. Who's all there?"

"Just Claudia, Alphonse and me,"

"Wow, the A team. Good morning again then guys."

"Good morning Tony, thanks for making yourself available."

"Aw, look, you've done me a favour. Bree wasn't too happy about me fixing to play golf on the last Sunday here. So, what's the problem?"

Alphonse looked to Peter, who dropped the bonhomie quite quickly, "I think we all know what the problem is, or what the problems are, I should say. Funding for property and resort expansion comes from our own funds, augmented by the bank, I will not dilute control beyond that. And the investment of new funds is conditional upon meeting profitability targets as we expand. If I understand it correctly, you've been having conversations with the bankers trying to sell this resort chain and you've been talking to your new investors about putting money into resorts as well as your funds."

"Too right!"

Peter coloured up and spluttered, "You have no right to do either of those things," his response wasn't helped by both Alphonse and Claudia having to stifle giggles at Tony's apparently deliberate offensiveness. "We have clear guidelines about what we agree before we take anything outside, and this whole plan is a non-starter. You're making yourselves look ridiculous."

"Only one person I can see making themselves look ridiculous, mate. What's happened to the great entrepreneur?"

Somehow, Claudia thought, Tony's addition of the extra syllable — he finished the word with 'newer' — made his response a little comical and seemed to decrease the tension slightly, although Peter wasn't finished yet, "The great entreprenewer," he mimicked Tony's pronunciation perfectly," is following his well-established principles and guidelines, which have enabled him to create a forty-billion dollar enterprise."

"And one of his principles is to employ creative people who think outside the box and challenge but, mate, I wasn't really ready for this conversation yet. We haven't got our ducks in a row."

"We?"

"Alphonse, are you just going to sit there playing with yourself, or are you going to say something?"

Claudia snorted, but Alphonse looked uncomfortable, "As you know, I wanted to find out a little more before we floated the idea. I wanted to explore the idea of changing our guidelines first. As we discussed overnight…"

"Yeah, thanks for that mate, I'm at my best at two

a.m."

Alphonse smiled now, "Couldn't be helped, but that was a discussion I'd been planning for tomorrow, but when you flagged the issue to Peter, my plan got somewhat derailed."

"You know the issue, though, this opportunity won't wait around, and neither will my new investors. Peter, mate, you're a legend, they look at all you've done, and they think you're fucking Midas. You wouldn't be losing control, you'd just get more flexible funding than with the bank. Don't let them think you're losing your golden touch. At least let us push it to the next stage, put a proposition together for you. And maybe you have to push a few guidelines."

"And maybe we have to abandon our principles."

"I don't see what principle we're abandoning," said Claudia, "you're happy to dilute your investment in Group businesses."

"But I've got the owners in place."

"You'd have me in place on this," said Alphonse.

Peter still looked very uncomfortable, "Well, you'd better put some proposals together, but I want to be on record with all of you," and he was looking directly at Claudia, "that I am strongly opposed to taking on extra investment for resorts, or ceding control of the expansion and development programme."

Alphonse looked troubled, but Tony remained breezy, "That's fair. Hell, I don't even know if it's a good deal yet. I'll work on that with my allegedly gay friend."

"Your what?" coughed Peter.

"Well, mate, there are some ladies down here who aren't convinced by that pose. But that's OK, at least our little group knows he's queer. I'll call you later Alphonse. What's our target date, Peter? You in New York soon?"

Peter, nonplussed, said, "Two or three weeks."

"We're talking to Tania and Will about Group expansion on May 17th," said Claudia, "that's a Friday."

"Shall we say the Thursday? Can you make that Alphonse?"

"Er, yes, I think so," said Alphonse, still looking slightly dazed.

"Good, we can get our bids in first."

"Do you people think you're going to dispose of my entire war chest?"

"There was a time you called it investment. Don't start being a pussy now. I'll see you all on the 16th, then. Call me when you're finished there, Alphonse, will you?"

"Yes, yes of course."

"Are you done with me now?"

"Yes, Tony, thank you," Peter seemed somehow also to have been caught off guard, "and I'm sorry you've had a disturbed night."

"Oh, that's OK, it had its compensations, but even they're a bit limited when you're told you don't have oral skills to compare with Alphonse. See ya guys," and, with a click, he was gone.

There was silence and some shaking heads around the table.

Claudia was pondering Tony's approach. Was that simple artlessness? She didn't think so. He'd deliberately chosen to handle it that way, he liked to use his brazen Aussie schtick, and it had worked brilliantly this morning. Peter looked unsettled, but at least his mind had been opened. Alphonse, who gave so little away normally, had clearly been shocked by the publicity. And Claudia herself, after feeling relief at having got Peter out of the hole he'd dug for himself, now began to feel a little possessive jealousy about Alphonse's apparent exploits.

They were all taking time to adjust their thoughts, after a while Peter asked, "Do you want to get Raymond in now, or shall we take five?"

"Taking five is a good idea," said Claudia, thinking she could really do with longer.

Chapter 11

Tania had missed the April meeting. She felt she couldn't miss May, especially as it was the time when they traditionally discussed the longer-term perspective for the Giddings business. Perhaps a day or so away from New York would help her get her thoughts on the Group project clearer, but she didn't really believe herself, she was too honest to rationalise.

She only just made the six o'clock from Newark; having to head to La Guardia for the nine-fifteen would have been wrong for so many reasons. As it was, her mother would protest about her arriving home after nine: 'no chance to chat' — but they would have, on Friday night, thought Tania. Her father would also grump about her inadequate preparation for an important board meeting, as he would put it, but their recent conversations had been awkward anyway. She should find time for a deeper discussion with him, the irritation they displayed to each other in their phone calls was a symptom, she knew, of bigger issues.

As it was, his gritted, "We should meet in my office at four, young lady," muttered to her as they all went to lunch at the close of the board meeting, seemed to have opened up the opportunity to broach the topics. "I don't want these things spoiling dinner at home," his follow up comment, certainly made her think it was a view he shared.

The difficult atmosphere, for that is what it had become, didn't spoil the directors' lunch for her. Tania wondered if her father kept their number at eight because that was all that fitted comfortably round the table in the executive room. It was a large enough number anyway for her to be captured by her two habitual supporters in the group, both of whom had offered her positions on their boards in the preceding year, and both of whom had been supporting her questions that morning. Her father was opposite her, glowering occasionally. She got the odd glance from Rod, but he had asked for time with her after lunch anyway and had booked the guest director suite for them. It would be their first serious conversation since the negotiations over Peter's divorce, although he'd managed to find a reason to call her most months 'just to keep in touch' — keeping his enemies closer, she always thought — and he was always civil and, on the whole, supportive if she raised contentious issues in the Giddings board meetings that they both attended. Today might be different; David, his nephew, had come under fire when, as guest presenter and planning VP (a recent appointment, and not one she would have agreed to) he reviewed the five-year plan. In an unusual move, Arthur had accepted Rod's request that more work be done to enable further discussion at the June meeting. The debate had begun to get heated and would certainly have proved inconclusive, she thought.

They were still drinking coffee when Rod stood up, moved behind her and asked, "Could we get started?"

"Of course," she said, and just caught her father's questioning glance as she stood to leave. She would talk to him later.

"Are we OK, Arabella?" he asked, without slowing, as they passed her desk on their way into the suite. When Tania looked to Arabella for confirmation, she gave a resigned shrug, Rod had moved past anyway without breaking stride.

He opened the door and made an oddly deferential move to guide Tania to the chair behind the main desk. "I think we'll be more comfortable around the coffee table, don't you?" and she sat down without waiting for him to agree. "Are we talking about this morning's meeting?" she asked, knowing there were a number of other topics he might wish to discuss, "And how long do we have? You normally fly mid-afternoon."

"I'm staying over." She looked questioningly, "Oh, don't worry, I won't be imposing on the Gunters for dinner."

"Marybeth?" she let slip out, it was probably cheekier than she'd meant to be, but it was never a bad thing to keep him on the defensive.

Rod was ready, as he almost always was, "Of course," he said calmly, "HR is my specialty area."

"That's what I thought," she said. He didn't make the mistake of smiling, so neither would she. It was a long time since she'd spoken to Marybeth, six months at least. That wasn't good — and it was her turn to call. But his dinner appointment at least gave her some information on Marybeth's private life, but she hoped there was more to it than an occasional tumble with Uncle Rod.

"Anyway, Arthur's asked me to see him at four."

"Oh, I only want half an hour, max. But Arthur? Not Dad? This is just us."

She smiled, "This is just work, I think, he's Arthur here."

"I admire the way you keep those things separate."

"Thank you, I sometimes think I do that better than he does. He seemed to take some of the points in the planning session quite personally."

"I think David may have done, too. That's one of the things I wanted to talk about."

"OK," she felt a little uncomfortable, she knew she'd been slightly aggressive but some of the assumptions were so complacent; no planning for disruptive changes, little vision, "but do you have a list of topics you want to cover?"

"Yes, of course. It's mostly about how this board works. It's a little bit about David, but I'll say up front I'm not trying to get defensive there, and it's also about Lavinia."

This was a time to be careful. It might be a simple New York project question, but Rod would never tire of trying to discover how much help Lavinia had given Tania on the divorce case. "Should we start with Lavinia?

It may be simplest."

"Happy to start there, but I doubt whether it's that simple."

Yes, it really was time to be careful, "I've had a little contact with her, but Claudia and Jack have had more." He smiled, presumably trying to provoke her to react about the other side of the Jack relationship, or maybe just hinting that he knew they'd colluded. "She seems very good and I need someone to help me pull a project together. She was interested enough to offer to take a week's holiday to help me."

"It doesn't have to be holiday."

Now she did smile, "Two reasons why that's not a good idea: one, you'd bill me; and two, you'd have rights to know what she's doing." He nodded slowly. "I'm happy to tell you more about it, nevertheless. It's still Dickinson, and you still have a business relationship there, don't you?" She let the question hang in the air. She knew he did formally, that was one of the points negotiated in the settlement, he hadn't wanted the publicity and questions around losing a major client, but she doubted whether Peter had spoken to him since.

"You know I do."

"Well, now they have the cash in from the Personal Care sale, and the Group looks very different now, they've asked me to look at what we might do with it. I'm seeing them in two weeks. I need some help and I know Lavinia's good at pulling information out of all sources and at putting it together well."

"So, what's likely to happen?"

"To the project, or to her?"

"Or to you?"

"I can picture a bigger group. It should be more coherent, it's got some great technologies, but they just learn from each other, they don't try to work with each other and integrate their skills and competences. There are areas they could and should move into, they could even tie in with Giddings here…"

"That was what you were getting at this morning…"

"In part, yes, I just didn't see any boldness, any desire or plans to push out, or even recognise how the world's changing."

"It sounds like you think they could both do with a dynamic CEO, the Group and Giddings," he managed one of his nearly-smiles.

"That may be my view. It's certainly not my decision in either case."

"So, Peter wants you to run the Group."

He must have surmised that, Peter just would not have told him, but she supposed she'd made it obvious, "That's a possibility, but I wouldn't want it without a clear commitment to spend money and grow. I've said I'll offer a plan in two weeks and I think I'm going to find a week of Lavinia's time very helpful."

"Would there be something permanent for her?"

"Could you ask me in two weeks' time?"

"I'm asking you now. She's very valuable to me."

She risked a slight smile, "Then she might be very

valuable to me." He exhaled, as if he respected being caught in that trap. "I would need someone with her skills if anything comes of this. The fact that she's giving me a week tells me that she's not averse to considering a change. Would that give you and me a problem?"

He gave a hollow laugh, "Bigger than we have already, do you mean?"

She stayed calm, "Do we have a problem? You've asked for time today."

He seemed to consider for a long time, "No, I wouldn't have said we have a problem. I wouldn't want you stealing my best resource, but I could understand her finding a change attractive, to work with one of the best young leaders I've ever encountered."

That would, two years ago, have been a massive boost to her, and it would be later today, she knew, when she thought about it quietly at home, but now there was Rod to deal with, he of the indecipherable agenda, "Thank you for that but, if I'm hearing you right, we let Lavinia make the decision herself if a position opens up."

He nodded slowly, "I agree with that."

Then they moved on to Giddings. He agreed with much that she'd said, and he felt her questions were well-directed, "I think my poor nephew rather took one for the team. I've encouraged him to be more forward when raising his concerns in the preparation of his presentation, but your father was reluctant to expose them, and David didn't want to be seen rocking the boat."

"I know it happens a lot, Rod, but for VP status and

that salary, I'd want more than a yes man. I know he's a smart guy, and I've always liked him…"

"But you think he lacks balls," he waited for her nod, "and I wouldn't disagree with you. He's not the future leader of this place, even if you don't come back."

"How long does the current leader have, in your opinion?" It felt strange to be asking that question about her own father, and she wouldn't expect a straight answer from Rod, but she had to find out as much as she could in order to protect him.

"Well, he can stay until the business is bust, he has enough cronies on the board. That's not quite true, of course, he also has shareholders, but most guys in his situation could survive a fifty percent drop in their share price if they put up a plausible recovery plan. But if he doesn't listen to you, that fifty percent drop will likely happen, and maybe sooner rather than later, and he won't have a plan that convinces anybody. So, no pressure, but a lot depends on you, but you do know that the board meeting's not the place to challenge him, don't you?"

"I know that. I was just a little caught out by the lack of vision, or any awareness of what might be happening in the world around them. Are you saying David's actually more aware of that than he let on?"

"I think he is. It wouldn't hurt to have a little chat with him and form your own view. You might heal his wounds from this morning and get a better picture of some of the thinking that's going on."

"I will. I'll grab him when we're finished. I'd like to

be reassured. I know there are some good things in this place. There's a brilliant IT group, and that ties in already with Collins and it would link with some of the stuff I'm looking at."

"I think you'll find David pretty receptive."

"I'd like to find him pretty effective, that's what I'm not seeing."

"He could do better if he knows you support him. We always thought you'd make a good team, your parents and I."

"You made me very well aware of that," she gave him a frosty look.

"I'm sure your New York friends are more interesting," now it was his turn to look coldly at her. But that was fleeting, "That's irrelevant, however, but I do hope you'll get something out of a conversation with David."

"I hope I can. I'll give myself a little time to think and talk to him before I see Arthur. So, Lavinia in New York for a week and if there's a permanent position, it's her own decision," she looked directly at him, he nodded, "I need to keep pushing for change at Giddings, but I should tackle Dad outside the board meetings…"

"Not Arthur?"

"This is getting too personal for that. I have to care for him as well as the business," he pursed his lips, but nodded, "and I'll see what David's got to offer."

"As always," now he was standing up, "perfectly summarised."

She stood up too, "That's everything?" he nodded, "well, thank you for that. You're being very supportive."

"I do try," he said, and tried a boyish smile, but with little conviction.

"I hesitate to appear cynical, but I think it has to suit you for you to be supportive."

"I think we understand each other well," he said.

She smiled now, "That's what worries me. Am I getting to be like you?"

He almost laughed as he left.

* * *

David was keen to talk, and she found Rod's comments reasonably accurate, he did have some ideas, she just wished she could have believed in a greater willingness to confront. But it did give her more confidence about approaching her father.

"He's waiting for you," said Arabella when Tania approached her at four. He was on the phone, nevertheless, when she went in. He motioned to the chair in front of his desk. She went to the large meeting table and sat down. He looked slightly annoyed and continued his call, seeming to spend an unnecessary time on pleasantries. But now he was standing, trying to put the phone down, maybe she was being too sensitive.

Now he was finished and moving around his desk with his arms open, smiling, "Give your father a big hug, you horrible child!"

And about fifteen years fell away as they wrapped their arms around each other. But it hadn't made her any less obdurate then than she felt now — just clearer this time that she was doing this for him. In her teenage years she was fighting for herself — but she'd nearly always won then, she reflected. She gradually untangled herself, "You do know I'm trying to help, don't you?"

"Of course you are," he said, slowly disengaging himself, "sit down, sit down, but I just don't think you're being realistic."

"Well, that's what we need to talk about," she said, firmly.

"OK, OK, that's why we're here," he said in his mollifying voice. Strange he still tries that, she thought, it never really worked before — or maybe it used to with Debs and Ange.

"I talked to David just now. I know I was a little hard on him."

"You were certainly that!"

"I wasn't that bad, Dad, you're his big problem."

"Well, I'm glad I'm Dad again, but you'd better explain yourself. How was I hard on him? I supported everything he said."

"That's because he was saying what you wanted him to say, not what he truly believed. I'm not giving him any credit for standing up for himself and his views but at least I think he was being honest with me just now. That's a reason, incidentally, while he'll never be a CEO. Well, not a successful one."

"And you will, I suppose," now he was tetchy, "listen, young lady, you have to bring people along with you. You were attacking all the time this morning."

Her younger self would have responded aggressively — and won, she thought — but that wouldn't bring her father along, he did have a valid point, "I accept that. I've spent some time talking ideas through with him just now, so he's better prepared for the next meeting. I thought you did well to take Rod's point there."

"How are you so close to him all of a sudden? I thought you had the same opinion as your mother?"

"I do, I think he's dangerous, and maybe even evil, but that's a good reason to stay close to him, not avoid him."

He looked at her, slightly astounded, shaking his head, "What monster have I created? Where has all this come from?"

"It's all come from you and Mom," she smiled, "mostly Mom."

He guffawed, "Oh, that's so true. But what are we going to do, girl, you think the problems are that bad?"

"No, but one of the problems, Pops, is that you're wonderful and everyone wants to make you happy."

"Well, all except one, maybe, and you haven't called me 'Pops' in years — and it was only when you were being cheeky then! You think I'm a problem?"

"You're the major reason this place works, but I think some big changes are needed. I just need to convince you of that, or David does, or someone. If you could see that clearly, no-one could make this place change direction like you could."

"You could come back," he said hopefully.

"I don't want to yet, Dad. You've got plenty energy to do what needs to be done, at least you seem to be agreeing that changes are needed."

"Maybe," but now he seemed to withdraw, "but I come back to my original point, you have to stay realistic."

"That doesn't seem to inhibit the best people I see."

"Maybe I'm just not one of those."

"That, my most wonderful old man, is just a tiny bit pathetic. You bought Longshore six years ago. You led a big culture change here after you got Claudia in five years ago."

"And you left four years ago, and I've gone to sleep since then. Is that what you're saying? This is still a profitable business, you know."

"I wasn't saying you'd gone to sleep," she thought for a moment, "actually, there's no point in having this conversation if you're manipulating me into being nice. Maybe it's because I'm no longer close to it, but I can't think of one major change or initiative that's taken place here in the last four years. Am I being unfair?"

"You're being irrelevant. It ain't broke. It's not just profitable, it's growing!"

"Not even two percent last year, and you're losing share."

"We don't chase unprofitable business."

"I agree with that, but that's only one element, and your shareholders aren't overwhelmingly impressed, you're down five points this last year."

"The sector's down in the market."

"By one percent. This isn't getting us anywhere. I thought you were starting to accept that things had to change."

He put his hands to his face and rubbed his eyes, "Maybe. But I just don't know if I have the energy."

"You don't have to do it all yourself. David's got enough ideas, you need someone who can implement the changes. Don't you have anyone with some energy?"

"You left."

"You cannot have let the future of this place depend on one daughter, aren't there more Davids? Just ones with energy and balls. What does Marybeth say?"

"Have you spoken to her?"

"No, and I feel bad about that. But don't you get her in to do a people review at one of the next meetings?"

"Yes," he said absently, "it's a mid-year thing. Would you talk to her?"

"I would. I will, but I'm not yet hearing you agreeing with my diagnosis."

"Let's just say you're mostly right," he said wearily.

"That's not good enough, Dad, if I'm…"

"Dammit, Tania," he exploded, slapping his hand down hard on the table, "that's got to be good enough. You've got some points but I'm not going to be undermined in my own damned board meetings again."

She was a little shocked but knew she had to keep her composure. He'd always been more robust than this, but here he was being inconsistent and now fragile. She could remember few instances of either in the past, now he was being both. She wanted to help but that would need lots of her time, and the New York project, as she worked more on it, was looking much more exciting than reviving Giddings. But this was the family business, and he plainly needed help.

"I'll come back in two weeks. That's the May twentieth week. Can you block two days with David and Marybeth? We'll work though everything, plans and people. Let's get a clear picture of what we need here, and let's you and I agree on it. David has to do the work anyway for the next meeting."

He was nodding absently, "Arabella," he called, too quietly for her to hear. Tania went to the door and asked her to come in. "Arabella, my dear, week commencing May 20th, what have we got on? My boss here," he nodded towards Tania, "is telling me to find two days with David Wilkins and Marybeth Porter, so you'll have to check their availability." He looked to Tania, who was thinking that just checking availability was not good enough but tried to keep that thought to herself. She seemed to be succeeding, he turned back to Arabella, "I'll rely on your charm and tact to make it absolutely clear to them that diaries have to be cleared for the Thursday and Friday," he looked to Tania, she nodded, she had no idea but would have to adjust her plans to meet his commitment, "and then maybe we can entice my daughter to stay for a weekend instead of rushing back to New York on a Saturday." Here Tania screwed her face up a little, there were other things in her life at weekends, and too many constraints already imposed by the Group project. At least Robert had been relaxed about moving their lunch back to Sunday once she'd realized she would have to stop over after the meeting to spend time with her father. She'd been pleasantly surprised at how amenable he'd been, and she was intrigued by the lunch date with the new little vibrator.

"I'll get on to it right away," said Arabella, and left them.

"Weekends here too boring?"

"It's not that, but the little social life I have is being squeezed into ever smaller lumps of weekend time."

He looked pensive, "I guess I'll let your mother interrogate you on that one."

"Thanks, now I'm beginning to wish you had invited people to dinner."

"Your mother's finally got her way on Rod, and he's not been pushing for an invitation anyway. Funny, I got the impression he was trying to avoid you, but there you are today, thick as thieves. There's more to that, isn't there?"

"Yes, and it's not pretty. Do you want me to tell you about it?"

"Do you want to tell me about it?"

"I'd feel bad about us having secrets."

"But if I don't want to know, it's not a secret."

She thought for a moment, then laughed, "Was that your successful formula for bringing up daughters?"

He closed his eyes, "Oh, God, don't remind me. And you were the best. Mind you, once they'd seen what you got away with…" now he shook his head, "but I'm even proud of those two." He stood up, "Shall we head home, let's not be late, I don't want your mother turning against me too,"

This felt like a barb too many, "Dad, I am not against you. I am seriously trying to help," it was hard to stay calm.

But now she got his big disarming smile, and his arms were open for her, "I know you are, chicken," now he embraced her, "and I'm unbelievably proud of you."

They stayed there a few moments. She was slightly embarrassed by the tear that dropped on to his shirt but when she leaned back to look up and apologise, she saw his eyes were welling up a little too.

Chapter 12

It was the fifth resort they'd seen in five days. It was a punishing and expensive schedule. They had managed three regular flights, but all other transfers had been by plane or helicopter hires. In two cases both. It was possible someone in the chain's reservations department would wonder why two men were making such strenuous efforts to see so many widely spread resorts in such a short time but there wasn't much in the management of the hotels that made him think the people would care that much.

"Could you do anything with the people?" he asked Raymond, once they'd checked into the fifth and had their first quick look round, "It seems like a uniformly mediocre culture."

"That's what's so exciting."

Alphonse shook his head and smiled, he loved this man's indefatigable enthusiasm. He'd been a wonderful discovery. He could only imagine his previous company had let him go because he wore them out. And in truth, thought Alphonse, I'll be quite glad to be heading out tomorrow. "You're now going to explain how mediocre people are exciting, aren't you?" He got, as expected, Raymond's beaming smile.

"We will probably change all the managers, but I

would even give them a chance. Once people see what your plans are and we run a training course at Morkuda, their attitudes will change completely."

"Not Teluk?"

"No, Morkuda is our design, not an upgrade of an existing," he hesitated, "I keep making the assumption that we bulldoze these places. You are still thinking that way, aren't you?" and a flicker of concern crossed his face.

"Oh, more than ever, but it makes the whole programme even more expensive and heaven knows what it does to the timetable."

"That's not too bad if you can find the money. Morkuda is the template, we just clone that in each place."

"Raymond, my dear man, I'd first of all like to clone you. I don't know how you'll cope," another flicker of concern from Raymond, "but I'm sure you'll put the right teams in place. I have to say, though, that finding people with your talent and energy isn't easy. It wasn't until I met you that I pressed the button on Teluk. We'd talked to more than two dozen people before we found you."

"We?"

"Yes, it's a different Dickinson business, run by a man called Sandy Nicholls. You met him once, he'll be helping you recruit. He'll actually help you think about the organisation you need, his people will recruit for you. More of that in a minute, can you sum up where your thoughts are now?"

Raymond, unusually, paused for thought and took a deep breath, "I've not had too many surprises, I knew a couple of the resorts anyway, not any that we've seen on this trip but they're essentially the same: fabulous locations, cheap buildings and demotivated staff. It's perfect!"

Alphonse laughed, he would normally be sceptical of cheery optimism, but Raymond always had a well-argued case for it, "Go on!"

"The poor building stock and the staff explain the poor occupancy numbers. We can change the first and remotivate the second. My only worry would have been if the locations had been poor but every single one, all five, and the two others I know, are remarkable. OK, some journey times are not good, but when you put the VIP heli-transfers in, that becomes a plus: we're targeting different guests."

It was one of the big draws of Asia for Alphonse, the sunny, positive attitudes of most of the people he met. Raymond was exceptional, but he wasn't unique. Alphonse had been truthful about the number of people he and Sandy had rejected, but their search had become rapidly successful once they'd stopped interviewing ex-pat Europeans and Americans.

"You're going to get tired of this, if you're not already, but you'll get so many questions on it from Peter. He'll call you to check up on me."

"And you don't mind?"

Alphonse half-closed his eyes, "Raymond, if I got

upset about that, then you'd have every right to get upset about me talking to your team. Trust is good, but…"

"I know, I know, so, you want me to say again why it didn't work before?" Alphonse nodded, "Well, Smith was a visionary, like yourself."

"He may have been just a dreamer," Raymond looked puzzled, "I like to think visionaries actually make things happen, dreamers just…well, dream."

"I think Smith would have made it. He bought all the plots, for good prices too, and the first two resorts were quite high class for their day, but that was twenty years ago. It was only after the plane crash when his family took over that they started building cheap and they never got the numbers. If he'd carried on, with all the Chinese travelling now, you couldn't buy this chain for ten times what they're asking. So, have we got our story straight?"

Alphonse was a little distracted, a compelling vision obliterated by a freak accident, no point in thinking about that, well, not now, "Yes, can you produce a little fact sheet on that story? You and I must have identical details, Peter will want all of that stuff, he's an inveterate fact-checker. He displays this wonderfully charming, care-free persona, that wasn't typical behaviour last week, but he does work extremely hard — but hides it. You must expect the odd call about minute details in your accounts."

Raymond laughed, "I've had that already," Alphonse laughed with him, "but I also know that you've checked up on me too!" Now they both laughed louder,

"Control is better, yes?"

"Yep, control is better."

"I have another question."

"Yes?"

"Smith bought six more sites. Why are they not in the package?"

"I didn't know that. Are they any good?"

"I don't know, but we've seen seven of the twelve he built, and all the sites are wonderful. There's no reason to suppose these won't match them."

Alphonse was thoughtful, "I guess that's what I'd recommend if I were the bank. If we make a success of this, their selling price on the other six rockets up. We'd better bring that up. I'll talk to them."

"Do you want me to do that?"

Alphonse shook his head, "We've already cocked things up slightly by Tony talking to them as well as me. I hope I've stopped that now. We'll do good cop, bad cop later, but if I get the locations from them for you, have you got someone you can trust to check them out?" Raymond nodded, as he almost always did, thought Alphonse, "I'll need a report two or three days before the Peter meeting, that's on the sixteenth."

"Oo, they're well spread out."

"I'll get you the information before I fly off tomorrow. Get your man to look at as many as you can."

"Will do. So, we're going ahead?"

"We're going to try," and he looked out through more palms, across more white sand and blue water, to the deep red dipping sun. It was always a thrill wherever he was, and he knew that the guests in his little heavens might, in truth, not all be the stylish sensualists of his imagination but self-centred, spoiled sybarites, terrorising the lives of the staff… but that was where, he knew already, good local management would make a huge difference. But now was the time to drink in the evening, and imagine the new villas stretching out north and south of him along his mile of beach.

His contact man at the bank had been guarded on the topic of the extra locations when he called him the next morning. "We're selling the chain as a going concern, Mr Newman. Other locations are not part of the package. They no longer belong to the family."

"Who owns them?"

"I'll have to get back to you on that."

"Because you don't know, or you can't tell me?"

"I don't see that's a relevant question."

"I'm going to make a wild guess here. When the family ran into difficulties, they disposed of some assets. The assets were acquired by the bank, and, since it was a fire sale, probably at a very good price. If you're still hanging on to them when this sale doesn't go through, because I won't progress it without the other locations, you will have some explaining to do, won't you?"

"I don't recognise the scenario you're depicting, Mr Newman."

Utter bullshit, thought Alphonse, "I do hope you can email me the locations in the next hour, and then let me know the ownership situation by tomorrow. Is that possible? As you are aware, if you've checked us, we can work on very short decision timetables." There was a delay, the man was clearly talking to a colleague, probably a superior listening in. "Which also means we move on quickly to our next targets."

"Er, no, no, just a moment, please." Alphonse was smiling to himself, there was another pause, "Er, we can certainly let you have the locations within the hour," now another delay, "but I don't think we'll get a response from the owners within twenty-four."

"Are you telling me that it's not the bank?"

"Well, the ownership situation is, as I understand it, quite complex."

"You two are making this difficult for yourselves," he was sure there were two, at least; two was probable, "these things have a market value to us if attached to the package now. I know I don't have to explain this to you, because you've thought this through already. You also understand why it's important to me. You think you can wait five years and, if my project succeeds, you can sell them for five times as much, to me, or a competitor. Well, guess what, my deal is not going ahead without them. I will pay either twice what you paid, or fair market value. Which is it?"

Another long pause, which settled the question about how many he was talking to, "We just don't know what a fair market value is."

"So, accept twice what you paid." More hesitation.

They wouldn't know whether Alphonse knew what they'd paid or not. He could afford to bluff, since they'd almost certainly bought very cheaply. "I'll leave that offer on the table for twenty-four hours. You will agree, in principle, to add the locations to the package. If the deal goes ahead, you get the better of either twice your cost or fair market value. That gives us two weeks to work out what they're worth."

"Two weeks?"

"Yes, that's when we make our decision. Unless the deal dies tomorrow, and you have to explain how you turned down a double-your-money offer on a speculative real estate deal that your bank probably doesn't like being in. Will I hear from you tomorrow?"

Another delay, "Er, yes, yes, you'll hear from us tomorrow."

"And I'll have the location list within the hour?"

"Yes, of course."

"And you're in luck. I'm travelling overnight and not in my London office before late afternoon your time, so you have nearly two working days to sort yourselves out. I'll look forward to hearing from you, goodbye."

"Goodbye Mr Newman," and he heard the second goodbye just before the phone clicked down.

He smiled to himself, was that a silly risk, he thought, they could have been bluffing, maybe they'd paid a high price for the locations and doubling that would be ridiculous. He couldn't not pay, he would have to kill the whole deal, but they would know that too, that was a risk they couldn't take; they may have other buyers in the pipeline for some resorts, but probably not for the whole chain. He felt almost certain he would be asked to pay market value, which, of course, was also subjective and negotiable, but, he shrugged, probably more than twice what they'd paid. Why worry? Sometimes you doubled your money on property.

It was time to meet Raymond for one last conversation on this trip. He wouldn't risk a midnight call to Tony in New York, that would have to wait until he landed in the UK tomorrow.

Breeana was obviously still in Brisbane. It had been a very sweet email the day before. Sweet, but not truly welcome. Receiving one from Sue earlier in the week had been more of a surprise, but she, at least, seemed readily to understand the opportunistic nature of their relationship.

Chapter 13

By the end of the day, Tania would find herself surprised at how well they got on. She'd admired Lavinia immensely through their dealings on the Dickinson divorce, even more when she realised it had cost Lavinia a relationship, but the woman had seemed somehow cool and formal so, for all the valuable talents ascribed to her, Tania had not expected to form a great personal bond like she had with Claudia.

But Jack had loved both women, perhaps there was an unseen side.

It wasn't immediately apparent when Lavinia began work on the Monday morning but then, Tania admitted, she was having re-entry problems herself. The Atlanta trip had been a major distraction, some complex business issues and the still unresolved tensions with her father, with her mother finally pleading 'haven't you two agreed to meet again on this?' And Mom seeming unnecessarily happy that Tania would be meeting the same man for lunch for the second consecutive weekend, that was enough to escape censure for leaving Atlanta on the Saturday. She'd had to describe Robert's age, looks, marital and financial status which, taken together, just about compensated for the flaky career, 'an art dealer, dear, well, that must be very interesting'. It was of course, but probably less interesting than Robert's sexual life, or her own, for that matter, which, fortunately, did not come up as a topic. She'd had to talk about Andy, mothers forget nothing, and the potential complications there but, since she felt comfortable herself, no further questions were prompted. She had to talk to them more about the Group project, which concerned both of them, not just for its implications for her future at Giddings, but she had the clear impression of them both being slightly awestruck at what she was doing.

She'd been a little awestruck herself at lunch the next day when Robert began playing with the controller in his pocket. She'd almost forgotten the little vibrator as they'd settled in to the first course; walking in, it had merely felt like slightly uncomfortable underwear, but now, just starting the scallops with a creamed wasabi sauce, the tingling began. It was easy just to smile at him first, but she began to squirm as the buzzing intensified and he switched vibration modes.

Threatening, as good naturedly as she could, to leave the table halfway through the main course to remove the device in the ladies, had at least made him turn it down to a faint, and strangely pleasant, stimulation. Her hissed protestation: 'I am not having an orgasm in this restaurant', had made him laugh and give in.

They'd had another very long afternoon together so the work she'd planned for the evening was curtailed. But they'd avoided the difficult, for her, topic of the event at

Noah's the following Friday. After two weekends of their new, 'non-exclusive' dating relationship, how would she feel about seeing him fuck other women, as he undoubtedly would. And she had no idea now about how she would feel about fucking other men. She assumed she would still want to. Friday would be intriguing.

But now it was Monday, and Lavinia was here.

So was Will, which was fortunate; he was able to give a more succinct introduction to the project than Tania could have managed, but more impressive than that was the focus of Lavinia's questions. She'd rapidly grasped the summaries of each of the current Group businesses and how some might operate together 'but you'll be firing that CEO anyway, won't you?'. Will had smiled at that, 'that would need a hefty buy-out, that's more expense, I'm afraid'. 'Cheaper than keeping, though', she'd said.

"There will be a cash constraint, overall."

"Is that one billion, or three point nine?" Will had gulped at that, Tania noticed; this woman was sharp, and Tania was interested in what Will would say.

"Well, I've had some conversations with Peter where he wants to know if we could work with even less."

"But what's your view?"

"I thought the Funds, Property, Group balance was about right, so I'm in favour, in principle, of the bulk going to Group, but with Peter trying to pull back a little to reduce his own workload, I think he's looking to be a little more conservative."

"But won't that leave you with an unbalanced rump of a business in the Group?" She looked to Tania before turning back to Will. Tania was enjoying this, she knew Will had to be neutral but now she felt she had a real ally, quite a powerful one.

"Most of it's focused on technology."

"But you still have two food businesses, four consultancies and two large shareholdings that you can't effectively integrate into operations. Couldn't they be sold if we identify things that fit our long-term aims better?"

The idea had occurred to Tania, but she'd been circumspect, wanting to be clearer about Will's position before she asked him — he might think it attractive to sell them anyway and have an even smaller group. After all, if Peter was not going to involve himself with the Group and its people, why would he want the risk of less sure returns. But now Lavinia, in her first hour, had asked the question anyway. Tania was nodding.

"You're right, of course, food makes no sense any more, and I suspect his attachment to the two big tech businesses is more emotional than strategic. They've delivered lower returns over each of the last five years than the funds have. So, I'm thinking here, if we put a convincing plan together with appropriate targets — and I mean they genuinely fit with our operations and not just fit with our Group's personalities — and that plan costs more than Peter thinks he wants to spend, well, then we bring the other into play."

"Which would yield what?" Tania wasn't quite open-mouthed, but she was very impressed by the points Lavinia was making, and by how positively Will was responding.

"The tech shareholdings are easy," he picked up a remote and pointed to a monitor on the wall behind them, Tania berated herself for not taking more interest in them, but all that data, the coloured graphs, the myriad numbers, real time, looked more than a little nerdy to her, "about one point seven for the two together, we'd have to sell carefully, and we'd lose a few points in the process, but you could pretty much guarantee one point six. The food businesses would get us far less, in total less than a billion, I think, and the majority of that would go to the owners. But that's probably worth doing anyway, they just won't fit."

"So," said Tania gleefully, "that's around two billion we can add to the war chest, thank you Lavinia. This is looking really promising."

"Woah, steady," said Will, looking concerned, "our first aim is to define a coherent plan. We've just got loads of ideas here," and he pointed to the sheets that he'd replaced on his wall as his first task every morning — he took them down every evening and locked them in his desk.

"Well, you guys will need to do that," said Lavinia, "looking at these pictures, I think what I'm best looking at is the targets on your first three sheets, the ones you've written priority on, and seeing how much more in-depth information I can get without alerting anybody."

"I think that's exactly right," said Tania, and looked to Will, who was nodding, clearly impressed.

He was even more impressed at the end of the day when they sat together for their six o'clock debrief, which was their innovation for the week. They felt they needed to be more disciplined anyway as they brought ideas together and Lavinia's arrival had pushed them into more formal time management. She handed them thick files as they sat down, "I thought paper would make it easier for us to jump around," Tania smiled, she understood, but she knew Will would be happier in front of a screen, "this won't get thicker as we go through the week, I'll just be filling in more blanks. There are three sheets for each business on your list. Loosely, the first sheet is the data you already had, supplemented by more facts I've gathered. The second sheet is mine, I'm attempting to pull together everything available on people, senior people especially, product and service performance, markets served and routes to market used. The third sheets are mostly blank, I think that's where you have to say how these things will fit into what you want to do."

"This is excellent stuff, but you've put your finger on the big issue. We will need a compelling vision of what this big group looks like, where does it focus, and that's where we're groping a little."

"Would you take input on that?"

Tania was a little alarmed and Will's expression

mirrored her feelings.

Lavinia laughed, "Oh, good heavens people, I didn't mean from me," and it was a lovely, self-deprecating laugh that had Tania instantly warming to her. Everything that Lavinia had done so far had impressed her, both with Rod and with this project, but this was the first time she could also smile and laugh, "We know someone at Columbia who's brilliant at getting senior people to refocus. I'm not talking about a six-week McKinsey study, I'm talking about a day with you, making you think your options through. Would that help?"

Tania and Will looked at each other and nodded.

"So, Thursday? Friday? Would you do Saturday? He'll likely have commitments on weekdays."

"I can do Saturday. Will?"

"Sure!" Yes, thought Tania, he would just tell Martha. She admired that, even more so since she respected Martha so much.

"And you Lavinia?"

"You'd want me here for that? I normally just organise him. I don't sit in."

"We'd like you here," said Will firmly, then hesitated, "if you possibly could, of course. After one day with you, we're deeply grateful already. And we'll need to feed these fantasies with facts." He smiled, "I know that's a strength of mine, but I like the idea of being able to vote quickly and two people can't do that."

He looked at Tania, she smiled and nodded,

"Especially as we usually disagree," and that was mostly humour, she thought, laced with a sprinkling of truth.

"OK, well, thank you for that," she hesitated, "I really do mean that, by the way, I'm already having fun. I'll get on to Kretzmer straightaway. Best if I do that now while you read through the sheets." She left the room.

Will and Tania began reading, "You've done a really good job pulling her in," said Will after a while, "this is excellent. I might have to offer her a job on my team."

"Will Uprichard, don't you dare!" and they were laughing when Lavinia came back in.

"He can only do Saturday, I'm afraid, and he's not cheap, he's learned what he's worth. I've agreed ten thousand, is that OK? And what have I missed?"

Tania laughed again, "Well, I was protesting because Will was about to offer you a job, but now he's seen how liberally you would splash his money around, I suspect he's changed his mind."

Lavinia looked alarmed, "I hope I've done the right thing, I can always…"

"Oh, no, no, no, please. I'm very sorry if I gave that impression. No, it's a brilliant idea, it'll be just what we need by then, and it's cheap when you compare it to Will's salary."

"You're not underpaid, Ms Gunter," but he was smiling broadly, "no, Lavinia, that's perfect, I assure you it is. I'm with Tania, it's an excellent idea. I'm only sorry it's costing you an extra day."

"Oh, that'll be fine," said Tania, "she's coming to a

party with me on Friday anyway." And that may have been one big step too far, thought Tania, but there was something about this woman that told her that this strange intuition might not be entirely misplaced. Lavinia, nonetheless, looked a little nonplussed, "Do you have plans for this evening?" Tania continued, "There's an Italian round the corner and I'd rather do that than cook for myself."

"That would be lovely," said Lavinia.

"You're excused, Will, it's bad enough for Martha when you spend time with one beautiful woman. Two would send her into tilt."

"I'll let you bad girls talk parties then, but can we spend some time on these before you head off?" He waved the sheaf of papers.

"Of course," they both said.

It was two hours later before they sat down and ordered. "So, Kretzmer, what's the story? How do we get a Columbia professor on a Saturday at short notice?" asked Tania.

Lavinia eyed her with a careful half-smile, "Networks has a relationship with him, and pays above the going rate."

"And the real reason?"

"It's a connection of Rod's. Do you want to know more?"

"I probably should do, shouldn't I?"

"I don't think you're going into a job where you can preserve your virginal purity."

"I think I lost that, in professional terms, when we managed Rod around the divorce. I still don't think he knows what happened exactly, by the way, but I get the odd question where I'm sure he's still trying to find out."

"I think you've managed that very well. I think he still suspects but can't prove anything — and he offered Duane a promotion and a move to the west coast. So, he was guessing right, but Duane's come out of it OK. He still messages me, but very securely. Anyway, Rod has something on Kretzmer, I don't know what exactly, but it's enough to keep him tame. And he is very good, from all I hear."

"We do need some process, it's hard to manage yourself like that, it can only help. Now I need to 'fess up."

"About the party?" Tania nodded, "Then I've guessed right. It's at Noah Reid's."

Now Tania laughed, "Is that too bad of me? I knew you'd met him — and you had warned me about him."

"And you took not a blind bit of notice of me!" Lavinia tried to deliver the line censoriously but was smiling at the end of it.

Tania laughed too, "It's only an option, we can do dinner instead. In fact, part of me is looking for an excuse not to go."

Now the waiter came with the wine while they spent a moment trying to read each other.

"I've obviously heard a little about what goes on, that's why I warned you, but I'm intrigued enough to find out for myself. Have you enjoyed them?"

Tania eyed her carefully, if they were to go, there was no point in hiding things now, "I've enjoyed them, and I'll admit I've shed a few inhibitions," she hesitated, "can we do a deal? If, once you've satisfied your curiosity, you find you've seen enough, we come away and have dinner together."

Lavinia thought for a long while, "That works for me," she said, "but shouldn't we know a little more about each other first?"

Tania raised her glass, smiled, and said, "Cheers!"

* * *

Two bottles were at least one too many mid-week, she thought when she woke up feeling blurry, but she couldn't remember the last time she'd had a real girlie talk. And she'd never had one that covered so much ground. My God, had she really talked about Andy and the onsen? At least she'd kept silent about Claudia's boat trip with him. But talking about Jack Stephens, as they inevitably did, took her into that area that she still failed to understand. Maybe she lacked the necessary submissive element. It nevertheless still surprised her that the three women she knew, all of whom apparently enjoyed that kink, were confident and powerful women. Lavinia was as different from Claudia and Martha as they were from each other, yet she failed to identify at all with that need they evidently shared. She'd found it easier yesterday at Robert's, when rummaging through his bedside drawer, to be intrigued by the strap-on device she'd found under the other paraphernalia. Maybe some later time for that, they were still exploring each other. But that was something she could envisage trying. And presumably Robert had.

Lavinia had talked a little about her marriage. Tania had met a few bullying men, but quickly broke up with them at the first hint of coercion or aggression. She had no undue modesty about being tall, pretty, clever and outgoing, dates had always been very easy to come by, but few had ever really appealed. That's why Andy was a troubling memory, and, beyond the onsen story, she said little about him.

And Lavinia said little about Jack. Tania was intrigued but, even near the end of the second bottle, it would have felt like a betrayal of Claudia to have pushed any enquiries.

But, heavens, they'd covered enough, and they might discover more about each other on Friday, but in the meantime, there was work to be done. A lot of work.

The next day was intense and the six o'clock session was both satisfying, lots of information was coming together, and overwhelming, there was still so much ground to cover.

At Will's suggestion, they tried to formulate some groupings that might work and give the projected enterprise focus but, by eight o'clock, it was clear they were getting nowhere, and with his observation that

Saturday was looming ever more important on the horizon, they decided to wrap up for the day. Tania found herself hoping that Kretzmer was as good as Lavinia had suggested, but they'd made that decision, there was no point in adding unresolvable doubt to incipient uncertainty.

She also needed a quiet evening at home and was delighted when Lavinia plainly also wanted time to herself.

Wednesday was a good day. Lavinia had added some new businesses to their list that she thought would be worth considering, so her six o'clock file had grown, and the blanks on her first two pages were filling in rapidly, but the third pages were embarrassingly weak, she knew.

As they left Will's office, leaving him tidying away his sheets, Lavinia said, "Will's asked me to dinner with him and Martha tomorrow."

"Wow, excellent, you'll enjoy that, she's fabulous."

"Really?"

"Oh, I was so impressed when I saw her in action in Tokyo," then thoughts of their interests went quickly through Tania's mind, not a subject to pursue, "I didn't put her together with Will, though. The boy's a dark horse."

"Talking of dark horses," Lavinia looked a little uncertain, "do you have time for a drink now?"

"I've time for a meal if you like but…"

"A one-bottle limit?"

Tania laughed, "Absolutely!"

They even had the same table and ordered the same wine. The waiter smiled when Tania forbade him accepting any orders for a second bottle later. They quickly dealt with food choices, Lavinia clearly had conversation in mind.

"You're looking troubled."

"It's Friday night."

"Oh, good heavens, we don't have to go to that."

"It's not that. A large part of me has been looking forward to it. I even went shopping yesterday evening for something to wear," then she laughed at herself, "not that I've any idea what one should wear to parties like that, if I've understood them correctly," and Tania giggled with her. "But I've had an email asking me to be somewhere else." She looked very serious.

"You've already made a huge difference here. If you need to go, we'd still be immensely grateful. We'd thought two thousand a day, by the way, I hope that's all right."

Lavinia looked shocked, "I hadn't… I was just…"

"I'd been told you were good, but you've actually been amazing. Anyway, enough blowing smoke. You're looking concerned and I'm going to guess you're like me, not many people to talk to," she chuckled, "I still live with my sister, but she doesn't know half of what you and I talked about on Monday. Anyway, is this DC?"

"How did you…"

"I didn't, but I'm finding with Andy that skeletons in cupboards don't die. I'm guessing this is something to do with Jack?"

Lavinia nodded and then began the story. The details of how they'd broken up reflected even less well on Jack than Tania had originally thought, two of her most admired women, so casually disposed of. At least Andy was still trying and had the excuse of a wife. But, without understanding the kink, she could understand Lavinia initiating contact again. Tania thought she'd been rather clever; define a little compartment in your life, let yourself be content in that, then it wouldn't distract anything else.

"But now he's asked to see you?"

"Well, it's not quite like that."

"Is he straying outside of the box?" when the double entendre struck Lavinia first, she giggled a little hysterically, and Tania joined her.

"As you'll have gathered, what was excluded was straying into the box," and they were laughing loudly now, but when the waiter waved their empty bottle at them, Tania resolutely shook her head, "But I will have a grappa with a decaff espresso, please. Lavinia?"

"Why not; me too, please." She turned back to Tania once the waiter was out of earshot, "It was set up to be a traditional dom sub relationship, which was my plan, so if he feels free to instruct me to be somewhere, it sort of fits the new pattern. Not that there's a pattern yet. It's only happened once."

"I'm obviously not very good on this stuff, even though three of the women I admire most seem to be into it, but is this about control, or just the kink?"

"Well, everybody's different, I guess, but they're somehow related for me."

"But when does that move from erotic to abusive, or exploitive?"

Lavinia thought for a while, Tania didn't want to push her, and then reflected, surely this was at the heart of a relationship like that. It was a kink, but you practised it to make the other person happy. Lavinia was still thinking when the coffee and grappas reached the table, finally she said, "When you're in the moment, you want to submit, you want to be controlled, it's only when you've given in completely that you seem to rise out of yourself. I have to admit Jack was always very good at that, tuning in to what I wanted."

"But this isn't tuning in to you, is it? Dictating when and where without knowing if it suits you. Does he know you're in New York?"

"No, he knows nothing, I ruled that out. I thought if we just focused in that narrow area, it might just be a little fun for both of us, and I didn't want to get into that emotional area again. It was very painful," she looked troubled, but then a smile spread slowly across her face, "and not a good pain." Even Tania found that funny.

"But this has come up sooner than you expected, hasn't it?" Lavinia nodded, "I need to be careful. I'll admit I am desperate to have you here still on Saturday, and I'm very keen for selfish reasons to have you with me at the party. So, I have an agenda…"

"Why at the party? You've been before."

"Robert will be there, he's the one I've had two weekend dates with," Lavinia nodded, "and I just don't know how I'll feel about seeing him with other people. I don't need to be indelicate here, do I?"

Lavinia laughed and shook her head, "I think I get the picture. You'll also have your own activities to worry about with him being there, right?"

"You do get it," and they giggled, "so I'm thinking, I'd kind of like to have your support. But all that's much less important than what you're going to do with this. You want to go to Jack, don't you?"

"I do," she said slowly, "but I only want to give up control in that narrowly defined area. I don't want my life taken over."

"Bingo, now I get it. I can understand that, I think. Thank you. You've helped me, even if you haven't helped yourself yet." Now Lavinia looked perplexed, "I think I get the control thing a little better now. I mostly like to control things myself," she laughed gently, "I let people know what I want, but sometimes I want them to push me. I want to be made to try new things, I find it kind of thrilling. I think I told you, I worked through some old inhibitions at the parties and one of my oldest, deepest fantasies was a little victim-orientated, but I can't imagine any of it being fun outside that party context. Well, quite a lot of it would have me reacting violently and squirting mace but, once you want to give yourself to it for a while, you have to go for it." Lavinia was nodding a little, but not looking convinced, "But the point is, you have to say when, it has to be your choice. Only then is your dom allowed to be a dom."

There was another long pause, Tania's grappa disappeared, Lavinia followed her slowly, "You've made a very good point, actually. This is an occasion for me. I'm allowed to be selfish about it. He's very good at it when we're in the zone, so it should be fun for him too. But it's my session, my obsession. It's my ass," and then came that Lavinia laugh that Tania had only heard that week for the first time, so warm, so self-aware. It was like a female Andy. "I'm staying here! Thank you. He can come when I tell him. One more grappa?"

Tania nodded.

* * *

Tania booked the Plaza table for eight-thirty on Friday. Somehow the ritual appealed. She was first there and ordered the Bollinger and canapés. It wouldn't be Rod's bill tonight, but she never normally had time to spend her own money.

Lavinia arrived soon after, looking stunning. A simple deep cream dress with a perfect cleavage, accessorised — belt, bag, shoes, brooch — to match her dark hazel eyes. The six o'clock meeting had been brief, they'd both stood abruptly at six thirty with Will in mid-sentence, open-mouthed. "Party-time, Will," Tania had said.

Lavinia had used her two hours very well, she glowed, and if she was in any way hesitant about the evening, it was undetectable.

"You look amazing," Tania said. "I've ordered Bolly and canapés, is that OK?"

"Perfect, but that's our alcohol ration for the day."

That was the strict Lavinia, thought Tania, I wonder if she switches — but that was only a word Tania had heard, she couldn't relate to it. The thought nevertheless prompted a question, "How did last night go? We haven't had a chance to talk about that."

"We had a lovely evening," said Lavinia warmly, "she's a very impressive lady. She's obviously been on my radar, one way or another for a long while," she paused and shrugged, "I thought I'd trained myself not to feel guilty about things like that, knowing too much about people you meet, I mean, but I did feel a pang meeting her for the first time. But any woman less like a victim it would be hard to imagine."

"Did you get on to that kink stuff?" Tania couldn't quite believe she found herself asking that.

"No, it would have been hard anyway with Will there, but she did ask if I'd like to talk about our bad boy, that's how she put it, 'our bad boy', some time. Will was out of the room then, she asked me to call her on Monday before eight — she was teasing him a little about the amount of time he spends with you."

"Do you think she's really worried? I wouldn't want her to be at all. I kind of love him like a brother, and he's wonderful to work with."

"Oh, tell me about it. I think he's brilliant, he's so calm and yet incisive, and I've never known a brain hold so much detail. I give out the sheets every day, but he seems to know every number on them without looking. Scary!"

"But his kink? Have you spotted evidence?"

Lavinia smiled, "A little bit, I think, it's the way they interact sometimes. It's very sweet. It gives me hope, I need to start looking at men in their early twenties," and she laughed.

"Any repercussions on the DC communication?"

Now she looked thoughtful, "Yes, that was good, actually. I was glad I took your advice. I had an almost apologetic email back. Well, it was apologetic, he said he was very happy for me to determine both the terms and the times in the relationship and he was aware that his timetable is fully transparent to me, so he would wait for my proposals, but hoped our next meeting would be soon."

"What will happen if you come here?"

"I suppose I'm looking for potential replacements tonight then, aren't I?" she laughed. "You'd mentioned the Red Room."

Now Tania was a little shocked, "You're thinking about that?"

Lavinia smiled, "And I'll promise not to be shocked if I see you involved in one of your gang bangs," she dropped her voice very low as the waiter approached, "but I've decided to look forward to it. I'll ask Noah to nominate someone."

"He'll want to watch."

She was thoughtful, "Yes, I'd heard that was his kink."

"It's disturbed me much less than I thought it would," said Tania, "I get too caught up in the moment."

"I'm hoping that would happen to me too. I'm not used to audiences, but at least it can't get out of control. Well," and she paused, "that should have been the case when my ex had friends in but that…" and she shook her head, "that wasn't good."

The glasses had been poured, Tania raised hers, "I want to say the biggest possible thank you for this week. You've been amazing, Cheers," and she raised her glass.

Lavinia appeared momentarily thunderstruck and seemed to be choking slightly when she said thank you. She put her glass down and reached quickly into her bag for a tissue, dabbing her eyes while she sniffed. "You shouldn't do that to me," but she raised her glass now, "thank you very much, I've been having a ball, so cheers."

They drank and put glasses down — *we use the same technique to help us drink slowly,* Tania thought, "In the middle of my interrogation back there I tried to drop in a subtle question," Lavinia looked puzzled. "I would like to know what you'd think about coming here permanently."

"Wouldn't that depend on the project, and your

meeting next week."

"Yes, and that's interesting. They've got Tony, Henry and Alphonse here the day before, so they can think everything through next week. We should know by Saturday. But would you come? I'm about one thousand percent desperate for you to come — and Will would offer you a job if I can't have you. What do you think?"

"Well, I know that's why I'm here, really, but the project's been such a focus, it's completely absorbed me," she paused, "well, that and thinking about what to wear tonight."

"You're perfect. Absolutely perfect, and don't worry too much about the underwear, it never seems to last that long," and they laughed a little louder than they should have done, but Tania was not unfamiliar with disapproving glances in public places. "But back to my question. Would you come?"

"But in what sort of a job? My role looks like a PA at Networks but…"

"Planning director, reporting to Group CEO, office next to mine if the project comes off. Double your salary."

"You don't know what I earn," but she was obviously taken aback.

Tania smiled, "You're not the only one who spies. Of course, Rod could have been bullshitting me, that would be typical, but I've sense checked elsewhere. I'm saying three hundred, would that do it? With some bonuses, of course, if we earn them."

"I'm flabbergasted. Yes, that would do it. Let's hope tomorrow goes well and we get some clear pictures of what's ahead. I'm stunned, thank you, I mean, I like the money, and I like the title, but I'm not sure…"

"This thing has got to grow, and it will take more acquisitions and realignments. We need someone who can identify the targets and research them properly. I've never met anyone like you. You can tell that bastard Jack Stephens he'll have to come to New York for his pleasures."

Lavinia laughed, "Well, it's what Oscar used to do, isn't it?"

"Anyway," said Tania, nodding, "you might find someone this evening better able to meet your needs."

* * *

The party started slowly for them, they were captured by Noah when they arrived, he was clearly surprised and intrigued to have Lavinia there. He would have seen her name on the guest list as a friend of Tania's but perhaps not have made the connection with Rod's DC operations. Lavinia was getting the full focus of his saturnine charm when Robert came up to them. He kissed Tania's hand silently and mouthed 'see you in there' pointing to the drawing room. She'd nodded and returned to Noah and Lavinia, "So would you be living in New York?" he was asking. Lavinia looked to Tania.

"That will depend on our joint project. We should be

clear by next weekend."

"Well, I'm thrilled to have you here. I hope you have as much fun as Tania usually seems to," his smile was wicked, but still friendly.

Tania wasn't sure how she could best help Lavinia, "Noah, I'll be showing Lavinia the Red Room later," his eyebrows were raised, "this may sound like an absurd question, but do you have any sensitive doms in attendance?"

Noah was looking piercingly at Lavinia, she was holding his gaze, "I do," he nodded slowly, "I think I know exactly what you require. Why don't you look around for a while? I'll come and join you in half an hour or so," now he looked to Tania, she nodded. He smiled at her, "Just don't let Robert distract you before I get there. Although I gather you may have had more than enough of him recently." She smiled at him. He took Lavinia's hand, brushed it with his lips and murmured, *"Á bientôt."*

The ladies managed a conspiratorial grin as he turned away. "Let's go through," said Tania, "your first conquest. He's not normally like that."

"Hmm, not convinced. He's probably looking ahead to my gorgeous big ass being spanked but, know what, I just don't care," and she laughed quite gaily.

Robert and Ray were with two young women when they entered the drawing room but, no sooner had Lavinia said, "Isn't that a Peter…"

"Doig, yes" said Robert. "You must be Lavinia," and he held her arms and kissed her cheek.

"And you, very clearly, are Robert," he smiled and looked very slightly awestruck. Tania was impressed, Lavinia seemed completely in command of the situation.

"Ray," said Tania, guiding him towards Lavinia after he'd kissed her cheek and said hello, "this is my friend Lavinia."

He took Lavinia's hand and kissed it, "I'm delighted to meet you."

"And, just so we're clear, she has no interest in what you have to offer."

"Well," said Lavinia slowly, "I may not be averse to alternative entertainments later, but," and she turned back to Robert, "I'm sorry if it's inappropriate at a party like this, but could you tell me more about the picture? And the Architect's Home one on the other wall?"

Robert was enthralled, Tania would lose him for the half hour now, she knew. One of Robert's greater attributes as a lover, she'd found, was that he never rushed — he always made her feel that they were working to the dictates of her body, even when those dictates surprised her. He seemed to understand her body better than she did herself.

Patience was not a virtue of Ray's. He returned to the two discarded young ladies and they were soon joined by some of Robert's other friends. He was in front of the canoe painting, talking animatedly to Lavinia. She seemed engrossed. Tania tuned into them for a while, declining the offers of passing trays of champagne; the butler didn't even attempt to disturb Robert and Lavinia.

"I do rabbit on, I'm afraid," said Robert after what seemed to Tania to have been a long time, "would you like to look around the party, we can come back to the Architect Home later, although I have to admit, that isn't the main painting. That was a study I persuaded him to sell. I should say I'm embarrassed about what I paid but I'm afraid I'm shameless about that…"

"And much else," said Tania, "come on, we're going to look in the Red Room," and she relaxed a little when she saw how easily Lavinia moved with her, and how undistracted she was as they walked past the girl on the sofa having sex with two men.

They paused in the corridor, Lavinia smiled, "It's easy to get my bearings, the noises are calling," and above the ambient cool jazz there was the vivid, unmistakable sound of a cane striking flesh followed by a loud moan of pain.

But the moan had sounded strange, half-preparing Tania for the sight as she entered. There was a man strapped to the bench and a tall blonde woman in leather underwear behind him, wielding the cane. Lavinia seemed unfazed. Robert guided them to the same red leather bench as before. The audience, predominantly female this time, were too engrossed to offer a clear view, so Tania stood. It had never occurred to her to watch a scene like this, and she was convinced she never would again unless, like this, by accident.

The man was fully strapped on at wrists, knees and by a belt around his waist. Tania was briefly captivated by his bunched genitalia, squeezed evidently by a large cock ring around his member and under his testicles, which bulged absurdly; his cock, by contrast, was suffering in the comparison, it was small and not stiff and altogether forlorn and unenticing.

His bottom was a fierce red with deep livid welts across it, mostly horizontal with an occasional, and deliberately well-placed, diagonal. The red light was dim, but Tania was fairly sure she could see flecks of blood on some of the marks, but the blonde woman continued with constant, unrelenting intensity. When Tania turned briefly to look at the other two, they were sat talking, Robert holding Lavinia's hand. Tania turned back to the scene, she knew Robert well enough by now to know that he would just be calming her, helping her relax.

The man's groans were as constant as the woman's strokes — was there no climax to this? Another aspect Tania failed to understand. But suddenly the woman cried 'fifty' and delivered a particularly vicious swipe. The man cried out, no mere groan this time, and the audience began to clap, quietly and politely. Robert and Lavinia stood and joined in the applause. Tania gave him a quizzical look, "Climax?" she asked.

"Not everyone needs it," Lavinia said, "some like it just for itself."

"And you?" asked Robert.

She looked to each of them in turn, "I like to come at the end," now she looked just to Robert, "do you have a friend who would help, maybe?"

"I'm certain that could be arranged. Do you like to stay on the horse?"

"I've almost never used one, to be honest, but I do like to stay in position. I'm usually very near coming anyway when the spanking's finished," she hesitated, "but if your friend would need to go on for longer, that would be good too. Just no anal tonight, OK?"

"Clearly understood," said Robert soothingly.

"I like it, but I like to get myself ready."

"You are a beautiful woman, Lavinia, I doubt whether any of my friends would be able to wait long anyway."

"Would you do it, Robert?" Tania was looking directly at Lavinia as she asked him. Lavinia looked puzzled, "You wouldn't mind if it was him, would you?"

"No, of course not, but…"

"But nothing, he'll be thrilled," said Tania. She was confused about why she'd asked, but she knew it was what she wanted. This was turning out to be an extraordinary week, watching Robert fuck Lavinia would truly climax it. Well, maybe not quite, she thought, she would have to get seriously fucked herself later.

But not spanked, she thought, definitely not spanked, as she saw Noah walking through the dwindling numbers in the room with a tall, older man.

"Lavinia, may I introduce Geoffrey?"

The older man took her hand and kissed it, "I'm honoured and delighted to meet you my dear. I hope we can have an enjoyable time together. Would you care to

198

step over here and talk to me for a while?"

"Of course," said Lavinia, looking, for the first time thought Tania, a little flustered. Noah and Robert continued chatting idly. Tania looked to the far corner where the two were talking intently, Lavinia seeming to lose her nervousness and becoming animated, nodding and smiling occasionally as Geoffrey seemed to ask questions and even, to judge by their reactions, to be making light jokes.

"Robert," Tania interrupted the two men without her gaze leaving the couple in the corner, "would you mind asking Ray to join us?"

He smiled, "Are you worried I won't be enough for her?"

"I'm sure you will, my darling, but I want to make it an even more memorable experience for her."

"I understand," he said, and went off to find Ray.

But he didn't understand. Yes, she wanted to make the experience memorable for her new friend, but she didn't want to take away a memory picture of only Robert fucking her. That might, at some time, get too personally painful. And besides, she thought, without quite believing herself, if I were ever spanked, I would want three or four of them fucking me afterwards.

But, as Lavinia was stepping elegantly out of her dress, Robert returned with a tall black man. Tania raised her eyebrows, "I'm afraid friend Raymond had just finished dealing with the two young ladies you saw earlier. I thought Lavinia deserved better. This is Amos.

Tania looked up into a beaming smile. Amos took her hand, and said "It's lovely to meet you, Tania," in a gorgeous, deep bass.

Tania tiptoed to kiss his cheek, "You too, Amos," *oh, voices, voices, girl, how sexy are voices*, and now, instead of feeling discomfort about what she might be about to impose on Lavinia, she felt a twinge of jealousy.

But Lavinia, now in only bra, pants and shoes, was being guided to the horse by a now stern-looking Geoffrey, who had shed his shirt to reveal an impressive torso for a man of his age, a silver-grey fuzz blanketing his well-defined pecs. Lavinia turned to face the device, unfastened her bra and threw it nonchalantly to the side.

Her thong revealed two generous, but perfectly shaped, buttocks. *If I were into it,* thought Tania, *that is a bottom I should love to spank.*

Geoffrey tapped the horse with a leather paddle. Lavinia lay herself along it. He made two quick adjustments to the knee rests and whispered something to her, she was evidently comfortable. She then wriggled her hips and then her knees to allow him to pull off her thong, which he then placed on a side table where he also placed her bra when he'd gathered that from the floor. He was moving very slowly and deliberately. Tania could feel the tension rising and, when she looked around, in the gathering audience, Robert and Amos were looking intensely rapt. Noah was at the side of the room, holding the hand of a woman, but focusing completely on Lavinia. Tania looked back to the voluptuous bottom and the sweet naked lips beneath. It was the first time, it struck her, that she'd studied this particular view. For her, it was just a female body, but she had a sudden sense of why it seemed to captivate fifty percent of mankind.

Geoffrey had tightened the straps at knee, wrist and waist, "Are you ready, Lavinia?" he intoned. There was only a murmur in response.

The paddle's impact was so loud that Tania was shaken. *Wow!* But from Lavinia there was only a deep sigh. He waited, and slowly a deep red mark appeared across her bottom. Now he stroked her, running a hand down each cheek. He leaned down toward her and whispered something. Tania could not even hear a response. He stood back and delivered the second blow, even louder this time, and this time there was a gasp from the victim.

But was she a victim? Geoffrey was plainly adjusting to her wishes. As with the man before, the strokes now came with a leisurely regularity, the gasps were of consistent volume, only the colour was changing, deepening, spreading.

The she heard Geoffrey call 'twenty' and he delivered a harder swipe, but this time there was a loud sigh, and not a gasp. One or two people clapped but Lavinia stayed still, seeming, if anything, to relax even more on to the horse.

There was another whispered conversation between master and slave, but Tania was left bewildered, wondering which was actually which. It was almost as if

Lavinia were in control.

Geoffrey placed the paddle on the side table, beside Lavinia's underwear, and picked up the cane. He waved it slowly in front of her face. Tania could see her nodding slightly. Now he moved behind her.

The first swipe was, for Tania, startling. It seemed much louder than the paddle before, and Lavinia's gasp was almost a squeal. Geoffrey whispered to her again, returned to his position, smoothed his hand gently over her, and delivered a much harder second swipe. Tania could easily see, as the second mark became evident above the first, that the intensity had been much higher, but Lavinia's response this time had been a deep groan, almost, it seemed, of satisfaction.

There was no more verbal communication. Lavinia seemed to elevate herself into a trance and Tania almost felt that she was rising with her. The sounds in the room were simplified; the swish of the cane, the smack of the impact, the gasp from Lavinia and, most peculiarly, the collective intake of breath of all watching. Tania managed to look to her side for a moment to capture the transfixed expressions of Robert and Amos. She could even feel herself growing very wet.

The red lines, as they were layered on top of each other, were violently vivid, but none had seemed to bring more than a deep groan from Lavinia. Indeed, she seemed to be wriggling more from the onset of ecstasy than from any discomfort. Tania had lost herself in the moment, she was somehow elevated too, and Geoffrey suddenly calling thirty had felt almost like a slap. The next stroke came, and this time Lavinia did cry out. Geoffrey leant across her and kissed her cheek. She seemed somehow to settle even more into position. He turned towards Robert and nodded. The spectators this time didn't clap but moved collectively to the sides of the room. Tania moved with them and stood beside Noah, still looking transfixed.

Robert, with no apparent haste, was behind Lavinia, naked from the waist and condom-clothed. Tania felt only curiosity, no jealousy. He pushed quickly into her, she was breathing very heavily, very quickly, she'd been clearly on the brink and very soon gave herself to her own orgasm, followed quickly by the sounds of Robert coming too. For Tania it was fascinating, but oddly familiar.

Lavinia sighed deeply as Robert stepped back, cock subsiding, the ridiculous condom dangling and a sheepish smile on his face, but Tania's gaze soon left that. He was replaced by a fully naked Amos. *Christ!* Thought Tania, *he is a big man.* Lavinia had not even opened her eyes but twitched when she felt a new pair of hands on her waist. Amos pushed the first part of his cock inside her, then leaned fully forward, his chest on her back, and whispered to her. Her eyes were still closed but Tania could see her nodding. Amos stood upright and fed himself more deeply into her. She heard Lavinia squealing slightly, but only after Amos was absurdly deep, she thought.

But now he pulled out and kneeled down. He buried

his face slowly into her, seeming to take great joy in her body and its juices, but Tania was transfixed by the enormous cock, waiting to be put into service again. It seemed absurdly soon when Lavinia's moans were growing louder. Surely not again already, thought Tania, but Amos was up again, pushing all of himself, it looked like, up into Lavinia's stomach, and she was squealing, but in ecstasy, not pain, and they were coming together.

Tania felt captivated, and almost insanely jealous. She looked to Robert, still half naked and staring at the scene. 'Come on', she mouthed to him. He was quickly beside her, "Green room, now!" she hissed and took his hand. When they got there, there was a bed empty. She lifted her skirt, ripped her thong off quickly and threw herself on to the bed with her legs wide open, "Eat me now, you bastard," she yelled. He, thankfully, threw himself on to her and buried his face into her pussy. Oh, he was there, now, perhaps, she could relax a little — but she was too excited, she pushed her clit at his tongue — he, sensing her urgency, gripped her thighs and spread his tongue all over her. She was screaming completely uninhibitedly — and coming and coming and coming.

When her breathing finally slowed he was lying beside her, his face still glistening from her. "Wow, thank you," she said, "I'm sorry I was so desperate."

He laughed, "I liked that, no more Tania the dictator. I liked you being desperate. More, please."

She smiled, but something in his remark lodged inside her.

Chapter 14

Will wondered how they would be together, the two women he was now closest to in the world. Tokyo was two and a half years away — and they hadn't met that often then.

Tania seemed superficially relaxed as they waited in his office for Martha to arrive. But she was flicking across the screens on the wall opposite his desk and then running through their menus and channels. That was something she never did, almost seemed averse to. He took that as a small symptom of nervousness and tried to hide his irritation. He had favourite settings for each screen, and they would probably take a few minutes to recover in the morning. He doubted whether she was interested in anything that came up, she was like a child channel hopping. It was so unlike her.

But she'd really impressed him over the last four weeks, even more so than before. She'd shown a clear-headedness that he'd seen in few others, almost matching the Peter Dickinson of the old days. Part of him was dreading Friday. Of the people running Dickinson, he was closest to Henry, and what he'd heard from Henry about Peter's Asia visit did not bode well for the next two days. But he would be sitting in with them in the Funds and Property conversation the following afternoon, prior to the Group meeting on Friday. In principle, he was entirely neutral between the three areas, but he and Tania had worked so hard on the Group plan, it was coming together so well after the Saturday session, and he believed anyway in keeping a balance between the areas, so his commitment to a big investment in Group was strategic, as well as emotional.

But it looked currently like an unviable hodgepodge. Lavinia had been quite right about selling the bits that wouldn't fit with the new core. It had taken her to raise the point that he knew had been on Tania's mind as well as his own — and he fully expected his wife to spot the same point when she arrived for their discussion shortly.

He looked at Tania and was distracted briefly by memories of the previous Saturday. He'd arrived home glowing from the day they'd had with Kretzmer to be confronted by a particularly brattish Martha making lurid accusations about what he'd truly been doing that day. His combination of fatigue and euphoria had almost made him miss the point of the game, and it had only been a hint from some look in her eye and a slight change in tone in her voice that made him risk that 'go into the bedroom at once' command — and her little smile told him that he'd been very successfully manipulated. He smiled at the memory. But it would be a very different Martha who would arrive in five minutes. They would be offering her information and insights that he really shouldn't take to the bank before the owner was in clear agreement, but he trusted her completely and her input could be invaluable. And, fortunately, they could look at the Group in isolation today. He would know nothing clear about Funds and Property until tomorrow, although Henry had given him an extensive briefing on Monday evening.

He felt much closer to Henry than to Tony or Alphonse. They were both Oxford, both maths, both investment banking in London, albeit with a ten-year age gap, and Henry had become a very supportive friend when Will's problems with Merle had reached their crisis. But Tony's brash Aussieness — Will knew that was mostly an act, but he didn't know what underlay it — and Alphonse's, well, what? Will found him to be the most disturbingly smooth man he'd ever met: always elegant and with a serene unflappability that Will initially feared was a triumph of style over substance, but he'd never found him wanting in the mastery of any detail of any of the deals he was putting together, and Will was becoming enthusiastic about the projections, which seemed ever more solid, for the resort programme.

But Henry's version of the recent Asia conversations implied a different Alphonse and, more disturbingly, a very different Peter, from the men he thought he knew. Henry had trusted him with the legal view they had commissioned about the constitution of Funds and how much control Peter actually had, but the simple outline, that Peter must represent ten percent of total holdings and that Tony and Henry were fireable employees, seemed unchallengeable. Will had been relieved and so, he sensed, had Henry, who'd been trying to rein in the more gung-ho Tony and commit themselves to finding a harmonious solution — clients and investors would hate disruption, or even disquiet. Tomorrow had to go smoothly for everyone's sake, not least for their Friday session.

He'd only just caught himself at the end of the Monday conversation, "Henry, I'm sure I've been giving you support signals for the resort programme and more leveraged investments for the Funds all evening, but I will have to put it in the context of what Peter wants to do with Enterprises as a whole, you know that, don't you?"

And Henry had smiled, teasingly slowly, and patted him on the arm, "Of course you do, of course you do." Then Henry had let him pick up the tab, saying, "Enterprise business," with a smile, "just helping you preserve your Olympian independence."

But now Martha was in the doorway, smiling at him, but stepping instantly towards Tania, who leapt from the chair to embrace her like a lost sister. He was used to Tania's effusiveness, but his wife's equally warm response surprised him. He sat back in his chair as they began trading Tokyo memories, their evident connection strangely at odds with the comments he'd had to endure from Martha over the last four weeks in particular. It flashed briefly though his mind that he would buy a new hairbrush for her for the weekend.

Finally, they both turned to him with a 'what are you doing here' look. "Yes," he said, "welcome to my office, make yourselves at home," and they both laughed warmly at him. They sat down in the chairs in front of his desk, Tania turning hers back towards him, away from her screen games.

"We'll go over there in a moment," said Martha, pointing to the sofas, "I just want to capture this picture of the major conglomerate finance head for my memories." She looked around, "It's impressive, husband dear, but it's not lavish. I'm afraid I meet CFOs running smaller operations who want their PAs to have bigger offices than this; the bespies."

"Bespies?" asked Tania. It was a new one on Will.

"You know, big ego, small penis," and they all laughed. "Do you have the same as this?" she asked Tania.

"I have nothing yet. Well, in principle I have the same in the opposite corner, but I refused to occupy it until I accept the role. Does that make me principled, or stupid?"

Martha smiled, "They're not mutually exclusive, you know."

"I know, but they're not such common bedfellows as being unprincipled and stupid."

Martha chuckled, "Tell me about it! So, how do you want to do this?"

Will looked slightly embarrassed as he handed a file to Martha, "I've been persuaded to offer you a paper version," he looked to Tania, "it's easier to jump around, apparently."

"And I have a record to keep, splendid!" Will groaned. She turned to Tania, "He used to do it on a computer screen and make me sit next to him so he could look at my cleavage…"

"That is so…" but he was stopped by their riotous laughter, not so much at her comment, but at his reaction. There was no point in getting irritated, he thought, he knew that each of them could switch into the topic in hand with dazzling speed and focus. "Let's go sit there, then," and it seemed natural that Tania joined him on one sofa, while his wife sat opposite them.

"We thought I'd go through current status of the Group, how we're looking after the Personal Care divestment and where we see issues and opportunities, then Tania will cover how the Group of the future might look, what its areas of focus might be and what we'd need to add to give it real clout. OK?"

"Sounds good," she nodded, yes, that was her game face.

He covered the status quickly, she knew the Group anyway and was very clear-sighted about businesses.

"But you'd sell food, wouldn't you? And would you hang on to his old tech investments?"

Will breathed deeply, "Yes, and no are the probable answers, but we didn't want to front that with Peter before we present the acquisition programme. We're thinking that might swing it if he hesitates."

Martha's eyes went to each of them, "Could you do anything else with them?"

Will felt awkward, he'd had an idea that he hadn't discussed with Tania, "Technically, we could offer the two big tech holdings to Funds, but they haven't met Funds return targets over the last five years." He kept looking directly at Martha, but he was aware that Tania had shifted position and was staring at him.

"So, you wouldn't recommend that?"

"No, definitely not. We have ambitious returns, they don't meet the criteria anymore." He could feel Tania relaxing.

"Can you think of why Funds might want them?"

"I can, but why do I get the impression there's something you're not telling me?" He could feel Tania bristling again.

Martha hesitated, looking to each of them again, "Tony King talks to me sometimes; he knows he shouldn't, I know he shouldn't, but he has some hope I might, on the odd occasion, influence Peter or you. I generally don't, of course, but I don't mind knowing a little more about what's going on. So, what do you think might be on his mind? Are you ready for tomorrow?"

"I'm ready," said Will, "but I wasn't expecting them to pull that one."

"What do you think they might do?" asked Tania, looking concerned.

Will now looked straight at Martha, "If they persuade Peter to switch the one point six billion into

Funds from Group, then they can take on an extra sixteen," Martha raised her eyebrows, "well, fourteen point four, without breaching Peter's ten percent barrier. Are they really going to try that one?"

"I have absolutely no idea," said Martha, but she was nodding her head and smiling.

"The bastards," said Will, not without some grudging admiration, but he felt a lot of irritation.

"I've told you nothing," said Martha, "we're clear on that, aren't we? What are you expecting tomorrow? It will have a bearing on Friday, you know?"

"Oh, we know that," said Tania. Will was nodding.

"I'm expecting them to argue for pulling in lots more Asian money, enough to threaten Peter's Funds limit. That will be partly to enlarge the Funds and partly to invest in the resort programme. Henry was briefing me on Monday, but he didn't mention the tech investment swap idea, and I certainly didn't feed it to him."

"Where do you stand on all that? I'm sorry Tania…"

"No, no, I can see why it's important for us. Well, for me, I should say. I can't expect Will to be anything but neutral."

"Being neutral doesn't mean I can't be enthusiastic about the Group proposals we're putting together. I am, that's why we want your views on what Tania will talk about soon, but we're talking three to four billion over the next two years, that's why it would be handy to pull two billion out of the hat with disposals. I just thought it might be a good way of swaying Peter."

"But if your friends steal one point six from under your noses?"

"I'll argue against that."

"So, what will you recommend to Peter?"

"He cuts his threshold Fund level to seven point five percent. He'd stay the biggest and he's still their glamour investor, his reputation brings in loads of new money, Tony or Henry could start up on their own, but it's the D in GKD Funds that attracts and keeps most of the money, but ten or seven point five doesn't change that from his point of view, in my opinion. On resorts I like the programme, not just because it helps Tony pull more money in. I'll recommend to Peter that he can loosen control here, he'll just have a more flexible source of money here than, forgive me…" he smiled at Martha.

She smiled back, "I know, I know, the bank — and I don't think we'd mind him having an additional source of funding that was more at risk that we were…" she raised her eyes at him.

"That's the way we'd set it up, yes, if that's what you're asking."

"That's what I wanted to hear, yes. So, I'd be in favour of that, after all, you have to admire a man who's arguing to invest in the business of another man who's having sex with his wife."

Will and Tania were both open-mouthed.

"That's something else from Tony that you didn't hear from me. But you do seem to have a clear head about all the other stuff, if you can stand a moderate

213

compliment from me." Will smiled and nodded, "Now I think it's time we listened to Tania. You must have quite an impressive plan if my boy's swinging this much effort behind you."

* * *

Dinner became a fun event but stayed, as was common midweek, relatively abstemious. There was lots of trading Far East memories with Martha having, of course, the dominant share. Some of her stories were new to Will, but he knew there were many more that would probably always remain secrets. Not that she wouldn't tell him if he asked, he thought.

But she circled back to the project late in the meal, as he knew she would. It was an endearing skill of hers and made her, he assumed, very effective in what she did. She'd already given an enthusiastic summing up at the end of the office session, after some, even by her standards, fierce scrutiny, but now she returned to the topic. The meal was, as always, a business occasion.

"I really do like the two groupings in software and hardware businesses," she said, now she looked at Tania, "I'm sorry I pushed you so hard on whether Molloy should stay separate, you know I had to challenge you on that," Tania smiled and nodded, "but on balance I think you're right; it is sufficiently distinctive — it has that end consumer element the others don't have and it has Japan, of course, that makes it unique. So, yes, leave Andy alone," and she smiled at Tania, "and pick group heads for the other two. You'll be busy enough yourself acquiring the new targets and disposing of food. It sounds like you've discovered a star to support you, or is that just my boy being distracted by cleavage again?"

"I thought he was an ass man," said Tania. *That was risky,* thought Will, *this is still our senior banker.*

But Martha's sense of humour was, as almost always, robust enough — and he could tell she admired Tania greatly, partly for her cheek as well. So, she laughed gently at the remark but got back quickly to the thread of her argument, "I liked the software grouping, particularly that Radius acquisition if you can pull the IT team out of Giddings. I'm assuming they're as good as you say they are. But you will need to move quickly, AI will make a big difference to logistics management and you're right that it's more talked about than acted upon, but you have to make Peter realise he can't wait. Here's the big question for both of you: has Peter still got it?"

There was a silence from their sofa. Will and Tania looked at each other. That was the big unasked question. "I am a little worried, I have to admit. In principle I think it's a good thing he's trying to stand back a little, but he will need to loosen control, or we lose our entrepreneurial dynamism."

Tania merely looked a little taken aback by the question, but then added, "I'm having the same thoughts about my dad, he doesn't seem to see the world changing either. Well, he may see it, but he's not keeping pace with it."

"Well, we get three bites at it this week."

"Three?" said Will and Tania together.

"Yes, I called Claudia yesterday. They're coming to lunch with us on Saturday; darling, I didn't think you'd mind. Claudia has the same worries as you do. She worries about him mostly, of course, but she's got lots of sympathy for what you're all trying to do, and she thought it would be a good idea to organise a working lunch at the end of the week." She took hold of Will's hand, "So, try to make sure your friends don't force him into an irrecoverable position tomorrow, keep it fluid if you need to," now she took Tania's hand too and looked directly at her. "It's not a mistake you would make, my dear, you manage your ego much better than most of the men do but, unless you get all you want on Friday, and I think your plans are too imaginative and bold for that to be likely at first pass, don't give up. We get another chance on Saturday. But thank you both very much for today. I know I think very highly of you anyway, you know that, but you beat my expectations. It could be exciting, couldn't it?"

Chapter 15

Dear J,

Thank you for your understanding last week, and for helping me to establish clarity about how future dates will be organised.

As it happened, had I been available, I would very much have enjoyed the experience and may well have been approaching you myself.

I note now, however, that you will be leaving on a long tour on Friday and that a meeting before then might suit us both. Would you be available tomorrow (Thursday) evening? I would prefer six p.m. but if later suits you better, I could manage that.

Another point I should like to raise concerns how we close the session. We both, in our last emails, described the last event as perfect. I will admit now, however, that I might have found one variant perhaps even more satisfying. I had requested that the arrangement be non-penetrative, that is a restriction I might enjoy lifting, if it would also appeal to you. I can assure you also that I have not had unprotected sex for more than six months. In the unlikely event that this also applies to you, I am comfortable to receive you with no condom.

Non-verbal and non-visual worked very well for me,

and these are conditions I do not envisage relaxing.

Please let me know if the date is suitable for you. In any event I will use this opportunity to say bon voyage and I will see you in a month or so, all other things being equal.

L

He smiled when he read the email. At the best of times she had a formal, slightly stilted writing style which seemed even heightened in these communications, but that somehow enhanced the experience. It was almost like being invited into a headmistress's study to deliver, not receive, a spanking.

And yes, although there had been some joy in watching the blobs fall on to her bottom, he had to admit that, at that point, it would have been intensely exciting to have pushed deep into that sweet, wet cunt and to have come with wild abandon. But he would have to insist that he was allowed to make her come first. This was, primarily, her experience; he'd come to see, in the wake of last week's frustrations, that the sub should specify the event. To the extent that the relationship matched the usual gender lines — and this one plainly did, even if some were different — he had decades of male history telling him that the male light was easily switched on, if not permanently illuminated. So, yes, tomorrow, definitely.

But that took him on to the second, bigger point. She was a lovely, caring woman, but maybe a calculating one too. Was this a way of being snared? If he'd wanted that, wouldn't he have called her? Just because he'd behaved — how had Tania so sweetly put it? like a total cunt — didn't mean that he couldn't say sorry and try again. It was silly to hope that someone else might be like Claudia; would he simply rotate through sub-optimal relationships for the rest of his life, never matching that memory?

But that wasn't, on the face of it, what Lavinia was asking for. Something in this was working for her. It certainly worked for him, although it hadn't, as he'd first thought, simplified other dates for him. Yes, the pure dom experience with Lavinia had satisfied a deep need but when his Saturday date had objected to a minor slap (well, the paddle had probably surprised her) he found her outraged response deflating and the woman herself, somehow, subsequently uninteresting. These little kinks were the sauces and flavours of sex. They were necessary. But could you eat just sauce, if that's what Lavinia was offering.

Dear L,

I'm always slightly unnerved by people knowing my timetable better than I do. I should have got used to it by now. But yes, when I checked, I found I would be away for three weeks from Friday so I would be delighted with a Thursday appointment, and six o'clock tomorrow will suit me fine.

I will also be happy to try your suggested variant, as long as you will permit me to put your pleasure first.

I also enjoyed the rather formal nature of this process, it somehow heightened the experience for me, and I hope it did so for you. So, non-verbal and non-visual (for you) again and, I assume, the same pose and implements (and whisky) as before.

I will also be neither bringing nor requiring a condom.

J

It was hard not to lapse into more human details. He was leaving Friday to see his boys in the UK. The tour was then global, any three day stay anywhere was a relaxing luxury, most were one or two, and there were two regions, Europe and China, where the five-year views of the teams he'd been through recently had seemed problematical. He needed a clearer view of whether the problems were in the markets, the products, or in the teams — and their leaders — themselves. He'd found himself reluctantly drawn to taking input from Henderson. He hated what the man did, part of him resented losing Claudia because of him, but Jack knew that was truly his own fault and maybe Henderson only confronted him with his own failings. He certainly seemed to seek out those in others, and he was pointing fingers at a key person in each of the European and China teams who was being disruptive. Davis should be telling me this, thought Jack, not our outside hired spy.

But an evening to look forward to tomorrow. It

would likely help see him through the next three weeks, which would almost certainly be celibate, if not through choice, then through attenuated opportunity.

Chapter 16

Alphonse felt very nervous about the meeting. Tony would be mercurial, even impetuous, although that was always, Alphonse felt, by deliberate intent. Henry, to whom he should have been closest, was a closed book to him, but not normally prone to injecting surprises, although there had been so little overlap in their interests that it hadn't seemed, before today, to have mattered.

Will had surprised him. Peter had obviously seen something in him very early. In the few studies where he'd helped soon after he'd joined, Alphonse had always found him quick and accurate and gave little thought, at the time, to Will apparently having expert knowledge of the property market and all its regulations, for this was Alphonse's language. It was only after their third project together when Alphonse realised that the young man had apparently learnt this foreign language in only weeks. He'd nevertheless been surprised at the rapidity of Will's ascent to head of the research team and then to CFO. Peter had, in his old style, pushed the previous incumbents quickly and ruthlessly aside. But Will never seemed to miss a step: any of Alphonse's plans were always subjected to rigorous and scrupulous, and always exactly fair, examination. He had never reached a point where he wanted to involve Peter in the resolution of any disagreements because he'd usually found that any objections of Will's had some merit. And he also felt sure that, long as his association with Peter was, he would more likely come down on Will's side.

And if Will disagreed today, they would have no chance.

Even Claudia wouldn't be able to save them. He was glad she would be there, but his feelings weren't simple. He did love her, he knew, the word was not wrong. For him, the word meant always wanting and doing the best you possibly could for someone, at all times, and in all circumstances. And he was fairly sure she was happy now. But he sometimes wondered if she still thought about Jack, yes, he felt sure she still thought about him. His guilt about Breeana was not so much about enabling her to be unfaithful to Tony — Tony had been unfaithful to her almost serially — but more that he'd let her briefly fulfil a Claudia dream for him; she'd been a surrogate, and he disliked using people, no matter that she'd come naked into his cabin. She had a prettiness and a bearing like Claudia, and, for that hour, she'd become Claudia. His memory of Sue was much simpler, the woman had wanted his body, and he'd been happy to enjoy hers — she was Sue, she made him laugh, and she was now a friend, a friend he would sleep with again when the occasion arose, she understood his body and his needs well enough to make that work — and he understood her well enough, he thought, to make it fun for her. But Bree?

That was more difficult, and he would be joining Tony and the others in ten minutes. And Claudia would be there, probably the most important person in enabling them to manage Peter. But that would cost her, emotionally, he knew. He was sure she loved Peter, but it was not a simple love. She would have to catch him if he stumbled on this one.

And fall he might. There was a strange querulousness that had begun to afflict his friend and mentor. It wasn't age, he didn't think, Peter was still very sharp and active. No, he'd meant what he'd said to Claudia, Peter's love for her seemed to have made him aware of his vulnerability. If he'd lost the five hundred million and all the collateral and contingent damage on the divorce, he would have seen that as a bad defeat, but he would have been in an office next day planning a recovery with a lesson learned behind him. But now he seemed aware that he had something to lose which would be utterly irreplaceable, and it was leading to strange changes in behaviour. At least, that was how Alphonse saw it. But the cause was irrelevant, they had a meeting to get through which would have been pleasantly challenging a year ago but was now fraught because of the changes in Peter.

But the man strode into the Fund's main meeting room in all his old magnificence. It was an entry! He should, of course, have ushered Claudia in first, but he was the great pasha, striding round the large room, shaking the four hands with an unusual formality.

Claudia's progress took longer, there being a kiss and a few words with each of them. Peter took station at the top left of the large table and looked slightly impatiently at her. She remained oblivious, probably deliberately, thought Alphonse. She took the seat opposite Peter and next to Will, who was on Alphonse's right. Tony had engineered Henry into taking the seat beside where they knew Peter would sit, but they would have agreed that as a sensible tactic.

"Whose meeting is this?" boomed Peter, when Claudia had finally sat down, "is there an agenda, I've seen nothing."

That was a cheap tactic, thought Alphonse, designed to put people on the back foot. They'd all used it at different times, but it was never good.

"It's mine," said Will calmly, "I need to plan for the disbursement of funds arising from the disposals and I want to take submissions for those and in that sense, there is only that point on the agenda."

That caught them all by surprise, even Peter, who'd probably been looking to Will as the minute taker and for some analytical support. Alphonse was curious to see how this grab for initiative played out. He felt reasonably comfortable, he'd kept Will fully informed of the resort performance and its plans; he'd received, and responded to, a number of detailed questions and had received also some very supportive comments. He knew that Henry kept Will a little in their loop, but he doubted whether Tony ever had much contact with 'The Boy' as he called him.

"I am of course aware," Will continued, "that there are ideas in circulation which would spring the bounds of our current arrangements, and I would find it helpful to give those an airing to help us plot a longer-term future. You are all more aware than I am that the Dickinson past has been characterised by a number of bold steps and I will be interested to see if the ideas we should discuss today fall into that category…"

"Or if they represent some of the nonsense that Dickinson has had to reject in the past to keep itself solvent and growing."

"And I completely agree with that," said Will quickly. Much quicker than Tony, whom Alphonse was closely observing; that was where the first explosion might come from. Peter had tossed a grenade, but no-one was pulling the pin. Will had effectively picked it up and pocketed it, unprimed, safely.

"As you are aware, the Personal Care sale has generated, net, three point nine billion. Our provisional allocation was one for longer term securities, one for Funds—"

"We'd said two," interjected Tony sharply.

Will stayed calm and smiled, "I know you'd assumed two, Tony, and we'd always said that these numbers would be up for discussion, but at no time have Peter or I formally communicated anything other than the numbers of the chart on the screen," he pointed to the end of the room. He smiled again, "I'm not proposing to use the screen as a presentation, I'll simply try to put up relevant facts and data if we think them helpful to the discussion. These are the numbers from the guideline memo I sent you immediately after the sale, where I also asked you to think about what different levels of investment might bring PDE if you foresaw activities which might be very attractive to us. Shall I continue?"

"Please do!" said Peter beaming; his boy's script was plainly pleasing him.

"We'd said we would allocate two tranches of half a billion to Properties, or P and R as I would now prefer to name it, since Resorts is now a significant and, early doors, a successful component of that."

Thank you Will, thought Alphonse. He was happier with the introduction than Tony, who was quite clearly annoyed with Will's comments on allocations.

"Now, in fairness, I should say a few words about Group. That will be discussed tomorrow but I need, I think, to tell you two things, beyond the initial point that we were mentally allocating between nought point five and nought point nine to it. The first point is that the previous balance between Funds, Properties and Group has always seemed healthy to me, from the point of view of spreading risk for PDE. The second point is that I have been working closely with Tania Gunter over the last four weeks and there will be proposals," he turned here to Peter, "this shouldn't surprise you, Peter, there are proposals which could see a two to four billion expansion of this sector over the next few years."

"Four billion!" Tony exploded.

"I would only say at this point that such a move would merely restore Group's relative position within PDE. Although I think I'm right in saying that there are other ambitious numbers for some of your plans."

"No, mate, we're talking about bringing money in, not splashing it about."

"We're talking about money that produces direct returns for PDE, Tony," said Peter coldly, "not money that makes money for your clients and puts you in the top ten list."

"We'll put GKD in the top ten, Peter, we don't forget what the D's for," but he settled quietly down again, this was barely a skirmish, thought Alphonse. Tony, for all his sometimes outlandish, interjections, was usually a smart tactician.

But Peter wasn't reacting to a very large number Will had just spoken of, thought Alphonse, *had he been briefed? Had Claudia been briefed?* He knew she and Tania were very close — and he'd not spoken to her for a week or two, not since the Morkuda meeting where he'd noted her reaction to Tony's indiscretion then. She'd looked surprisingly troubled, although, in that moment, he'd been rather preoccupied with his own shock at the public disclosure of the Bree event.

"Tania will have a chance to take Peter and Claudia through her ideas tomorrow…"

"Hers or yours?" asked Tony, sourly.

"We've worked on them together. In themselves, I

think they are very good ideas but, in order to fully support them and make a recommendation for Peter's consideration, I need to set them in the context of what we want to do with the group as a whole. Is that a fair statement, Peter?"

"That's true, and we need to acknowledge the constraints of finances and the guidelines of well-founded principles. We do business the way we do for reasons we should understand."

It was assertive, Alphonse would give him that, but he wasn't detecting a ready acceptance in the faces of Tony and Henry opposite.

"That's entirely understood," said Henry, which was not what Alphonse had just been reading his face, "should I talk about where we are?" he looked, interestingly, to Will.

"I was hoping you'd start."

"We have a pipeline, predominantly in Asia, a lot of it arising from the Teluk meetings eighteen months ago, and we would anticipate bumping up against the ten percent rule quite soon. The addition of a billion from you, Peter, would lift us well clear of any restrictions for a while yet and it would, as you rightly point out, put us in the top ten. That actually would not appeal to me, our clients might worry they would lose the personal service."

That was probably an outrageous fib, thought Alphonse, *but quite a clever one. Fibs weren't lies, fibs were ethically tolerable misrepresentations — you couldn't work in property for twenty years without understanding that.*

"We have new strategies coming on stream which will enable us to tailor our programmes to meet a wider range of individual client wishes and if you give me time on another occasion," here he looked between Peter and Claudia, "I can demonstrate that your second billion would be better placed here than in securities."

Peter was pursing his lips and shaking his head, probably thinking that Henry would be raising their ceiling by another ten billion. He didn't pursue that tack, however. "Of this new money you're talking about bringing in, how much of it comes with caveats?"

"About half would come with caveats, which is unacceptable unless we agree to change some rules."

"I think you're talking about abandoning principles, not changing rules, Henry," said Peter.

"I accept that's a vital point, Peter, but would you be prepared to come back to that point when we've finished the summaries?"

"Why, so we can let the dazzling sizes of the illusory prizes blind us to the principles that have built us into what we are? It's better to have the principles discussions now."

"Are you guys comfortable with that?" Will looked around the room. *That was bold*, thought Alphonse, Peter plainly hadn't put that point up for approval, nor did Will truly wait for responses but clicked on to a fresh chart on the screen.

"I've tried to highlight what I think are the two critical issues, but I present these only tentatively. There may easily be points I've missed, or perhaps misunderstood. Could we deal with the ten percent ceiling first? I have always assumed this is to ensure that Peter is your major investor, this is especially important as it's his name that is a major factor in attracting new clients and new money," Tony and Henry were nodding emphatically, Peter was looking sceptical, as if suspecting a plot, "but your next biggest client is…" and he looked at the two of them, they looked at each other, hesitating slightly, "it's Arbuthnot Life," said Will, "and they're at less than five percent — four point eight to be exact, but you've three pension businesses just behind them. My point is," and he looked at Peter, "if you reduced the ceiling to, say, seven point five, you still remain the dominant source, and therefore the star asset. It's only five years since you brought the ceiling down from fifteen to ten. I think we shouldn't get caught up on a number so much as on the principle of Peter remaining the major investor, am I seeing that right?"

Alphonse struggled to read Peter's narrow-eyed stare. It could be resentment, but there could be some grudging pride. There was only suppressed glee on the faces of Tony and Henry. It took Claudia to break the silence, "That makes sense to me, Will, I think it's a very good point."

Peter's face crumpled into a grin, "OK, maybe there's an option to move to eight. I want a whole number, decimals feel like dirty underwear. I'm prepared to park that, without saying I'm accepting it."

"That's helpful, thank you, but it's the second issue that I think may be more troublesome, and I think it links to the caveats you referred to before."

Peter, without looking at the slide Will had put of the screen, leaned forward, his elbows on the table, his fingers interleaved, looking directly at Alphonse. "I have built these three groupings, principally because I was interested in them and also because I believed in the people in this room, principally in the three of you," he looked now at Tony and Henry, before focusing on Alphonse again. "I enjoyed putting the Group together because I believed in the individuals who ran its rather diverse businesses. This overall diversity gave me, it is true," here he nodded to Will, "a consistency of business performance that more focus might have denied me in some years, but it was never really consistency that appealed. What appealed was long-term growth, underpinned by sustaining our independence. If you look at what we can and can't do, gentlemen — and Claudia, of course — it is all determined entirely by the people in this room, and that is why," his voice was rising now, "that is why the fundamental principle we observe is that we retain the freedom to control everything we do."

"That's an old speech, Peter," said Tony, "and nobody's talking about giving up any control. We can just make more money available for property and resorts, no-one's trying to tell us how we use it."

"I hesitate to accuse you, of all people, of naïvety, Tony, but the mere linkage of Fund investment to Resort investment, tells you they are bent on imposing conditions and exerting influence."

"What the fuck influence do you think they're trying to exert?"

"Then why are you talking about linkage and caveats?"

"May I ask a question?" said Will, his mildness a stark contrast to the rising voices of Peter and Tony.

"Go ahead," said Peter, waving a hand airily at him, without looking at him.

"Tony, are your investors genuinely interested in the linkage, or are they hoping we'll see that as an inducement to let them sit at the property table?"

Tony shook his head, but continued staring at Peter, they seemed engaged in a battle of wills, each daring the other to blink first. "Don't understand you, mate."

"I'm asking if they've shown an interest in Alphonse's plans and you've told them they'd have a better chance of investing in that if they top up what they're putting in funds."

"No, mate, no," and he waved the question away.

Peter, however, now turned to Will, "What's on your mind?"

"I'd be surprised if that linkage actually existed in an investor's mind. If they're interested in a resort programme, they could pursue that independently. I know you've set the sector up to be funded only by your own money and the banks, Peter, but, in the event of any downturn, you'd soon be getting parenthetical help from that source and our precious freedom would be quite severely curtailed. There should be a way, I would have thought, of structuring the external investments to give them a potentially higher return than we give to the banks, of course, but under conditions where we retain at least as much control as we have now with the banks in the picture."

Alphonse grasped the point immediately. It was clever. But both Peter and Tony had made mistakes in their assumptions and approaches, they needed time to climb out of their trenches, or someone had to pull them. It couldn't be him, he was too interested to be seen as neutral.

"Could I try to understand that a little better, Will?" *Thank God for Claudia,* Alphonse thought.

"Are you saying you would offer them Resort investments with flexible returns that were results-dependent, but they'd be excluded from development discussions?"

"That's a little too black and white, I'm afraid, after all, Alphonse gets a bank sign-off on all the loans he takes from them, isn't that true?" Alphonse nodded. "But the principle is right as you've outlined it."

"You're right, Claudia," said Henry, "these are investors who are obliged to seek returns from a spread of categories. Our funds are the best place for returns, but they need other sectors to invest in and some of them like property and, particularly now, resorts." He laughed a little, "And a few just can't stand our impenetrable mathematical mumbo-jumbo, they prefer to see buildings. But I have to admit, these are people that Tony has been dealing with, I don't know what's on their minds. It may be, as Peter says, they have designs on exercising influence in nefarious ways, but I'd start off in Will's position, I'd assume we could structure some sort of resort investment vehicle for them that they could invest in independently of other things. What do you think, Tony?"

"It might work," but he was glowering at Will. But now Alphonse himself was feeling cross, had Tony set this up to squeeze additional funds investment on the back of Alphonse's resort programme? Was that some sort of payback for Breeana? He felt the need to calm down before he commented. Fortunately, Will took over again.

"Peter, I think I could structure something along the lines that Claudia and Henry are suggesting. The investment could be developed to be no more onerous than bank oversight. It would offer higher returns in good years, but not as high as we'd be earning ourselves. In any downturn, however, their returns would drop, but they, unlike the bank, would have only limited ability to withdraw or foreclose. Is that worth pursuing?"

Peter looked hesitant, but thoughtful, at least.

"I don't know if they'd go for that, mate," said Tony, sourly.

"Isn't that something we could at least put to them?" said Alphonse.

"So, you want to smooth talk your way into their knickers too, is that it?"

Alphonse stayed cool, "Why not?"

Tony shook his head and murmured, "You bastard," but then smiled slowly. "It's worth a punt, I reckon, as long as you make the top end attractive enough."

"To the extent that I've understood what's going on here, I am prepared to substitute or supplement bank investment in the sector, I would still insist that fifty-one percent is ours. You can write what you like about our freedom to control, Will, but it doesn't stop the bank calling us whenever they get twitchy."

"Does that mean we've found a way forward without compromising our principles?" asked Alphonse.

"As long as you don't forget the principle of sustainable, attractive returns, and you've yet to convince me of that in your holiday camps."

"Accepted," *no point in rising to that jibe,* he thought, "but it does mean, I believe, that we could move on to the discussion of the plans themselves later."

They all looked to Peter. It took him a long time to nod slowly.

Chapter 17

No two situations are ever identical, Jack thought as he closed the front door with a firm click behind him, but this, in its formality, had a greater sense of déjà vu than most. She even had the same aroma in the hall.

But she had defined a variation this time, one that appealed immensely to him, and meant that his hands were again trembling lightly as he opened the doors.

There she was in an identical pose, one he found preternaturally thrilling: that beautiful bottom, the lifted skirt, the framing garter straps and stockings. His response, this time, was even more startlingly quick than before. In a similar situation, a year or more before, he would have managed a quick poke before even slapping. But here formalities had to be observed, the reward would be in how vividly the memory would stay with him, as it had from six weeks ago.

Now he could stand and admire the perfect sumptuous pale cheeks. He cast his jacket on to a chair near him and went to pour a whisky. He assumed she liked these moments of him contemplating her, although he smiled as the occasional memory returned of her crying 'for Christ's sake, Jack, stick it in me', but now she was calmly presenting herself; there were, as yet, no detectable movements of thighs or hips. He took a sip, put the glass down and stood beside her. His hand moved sensuously across her bottom... and then again... and then again — he was feeling a number of faint ridges, and when he studied more closely in the little light let in by the fully drawn drapes, he could even see the delicate changes of texture on the normally perfect skin. *But six weeks, Jack,* he thought, *six weeks!* He knew how quickly she recovered from their times before, almost never could he detect anything a week later. She'd been caned by someone recently, he was suddenly gripped inside by that strange snake of jealousy when everything rational was trying to tell him that she had every right to enjoy herself like that. She had probably been busy on the very night he'd tried to paddle the lady he would never again meet. On the night, maybe, when she'd been unavailable. But the snake wriggled. Oh, this could enhance his enjoyment. The woman must be punished, of course she must be punished.

* * *

When he closed the door later, the void he felt was almost paralysing. There had been intense erotic fulfilment for him and, probably he thought, for her; she'd certainly come quickly enough when he touched her, and that last line across her bottom, the one that had provoked the first shriek he had ever heard from her, the one with small flecks of blood along it, had been the one he'd focused

238

on so closely when he was pushing as deep inside her as he could, and coming, he'd felt, almost unceasingly.

But now, sat in the car, unable to start the engine, he felt overwhelmed and immobilised. Could he do that again? How detached could such an intense experience be? It was not detached, it had released other primitive emotions in him, even a little shame, maybe even disgust. But only self-disgust. Wonderful preparation, he thought for a three-week world tour.

He'd rung the bell but was now rapping the door with his knuckles. Was she avoiding him, how long was she taking, how insane was he being, how bad an idea was this, how disgracefully unfair and selfish was he trying to be? He turned away, pressed the elevator button and waited. He heard a door click open behind him as the elevator arrived.

"Jack?" he turned to see her standing in her doorway, her eyes red-rimmed, wearing a bathrobe.

"May I come back in?"

Chapter 18

Claudia, behind him, could nevertheless sense him swelling with pride as Tania ushered him into her office.

"Are you giving me a message, young lady?" he boomed.

"I'll admit, good sir, this is the first day I've been in here, but," and Tania, for all her usually, now, commanding presence, could still manage a quite charming coquettish smile, "since it might also be my last, I thought I should get one day's enjoyment out of it."

"You think I might be susceptible to emotional blackmail?" asked Peter, plainly charmed.

"I ask only that you remain, as ever, susceptible to powerful business arguments and committed to your principles of entrepreneurial dynamism."

"That's not written on the list. Where have you seen that?"

"In your mind, of course, and in your deeds."

Peter laughed uproariously. It was one of the sounds Claudia most loved to hear. It was a wonderful atmosphere to enjoy, but she knew today would have its difficulties. Even with the relatively and unexpectedly positive outcome yesterday, she could not see the numbers adding up in a way that would have Peter feeling at all comfortable. And she herself didn't want them taking on speculations and adventures that she knew would pull him once more into taking back closer control of his unruly business leviathan.

But Will, above all others, had helped him feel comfortable yesterday. Maybe he had similar magic ready for today, and anyway, there would still be tomorrow with Martha to maybe resolve some doubts or clarify imponderables. The Tuesday call had come out of the blue but had felt so entirely natural, and so utterly like a friendship that Claudia worried, subsequently, whether she'd been caught being too naïve. But that was silly, that was an area where her judgement almost never failed her. Only with Jack, and maybe that had been only wilful blindness — still a misjudgement, she thought.

The room had been rearranged since their last visit. That must have been Will. She and Peter were placed on a sofa opposite a screen that hadn't been there before. Tania and Will sat on either side of them in armchairs, Tania next to Peter.

As Will and Tania went through their assessment; Will on status review, Tania on vision, she found herself asking even more questions than Peter, almost surprising herself by how embedded her own sense of ownership was — and by how much she'd felt challenged by some of their observations on the performance weaknesses and the changes needed. But, ultimately, she had to admit there was nothing with which she seriously disagreed, they were touching on problems she'd discovered, but found intractable.

"Well, children," said Peter leaning back and looking at Will's last chart — the bill for the whole programme, but then he closed his eyes, "I am so sorry," now he looked to each of them in turn, "I hope you will forgive me for that slip," now he focused on Tania, "I sometimes have to apologise to Will for calling him 'my boy', but I hope you'll excuse my inappropriate terminology on the grounds that it's prompted by an almost paternal pride in what you've done — and in only four weeks. It's a magnificent piece of work, very well done, both of you, I expect the amazing from him now, my dear, but I didn't truly know what to expect from you, but you've plainly exceeded even him," and he relaxed into a laugh. "But now we have to manage the soft landing and try to save bones and egos." He took off the glasses he sometimes wore in meetings and placed them on the table in front of him. "The whole programme, as you've outlined it, makes sense to me and you seem, from your detached perspective, to have identified the weaknesses we have also seen in some of our people," he looked to Claudia, who nodded, "so you'd be firing the right ones, but you've come up with a bill that is beyond what I can make available, even supposing your estimates of buying costs are right — and some of them look very optimistic to me. But there's also a level of risk that leaves me feeling uncomfortable."

"Can I broach a sensitive topic?" asked Will.

"Ah, your unshakeable politeness, my boy. Would it

stop you if I said no?"

Will smiled, "I hope you already know it wouldn't," and Peter laughed again. "The point is, we can meet half of the costs from the Group itself. We don't need the original tech investments, and the two food companies just look out of place. They're good, but they no longer belong."

"Do you realise what I've earned out of those investments?"

"I do, and I admire it profoundly, but they no longer provide the returns to match the rest of your businesses."

"Really? I know I've tended to ignore them, but they even pay dividends now. Besides, they might fit into Funds in one of their more conservative portfolios. That might suit me."

"They would nominally remain with you for a time, yes, but you'd be giving Tony and Henry the right to trade them whenever they wanted, you'd lose whatever emotional connection to them you still have."

"Are you saying I make emotional decisions?"

"Of course you do. It's one of the things I admire the most. I'm just relying on you getting more emotionally attached to the future than you are to the past."

"Now you're going a little too far…"

"My boy," said Will, smiling, "you've had no direct input into those businesses for years. I'm guessing the emotional connection is much weaker."

Peter was shaking his head, but grudgingly muttered, "I suppose you're right."

"And food?"

"We like the people," said Claudia quickly, "but it would just be a distraction for you, and I think they're feeling a little detached anyway."

"I'd meant to add to them," said Peter, "but whenever I found businesses I liked, they had people I knew wouldn't fit with us, so it makes sense to find better homes for them." He turned to Tania, "Make sure you talk to them about who you want to sell them to, will you do that?"

"Of course," she said, "but they have an input, not a veto, right?"

Peter laughed, "My God, you have everything don't you? I'd already offered you the job before." He turned to Claudia, who nodded, "I'm double offering it now."

"With the net two billion investment?"

"Over three years," he said.

"I don't think we could move quicker than that anyway," said Will, "but if one of the big components makes itself available soon, we'd like the flexibility to go after it."

Peter raised his eyes and breathed deeply, "Well, you'd refer it to us."

"Of course."

"Well, yes, with flexibility. Dammit, man, you control the money!"

"Thank you."

"For giving you flexibility?"

"No, for calling me man!" and they all laughed.

Then Peter stood up, turned to Tania, and opened his arms, "Do I have a new Group CEO?"

She threw herself at him and squeezed him very tightly, "Oh, yes, yes, yes," she eased back, looking slightly teary but with a very big smile, "and thank you," she moved to Claudia, who was standing by now, and hugged her equally tight, "and thank you so much too."

"Oh," said Claudia, "you're doing me the biggest possible favour, I'm thanking you."

Chapter 19

"Can you come? We're going ahead!" Even had she been a master of suspense and subtlety, Tania's feelings were overwhelming her.

"Wow, he's said yes already?"

"We had to offer up the two billion, but then we can go for everything. You will come, won't you? Conditions as agreed."

"I felt sure he would think it too ambitious, I fully expected you to bring me bad news."

"Vinia," it was Tania's new name for her, and Lavinia seemed to quite like the intimacy of it, "I know I need to calm down, I'm so hyper after these four weeks, but what am I sensing? Has something changed?"

There was a pause, Tania was slowly feeling uncomfortable, "Oh, T, please don't let me worry you. No, nothing's changed there, I'm completely overwhelmed by it, but I'd be thrilled, really I would."

"You would, or you will?"

"No, I will, I will, as soon as you like."

Tania breathed a big sigh, Lavinia would be vital to enable her to do all she needed to do, "But something else has happened, is it something to do with last weekend?"

She heard Lavinia take a deep breath, "In a very

strange way, yes, do you have some time now"

"Will and I are going for a drink when he's wrapped up, but he'll be ages yet. I sometimes forget I've been borrowing him from his day job."

"A drink with Will, eh, and Martha doesn't mind?"

"Oh, now she's met me, she's realised I'm no danger," they laughed, "little does she suspect that you'll be her big worry."

"Well, possibly not, I nearly had a visitor this evening."

"You asked Jack to come and deal with you!"

"No, that was last night."

Now Tania, who'd been pacing the room, agitated by adrenaline, sat down. "So, who would have been your visitor?"

"Jack."

"Now you're enjoying teasing me. What's happened?"

"I'm still trying to process that, and it's not making a terribly noble picture, however I look at it — and it's also going to make no difference to me coming to New York. Now it's sinking in and I'm getting more and more thrilled."

"But is Jack trying to rebuild?"

"T, he's a man, he has an imagination no bigger than his penis, which is fine, but it certainly doesn't match my new, New York friend that you organised for me," and now they both lapsed into dirty laughter, "but he was here last night, and something triggered some sort of epiphany and he came back later, saying all sorts of sorry — and he stayed, wanted my arms around him all night. Well, he also woke me once or twice, of course, but I'll have to admit to having been very happy about that too. But this morning he wanted to see me again tonight."

"But you stopped him?"

"Yes, I did, and I was lucky. I knew he was flying to the UK, I have all those lists, so I guessed he'd be seeing his boys and I told him he couldn't break that commitment. I do believe that, but it also helped me. I know I wanted him back — and I wanted him desperately badly yesterday — but he is dangerous, I'd be so vulnerable again, and I don't want that, so I'm glad he's away for three weeks and he can think, and I can think."

"It's almost impossible for me to tell you how much I admire you. I find it hard not to ring Andy, but you had much more with Jack than I ever had there, but you still walked away for something important."

"Well, I wouldn't want to exaggerate that. Yes, I thought he was behaving like…"

"A total cunt!" and they laughed.

"Yes, you did put it rather well — and I was concerned about Claudia, and very angry at Rod but, it was a lot about me, too, so please don't make me out to be noble. I just knew I'd feel bad about myself if I hadn't stood up for that, and I knew I couldn't let him not respect me. But yes, I pulled him into bed again as soon as he knocked on the door. But I don't know really why he's there. I'd offered the kink and I thought that might have worked but, there we were, both wanting more, apparently. But I know I'll always feel vulnerable if I don't control this. It's funny, after these few weeks, and especially in the conversations with you, I've come to understand myself better. I do like to control, and then I love the thrill of giving that up for an hour. But then I want it back again. So, sorry to ramble on. But, New York, I'm ever so proud of you, and I'm telling Rod on Monday. When do I start?"

"Monday? Call him from here," and they both laughed again, "as soon as you possibly can, is the simplest answer. I'll get the paperwork processed through the Sandy Nicholls office and get it to you early next week. It'll be official then. Fuck!"

"What's up?" she sounded alarmed.

Tania laughed almost hysterically, "I really ought to sort out my own paperwork at the same time. I have a double motivation for nine a.m. Monday. When will you tell Jack?"

"Not until he gets back. I don't know what triggered last night, lust, or remorse, or something even darker, but I do know he's a man I need to be careful about, *mais, faute de mieux.*"

Tania laughed again, "I've no idea what you're saying, but I completely agree. Shall I call you Monday?"

"Please, and I'll be getting started on our stuff even from here. Talk to you then."

Chapter 20

Will had seen the advisability of her booking Peter and Claudia for lunch, although, had the week gone badly, Martha may have overestimated her ability to help rescue it. But, after the early tensions of the first meeting, Peter had seemed back to his old self. Martha had not been exposed to some of the comments he'd made about the others when he'd spoken to Will about his concerns.

His alleged desire to pull back from too much direct involvement had seemed, to Will, to be superficially plausible, but the level of control he'd enjoyed was high. *That word, control, was the right one,* Will thought. As he'd had grown closer to Peter, he'd been astonished at the level of detailed awareness he had about all the businesses they managed directly. The persona he projected, suave, sociable and effortlessly commanding, was what most people experienced of him, he loved the theatre of himself; but Will had come to see the actor studying his lines, the careful analysis and preparation that went into each part he played. Will, himself of a more obvious introvert bias and deeply meticulous, had appreciated very early on the hidden side of Peter and that had helped their bond. He'd had a valuable lesson when an error he'd noted but failed to correct in the appendix of one of his first reports came back red-circled with the comment: 'there are no small errors, only errors'.

When Peter had appointed him CFO, he'd referred to that mistake in telling Will of the reasons he would be replacing his predecessor: 'too many errors sneaking through — that's what destroys the confidence — and you've had your one chance, remember'. But Will had assumed that was only part of the story, but it did give an insight into the prodigious amount of background work Peter put in to exercise his apparently casual mastery. But pulling back and exercising less control would be inconsistent with his nature and would leave him troubled. It was a related thought that he'd also been troubled by the Fund's machinations with their potential new investors. Will himself had rather sided with Tony and Alphonse, they didn't seem to have given any firm commitments to anyone, and if they embarrassed themselves by appearing to make offers, they ultimately couldn't deliver on, so be it; their own reputations would take the beating. Peter seemed to be wanting, however, to peer more deeply into their operations even as he purported to be pulling back. But Will had seen a disconcerting ebbing of trust between all of them, which was unfortunate because the plans, as he saw them, looked very attractive.

"I'll tell you Martha, I was dreading this week, as you obviously had realised," his hand was on hers as they sat under the huge parasol, shaded from the late May sunshine on the terrace. They had just sat down, Peter's champagne glass was the only one not at least half-full. Will knew there was deep respect between the two of them, but some necessary circumspection too. They had an abiding sense of what could and could not be discussed. Will was taking time to get used to that and was often guided away from some topics by his wife in their private conversations; 'it's just easier for me if I don't know that'. But she'd been very forthcoming about the non-business side of relationships, she'd told him early on about Jack Stephens and their Singapore relationship, she'd even talked about Peter and an outrageous Tokyo night club visit. She'd only been decently coy about Claudia and what had gone on in her life, but that hadn't mattered, he respected the diplomacy and wasn't, by nature, overly curious in that area anyway — but there were obviously tensions between Tony and Alphonse that he might need to understand better — that would fall into 'the colour of decisions' area as Peter liked to refer to it.

"Your man has had an amazing week," and Peter looked proudly at him. Will was taken aback. He'd stayed so tightly focused all the time, recognising in advance how interests and egos might collide, and how fruitful it might be simply to assume the initiative early on. "I couldn't pull back if he weren't there. He's quiet enough to get underrated, and they find themselves snared in his net."

"Tell me about it!" said Martha, looking at him, and the ladies laughed. Peter blinked, then caught quickly up with them.

"I'll clarify it in the next three months, but this loose board idea I've had of Alphonse, Claudia and me exercising overall control needs to be formalised, and you need to be part of that."

"Well, I thank you, I think that's probably flattering, but will you have Tony and Henry sitting outside the circle?"

Peter looked to Claudia, "That's one of the things we're discussing. They'll both make the point that it's their business to understand all business and they have plenty to contribute to the other areas, but theirs is the area I'm most involved in, they do wheel me out to meet people quite often. But there are egos and personalities to manage, as you've seen, and we need to give that some thought."

"Well, I picked up some tension between Alphonse and Tony. What was that about?"

Peter looked to Claudia, who seemed mildly embarrassed. Martha's face lit up, "Is there something interesting here?" but then Claudia seemed to catch her eye, and Martha looked almost pleased to welcome the waiter arriving with platters of food at the table and help her off the topic, "Excellent, we thought we'd just put cold out for you. It's easier for those of us on diets to manage our intake." She looked around, "I say us, good people, but apologise immediately. I am referring, of course, only to myself."

"I think you're referring predominantly to me," said

Peter, stroking his stomach, "but this looks so scrumptious I'll be incapable of exercising any restraint." He looked up at the waiter, now pouring wine, and mouthed 'thank you'.

"But you're happy with the week, you were saying."

"Oh, I'm delighted now I've had Will's note explaining to me how wise I've been."

"Have I seen that?" said Claudia.

"I've just sent him a draft of what I think we've agreed and what limits we've set on what can happen, but I wanted to know if he saw it the same way. I only sent it an hour ago," he turned to Peter again, "you've obviously read it."

Peter smiled, "You obviously wanted me to, so that I wouldn't spoil you wife's charming lunch by too much business interrogation."

"So, you spoiled her Saturday morning instead, now I know what he got up early to work on," but Martha was smiling, "I rather like my weekend lie-ins. I see precious little of him mid-week. He's with that other woman all the time." At least now there no longer seemed to be an edge to the comments — and he was seeing more similarities between Tania and his wife and, after Wednesday, a budding friendship. "I must say I think you're making an inspired choice, I didn't get to know her that well in Tokyo, but she has a wonderfully clear grasp of business. Whether things will fall into place quite as clearly as the two of them hope…"

"Or as cheaply," said Peter.

"Quite! Even if you can buy your way into Radius, is it?" Will nodded, "You still have to get her father to free up his IT team and his client base. Radius is still quite regional, as I understand it."

"That's true," said Will.

"You've been through all this, Martha?" Will detected a slight edge to Peter's question.

Martha was unfazed, she'd picked that up too, she put her hand on Peter's, "They wanted an independent view of their thinking. They obviously didn't want to confront the Lord and Master with something half-baked."

Peter, not quite mollified, countered, "You're not exactly independent, are you?"

"You know you have to think of me as free expertise in this area, it's where I really am closest to independent. It's in Funds, where my bank is competition, and in Properties, where you have lots of my money, where I have much more interest," she turned to Will, smiling, "and he has a special way of dealing with me if I get too nosey there, don't you my love?"

Will could feel himself colouring up, he wasn't used to even hinting at their kink in front of others, but he had to remember that the other three had at least one common experience in Tokyo, "I sometimes think you just raise those questions to provoke me."

"Damn you, Will Uprichard, for your lack of chivalry. Of course I do, but you've no need to tell on me." At least that seemed to make Peter relax, and

Claudia was smiling.

"I meet Tony and Henry occasionally here at various gatherings. Oh, maybe I am telling tales out of school," she took Peter's hand again, "but I get much more out of Tony than I ever get out of Will. I think he thinks I might influence you," she raised her eyebrows at him.

Peter was relaxing again, "Then he doesn't know either of us very well, does he?"

Martha smiled and shook her head, "Alphonse is the one I don't really know, which is quite clever of him, since he has most of our money."

Peter's eyes narrowed, but he still smiled, "He's a sly one, our Alphonse."

"That's not fair," said Claudia, slightly animated.

"Ah," said Peter, looking amused, "but Claudia, you see, is in love with him," now Claudia looked embarrassed.

Martha was a little surprised, "But I thought he was…"

"He is," said Claudia emphatically, not quite concealing her irritation, but then she softened and looked to Martha, "He's a girl's best friend, really. He takes Jonah to football and Pat and Abbi think he's wonderful. Abbi has no shame about the presents he buys her. I told them both, an Hermès bag is not an appropriate 'getting to university' present but they both laughed at me," now she was smiling warmly.

"You see," said Peter, mock triumphantly, "a ticket to Chelsea and a handbag and I can't match that with a motor yacht."

"Oh, you're outrageous, you know how excited they are about the summer, and I don't want you perving too much about Abbi and her friends." If there had been any tension, Will thought, it seemed to have quickly abated.

"Does that appeal to you two, by the way? A week on the yacht with us later in the year."

Will was uncertain, fortunately Martha had views, "The boat appeals very much, and I love you two more than any other couple in the world, but we've already found in one lunchtime that there are actual and inevitable business sensitivities in our conversations, and there are also the ethics of what might be seen by the bank as a gift, or an effort to influence. So, I thank you so much for the offer, it would be wonderful, but we couldn't."

"You're quite right, of course, I should have thought of that. I sometimes lapse into thinking of friendships first, But," and he smiled rather cheekily, "the bank doesn't scrutinise your domestic arrangements too much. They gave permission for your marriage."

"Oh, I had to sign a paper saying I was the top and he was the bottom and that made it satisfactory."

Will was now aware of colouring very brightly, but the others seemed to be laughing easily enough and Martha's wine glass was being refilled again. It was Saturday, they really were with friends, there was no point in worrying.

"Fortunately, it's an impression my demeanour can easily give, so my word was accepted without me having to spank the HR head as proof."

Will tried to laugh with the others but his embarrassment had not yet subsided enough to make it easy.

"There have been times when I've wished I could spank him, heaven knows he's deserved it, but it's nowhere in my nature," now she turned to Will, "and I haven't yet detected that my man here wants to switch, do you darling?"

He could feel the colour rising again, as he was muttering 'no' Claudia came to his rescue, "I didn't even know I was a bottom until I met this monster here, and I still don't actually think of myself that way, I just got more relaxed about trying different things out. But being a top is one thing it's never appealed to me to try. Have you switched, my darling?" she asked Peter.

Wow, thought Will, happy not to be participating in this part of the conversation.

"I've tried it, of course, my first wife was keen on switching, but that abandonment of control was something I could barely submit to, let alone enjoy."

"Oh, if you can't do that, there's no point." She looked at Claudia, "when it works well for us, I get to a point where I'm almost outside myself, feeling that I'm controlling him." Now she looked at Will and took his hand, "And you are very good, darling," now she turned back to Claudia again, "he had a very good trainer before he met me."

Claudia smiled, and took Peter's hand, "I think I met

an expert to introduce me."

And they'd both shared an expert too, Jack Stephens, thought Will, and prayed that the conversation wouldn't move there. Peter seemed to sense his discomfort, "I think you two ladies have said quite enough to deserve whatever happens to you later today, and I'm delighted we've managed to move on to serious topics and leave the frivolous world of business behind us. We should just, however, be sure that we're happy with the week. If I appeared to be doubtful or questioning about your input earlier, Martha, that was inexcusable of me, and I apologise."

And he brought the conversation quite decisively back and they began to speculate again on how the Group could be brought together. Will was again surprised at how quickly they could all refocus, "I do like their ideas in logistics management," said Martha, "if you could get a major customer to buy in and sell its logistics management function to you, put it into your business, I mean, you could give real impetus to your new creation. It's not as if it's an area where big businesses try and differentiate themselves."

"If you're thinking about who I think you're thinking about," said Claudia, Martha nodded, "You need to remember that the last time Tania spoke to their CEO, she called him a cunt!" Even Will joined in the laughter this time.

The catering team had gone before Claudia and Peter said their leisurely goodbyes. Will poured the last of the wine into their glasses when they sat back down on the terrace. Martha pulled her chair towards his, "Was I outrageous today, my love?"

"You were a little, I had no idea where that was going."

She drank, "It doesn't matter. The key question is," now she looked directly into his eyes, "was I outrageous enough?"

Now he smiled at her, "Oh, I think you were easily outrageous enough. Go in there and wait for me!"

She smiled, put her glass down, and moved to kiss him.

"No, no, I've told you. Go into the bedroom and get ready. Kneel on the ottoman, naked to the waist."

Chapter 21

The plane's delay meant she didn't get home until ten thirty. Mom was still up, of course, but Arthur had gone to bed. "He mooches off soon after ten most nights these days," said Samantha, and Tania couldn't judge what was behind the little shrug her mother gave. But Mom had always been the one waiting to have the late-night conversations. "We had the champagne ready…" and she raised her eyebrows to ask the question.

"I think just hot chocolate, don't you?" said Tania.

Her mother nodded and they moved to the kitchen, "He is very proud of you, you know," it didn't need saying that Samantha was too, "but you are giving him a big worry about this place."

"How long does he want to keep running it?" this was a question about her father, his state of health, his state of mind. For Tania, the 'it' would have to change, the question of whether her *father* could change it was a different one.

Her mother sensed there was something more behind the question, "It's so hard to say really. He gets there every morning before eight, and he travels as much as he used to, but I do see him getting tired more often and," she hesitated, "now please don't take this the wrong way, because he's very proud of you, but worrying that you might not come back to run the place has taken some air out of his balloon."

"Does he worry more about whether I'd come back, or what I might want to do if I came here?"

Her mother stopped pottering with pans and milk for a moment, "I don't think what you might do worries him, although he did harrumph a little after that last meeting," she paused to consider, "and that's not the first time he's talked about your ideas."

"But not in a good way?"

"Sometimes he just needs some time. You remember when Claudia first came?" Tania nodded, "He said afterwards that you'd been telling him Giddings needed something like that, so he's shown he can listen."

"But it seems to take too long."

"I've never found it possible to hurry him by pushing him. You've more than one string to your bow, child, you can charm him. What's so funny?" Tania had laughed.

"Oh, Mom," and Tania hugged her, "that was a perfect reminder. I've just been made CEO of a multi-billion business and I'm still 'child' in this kitchen."

"Now I didn't mean it like that."

"I know you didn't, but it helps me keep my feet on the ground. My worry is, though, that he might still think that way."

"Oh, you don't need to worry about that. He does take your business ideas seriously."

Tania laughed again, "Yes, he just plain old

disagrees with them. Anyway, I'll spare him in the morning, I'm seeing Marybeth and David first, but I will go with him into the office."

* * *

Arthur had been bright and cheery on the way in to work. He'd spent the whole journey interrogating her about the new job. She'd flagged that she saw an opportunity for collaboration, but he'd merely looked sceptical and said, 'no doubt we'll come to that'. He avoided any private life questions, she knew she'd have to face her mother's interrogation about Robert later — but she didn't think she'd tell her about the call from Andy on the Monday. After all, she didn't really know what to think herself — she'd become better over the years at letting some issues sit and gestate in the subconscious for a while. That usually had one of two happy results: either she had clearer thoughts and feelings when the issue re-emerged; or the issue merely sank into irrelevance. But she didn't expect the Andy problem to be easily resolved. Anyway, it would be Marybeth first, and then David.

Arabella was putting flowers in the guest director's office when Tania came in. She seemed to glow with pride when Tania hugged her and put her cheek to hers, "I have you with Ms Porter at nine and Mr Wilkins at eleven, that right?"

"Of course," said Tania smiling, "if I thought any different, I'd still assume it was you who was right. I'm going to her office, and then David's in here."

Arabella nodded, "Oh, and I had a call from a Mr Molloy ten minutes ago. He just wanted to catch you for a couple of minutes before you got busy."

Tania frowned and shook her head a little, "If he calls again, please say I had to go straight into meetings," she hesitated, "but say I'm sorry."

That was truly a project for the subconscious, even though she wasn't hopeful of a clear resolution in its subterranean depths. And in the hour, she'd given herself to deal with Group business, she found that the subconscious was not always keeping the issue below the surface.

A small cloud of guilt oppressed her as she walked to Marybeth's later, she really should have returned the last call, but it was instantly dispersed by the reaction, "Come here, you bad girl," Marybeth was smiling and moving quickly round her desk, beaming, with her arms open, "I am so proud of you," and proud had acquired a few extra syllables. She released her only slowly, "and look at you, all this New York elegance."

"Ha," Tania laughed, "not guilty. Every time I get home, I find that Mom's put something new in the wardrobe," she twirled round, "and I always love it — and it's usually a label I tell myself I couldn't afford."

Here Marybeth raised a sceptical eyebrow, "Well, maybe that's not a bad attitude to have, but I don't think it's too forward of me to observe that it don't relate closely to no facts," and they both laughed.

"I know, I know, I just don't get time to spend what I have but it's funny, even when I do buy, half the time I don't like it when I get home, but Mom hasn't made a mistake yet."

"Well, she certainly hasn't today. Now what's this new job of yours? Not everyone's totally thrilled, you know?"

"Oh, Arthur's been quite good so far."

"I'm not talking about him, missie, I'm talking about me!"

They laughed again, this was good, "Well, that's something to do with what we have to talk about. But David must be happy."

Suddenly Marybeth looked serious, "Come on, that's a good place to start, let's sit down over here," and she pointed to the low chairs around the coffee table.

"I was kind of hoping we'd start with an overview of the senior levels and a review of the talent pool before we get on to specifics."

Marybeth nodded slowly, "I got that from your email, and I'm ready for it, but I wanted to deal with this one point first because it has quite a big impact on what we're going to talk about today and tomorrow."

"Well," said Tania slowly, "I'll tell you first where I hope we'll be tomorrow afternoon, and if your approach fits in with that, we'll follow your agenda."

Marybeth nodded slowly, as if she was coming to terms with a new perspective on who should be running the place. "I guess I should have asked you first, instead of just following my boss's orders." They stared hard at each other for a while, and Tania really couldn't say afterwards who had begun to smile first.

"Well, I think it was me who set up this meeting, but I should have called you anyway."

"Too true, honey, I'm gifted, but I'm not telepathic," now they were laughing, "but I do know you've been very busy. I'm just glad you made it for these two days."

"Well, we got stuck on a number of issues in the last board meeting when we were discussing a five-year future."

"And poor David had to take one for the team, I heard…"

Tania scowled and eyed her carefully.

Marybeth looked coldly at her now, "If it matters to you, I'll tell you straight I heard it that night from your Uncle Rod, but that doesn't alter the facts of the case."

Tania felt chastened, but had enough composure to respond, "Of course it doesn't."

"He's just a little in awe of you, by the way, if you want some more pillow talk."

Tania was now a little unsettled by this and found herself, unusually, struggling to find the right response.

Marybeth, having won the initiative, seemed to relax a little, but still kept the hard stare, "I'm pretty sure I haven't said anything that greatly surprises you. I'm just guessing you're a little surprised that I've said it at all."

"Right on both counts."

"So now you know I'm going to be pretty open with

you about things here. And you don't have to tell me a thing about your naughty New York parties, do we have a deal?" Now she was smiling again.

Tania, of course, smiled back.

"I really will review senior folks first, but we've made David a VP now, so he is on that list."

"Were you happy with that?"

Marybeth look slightly offended, "Of course I was, or it doesn't happen. Your father's too wise an old bird to impose an HR decision on me."

"But do you see him as a future head of the place?"

"No, of course not, I always thought that was going to be you someday anyway, then you'd have found him very useful. Hell, I'm not giving up on that, you will find him useful if you come. He has more knowledge of the business as a whole than anyone but your father and, here's the point, he has more ideas to do something about it than anyone."

Tania nodded slowly, "Yes, I got that impression when I sat with him after the meeting but…" she fixed Marybeth with a stare, "you just said you'd never let Arthur bully you on a people decision, yet it looks like David's just got himself bullied on his plan."

"Now there's a glory for you!"

"A glory?"

"A nice knock-down argument, it sounds like it, but it ain't. It sounds like you're making a plausible connection, but I'm talking about one single HR decision, what David's trying to put together is a plan for the entire business, and that's existential for your father. He made him a VP because he wants to talk to him directly about where we're going. Your father values him."

"Well, it sure didn't look like it."

"I know, that's why I was so glad you set up these two days. So's David, that's my point, he's not too proud to use your help. Don't underestimate a man who can manage his ego that well, you can't often see that combined with talent."

"And you think he's got talent?"

"Hell, yeah. You don't?"

"Well, I'll admit I was impressed with him when we were on our own, but it just made me worried that he'd been such a wimp with Arthur."

"Well, here's the thing, there's another view that, in the meeting, he was a bit of a wimp with you and some of the points you were making and yes, of course you know what my source is and Rod thought he should have hit back at you and not let some girl push him around," Tania screwed her face, "yeah, he's surprisingly enlightened in principle, your Uncle Rodney, but you scratch him and he bleeds testosterone. Now David's more subtle than that, he probably didn't let your sassy questions damage his ego because he wanted to use you to push some of the ideas through your father. You calling this meeting might help him change things faster if he can use your support, but he would have been pushing anyway. Of course, his Uncle Rod now questions whether he has the balls for a bigger job — see, case in point, why is that imagery always male? — and I've had to point out to him that most things are resolved by something other than a frontal assault."

That part of the conversation left Tania feeling warmer and more hopeful, but, otherwise, there was little really positive news. The attitudes had changed, and performance had improved since the Claudia intervention, but there were too many people still in the same roles and her father was showing as much reluctance to change his people as he was to developing his plans. Even Rod, who seemed to her to be more forward thinking, was not finding it easy to move him.

It felt, to Tania, like a clear-sighted and honest review, and they had time at the end for Tania to talk about her new role, and about some ideas for restructuring the IT part of Giddings into a joint venture with one of her projected acquisitions. She at least got Marybeth interested without, she knew, winning her over.

David seemed genuinely interested in her new job and she took time to describe how she foresaw reshaping it, including the possibility of forming a logistics intelligence group by linking a Radius acquisition with Giddings IT.

"And would you get major customers to link in to it? They have so much overlap with us in their logistics management, it adds costs and inefficiencies."

Tania was taken aback, "That's exactly what we'd been thinking."

Now David laughed, but he was clearly pleased, "Then, you're probably thinking about the same ideal candidate. Progressive, multi-national, high volume."

Tania groaned, "Oh, please don't go there. I've had limited exposure to the CEO in question and I think I've rather severed all diplomatic ties, well, I mean I'll have forced him to."

"Well, maybe Rod could use his influence."

Now Tania stared at him, "I doubt whether his influence is quite so strong these days."

"I know the CEO's changed, but Rod is still a director," Tania was still nonplussed, what could she say, "why do you think he couldn't first raise the issue?"

"We may have a better connection," said Tania quickly, without truly thinking that Lavinia's restarted relationship could actually have a business bonus, "but anyway, the first stage would be to get Arthur to agree to be part of setting up a new business."

David nodded, somewhat glumly, "Yes, as I told you before, I hadn't found him very receptive."

"OK, well, let's go through that again and you can give me a little more detail on what his objections are. I don't know what your thoughts are on how we tackle this afternoon?"

He smiled broadly at her, "I'm pretty sure you have a clear idea of how you want to approach it," Tania smiled back, of course she had, "but I have been giving it some thought, and I do have a proposal."

Tania felt curiously pleased, "Well, go for it!"

"First, we have a lot more time, thank you for that, but I'd rather get a clear picture by the end of today and use tomorrow to tidy things up while you're still here."

"That would suit me much better. I'm not short of other stuff to get on with and a day and a half of arguing with Arthur isn't exactly appealing."

"I'd like to keep control of the agenda, if you don't mind," she nodded vigorously, "I want to spend a little more time going over the challenges we're confronted with, and where we're falling behind competitively, in a way that will feed in to what these Radius guys are doing, but you can talk about that later, then I'll present a base case 'no change' scenario that actually computes the impact of doing nothing against competitive and market pressures," he paused and looked at her, "it looks pretty ugly but your father…"

"Let's call him Arthur, please."

He smiled, "Well, Arthur just smiles and says, 'nothing's ever as bad as any planner told me it would be'. But last year's out-turn was exactly as bad as I thought it would be, and we're falling behind this year. Also, one or two major customers, when you can get sales to talk honestly about it, are running trials with different providers.

"Anyway, he rejects my base case as unrealistic, but I have five areas where doing things differently could give us more growth, and firmer relationships with key customers. I'd like to go through each of those, each could make a two to five percent difference to the five-year growth picture. The last one, funnily enough, is exactly what you were talking about earlier."

She must have looked pensive to him, sat there, nodding her head slowly. He was frowning, obviously concerned. "That sounds like an ideal approach to me," now he looked relieved. Then she smiled, "I just hope your ideas are worth it."

"Well," now he looked doubtful again, "most of them got an airing in the board meeting and you didn't seem so receptive then."

"But you were just talking about areas you might look at. I think my frustration was that there was no conviction behind anything."

"I don't like appearing disloyal, but I had to fight to be allowed to mention them."

She snorted, "He's got that bad, huh?"

"Don't get me wrong, he's the heart of the place and there are contracts that will stay with us because sales will get desperate and ask him to call his old friends — not that his friends aren't above squeezing some extra discounts when he comes calling. But you know the picture, if we can get him to change direction, this whole place will immediately swing behind him."

She was nodding, "Yeah, they wouldn't do that for you or me, would they?"

"Oh, I'm pretty sure you'd get them there, but I am aware of my limitations."

She was slightly surprised, "That's very sweet, on both counts, but let's make use of your strengths now.

Let's go through your five growth steps…"

And by lunchtime she was almost comfortable about what he was saying, but his dystopian view of the current position had felt disturbingly realistic. In studying the Radius proposition she'd recognised many of the traditional failings they'd described in the industry, including paying too little attention to ecological issues.

That was only one of the issues where they had pushback from Arthur in the afternoon. He seemed unwilling to acknowledge the concerns David was describing, and Tania found him seeming almost resentful of her input. And Marybeth aligning with them seemed to make him more obdurate than ever.

They reached a point where Tania had to say, "Well, I think we've agreed that the accelerated tractor replacement at least generates worthwhile fuel savings, even if you don't agree on the PR benefits of being greener."

"But it's accelerated capex, too."

"That's factored in," said David, quite firmly.

"OK, we'll take that point. Did you want to take five now?"

"Good idea," said Tania sharply. They'd had two hours not seeming to get anywhere, with one or two quite waspish reactions from her father. She stayed with him in his office while the others left for a break.

"What is it, Daddy? Things seem to be getting to you more than they should."

"Oh, it can be 'daddy' when it suits you," but it took

one more second for his face to crumple and he slumped into his seat. He looked at her with his first kindly expression of the afternoon. "Could you close the door, chicken, please?"

"Ha," she said, smiling, "it can be 'chicken' too, when it suits you!" and now he even laughed.

"Look, you heard her make the point in the middle of that, about how shareholders are feeling about the stock price?" Tania nodded, it had been a valid point. "That's pure Rod Henderson, that threat, he's tried it before, you know, that 'do you want a job or a business' question, it's just unhealthy, them sleeping together, too much of the wrong things get talked about. It's an unholy alliance."

She leaned towards him and took his hand, "Are you getting a few things mixed up here?" she asked, as softly as she could.

He looked towards the window, but gripped her hand firmly, "What are you thinking?"

"I reckon you're probably worried yourself about the stock price, she perhaps should have recognised that and not made it seem like a threat. But the worry's real, isn't it?"

He still looked out of the window but was nodding his head slowly.

"And Rod's going to be poison whether he's fucking Marybeth or not." He guffawed, turned to her and looked shocked, but was smiling somehow. "Can't you get rid of him? His term must be up."

"Twice over, but he's better connected with some bigger shareholders than I am."

"I know you may not want a public scrap, but it's surely one you could win if you think he's that dangerous."

Now he was shaking his head, "That's not all he's got, chicken."

She put both of her hands around his, "Is this something embarrassing that a devoted family man couldn't possibly let his devoted wife and daughters find out about?"

Now his shock looked extreme, his mouth was open, and his face went white.

But she smiled at him, "I'm not going to find out that my beloved father has actually descended to behaving like a normal man on some unforgiveable occasions, am I?"

"What's he said to you?" he said almost angrily.

"Daddy, he's said nothing about you to me. He's said things about other people, so I know how he operates. It's Mom who's said things about you."

His anger subsided quickly, and his shocked look returned. "What…"

"She's just said you haven't been an angel — and a bit of me was surprised, of course, but only because I'd never thought about you that way. Then when I did think about it, well, who's the most charming, handsome, witty and fun man I've ever known in my life? What girl wouldn't?" He was shaking his head, but smiling slowly,

"And Mom..." she raised her eyebrows.

He shrugged, "No angel either?"

She smiled now, "Yup, no angel either. But it didn't do your daughter any harm to see you both, finally, as good old mortals. Debs is all cool with it too, by the way," he gasped, "Oh, but we couldn't possibly tell Ange," she teased, "there'd be a mammoth lawsuit coming your way for destroying her childhood," and they both started laughing, "of course, she'd have to park that BMW i8 you bought her out of sight of the court-house."

He was laughing now and stood up, "Come give your daddy a hug, child, and we'll let these monsters in."

"I'm going to open the door, but not before I've told you they love you nearly as much as I do."

He seemed to well up a moment, "Open that damned door, will you?" He was smiling again.

When the meeting closed, Marybeth and David followed her, unbidden, into her office.

"Are you going to tell us how you managed that, missie? We left you with Mr Hyde and we came back and found you with Dr Jekyll."

She shrugged and smiled, "Guess the serum just plain old wore off." Neither looked convinced. "Look, I know he's getting a little more sensitive, I don't want to say paranoid, but he's not convinced everyone's on his side," and she stared hard at both of them, "we know who he worries about, don't we?"

They both looked slightly shame-faced.

"Oh, don't worry, I know where you stand, and I

don't even mind Rod reminding him that he has to run the place for all the shareholders, not just for mister fifteen percent. It is about this business, not about his job, but he's gotten peculiarly sensitive about that." That should be enough, thought Tania, there was no need to mention the other threats, although she was certain Marybeth would know all about the sordid facts. "Are you going to sit down, or just stand there?"

They chuckled a little awkwardly and sat in the armchairs. "Now we need to be a little careful here, I know he got terribly enthusiastic about this new business idea, but I do believe we need the Radius technology to make it work — and I have no idea about whether they'd want to become part of Dickinson. They may find their own IPO more attractive."

"We could do it on our own," said David tentatively.

She nodded, "But do you think we've got time?"

"I have to say no, don't I? I feel I've been talking all day about how urgent things are. What are you thinking?"

"I need to talk to somebody there in the morning, to see if they're receptive at all."

David looked at his watch, "It's west coast."

She laughed, "Your folks were slave owners," then she felt sharply embarrassed, but Marybeth was smiling, "I need to get my head straight for that phone call and, honestly, I'm bumping into my limits. That was one of the more emotional days. Group hug?"

They laughed, but stood up and hugged each other. As they eased apart, Tania said, "Well, Marybeth, looks like we've got you a morning off."

"Hell, you just got one pissy-assed little phone call to make. It's poor David who's got all the work," and she looked at Tania, smiling, "I know who's the slave boss man around here!"

Chapter 22

Dear L

I know that last evening changed a lot. Well, it did for me.

But I mustn't presume that you did any more than show me kindness, so I should not, in writing this, jump any of the boundaries you have set for this new phase of our relationship (I'm not even sure I'm allowed to call it that).

But, since we're at least two weeks away from organising another meeting, I hope you'll forgive me for getting at least one thing off my chest. I want to say thank you for making me stick to my original schedule. I had a wonderful time catching up with my boys — and meeting the fiancée, as she has now become.

I am also trying to signal that, if you felt any inclination, I would love to chat some time. But I really must leave that up to you.

Yours,

J

He'd hovered over the last paragraph. How selfish was he being? An emotional weekend in London, three difficult days in Brussels, and now a lonely Friday evening in Singapore. It was only when he'd landed that he'd realised how the memories would overwhelm him. It had been easy to put Robert off dinner, 'could we just chat Saturday on the boat?' — but he wasn't tired, he'd realised, he just knew he'd be too distracted to make good company. But did that mean he should be writing to Claudia, not Lavinia?

After he'd pressed send, he realised that his winning argument: you can't even truly revisit the past, let alone recover it — was as self-serving as most of his other rationalisations. But he knew he'd love to hear Lavinia's voice again, so there was a core of honesty in his... offer... plea, what was it?

Dear J,

I was glad to have your boys as a good reason to force you to stick to your schedule, or I would have been tempted to lapse in my resolution.

I'm not sure if that last night (let's not be mealy-mouthed, it wasn't just an evening) really did change anything. I am very reluctant to hope.

I was happy to have recovered something of our past and to have given us both, it seemed, a safe area to enjoy something we both enjoy. But it was clear there was more on your mind that night, that made the initial exercise, how can I put this, a little more than satisfying, I think. I haven't fully recovered yet.

But we did spend the rest of the night enjoying something else we both clearly enjoy, but that enjoyment is something I find much harder to detach from my emotions and I must remain cautious. You sent the email at nine p.m. Singapore time: you're not out at dinner, you're in a hotel, you'll have had a drink, and you may be lonely.

That said, it's ten now (here and there), I've responded embarrassingly quickly and I'm having one of my last quiet days in the office here. So, do feel free to call.

Yours

L

He laughed a few times as he read it. He could picture that serious face as she'd been writing. He was amused by the guarded formality of everything — and by how unfortunately insightful she was; yes, hotel room, yes, drinking, yes… lonely.

But should that actually stop him? If he was certain he would do no harm?

"Can I start with some simple stuff? Like why it's a last quiet day?"

"Well, we're certainly not going to start with the hard stuff, like: whatever got into you? In fact, I don't think we'll get on to that at all. But I'm moving to New York."

"Wow! Tell me more, is what I think I ask here. New job, or is Rod moving things around?"

"New job, working with Tania."

"That sounds like a," he hesitated, "very interesting move." It did. He'd rung full of his own preoccupations

281

but other lives, as they always did, were going on elsewhere. Lives, too, that were important to him. "Are you happy about that, or are you escaping?"

"I'll admit things have been quieter for me here since," and she paused, "well, you remember when."

"Of course. I've never truly said sorry."

"Are you saying it now?"

"Of course, no, I mean yes definitely. It's not an of course…"

"You're mumbling, Jack."

He took a deep breath, "I know, not like me, is it?"

"No."

"I really am truly sorry. I even want to apologise to Tania. I can't possibly make up for what I did to you."

"Thank you, Jack, that's enough. Any more and I'll think you've been drinking."

He sniggered, there was now only one person in the world allowed to tell him off — that was something else he'd been missing, "I have been, but you'll tell me if I'm not cogent any more, won't you?"

"Of course." Now he assumed she was smiling, at least, "But, truth is, I'm really excited."

"About the job, or New York?"

"Well, both, now I think of it. But it's mainly the job."

"But New York also has more opportunities for fun than DC, doesn't it?"

There was a long pause, "I'm now going to tell you that you have had at least a drink too many. I am happy

282

to talk, but I think I'd rather you cleared your head. I'm at home this evening from six. If you feel like calling when you wake up, I'll be happy to hear from you. Goodnight."

"Goodnight," he said to the dead phone line. Yes, he had been thinking about the marks on her that evening. Yes, that meant he couldn't be a simple player at fun time. He had been that with Martha, he thought, but then he was her only outlet — although he'd managed the Smarts club evenings without these visits from the snake of jealousy. This was telling him something about his feelings for Lavinia, but it wasn't necessarily a good thing. Robert would be picking him up at nine in the morning. Plenty time to think and then call before then.

Chapter 23

"It's Mr Molloy again," said Arabella.

"OK, put him through," the afternoon meeting was about to start, it was easier to take the call when she had only five minutes.

"Hi Andy. Look, I've only got a couple of minutes now, but I didn't want to keep putting you off."

"Well, I'm glad to hear we're still talking. Have you got time later?"

"Could we say four?"

"Four is good. Will you call me? Then I'll know you're free."

"I'll call you, 'bye." She was still buzzing from the earlier call. San José on Monday, she couldn't say the guy had been enthusiastic, but they'd bandied a few ideas around and she'd realised, perhaps for the first time, that Gunter and Giddings and Dickinson in combination made a pretty persuasive entrée into a business conversation — and he'd been keen to meet and talk more.

The afternoon went well, Arthur not just accepting David's five points, but refining them and offering, this time, a useful critique.

"On point five," said Tania, "I did talk this morning

with Greg McGee, who owns Radius, well, he has some banks and backers behind him but it's his show."

"Do you know him?" Arthur was curious.

"No, Dad, but he works in logistics, Gunter and Giddings opens doors," Arthur nodded, "anyway, I'm going to see him Monday."

"Monday?" Arthur now looked shocked. Even David and Marybeth looked surprised — *but that's what we decided yesterday afternoon, people,* Tania thought.

"I'm not going to get carried away. I'm interested in them from the Dickinson point of view, but it doesn't make so much sense unless there's a tie-in with a national logistics network."

"Should we buy them?"

That was not what Tania wanted.

"I think you might limit their potential if you do that," said David. *Thank you,* thought Tania.

"Explain, please?" It wasn't an unfriendly question from Arthur.

And David answered, "This works best if it's seen as independent. It's an entity that sits in the middle of the industry and provides services to all of it and it makes it easier for it to work with the major manufacturers, it replaces part of their logistics function, something they don't put their best people into. It's a big idea, and you own part of it quietly, I don't know, Tania, but I imagine you'd want your father on their board?"

She nodded. She could have kissed him. Arthur was nodding slowly, "Well, you be careful, young lady, don't go giving away the family silver." They all laughed. For Tania, that was enough, but it suddenly struck her that she was trying to juggle a lot of balls at once. Still, no turning back now.

Arthur was standing up, "I've asked these good people to dinner tonight, chicken. I think that champagne we had cold for you on Wednesday could do with being drunk up." Tania raised her eyes heavenward when the others giggled at 'chicken'. "Harry and Arnold are bringing their wives too. It won't do any harm to let some of the other VPs see we've made some good progress, but we'll keep the business talk to a minimum. It's more about showing a united front." This was Arthur, the supreme people manager, back on his game, thought Tania, she was still going to learn a lot from him.

It was three thirty. She wanted to ring Andy, but she knew that would be a bad idea. She wasn't yet thinking straight. He may have thought he and Jen were separated, but couples often did that anyway, and who got hurt when they got together again? Always the other party. And how hard had it been to live without him in her life? New York was wonderful. So, maybe Andy part-time. It hadn't worked before, but her life was very different now.

She put the phone down at half past four trying to remember the last time she'd lost control of a conversation quite like that, maybe eighteen months before when she'd explained to a business head why Brodie Gunter Jeavons would not take him on as a client, fighting the urge to scream 'because we don't work with assholes' and finding that her diplomatic circumlocutions were not helping her find an exit. In the end just putting the phone down was the only option.

But she hadn't done that with Andy. Andy would be, and had she really agreed to this, she kept asking herself, 'picking her up in Atlanta' as he'd put it and flying her to San José on Sunday. He would confirm tomorrow when he'd got a plane sorted.

It only crossed her mind later that Molloy was one of her businesses now, and at some point she might need to protest about such an extravagant waste of company money on private jets. But it was his bottom line, she thought, and she wasn't ever going to micromanage.

But if Greg did want to talk about what it was like to operate within the Dickinson Group, then Andy would be a poster boy; a great deal of independence and the freedom and support to buy companies abroad. But that wasn't Andy's prime motivation, she knew, but he'd rather skilfully managed her through that. *The bastard*, she thought, as she smiled.

Chapter 24

"Six fifteen, I'm impressed, but that must mean you've got something on later," there'd been a time when Jack could have guessed whether she was just taking the piss, but he couldn't afford games like that now.

"My regional head is picking me up later, that's true, we're going out on his boat, but that's not for three hours yet."

"No man can keep it up that long."

There was a fair chance now that she was just teasing, "You do mean a conversation, don't you?"

"Nearly caught you," she giggled, and to him that felt like sudden sunshine.

"You were right to put the phone down on me last night."

"I know, but now you're going to tell me why, aren't you?"

"Yes, I am," there was no point in being unnerved. He was going to have to commit to openness if this was going to work. Ironic, he thought, given his history. "It wasn't just a throwaway remark about New York. I made an assumption that something had happened there, and it might threaten our relationship."

"I'm going to ask you in a minute what you mean by

our relationship, whether it's the one we were trying to re-establish, or something else that's in your head. But before you do that, I will say that something did happen in New York. I did enjoy it, and I didn't feel it conflicted in any way with what we'd agreed. But I'm not going to portray myself as the little innocent; yes, I wanted to see you when I knew you'd be going away and yes, I was aware that some evidence of my misdeeds was still faintly visible, and I wondered how you would react. But when you caned me like that, I knew it had produced some very strong reaction. I took it because I stayed in that zone, I was pleased I'd been so naughty and thought I'd earned a particularly hard thrashing. But when you left, I got instantly hit with all manner of thoughts and feelings and then, when I saw you there, I knew something similar had happened to you. So, say what you want now, because not all of my thoughts and feelings were nice ones."

"Can I deal with my two worst ones first?"

"I'm listening Jack, I always do."

"The first one was jealousy, I felt it grip my entire insides when I worked out something must have happened. And it didn't matter that my response was so insanely unfair, you'd only done as you were fully free to do," he paused.

"And the second thing?"

"Well, that awoke a demon that was strange to me and this one is, as I've thought about it, maybe even worse…"

"Go on!"

"Well, when I spank you or cane you normally," and he chuckled quietly, "I suppose I'm allowed to call it normal?"

"I think we've both shown we agree with that."

"Normally, much as I am always having a wonderful time, I am trying to give you as much pleasure as I can, but something else took over on that Thursday. My jealousy made me feel I had a right to punish you, and I got very vicious and here's the very hard part: for a few moments there I found it totally thrilling. It was only when the door closed behind me that so many other feelings came flooding in, remorse, regret, concern…"

"Stop, Jack, don't say any more, you might just let that one word slip out that neither of us is ready to hear. I'd like to say something now."

"OK." But there was a very long pause.

"What if I told you that was the most thrilling caning I had ever had?"

Now he was the one pausing, "Why would you say that?"

"Because it was. Whether you were justified in being angry or not, and neither of us is saying you were, it was a thrill to feel I was being properly punished. You made it hard all the way through but the cane, well, I got on to that high so quickly, I couldn't believe how much I wanted it. It was very seriously painful, of course, but I wanted it, I let myself believe I'd earned it, I would say I rejoiced in it. The only problem I have now is, I can't ever imagine those circumstances happening again. It was a false provocation, you had no right to be so angry, but I did guess you might be, but I had complete trust that you wouldn't go too far. I suppose I guessed that, somewhere deep down, you would have feelings to manage your anger, but that anger, while you were caning me, well, it was an extra thrill. But whatever we decide to do, I can't imagine ever provoking that in you again. I think we're going to talk now, aren't we?"

"I certainly hope so. That's why I rang."

"Oh, so you did," and he loved to hear her laugh.

"But I really do want to hear about the job. Before you start, I'll say I'm genuinely thrilled for you, as long as it's a big job. You could do so much more than you've been doing, you have some amazing talents. But I will miss you."

"Oh, Oscar used to manage New York fairly frequently and, without getting ahead of ourselves, I might invite myself to DC for the odd spanking if I think I've been too naughty. Maybe I should come a couple of days after I've let someone else spank me in New York," she paused a while, "this is too early for jokes like that, isn't it?"

He found himself laughing nonetheless, "Come on, what's the job, and take your time, tell me what it is, how it came about, and will Tania ever forgive me?"

"The last one's easy. She's just embarrassed about what she said."

"Well, please tell her she was entirely correct."

"She'll enjoy that…" and then she told him about the Dickinson changes, the deal with Rod, the plans for the Group, and what her own role would be.

"That sounds perfect for you."

"Do you think so?" she sounded uncertain.

"Oh, you are a girl, aren't you?"

"Of course, I'm a fucking girl, you've had enough opportunities to notice, but what do you mean?"

"Oops, no, I can't, I'd be gender stereotyping. Well, how can I avoid that danger? I know: I can't think of a single man who's ever expressed any doubt about his suitability for a promotion. There, that's a factual statement and you can make of it what you will. But this honestly sounds perfect for you. I'm very thrilled, but I will miss you."

"Like you have done for the past year?"

"Yes, like I have done for the past year."

"You could have done something about it you know."

"Probably, but the inertia of guilt was very strong."

"And now you've piled fresh lumps of jealousy and sadism on top of the guilt. Doesn't look very hopeful, does it?"

"Oh, the more daunting, the better, I always find."

"Shall I take you at your word?"

"Yes, please do."

"Well, I'll wait for your next call, at least. Have a lovely day, and don't drown. But Jack…"

"Yes?"

"I obviously don't know what's going to happen with us, or even what I want to happen with us. But even in that limited area of the game we like playing, we both learned some good things amongst the bad in your last visit, well, I did. I've often wondered what I like about it, and how I get high on it, but that last time I really did enjoy being punished — and it felt like you enjoyed punishing me in amongst all the other difficult things you felt. Do have a think about how you want to get the most out of those times.

"But I'm also going to confess that I loved you holding me afterwards. If that frightens you because you feel that drags you into a commitment, well, that's not my intention. I don't want to be hurt in that bad way again. But I do love our meetings, and I did love you being a little angry. And if I need to do some naughty things to help you get the most out of it, well, maybe that might be fun for me too. So, I was joking earlier on, about getting spanked before the next meeting, but maybe it's an idea. I could fuck someone and tell you about it, but you might think I was making it up. So maybe you need to see a few stripes to put you in the right place. But we should work on it. It's been pretty wonderful, that part of what we do, but it's never been quite like it was the last time."

"Why am I only learning this now?"

"About yourself?"

"Yes."

"Why worry, we've got two weeks to think and talk."

He spent some time thinking, "I can't really thank you enough. I—"

"Jack," she interrupted him, "don't say anything we might regret. Go and enjoy the boat, 'Bye." And she hung up on him.

Chapter 25

Tania had flown only once out of Peachtree, her father had a day in DC planned and he took Debs and her in the private jet to look around the capital while he did some business. He regretted it, of course, they were late for the return booking and Ange made his life hell when she found out what she'd missed.

Andy was waiting when she got there. "I'm not late, am I?"

"No, it's just the way the slots worked. I do pay some attention to economy, you know."

"Boy, Molloy, you can make a girl feel special, economy private jet travel, who'd have thought?"

"If you can look me in the eye and tell me you didn't think about the cost…"

"I can look you in the eye and say thank you," and they finally managed a kiss, barely a touch, but on the lips. "So, what's our story?"

"My story is we've got five hours to talk about all we want, so we should get you all checked in and get going."

They were soon airborne and had dealt quickly with the steward's attentions when she turned and said, "So?"

"Three things…"

"I'm going to listen for the third." He raised his eyebrows, "I'm fully trained on Dad's bullshit detector. He would say the first two won't matter."

Now Andy chuckled, "Well, the third is that my cock's going to do all he wants with Tania Gunter this afternoon."

"That may not be what Tania Gunter wants," she tried to sound a little cold.

"I don't suppose it is, at the moment, but your daddy's folk wisdom, and I grant you it's good folk wisdom, has obliterated all my careful seduction preparation. Do you want to hear about points one and two?"

"Not really," she smiled.

"You're going to anyway. One, this could work well for the Molloy business, if you can bring it off, as far as I can judge, and you talked about it in Boston. Their systems will work just as well for service systems as for physical product delivery. Two, you want to create a new business in the Group, and I figured the guy might be persuaded if someone tells him what working in the Group is like; he can go IPO and then have shareholders on his ass, or he can keep his autonomy with a little oversight and a lot of support from, in this case, you. Of course, there's no point in saying that if you plan to run things differently."

"No," she shook her head, "I reckon I've got two year's work on disposals and acquisitions."

"Disposals?"

"I told you, the food companies."

"But you haven't told them yet?"

"No, Claudia and Peter are doing that this week."

He nodded, "So they should, but that's what I'd expect of them anyway. Did they quibble about me remaining an independent unit?"

"No, I just had to promise I wouldn't fuck you." She got an Andy smile, "It's OK, Claudia sort of winked at me on that one while Peter was doing the stern parent thing."

"Which brings us to point three."

"Not so fast, buddy, wasn't there some talk of seduction?"

"This is it, babe, a private jet and a diet soda."

"You smooth bastard!"

But there was more business talk; she gave him Will's description of how the Thursday had gone and what tensions had arisen before and during that, then she talked about Lavinia and what she would be doing.

"I've been too preoccupied with my own shit, but what's all the background there?"

And it seemed worth stepping over a divide to give him the full story of the divorce and Rod's role in that, and how she and Lavinia had manoeuvred through that. If she was going to get him to talk about his shit, as he'd put it, it seemed silly to be coy about what everyone else had gone through.

He was shaking his head, "I picked up almost none of that. Maybe I was too preoccupied."

"Well, I hope nobody picked up too much of that. Part of the deal was absolute security. You can be disgusted with Rod Henderson walking away with twenty million instead of a jail sentence, but I'm learning to be a big girl about these things."

"And about Andy Molloy?"

"I hope so. It wasn't easy, you know."

"I didn't know, really, but, however you felt, and that's what I didn't really know, I always admired the way you handled it."

"How did you think I felt?"

He thought for a moment, then signalled for the attendant to bring him a beer. Now he looked at her, "I thought you had a lot of feelings for me and you got pissed off with me being dragged back to Jen, so you just saw an endless mess for yourself…"

"Go on, you've got more to say, haven't you?"

"Well, I think you thought you were making life easier for me as well."

"I did, Andy, I was, I thought. It took a lot of getting over," and she sighed heavily, "but I found plenty of distractions to help me and I found a few new things out about myself. Some quite fun things amongst them. But one of the things, unfortunately, is that I still have feelings for you, and I'd like to manage them without getting myself hurt again, or even seriously distracted, so your point three is a no."

He seemed to consider and nodded his head slowly, "I understand. But a no is not a no no."

She gasped, "Is that how you guys rationalise everything? She said no, Your Honour, she didn't say no, no."

"I guess I put that badly," and the slow Andy smile spread across his face.

"I was yanking your chain. We're here because you wanted to talk, and I do appreciate the lengths you've gone to — and it will help to have you there tomorrow, but I think we're on this plane because you wanted to talk about us — or you could have flown straight to San José. But I am having fun in New York in the little bit of time I get to myself. Well, I'm also having fun with the job, of course, I'm amazed to be doing what I'm doing."

"And you're doing amazingly well, I can see that — and Peter's a superb judge of people, so if you've won him over, you're in the right place. But, can I ask, have you got anyone special? I really don't want to fuck up your life in any way. I'm finding it hard to live with my feelings. I've been honest with Jen about that and that's made it easier for us to straighten things out."

"So, you're living apart?"

"Yes, I'm back in the city, in an apartment. I won't say I like it that much, but I wasn't doing it to relive bachelorhood. But what are you doing? Are you being coy with me?"

"I'm being careful with you, Andy. To answer your question, I see one guy a little, but it's a very open relationship and that suits us. I have fun, like I said, and I'm finding it quite easy to enjoy life as it is," she paused a while and looked out of the window. She turned back to him, "And that's partly, I think, because feelings don't get in the way of things. If I give in to your point three, then I have a messed-up relationship with you and I'm pretty sure it will affect how I live the rest of my life. It's fairly easy with Robert, that's the guy, to have an open relationship, because we're more committed to openness than to the relationship. Well, that's how I feel, I have some worries that he might be getting a little serious."

"Well, if you want that to get serious, I'll…"

"No, don't be silly, that's not the point. We were getting serious, Andy, us, that's what I thought, and it just got very fucked up. It's nice to be without that. I just couldn't do us in a situation with open relationships."

"Well, I obviously can't…"

"Ha, Andy, listen to yourself. I do know something of your history. Remember, first night, your 'most people seem to manage' quote. Thank you for the romantic jet flight, but you have history, my man." She knew she was smiling, that was why she was getting his grin.

* * *

"Are you saving him for something?" She was looking in his eyes as she held his cock, still stiff and huge, but very wet, on his belly.

"He and I are here in the service of Tania Gunter. Our memories are of her being somewhat demanding."

She waved his cock a little, it was hard to shake, it

was still so stiff, "Well, you should remember her being very careful. But I think I will want more. If I leave him alone will he relax a little while?"

He smiled, "That will probably help us all. I could have come just then, it was very hard not to, but, fortunately, you were pretty quick."

"That's ungallant," she paused, "it's undeniably true, but it's ungallant. Anyway, the second time's usually better."

"And the third? I remember your little fantasy."

"Yes, my little fantasy," and she drifted off into her memories. "Andy?"

"You're going to tell me something."

"This isn't easy, but I think I should say. I have tried out my little fantasy once or twice."

"I wondered, from what you'd been saying. Did you enjoy it?"

"I did, even when it got a little rough."

"But, let me guess, it was rough to Miss Tania's specifications?"

She giggled a little, "That's pretty much it." He looked a little on edge, but it would be silly to try to rebuild anything on a foundation of secrets, she thought.

"And did any of it include the fantasy threesome?"

"Well, I did even manage a four on a couple of occasions."

"And, for the avoidance of doubt, three quarters of the quartet were male, right?" He seemed now to be taking it quite well, but she was getting slightly embarrassed and buried her face in his neck. "Now this raises an interesting little issue for me."

She kept her face hidden, "Are you going to ask me about that thing you always wanted to try, and I didn't?"

"I don't think I need to ask. You've plainly tried the whole thing now, and I assume you enjoyed it."

"I did," she murmured.

"I think we'll have that a little louder, Miss Gunter, please."

She was silent. She felt a sharp slap on her ass, "Louder, please?"

"All right, I enjoyed it, OK?"

"I thought you would."

"Why do you say that?"

"Because we got as far as me playing with you there and two things happened. You started to squirm with pleasure when I touched you as you were overcoming your inhibitions; and you relaxed very nicely, it made it easier to play with you, so I thought you'd find taking the whole thing quite straightforward."

"I don't know about that. I'm usually getting quite carried away when that happens."

"Well now, here's the interesting thing, here we have Tania Gunter, control freak extraordinaire, with a gang bang fantasy. Whatever do we do with this?"

"What do we do with this?" He laughed, "What have I said?"

"Well, you didn't argue about being called a control freak, but here you are asking what happens next?"

"Look, I don't even know why I'm here."

"Yes, you do."

"Why?"

"One, you can't not take a risk with feelings, you have to find out where they lead you."

"And two?"

"If you stay a control freak all the time, you're never in a partnership. You know you have to let someone take over some of the time. You're going to take that risk too today."

"I am?" and she knew she was, "Where are you going?" He'd got up from the bed and began rummaging in his bag. He quickly turned to her, a large tube in one hand, and another condom in the other. "One of those you don't need."

He smiled, "Tania Gunter, that's your last instruction for the day," and he threw the condom back into the bag. "Now kneel on the edge of the bed here and stick your ass in the air."

She could see him kneeling down as she began to turn — at least he would start with licking it seemed.

But that wasn't quite true, she felt his hands on the top of her buttocks, stroking her gently, he was obviously staring, "Apart from your face," he whispered, "this is the most beautiful sight on earth."

Now he pulled her to him, and she felt his chest on the back of her thighs. She could feel the ridges of his pecs sliding up and down. The bed was a good height, it would make it easy for him to lick everywhere, and now she felt his tongue on her clit, still gloriously, embarrassingly wet. But now he moved to the new place. He pulled her cheeks wide apart and began rimming his tongue around her. It felt so thrilling as the sensations seemed to radiate out right through her. He pushed his face in and now she could feel his tongue entering her. Now the inhibition threshold was gone. It was tingling thrillingly, anything could happen now, anything he wanted. She was gripped by him, his hands now on her lower back, his forearms down her hips and thighs, she was almost immobile in his clamp, he just allowed her to wiggle slightly — with this much stimulation, a little movement was necessary. She was breathing hard and gasping, pushing herself a little higher, making herself more open.

Now she felt him move away slightly and then felt the cold dollop land between her cheeks, his finger rubbing it around and then gently, easily into her. His finger sliding in deep felt wonderful. "Gorgeous," she heard him whisper, but then came more lube, and now more fingers, it was still easy, but that little stretch felt voluptuous. He pushed deeper, but then began to circle her hole with other fingers. It was exquisite and became more startlingly thrilling when another finger was pushed inside her — *please don't touch my clit now,* she thought, *I'll come screaming straightaway.*

He was standing up now but still playing with her, pushing his fingers as deep as he could.

"I think you're maybe ready," said his soft, low

voice, "but I certainly know I am. You are going to take all of this great big cock, missy." And she felt a hand on her hip, and then that huge thing entering her pussy. "I just want you to remember for a while what he's like," and he pushed halfway in, enough to get a little uncomfortable, and he settled into a slow rhythm of easing in and out.

"Now the bad boy wants your ass. And the bad boy's gonna have your ass. He'll go slow. He'll go easy. But he'll go very deep. Your sweet little ass is gonna take all of him, and even if you squeal, he ain't gonna stop."

She felt more lube being dropped on her and his thumb was easing it in. This would probably get painful. It might even be impossible, but she was now in his hands — and for these moments, naked, excited, ass pushed as high as she could, she wanted to be in his hands, no-one else's, 'fuck my ass, Andy Molloy, stick that huge, fat cock right inside me'. *Just think it, don't say it. He is doing exactly what he wants. I am staying powerless.*

Now it was pushing at her. Oh, this was no Ezra, this wasn't just tingling, this wasn't just uncomfortable, this was getting painful now, really painful, "Oh, Andy, no! You can't!"

There was a very sharp sting on her ass where the slap landed, "Tania Gunter's a big girl, believe me, keep your ass pushed up. Nothing you can do to stop this."

The fantasies hadn't been like this. The parties hadn't been like this, now she was shouting louder and louder, way beyond the noises you'd ever let yourself make in a hotel room — or anywhere — this was seriously painful, a tearing ring of pain around the centre of her ass, and he was still moving, very slowly, tiny little nudges forward, his hands holding her hips, she could move nothing, focused only on this huge thing pushing in to her, feeling immense, unnatural, feeling, wait, the pain was easing, slowly she felt her insides filling up, but now he was pushing no further. She felt ridiculously stretched but curiously, gloriously full. He was making gentle to and fro movements, not pushing deeper. She still felt the stinging, but the other feelings were overwhelming her. Her clit was untouched, but she knew the feeling of an onrushing orgasm. My God, she was going to come, just like this. He was trying to restrict his movements, just gentle oscillations now, but the vice-like hands still held her, and she knew from his noises that he would soon be with her. Now she could let herself go completely and, immediately she started, she felt him pulsing into her, heard him calling oh, oh, oh, even still calling oh as she was subsiding, sinking down into practicalities; that thing had to come out, how would that be? The thing to do was stay still, surely, but she couldn't move anyway. And now the waves had washed over him.

"Try and be a little bit patient, my darling, he will soften and shrink, I promise you, but it will take time. I'm afraid this is just the most thrilling moment of my sexual life, seeing that most perfect ass with that fat boy stuck deep inside you."

Yes, she thought, *he didn't seem to be softening at*

all, even, never mind shrinking, but even on the dip slope of an orgasm, this was still a wonderfully voluptuous feeling. She felt his hands stroking her cheeks.

"Fondling that beautiful ass isn't going to help you soften and shrink, my friend."

He slapped her ass again, not so hard this time, "We'll take complaints in writing, Miss Gunter."

"I don't think I was actually complaining, but, wonderful as this is, I am going to be a little relieved when he leaves me."

And suddenly it was gone, and she felt disturbingly wide and empty. She collapsed on to her side, and he fell down into her arms. The telephone rang, he grabbed it, "Andy," she hissed.

"No, no, I'm awfully sorry," he was saying. "We were having a little fun and maybe got carried away. Please reassure the other guest there's no problem." He put the phone down.

"Andy, we're in my room!"

He smiled, "We can go to my room later and disturb some other people," but he wrapped her in his arms and kissed her languorously. "But I'm guessing you won't want that again for a while."

"Want to try: ever again?"

He pulled back a little and smiled, "I'm thinking, if you want me again, you'll want that."

She buried her face in his neck again, "I don't know, Andy."

"Don't know about me? Or don't know about that?"

307

Now she looked up at him, "Come to think of it, how the fuck did I let you get me into bed?"

"You didn't, I pushed you. You said no — and I know this is a terrible thing to say in this era, but you didn't mean it. Nevertheless, I think I've just given you grounds to fire me, and you can choose, insubordination or assault but, you know, I'd do it again."

She was pensive, "Maybe I would too," she thought some more, "I know you might have to be unromantic in answering my next question, but I'm not going to hold it against you this time," she looked at him.

"Go on, I believe you, but it doesn't matter, you'll get a straight answer anyway."

"Yeah, that's what I'm expecting. How often can you do that? I mean how many people can cope with it?"

He smiled, "Very few, most won't even try."

"And when they try and can't?"

"I stop, of course."

"I was virtually screaming. You didn't stop then."

"Well, here's the thing. Well, two things actually. First thing is, you have a beautiful little asshole, and on the few occasions I got to play with it, it did seem to relax so nicely — and I knew you were actually enjoying it so much, however many of my fat fingers I played with. Second thing is, I just guessed from something in your little fantasy there, that you really wanted to be taken past a no point. If I was wrong," and he looked serious now, "then I have erred grievously. I can't make amends, I can't make it up to you — I would just have to be very, very sorry. But a little bit of me is hoping that it's what you really wanted, just to let go for a bit and be taken."

"Mmmm," she found herself nodding, almost involuntarily, "but one more little question. If it has worked with a few people…"

"Yes?"

"Did it get easier the next time?"

"As long as you make sure and do it at least once a week." But when she looked, he had that big Andy smile, so she slapped him. "You may not want to hear it, sweetheart, but that's God's honest. If you want it again, stay committed."

"Woah, sorry for letting my mind run on, but that's way too big a question."

They lay silent for a while, she looked up, "Can we look on this as a bit of an experiment?"

"What's on your mind?"

"How d'you feel about staying in the same bed tonight? No phone call worries."

"Your mother?"

"No, but my room," she paused, "actually, I've no idea why I said that."

"I don't mind, but I do like the thought of wallowing in our dirty sheets. Wanna put a 'do not disturb' out so that turndown doesn't come in while we're eating?"

"Nah, I'd like to come back to a neat room and then make the dirty sheets all messy again. But I think I've had my fill of my once-a-week experience."

"Come on, let's shower before dinner and work out what we're going to do with Radius."

* * *

"I rang Greg while you were in the shower and said you were in town but had a couple of hours free and would he like to meet you." They were in the cab, heading for Radius.

"And?"

"You're going to get a big surprise, but you need a follow-on story for what you're going to move on to after 10.30, that's when I said you had to be away."

"And my surprise?"

"Is a surprise. Oh, one surprise I don't have is a feeling of having a hot poker in my ass, that's exactly what I was expecting," she whispered, "does anybody ever get used to that?"

"Nobody has, but once a week does help, honest."

"Was that Jen?"

"It was, in the eros phase."

"The eros phase? I suppose it's self-explanatory."

"Yup, you're not a stupid girl," he paused, "boss."

"Don't ever call me that." He laughed, "I'm serious. You own sixty percent of your own billion-dollar business. I'm a hired hand."

He laughed again, "It's less than sixty now, but we can agree that's a silly tease. I won't do it again."

It amused Tania when the cab pulled up in front of Radius Network Logistics. She looked vainly for a warehouse. That was what she'd grown up with. It seemed unnatural to have only an office building here.

Greg came to reception to meet them, medium height, wiry, dark wavy hair a little unruly, open-neck plaid shirt and chinos, mid-thirties, probably. He looked relaxed, "Morning guys, thrilled to meet you, wow," he was shaking his head, "two VIPs at once. Come on up."

He opened his office, the first door on the first floor, and Andy got his surprise: "Man, mark sevens, wow!"

"You're not cheap, Mr Molloy, but that's because my wife's a violinist and when she came and heard these, I had to buy another pair for at home. We're also fully wired with Molloy speakers through office and home. I'm not even going to guess what we've spent with you."

"Any issues, ever?" asked Andy.

"Well," he hesitated.

"Go on, please, one of the reasons we're here is to work out ways of managing the installed base better. Our installation and service performance isn't what it should be."

"Hey, I'm not going to say we've had big problems, but we have had some niggles, and do you mind me saying I'm impressed that you're asking?"

"Well, we have to get better, I've got a distributors' meeting later to listen to their issues,"

"Oh, sure, we should get on."

Tania tried smiling at Andy — cheeky bastard, is what she thought — but he remained completely impassive.

They sat around a large square table on some stylishly uncomfortable hard chairs. "Our office designers put these in, they say it keeps meetings shorter. It seems to work," he smiled.

"Greg, like I said on the phone," Tania wanted to take control — *it's usually right,* she thought, "we want to put a bigger unit together to manage logistics and service networks and we think you have the best ideas and the best technology. The Dickinson Group, as opposed to Funds and Properties, would have four semi-autonomous units, Andy's is one, we'll have groupings around hardware and software — all tech biased, and we're still defining those now and we'll build a fourth leg, but that would take us a long time if we just carve it out of Giddings and marry it to Andy's service management network, and we're way behind you so we'd likely never catch up. But before you and I get into that. I thought you'd maybe like to let Andy tell you what it's like running your own business inside Dickinson, because that's the way we'd see it happening."

And Andy was brilliant; he managed to cover everything, father's seed money, tech and audio obsession, facing bankruptcy, Peter's being the only offer that let him keep control, the support for the Japanese acquisition. Greg asked a few questions, but never quite seemed to escape from being a little star-struck by the man who'd made those magnificent boxes standing in the corners of his office.

When Andy had left, and it was a peculiar feeling for Tania, watching him go, Greg became much more hard-nosed. But that was good. In spite of all that had happened yesterday and overnight, Tania was ready for the discussion.

At one point, Greg had said 'sorry the chairs are uncomfortable' but there was no way of explaining the real source of her discomfort.

And there were other times when the source of her discomfort was more intellectual, she was trying to grasp technologies he was working with that went way beyond her experience, but Greg seemed relaxed about that, as if he expected it — and he also seemed impressed that her knowledge of logistics businesses and the industry in general was a lot deeper than his.

Over sandwiches at lunchtime they sketched out a few business models they thought might work and agreed they'd discuss them with their people and booked a Friday appointment for a video conference. It felt good when he waved her cab goodbye. *But, my God,* she thought, *my ass is sore.*

Chapter 26

Alphonse loved the view across to Hong Kong Island. It reminded him of his early days selling property. He'd always found it easier to sell a view than a location; a location was somehow in a buyer's head, a view spoke instantly to his heart. And he knew he'd make at least one journey across on the Star ferry, there was some elemental pleasure in joining the bustling passengers in the prickling humidity.

But it had been that bustle that made him opt for a swim in the Peninsula pool that morning. He'd tried running along the waterfront walkway, but he could never find a rhythm at any time of day, constantly needing to change direction for the busy workers early at rush hour or the ambling tourists later on.

He hadn't pushed to have breakfast with Tony, but Tony had been sketchy about his arrangements anyway, which was unusual. Tony's occasional mystery movements tended to be restricted to hours of darkness and Alphonse had a better than vague idea of what his plans involved in those circumstances. Yesterday's 'see you in the meeting at ten, mate, got a few calls to make first', had made Alphonse suspicious. He'd met Harry Li before at the initial Teluk meeting and knew him to be a client of Tony's from a long time ago, so he was alert to the danger of the meeting serving Tony and Harry's interests above Dickinson's — or his own.

And Tony and Harry were both in the meeting room when he arrived shortly before ten. Harry, perfectly groomed, dark-suited and tall for a Chinese, introduced him to Mei, his colleague, also dark-suited and well-groomed, and emanating a self-confidence that Alphonse was finding more common now in women in business in Asia. And 'Business Development Director' were the words on her card. "Mei will be the one following this project through, Alphonse," said Harry.

"Then I shall very much look forward to working with you, Mei," said Alphonse. She nodded without smiling — a little unusual, he thought, "let's hope we have a project we can follow through."

"Let's sit down," said Tony, "Harry's aware we have agreement in principle."

"You do understand our issues, Harry?" Alphonse asked as they were still organising their chairs. Alphonse picked the view, again. It would be distracting, but not too distracting, although he never tired of the Bank of China Tower — he'd spent half a lifetime in property but was still thrilled by the thought of making decisions to build buildings like that. Most of the Dickinson transactions were buying and selling existing units, only a few had they managed as redevelopment projects, and almost never had they built on greenfield sites, 'I want the money working, my boy' was Peter's usual comment.

But building his own buildings, for that is how he looked at it, was one of Alphonse's reasons for pushing the resort programme, but only one of his reasons.

"I understand," said Harry, calmly. The American accent was something Alphonse always expected here. "Peter wants to make sure you keep control of the programme, and my family entirely understands that. It's your skills and experience we're buying into, Alphonse, you're the expert."

Alphonse found it easily possible to ignore the clumsy condescension in remarks like that, but he noted them nonetheless for what they told him about the speaker. Harry was smooth and urbane, mid-thirties, but what he referred to as his family was the family he worked for, not the family he belonged to. Alphonse didn't rule out a distant connection, but he always had the impression, on the few times they'd met, of a boy trying to make his mark. It was important to form a clear view of what his motives were in this.

"Tony, are you going to summarise the options Will says we should look at, and what restrictions we have in the arrangement?"

Harry lifted a report from the small pile of papers in front of him, "We understand these already, do we need to go through them?"

So, thought Alphonse, *there probably had been an earlier meeting with Tony,* "I'll get a better sense of what you're looking for if I can understand your views on why you favour a particular course." Any sense of being hustled always made Alphonse slow down and look for what was being concealed. Sometimes there was nothing, he was merely dealing with 'make-a-deal' hustlers, but sometimes there was subterfuge; either way, this wasn't a time to rush. "I think Will is recommending the first two options for your consideration."

"Well, that's what we need to get into, because even the second one doesn't go far enough, in our view," this was Tony. It would be a cheap point to ask who the 'our' was — it was too obviously Harry's and Tony's and their objectives would not align with the Dickinson aims. Everyone had their own aims, thought Alphonse, the trick was to align them fairly closely. He was here because, in principle, there should be a deal available that would suit everyone — even himself, he thought wryly.

"Well, perhaps it's better if we start with what you are looking for. Tony? Harry?" It would be interesting to see who responded. Tony leaned back in his chair. *Yes,* thought Alphonse, *you do know what I'm worried about.*

"I think you probably understand what we're after, but I'll recap," said Harry. "The family fund, just like Dickinson Enterprises, spreads its investments over a number of areas. Tony's fund, in addition to being our biggest, is also, in most years, our most successful," Tony was looking smug, at least Harry didn't make the mistake of turning to look at him — he'd probably been briefed by Tony not to make it look too much like a tag team presentation. "Property, like Dickinson, is our second largest area but, unlike Dickinson, we've found it hard to make consistent returns. We want to put more money into property, but we want to make sure it works for us, so a tie-in with you seemed the ideal way forward."

"Have you discussed rebalancing? Putting more with Tony? Or even" and he paused to smile, "with other funds — that would give you some diversification."

Tony almost reacted, but he caught Alphonse's little smile. Harry caught up once he'd seen them smiling at each other. "The family maintains very strict guidelines on allocations between sectors."

"Guidelines you can't challenge?"

Now even Harry smiled, "My predecessor tried," and even Mei laughed now, a cold laugh.

"So, you have…" and he waited on them, although he knew the answer.

"One point five, looking for a home."

"This deal is two point five in total."

"I thought you'd knock them down a bit, mate," this was Tony, paying him back for his 'other funds' joke.

"I did, but then I got them to throw in the six other resort locations. That's the bank for you, they dropped their client's price for twelve fully developed going concern businesses by twenty percent so that they could take half a billion for six sites they'd paid a hundred million for four years ago. Maybe you should put your money with them, Harry."

"Even banks get lucky sometimes, Alphonse, but it's quite rare," and they were laughing again.

"OK, but before we come on to the big issue, what

did you think about the other elements of Will's model?"

"We'd need it open-ended. We accept you earning more always, but we wouldn't take the idea of a cap."

Alphonse was shaking his head slowly, "What about the zero return if we make less than two percent?"

"That's not such a problem if we're effectively insured against losses."

"Well, we need the cap to effectively pay that insurance in the good years."

"The family won't take a cap."

"Would you?"

"Doesn't matter. The family wouldn't buy it."

Alphonse smiled, "Sounds like you're working for Peter Dickinson, their approaches are very similar. But if we raised our no return threshold to four percent?"

He seemed to think for a moment, "That sounds steep. I think I could swing that in principle, but I'd need to look more closely at the numbers." Mei was busy on her laptop.

Alphonse already knew how much flexibility he had, he'd already cleared those arrangements with Will, so he would have an ally in the future debates with Peter. "OK, sounds like we might be able to make that work. So, let's kick the big thing around for a bit. It's Peter's money. He'll only allocate a billion, and he'd prefer half of that to go into property, rather than into my holiday camps, as he calls them, and he won't let anyone take him under fifty one percent participation on any property deal. I'm talking about this openly because I want to go ahead, all our data and projections are very positive," he stopped and smiled at them, "after all, that's why you're here. But we need to find a way thought this or around it, without threatening Peter's principles."

Alphonse tried to remain constructive but the next thirty minutes of discussion centred, effectively, on ways to circumvent those principles.

"Guys, I think we're focusing on the wrong thing here. We've heard about the family's principles and we're not going to challenge them," he smiled, "or we'd get Harry fired, but all we've really done for thirty minutes is to challenge Peter's." He looked at Harry, "I'm not saying your points aren't valid, Harry," and he smiled, "I'm not even saying I disagree with you. I'm only saying I won't get it past Peter."

"Can't you sell us some property?" said Mei, suddenly.

There was silence in the room.

Alphonse got the point immediately but needed to stay cautious. The other two men understood soon afterwards, "That's brilliant," said Tony, "you could do that, couldn't you?"

He nodded slowly, "It's a very good idea, Mei, thank you," and he got the first smile of the morning from her, "but we're not marketing anything at the moment. Well, nothing on this scale. You're obviously thinking of a half billion-dollar deal, aren't you?"

"Well," she said, "a quarter would do it."

He laughed, "Yes, of course, stupid of me, thank you

again." The men were looking a little slow. "You pay us 250 and we can each put one and a quarter into the resort programme and you have your one point five property investment. I like it." She was beaming and the men were slowly smiling. "We have to discuss caveats, boys, but at least we have something worth discussing."

"What do you mean, caveats? It works," said Tony.

"Be careful, Tony, don't get carried away. We're not marketing anything big at the moment because we're happy with our returns. You're talking on this scale here about big blocks of apartments and offices and, world-wide, we're getting very good lease rates that Peter would be reluctant to give up."

"But if he got an attractive price?"

Alphonse smiled, "I've spent twenty years in the game, and I've never found out what that is."

"But there's a price somewhere."

"Yes, there is, but I'm just warning that Peter would look at this very closely and I can't close big deals without him, and this is a big deal."

"What's your threshold?" asked Mei.

"I need sign-off above fifty and even pre-agreement for discussions above one hundred. I know what you're thinking," he looked at her, "and it's clever," *but utterly unscrupulous,* he thought, "but I act in awareness of his thoughts and interests. I'm not saying we shouldn't pursue the idea, but I will need him on board eventually. Bearing that in mind, we also have to recognise that he's not yet fully convinced by my so-called holiday camp programme. So, we can sketch out a deal, but I'd still have a lot of work to do."

But he felt hopeful nonetheless, particularly as he had two London developments not being marketed but where returns, because of the twin terrors of lower occupancies and declining prices, had fallen below his standards. The guys would see that when they got into detail, but they might be too committed to resorts by then. Caveat emptor.

He felt comfortable enough by lunchtime that he had something that, with Will's support, he could get Peter to agree to in principle. That meant that the bank meeting in the afternoon, where he would be discussing the timetable for the resort chain purchase, could begin to deal with specifics. He'd not expected to be so hopeful, he'd told Raymond not to come, he was relying for support from his local legal team. He would feel even better if he could talk it through with Will, but it wasn't worth waking him for. That could wait until the evening.

He'd asked the young lawyer to meet him in the lobby at two, they should arrive at the bank together, and in one of the Peninsula's Rollers — that message would make it up to the thirty third floor.

He'd briefed the young man on the morning's progress. He wasn't expecting him to do any more than take notes of the afternoon discussions, but he could be more effective if he was up to date on background — Alphonse had been pleased to note that he'd studied all the preparation documents diligently, people did things right out here.

It meant he could settle into the serene stillness for the journey through the hubbub and the tunnels, but his phone buzzed as they pulled away. A text read *'do you have a condom?'*. It was a six one number, it could only be Bree, surely — or some perverse trick of Tony's!

He texted *'???'* back.

'Tony's expecting me tomorrow. I'm either surprising him this evening, or you. B xxxx'

'I'll let the hotel know my wife's arrived. A xx'

He rarely did stupid or ill-considered things, he thought, as he now lost the island view, and they were engulfed by the tunnel. It intrigued him that the car's silence seemed to change, but it was still silence. He'd had no need to respond to her that quickly. Well, at least he wouldn't be disrupting Tony and Harry's plans for whatever excesses they had in store for the evening. Peter always told him that Tony's gambling was a mere habit, and not an addiction, 'It's the women that are the addiction, my boy, and that, at least for our business, is safer'.

The trip back to Kowloon was to have been his Star Ferry experience, but to arrive back feeling sweaty after the journey would not be the right way to greet her — she would be waiting in his room, he assumed. She can't have been in any doubt about what he fundamentally was, surely, but that would need to be cleared up first, condom or no condom.

But there was a condom, of course.

* * *

She was looking a little nervous when he entered the room. She turned to face him, she'd been looking at the view. He placed his briefcase on the credenza and held his arms out. She moved quickly towards him and let herself be embraced. "I'm sorry. Have I trapped you into this?"

He leaned back slightly, but still held her, "Well, it would have been pretty ungallant to have rejected you, and I did wonder what was on your mind."

"Not a lot, really. I wanted to see you again, of course, and maybe make up a bit for the boat. Well, I assume you didn't mind the boat experience itself…"

"The boat experience was wonderful," and he kissed her forehead.

"Well, I didn't know if I'd created any problems afterwards. Tony and I are pretty open with each other…"

"Like comparing his oral skills unfavourably to mine?"

"I never said that!" She looked quite shocked, he assumed genuinely.

He smiled, "I think we can agree that your husband's a bastard, just quite a funny one. I don't think the publicity has done me any harm, though."

"Publicity? Who was listening? Oh, shit! What did he say?"

"It was only Peter and Claudia, and they both know him well enough."

She looked troubled, "He says you're in love with Claudia."

"I am, but it's obviously not simple. Shall I get us a drink? When did you get in?"

"I texted from the airport, I was waiting for bags. I've been here an hour. I haven't unpacked." She pointed to her bags, waiting near the bedroom doorway. "I can still surprise him."

"No, no," he paused, "well, only if you want to. I'd rather we had an evening together." She looked up at him, frowning slightly. "Well, that would mean a night of course, but I think we need to get a few things clear first, don't we? Or were you hoping I'd be a little more romantic?"

She shook her head, but kept her arms around his waist, "I don't know what I was hoping... beyond just wanting a little more time with you. I know what you are," She shook her head again, "no, that's silly, I don't really, do I? But I suppose I was hoping there could be some sort of relationship there. Could there?"

He lifted her chin gently and kissed her lips lightly, "I think you're very lovely. But let's see what we both want, shall we? I think we've agreed you're staying here the night, yes?" He searched her eyes.

"Yes please."

"But, as cold and unromantic as it sounds, we'll find out a lot more about each other and what we want from this before we do anything like the boat, agreed?"

"Of course," she nodded vigorously and seemed to

be relaxing slightly.

He smiled at her, "But, in the event that it proves necessary," and he smiled, "I do have a condom," and he kissed her lips again, still lightly, but more lingeringly this time.

They'd settled on the sofa with the harbour view and he'd poured champagne. She was relaxing a little now she had only the residual anxiety of sleeping in the same hotel as her husband, but in another man's room.

She was very pretty, and a lot younger than Tony. Alphonse already knew she was a second wife.

"I'd always thought he was fun, and we'd agreed we'd be open, but I hadn't realised he'd pursue the alternatives with such obsessiveness. And I've found fewer and fewer people who appeal. Well, nobody for a couple of years now, to be honest, so it was funny to find myself reacting to you."

He smiled at her, he just wanted her to talk. Her dilemma wasn't unusual, but he found her sweeter than most. Well, sweeter than anyone since Claudia.

"So, I knew you were gay. Well, Tony had told me you were, and you're much too stylish to be straight, well, straight straight," and here she laughed gently at herself, quite charmingly, he thought, "but it's not that simple is it? He told me about Claudia too. Does that mean you're bi, or something?"

"My one to one relationships, have been gay, if that helps."

"But Claudia? Sorry, I'm not trying to replace, or

326

anything, I'm just trying to understand."

"No, that's OK. But it's not a one-to-one relationship, and now that she and Peter are together, it's not even physical."

"But I expect he still gets jealous."

He sighed and drank a little, "I'm afraid he does, and there's nothing I can do about that. Love just seems to make people vulnerable."

"Does it make you vulnerable?"

She seemed both concerned and curious and, if this was going to be some sort of relationship, she needed to understand. *Well,* he thought, *as well as I understand it myself.* "It certainly did, but that was a while ago. Maybe I haven't been in love since then. But that would be a bad definition of love, wouldn't it? It's only real love if it makes you feel vulnerable, somehow that just can't be right. I'll admit I feel a little jealous sometimes of what Claudia and Peter have, but I'm really happier for both of them."

"But didn't she have someone else?"

"Yes, and I think that also weighs on Peter's mind," he chuckled lightly.

"What is it?"

"For fifteen years he was the most sublimely, and justifiably, confident man I've ever met but now... well, I wouldn't say it's deserted him, but what Tony and I are struggling with here is not just whether we're putting together a good deal or not, but whether we can get Peter to judge it rationally and free of the distractions that now seem to afflict him. He's showing less trust in us."

Here she gave a small, bitter laugh, "Ha, trust Tony?" He raised his eyebrows. "Oh, that's probably unfair. I've not found him doing anything he hadn't told me he might do. I suppose I'd just expected us to be closer more of the time."

"And would he expect to find you in his colleague's hotel room? Are you going to tell him about this?"

"I'd rather not. Would that be bad of me?"

"Well, it would be, of course, but I'd rather you didn't. Or do you have a pathological commitment to honesty, the pair of you?"

She gave a hollow laugh, shook her head and looked down, away from his eyes, "No, it's almost becoming more about hurting each other. I told him about the boat partly to hurt him."

"Did you... did you come to me in the first place to hurt him?"

She shook her head again, vigorously this time and, when she looked up, her eyes were wet, "Oh, no, no, I wanted you desperately. I haven't felt like that in years, not even with Tony." She reached out and touched his hand, "I'm sorry, I don't mean to put any pressure on you."

"Don't worry," he said soothingly, hiding, he hoped, his concern about where this might lead.

"No, it was easier to feel wild because I accepted it was hopeless." She paused, "Sue's dealing with it better, isn't she?"

Now he laughed loudly, and she smiled, "Well, the two of you managed to put together the most remarkable night of my life. It was delightful, but utterly unexpected."

"I had no idea she was going to do that. I think she'd guessed I might. I don't know if she did it to help me or just told me to help me."

"Oh, I think she had some fun herself," he said, his vanity not really hurt, but he thought the remark would make her laugh — and it did.

"I am so sorry, of course she had a wonderful time. Tony wasn't wrong about your oral skills but that was honestly an invention of his."

"Well, maybe Sue told him."

That thought seemed to shake her, "Oh, that's possible, I suppose..." and she drifted off into herself for a moment.

"Do he and she?"

"Well, they used to a lot. Not so much now, I don't think. And I've never..."

"Jerry?"

"Yes," she shook her head, "there were an unpleasant couple of scenes early on, but I made myself very clear. Anyway, I just desperately wanted you then. Like I do now, really, but you're being all noble and good, aren't you, and a bit bloody unromantic, too," she smiled at him, "if you ask me."

* * *

They were lying naked on the bed after the shower. "You can call them for food now. And then you can tell me more about yourself. But I was so desperate to have your cock inside me I'm afraid I would have been a pretty poor dining companion. You're amazing, by the way, I've been dreaming about sitting on you like that, but I didn't know if it would work for you."

"You have the most beautiful eyes; of course it worked for me."

"But are there other things you like to do, aren't there? I want to make you happy."

"You made me very happy on the boat."

"Well, we can do that later," she paused, "but what else?"

"Am I educating you as well? Have you made some strange assumptions about what I might like?"

"No," she said quickly, defensively, then paused, smiled, and said, "I might."

"OK," he said, "I won't let you down. After dinner, and life stories, and a little more unromantic discussion about how we will behave with each other in the future, I will let you sit on me again. I love your eyes and your smile."

"But we just…" she hesitated as he smiled, "Oh, I don't know…"

"I'm going to leave it with you. I have lube with me. You can do with him what you choose, but if you're furthering your education, you really should try it." She looked doubtful. "Doesn't matter, that's for later. I'm ordering room service, then I have to ring New York."

"Am I a distraction?" she looked genuinely worried.

"No, we'll work on what we want for both of us. I want to do that with you," and that was near enough true, he thought, "but I do have a day job. It's just that it's a twenty-four-hour-a-day job."

She seemed to relax again.

He ordered two prawn risottos and a Meursault, then rang Will.

"I'm impressed," said Will, after Alphonse had described the morning's discussions, "particularly if you can get them to accept the four percent threshold. I was dreading your sneaky option. I tried it on Martha…"

"Peter doesn't like you talking to her about those things."

"I know. But I suspect he'd have liked your other scheme even less than that if it came to light, and I would have had to tell him."

"They would have been buying the six sites independently."

"How did they feel about that?"

"It never got that far. Their woman came up with this clever option. But why were you against it?"

"I think you know."

"I want to hear you say."

"Alphonse, old thing, they'd be holding something for us and the obligation on us to purchase later would have to be contractual. They'd be mad to agree to less. And they'd probably try to turn a big profit on it later.

Peter would see right through that, you know he would."

Alphonse was reluctant to agree, but had to admit grudgingly, "You're probably right. Anyway, we have a better option."

"At least we're not trying to slide something past him."

"But what did Martha say?"

"That even with a commitment to buy later, which would defeat your objective, because he would only effectively have forty percent of the total package, they wouldn't want to do it."

"The other bank did."

"Yes, but they were screwing their clients. This five hundred mill is a market rate, and the value could go down. They don't want to get their client into a vulnerable situation like that."

"I thought that's what you'd say. You're actually impressive, you know that?" Alphonse quite liked to tease him. Will remained almost infinitely good-natured with him.

"Thank you. Now what properties are you going to put up for them?"

"London. We're starting to struggle, and I don't see it getting better."

"I agree. I think he'll see it that way too. It's your best chance."

"And how do you rate my best chance?"

"Fifty fifty."

"Where are you on it?"

"About eighty twenty."

"Are you ever more than eighty?"

"Nope!" and they both laughed.

"OK, I'll take it. I'm seeing him next week, I'll send you details so you can be on alert."

"Him, or them?"

"I'm sure she'll be there."

"Have you thought of calling her first?"

"Yes," and he thought for a while again, "but you understand why that could fuck it up for everyone, don't you?"

"I accept what you say, but I struggle to understand it. If it comes up when I'm talking to her, would you mind if I give a progress report?"

"Honestly, I'd rather you didn't, but I'll have to leave that with you."

"OK, I'll mull it over, but well done anyway, sounds like a good deal."

And as he put the phone down, Alphonse realised that comments like that from Will now mattered to him.

"Were you two manoeuvring?" She was in a bathrobe, on the sofa now, sipping champagne.

He felt thoughtful, "A little, maybe, but we seem to have gone from waiting for Peter's insightful views to managing around his sensitivities."

"And that's all down to relationships?"

He shook his head slowly, "I'm unwilling to draw that conclusion, but it looks…"

Now she laughed gently, "Ahh, you are just an old fucking romantic though, aren't you?"

"Of course," and he laughed with her.

Chapter 27

Claudia had been grateful for Will's call. She'd guessed that his second point, Alphonse's deal, was the real reason for it, and she could understand why he and Alphonse were so keen. She also understood why Alphonse hadn't rung her himself.

That arose from her bigger concern. Peter seemed to get more and more sensitive about her relationship, even as it was becoming more distant — which disturbed her, because she missed her Alphonse times, and it probably disturbed him too, she thought.

But she wasn't entirely convinced the business should be rushing into resorts. All the data looked impressive, all she'd read around it seemed to indicate that the push Alphonse was striving for was timely, but surely, they should wait for more results from Morkuda to confirm the success of Teluk. And why did Alphonse seem so obsessed to make this work? A year before she would have rung him, or had dinner and talked it through. And yes, she thought, I would have wanted to sleep with him if I'd done that. Strange, when she'd stopped loving Dave, soon after Abbi was born, she'd gone off any idea of sex. But now she loved Peter, she was sure, but a chance to meet Alphonse alone would be thrilling. She laughed to herself as she had the thought, that was probably what Breeana was feeling now. She'd only met her twice but, now that thought had come into her head, she could imagine Alphonse being attracted.

And now she was spending too much time thinking about Alphonse and his project, and if she raised the topic at all with Peter, he would make his overly sensitive assumptions — and probably find rationalisations to kill the project. It would definitely be best to say nothing, as Will seemed to realise, he certainly hadn't pressed her. She smiled when she thought about him. He and Martha intrigued her. They seemed to have worked out a very successful relationship, in spite of Martha's evident vulnerabilities, but the structure of their lives now just didn't seem to allow the chance for her and Martha to sit together and drink and chat like in Singapore. That's silly, she thought, I should get over myself, she might be grateful too. That would be something for the next New York trip.

In the meantime, Alphonse had flown back in over the weekend, she knew, and was due to meet Peter. It would be best to say nothing, know nothing, until that meeting was over. But then Peter surprised her. "I'm seeing Alphonse tomorrow afternoon. Could you join us?" he asked across the breakfast table.

"What time?" *There might be a simple way out of this,* she thought.

"It's at three, but we can move it if it doesn't suit. When could you make it?"

"Are you meeting in town?" not so simple to avoid it, if he was prepared to be flexible.

"Yes, at Sandy's. Please try. Or tell me when you could."

"Four would be better. But why do you want me there?" she was trying not to show her concern.

He seemed to ponder his reply, "Well, he and I seem to sit on opposite sides on this one and, as you saw in Morkuda, there's a little background there. I don't like the way he and Tony are going about it."

"Well, we've talked about that quite a lot. I think you were right to reiterate your principles," now she was struggling a little.

He looked into her eyes across the table and smiled, "You think I behaved like an ass."

"No, I don't" she said, rather too quickly, "but I was surprised you were so sensitive. Anyway, I thought we'd cleared all that up in New York. What's this meeting about?"

"We'd agreed they could carry on talking. Now they have done, and it sounds like they have a deal in prospect. He wants to take me through it, but he wouldn't give me details over the phone so I'm naturally suspicious."

"What does Will say?"

"I don't know, I haven't asked him yet. How would he know about it?"

"Because, my sweet man, he and Alphonse talk, as they should do."

"Has he said anything to you about it?"

"He spoke to me on Friday, that was mostly about Tania's area, I like to get his views, not just hers — you taught me that — and he mentioned in passing that he thought Alphonse might be close to a deal, that's all."

His eyes narrowed suspiciously, "But he didn't give you any details?"

"No, he didn't." A fib, and this new need for fibs would have to be addressed soon, it was beginning to irritate, having to worry about more of Peter's sensitivities, but raising the problem now would endanger Alphonse's project.

"Did he have a view?"

"I think he's broadly positive. You could talk to him yourself, if you're worried."

"I know that. I just wondered what he'd told you."

It was getting harder to stay patient, "I think Will's the last person to express a different view to me to the one he'd give you."

"Who would do that?"

She thought for a moment, the conversation needed to go in a different direction, "Well, Tania would always check things with me first if she was going to talk to you. Oh, did I tell you that Andy had flown out to the west coast with her to look at that business she wants to buy? That's something she'll be calling you about."

"About Andy?"

Was he being deliberately obtuse, she wondered? "No, silly, about the business. She'd like the guy to meet us when we're in New York next. She'll tell you about it when she calls."

"And about Andy?"

Let's misunderstand this completely, she thought, "He was a great help apparently. He's a poster boy for operating autonomously in the Dickinson empire. She wanted to make sure the guy realised he'd still be very much CEO of his business, and I think it worked."

He seemed to ponder a while, she hoped he wouldn't ask more, she'd accepted Tania's white lie about Andy having a distributors' meeting but she'd taken that as a coded signal that Tania wanted to talk more about the Andy relationship when she next saw Claudia face to face. It had been obvious that she'd slept with him again.

"You think they're sleeping together again?"

He caught her with a cup at her lips. It led to an inelegant snort, "Ha, you haven't lost it, have you? All that sensitivity seems wasted on a man. I suspect you might be right. I think it's one of the things she wants to talk about next week."

"And do we have a view on that?"

"That's an interesting question," she smiled at him, "do we have a view on the relationship between Mr Peter Dickinson and Mrs Claudia Brodie?" Now he smiled back. "I would like to know about it, just so we can help them if it starts to interfere with business."

"And does our relationship interfere with business?"

It couldn't be put off forever, "I worry I'm starting to tread on eggshells sometimes and that doesn't feel right. Why don't we agree to talk about it this evening?"

"I thought Mondays were Jonah evenings."

"He has a twenty-twenty evening in London, he's starting to enjoy cricket."

"With Alphonse?"

"Yes, with Alphonse, and he stays there if they do anything like that," but now the atmosphere seemed to have cooled. She stood up, walked round the table, put her arms round his neck and kissed his forehead, "And that, my love, is one of the things we'll talk about this evening."

It was a busy day for her, which was fortunate. Putting off a difficult conversation seldom helped, she'd found, but they couldn't ignore the day's appointments. She felt no more ready when she got back to Barnes that evening and had no idea how to restart the conversation.

Peter was already back, talking to Hannes in the garden room. He stood and kissed her when she came in. "We have business, my love, can we go to my favourite sofa in the library?" He nodded.

"Can I bring you something?" asked Hannes, "Earl Grey?"

She smiled, "Thank you."

"I'll have a large gin, Hannes," said Peter.

"Splash of tonic?"

"Very small," he looked serious, but by the time they'd sat down he was looking apprehensive, maybe as much as she felt.

They were at opposite ends, "I remember my first evening on this sofa as if it were yesterday."

"I do too."

"I've always imagined you had lots of those conversations with troubled women in here."

He smiled nervously, "A few, not that many."

"Did you get more enjoyment out of solving their problems, or from caning them?"

"Caning wasn't a universal panacea. I just used to enjoy helping them understand themselves better."

"But now I need to understand Peter Dickinson better. Don't worry, I don't suppose it's going to lead us to the dungeon."

"Do you think it should?"

"I doubt that, for several reasons. When I sat here five years ago, you'd managed, in one evening, to tune into my feelings and into my buried fantasies, but I feel so helpless, sitting here, that I don't feel I can do either of those things for you, even after all this time together."

"I'm terrified of losing you."

She felt utterly shocked. He sat with his arms stretched out on the back and the arm of the sofa, a helpless smile on his face. It was what Alphonse had tried to tell her, but it was a thought she'd been unable to assimilate. Now Peter had put it into words himself.

Hannes walked into the silence and put the drinks down, "*Verzeihung, bitte,* but I hope you two aren't going to be stupid. To me it's *erstaunlich* that the two people I admire the most cannot understand each other a little better."

Peter had started laughing before Hannes finished

speaking. Claudia had been, initially, too shocked, but now she joined in.

"Thank you, Hannes, for your unsolicited but welcome input. *Nun, haue ab, und nimmst Du bitte Deine unverschämte Frechheit mit!*"

Hannes left, smiling. Claudia was puzzled, as she often was when the two of them spoke German. "I told him to fuck off," said Peter, smiling, "but he did have a point."

She slid along the sofa and leaned on to his chest. He hugged her to him. "You're never losing me. Tell me what I've done to make you think that. No, that's silly, isn't it?"

"Why do you say that?"

"Because I've done nothing, and I feel nothing that should make you feel that way. These feelings are coming from somewhere inside yourself." She hesitated, "I'm not Anne, you must know that."

It was a long time before he spoke, "But you have fucked one of my best friends."

"Not since you and I became a couple, even though you sometimes seemed to be pushing us that way." She sat up, kneeled and sat on her heels, "were you?"

"Part of me was."

"Well, I'm glad about that." Now he looked puzzled, as she'd assumed he would. "If I'd been wrong, then I would have been reading you wrong, and that would have worried me. But I still don't understand why you wanted that."

"I didn't, but I know what you enjoy…"

"*Have* enjoyed," she corrected him.

"I don't believe those urges go away."

"So you think I'd still like group sex on a boat?"

"Wouldn't you?"

"No!" she said indignantly.

"But would you like to sleep with Alphonse?"

"No, and I've no idea why you seem to want me to. And I don't know what you were feeling when we played that little scene on Yvonne. How were you feeling about me then?"

"I was in love with you."

Now she was the one feeling puzzled, "But you had no feelings of possessiveness or jealousy?"

"Of course, but they were easier to manage then. I could see you were happy, and you were finding out more about yourself. I also thought you were in love with another man. So, I was getting as much as I could out of you in the circumstances."

"How would you have felt if you'd been Jack?"

He looked pensive, "I tell myself that I'd be happy you were happy and doing something you enjoyed, just as I was doing things I enjoyed…"

"Go on."

"But I'd be lying to myself. I would have felt vulnerable, like I do now. It was easy to watch Yvonne being fucked, I even enjoyed that — and not just because it made her happy, I'll admit there were darker motives behind that. I don't know where they come from, but they're there. I did enjoy watching you on the boat, but other feelings were beginning to get mixed in with that."

"Well, I can relate to that. The first time I saw you in any way ecstatic was in Tokyo when that girl had your cock in her mouth, and I felt speared with jealousy. Her name was Kimiko, and I remember it very vividly. I felt quite comfortable about you spanking Martha, although I was starting to have some strange feelings about that. I don't think I found it too hard when you were watching her being caned. But it was too much to watch that little Japanese girl fellating you. It was horrifyingly fascinating for a few seconds, she seemed to be taking you very deep, by the way, but I had to rush away. I thought you were about to come in her mouth, and I would have hated that. Did you? I've always wondered. No, don't answer that now, you avoided it when I asked you before. I'll just assume you did, but I'd rather not know."

Now she turned and nestled into him again.

"Maybe I feel that way about you and Alphonse. Maybe I should just assume you do, but never try to find out."

"I've always fought against trying to live like that," then lots of memories of the Jack conversations came into her head, "but my way didn't work. But neither would your way. Alphonse and I are very happy as friends."

"But you do miss sleeping with him."

"No, I don't, and I don't miss orgies. I love my life as it is, even if the man I love appears to have a perverse aversion to being happy."

"It's being vulnerable he appears to have an aversion to."

"You're not, not as far as I'm concerned. There's nothing I want that you and I can't manage for ourselves — but I'm finding it hard to guess what you want. I would do anything for you, but you'll have to help me — it is silly that two sensitive and self-aware people can create so many difficulties for themselves."

* * *

She got to Sandy's early the next day. Alphonse was already there. "Thank you so much for yesterday evening. He was glowing this morning. Not just the cricket, but also being driven to school in your Cobra..." she shook her head, "I'll never hear the end of it. He's perfectly capable of getting a train back, you know."

He smiled, "But it was such a beautiful day, the car needed an outing, and I had business down there anyway with an enthusiast, so I tied up several things at once."

She was dubious, "The more reasons you offer, the less plausible your story."

"What story isn't plausible?" Peter strode into the room, "Good afternoon, darling," he kissed her, "good afternoon Alphonse, what's she accusing you of now?"

"He took Jonah to school this morning in that Cobra thing of his. I've been getting texts from my son all day about the stir it caused — and it's a school where plenty

Bentleys are the kids' taxis."

"Are you spoiling the boy, Alphonse?" — it wasn't a friendly question and Alphonse, having initially looked sheepish, began to bristle.

"He'd asked about it several times, and he'd studied the history of them, so he has a real interest. It just seemed a chance not to be missed."

"Which brings us nicely on to the topic in question. Your other chance not to be missed. Have you ordered tea, before we start?"

"Yes, I have, it'll be along shortly."

"Good, now where have you got to, and why didn't you want to tell me on the phone?"

"Even we don't make billion plus deals over the phone."

"I can stop you there," said Peter, and Claudia dreaded what would come next, "a billion plus is not even on the agenda. We're not considering deals of that size. You know the limit, we talked about this in New York."

"Shouldn't we hear what the options are?" asked Claudia, seeing Alphonse tense.

"Are you sure you don't know what's coming?" now his aggression was directed at her.

"I've told you, all I know is that Will's been involved, and he'll be interested in what you think of it. I didn't want to hear any more, I wanted to look at it with fresh eyes. Well, I didn't want to look at it at all particularly, but you did ask me to come," she needed to stand up to him, she was surprised the boorishness had

345

re-emerged, but she thought that pandering to it would no longer help.

"And is Will joining us?" he nodded to the phone on the table.

"I've asked him to be available. Do you want me to call him?" asked Alphonse.

"You have him lined up to support you already?"

Alphonse stayed calm, which must have been difficult, she thought, "I have briefed him, as I always do about anything in the pipeline and, as always, he's been incisive and critical in the best sense and he has advised, as I'd already guessed, that there are features of this that may not appeal to you."

"And do they appeal to him?"

"We can ask him."

"I'm asking you."

"He thinks it's early to push for this large an expansion, but the projections all make sense to him. He would support it if you were enthusiastic."

"But I'm not."

"Yet. That's why we're meeting." But Peter was shaking his head.

"Shouldn't we hear where he's got to?" asked Claudia.

"That's why we're here," he said, as if annoyed with her too. But then tea was brought in and at least the tension seemed to subside while that was organised for them.

"Shall I start?" asked Alphonse when they'd settled

again.

"By all means," said Peter, but not with his usual relaxed demeanour.

"The chain is available for two billion dollars. Shen's property division would like to take forty-nine percent of it."

"So why are you talking about one billion plus? I don't like your holiday camps, and I don't like your billion going all into that. I want half of it into traditional property."

"I don't want more than a billion, but this deal will look bigger than that." Now Peter looked as if he were paying attention.

"There are six further sites that the bank owns, and I've told them I wouldn't go ahead without these being part of the deal. I don't want them coming to me five years down the road, when our business is a success, and trying to squeeze a billion out of us for them."

Peter pursed his lips and nodded, "But we could go ahead without?"

"Not so easy. They've only agreed to the cut from two and a half to two for the chain if we buy the other sites."

"So, they're just fucking over their clients and the clients don't know."

"Of course not."

"That's shitty, isn't it?"

"They think it's business," Peter was shaking his head, Alphonse continued, "we've looked closely at the sites and we think five hundred is at the top end, but two billion for the chain is a steal, so I'm arguing for the package."

"And how do I have control of a two and a half billion investment without spending more than a billion?"

"They buy property from us for two hundred and fifty. I'm quite relaxed about selling some London developments for that, I don't think the next few years will be easy."

Peter took a deep breath, "I have to agree with you there, I've seen the trends in your data, but won't they see that too?"

"They probably will, but they're taking a longer-term view on a London recovery and they're light on property here anyway. They feel, on balance, they've got too much in the US."

"It's a clever ruse of yours but it would mean I'm into holiday camps for one and a half billion when I include Teluk and Morkuda and I've got one functioning business to look at data from. All because the boy who cheated on you owned a couple of hotels."

Claudia was stunned. Peter turned to her, "You didn't know? Didn't come up in the pillow talk? You're a very astute woman, my dear, but you may have a blind spot when affections are involved. It's important to get behind the bigger decisions. Nothing's driven by rationality. Where are you going?" He had turned back to Alphonse, who had stood and was gathering papers.

"That's it, Peter, case closed. Thank you for listening."

"Alphonse…"

But Alphonse left.

Claudia felt numb. She also felt like walking out but forced herself to stay.

"So that was news to you, was it?"

"The real news to me was that you can behave like that. That was astonishing. I didn't know what the love of his life had done. I'd only been told that he was a cunt, which was Alphonse's exact word, but as to that affecting how he wanted this deal to go ahead, I had no idea, but I would be amazed if that had influenced his judgement in any way."

"You are a very smart woman, my love, and your touching naïveté makes you just that little bit more adorable, but when these buried emotions affect a billion-dollar investment, I have to call them out."

"Are you happy with the way you chose to do it?" She was finding it hard to control the anger in her voice.

"He's a big boy. He'll think about it. Maybe it is a good deal, but I want it done for the right reasons."

"And your snide aside about pillow talk, was that appropriate?"

"I have to know what's influencing decisions."

She was shaking her head, flabbergasted, looking at a man who now seemed a stranger. She packed her papers into her bag and stood up, "Well, when you think about Alphonse being influenced by the past, you might give some thought to whether you were taking your own surrogate revenge on Clive; that was the name of your best friend who slept with Anne, wasn't it?" And she left quickly, unable to be in the same room with him any longer.

* * *

Part of her wanted to follow Alphonse, but most of her realised that wouldn't help him, either with his feelings or with the project. She didn't feel she could even talk to Will yet, but she did need to alert him. She texted:

Difficult meeting, didn't go to plan, awkward history dragged up. Could you talk later? I'll be home after seven. C

The reply was almost instant. He'd clearly been waiting to join the call:

Home is not Barnes, is it? I'll call then. W

She almost smiled. Will had an unusual sensitivity; it felt, for a moment, like a blanket to wrap herself in, but she hadn't been long in the car before she realised that he had to support Peter's position. It was Peter's money, just behaving vilely didn't change that. But it would change what people would do for him.

Will rang at seven; punctuality, which was usual

amongst them all, was almost a fetish with Will. "He has spoken to me," were his first words.

"What's he said?"

"Would you mind if I asked you to tell me what went on first? If I'm going to try to help sort this mess out, it's best I try to stay independent as long as possible. I'll call Alphonse later and see how he's feeling about it. You didn't speak to him afterwards, did you?"

"No. I wanted to, but I didn't think that would help."

"I think that was wise. So, what happened?"

"Alphonse outlined the deal, buying the chain and the other sites for two point five, selling London properties for two-fifty and using those proceeds to enable us to stay at fifty-one present resort ownership. I thought Peter was agreeing, they both seemed to think that London would be good disposals now…"

"They would be, judging by how things are going. I'll be slightly surprised if they agree."

"But Peter's main objection is that it's too early to be rushing into holiday camps, as he keeps calling them."

There was a long silence, she couldn't blurt out the other part of the story. She'd had time to convince herself that the rational objection was a sufficient one. "There's more, isn't there? Help me, Claudia, I need the full story."

There was no point in withholding, but it was a difficult story to tell without an emotional bias. Will would have to deal with that. "Peter got it into his head that the decision had an irrational emotional element, arising out of Alphonse's past…"

"About Éric?"

"I didn't even know his name."

"Neither did I until Peter called me. I didn't know anything about the relationship. Anyway, he managed to upset Alphonse. Then what happened?"

"Well, Alphonse left."

"And?" she said nothing, he waited a while, "didn't you have a few words?"

She hesitated, "You know I've been close to Alphonse?"

"Have been?"

"Still am, emotionally. I can't believe we're discussing billion-dollar decisions in these terms…"

He laughed gently, "My wife would tell you that most big decisions have a large emotional, irrational component. So, what was said?"

"Peter was very badly hurt many years ago when his first love slept with his best friend, Clive. It seemed to have completely changed his approach to relationships, well, until he met me, he says. But now he seems almost retrospectively jealous of how Alphonse and I were before he asked me to be his partner, but Alphonse and I have scrupulously avoided being with each other since then. It still seems to eat at Peter though, even though we'd been talking about it the evening before, so I asked him if he wasn't just making the same mistake as he'd accused Alphonse of making, attacking Alphonse as a surrogate for Clive, but I ended up being the one accused of naïveté and emotionalism," she paused, "is my story the same as his?"

"Actually, they're surprisingly similar…"

"But not the same?"

"No, but yours of course is more truthful and accurate than our esteemed leader's." She guessed he was smiling. "But now we have to pick our way through two major problems. How do we keep the deal alive? And how do we repair the relationships. Will you be OK with Peter, do you think?"

It seemed such a strange question to have come from him, but it was surprisingly easy to respond, "I expect so. I'm used to silly things being said in times of emotional stress, just not from him though. I'd been trying to get through this strange attitude of his, but I just seem to have made him more sensitive. But is the deal worth it? You can see the risks, can't you?"

"I can see bigger risks in not supporting people who are trying to make things happen for you and, let's face it, Peter isn't generating deals any more, not since the divorce. I think it's an excellent thing that he's effectively delegating that to Tony and Henry, to Alphonse, and to Tania and you, but he mustn't start blocking you."

"Aren't you supposed to be the conservative one?"

"I am. But being conservative is about managing risks, not avoiding them, for whatever reason. And these don't even feel like good reasons. Anyway, thank you for being so frank."

"What are you going to do?"

"Talk to Alphonse now and try to find out how much damage has been done and, as our leader would say *'was mich nicht umbringt'*…"

"Makes me stronger, yes, he's made me understand that much. OK, I'll see where he is in the morning, emotionally, I mean."

"Good girl," and that felt strange, coming from someone ten years her junior, but welcome, nonetheless.

* * *

"Alphonse, thank you so much for calling. I've been sitting here agonising about whether I should ring you, or whether that would just make things worse. I am so sorry about this afternoon."

"Where are you now? You are at home, aren't you?"

"Yes," she hesitated, "in my home."

"I've been wondering what to do about calling you. In the end I just thought, in case there was a danger of you fighting my corner, that you should have a little more information."

"That's what I wanted to do for you, but you first, you rang…"

"My sweetheart," he laughed, "I think we've trained you too well. Anyway, what he said was vile and hurtful, but I need to tell you that Éric's family did own hotels, and there was something competitive in our relationship," he laughed again, "he was even better-looking than I, can you believe that?"

354

"Absolutely not," and he'd made her laugh.

"But he was merely pretty, of course, I doubt whether his looks have lasted, but it meant we could play around easily. My stupidity was in believing that the deeper feelings I had for just him were mirrored. I don't know why he found it so amusing to tell those lies, it wasn't as though we weren't free to see other people. But anyway, I've always watched their family's business and I think Peter's aware of that. I still thought this would have been a good deal, but it wouldn't have been fair to you to let you think his accusation was baseless. So, what was your story? I do believe I'm allowed to ask you now."

"Of course you are, but first of all, thank you for being so open. I'm going to ask you about your talk with Will in a minute…"

"But first you have to give me your secret, but he did tell me that you and Peter had words after I left, and your versions didn't differ much."

"I just told Peter that he was guilty of something he'd accused you of. He lets the fact that we were once lovers destabilise him, part of him thinks we're Anne and Clive."

"I did tell you, didn't I?"

"I sort of believed you, but it seemed so improbable. Anyway, that's what I told him, then I left straightaway. I'll deal with that in the morning."

"There's a danger of me seeming self-centred here, but you'll deal with what in the morning? Peter, or the project?"

"Peter. I'm hoping Will is going to deal with the project. I get the impression he's in favour. What did he say? It's about managing risk, not avoiding it. But what are you going to do?"

"I've had my tantrum moment. Let's see how things pan out, but I like resorts, I feel I'm creating something."

"Would you go independent? Just use the Chinese money?"

"It's crossed my mind, but we're a long way from that."

"Alphonse?"

"Yes?"

"I wish I could just hold you."

"That's why I'm outside in my car."

Chapter 28

MDL

I've had an alcohol-free evening, in the hope you might be able to talk when you wake. You must be in the in-between phase now, waiting for New York to start — and that's just one more thing that's helping me clarify my thoughts. I'm finding I have two powerful and opposing feelings about your move.

I am genuinely thrilled, I think it's brilliant for you.

But I will miss you! Laugh if you will, I realise I could have done something about that before now. (Yes, should have!)

I have also been thinking a lot, however, about our last call, and I've been trying to come to terms with what I felt when we were last together — and I mean both the night in each other's arms again, as well as whatever our 'arrangement' did for us before that.

It did raise some interesting questions about whether that would be in any way repeatable, it was a peculiar set of circumstances but, true confession time, I've been perving about having you again, including the full night, ever since then, and, if you're up early enough to respond to this, I'd rather talk to you about all that than get reacquainted with my right hand once again.

YLJ

"You are going to help me with these three letter acronyms."

"Didn't you guess?"

"I am definitely not falling into that trap. You tell me."

"Sometimes I wonder who's the dom."

"I'm very happy ceding you that role in one particular area," she paused, "although, maybe even there, I could think about switching. Has that ever appealed?"

"I wouldn't say it appealed, but I have an open mind, is it something you've wanted to try?"

She laughed, "I did when you were such an asshole last year. But seriously, no. The playtime should never be about real punishment anyway, or real anger, should it?"

"Well, no, but you said that was such a turn-on for you last time…"

"It was, but I always thought your self-control would eventually take over. It's a good job it did, I don't think I'd ever have said stop, I was floating. Anyway, acronyms first. MDL?"

"My darling Lavinia."

"OK, I'd guessed that right. YLJ?"

"Is that so hard?"

"I can make a guess, but I'm not going to. You're in the middle of a three-week road trip, with some difficult conversations, no doubt, and some lonely evenings. And if they're not lonely, then I hope at least your arrangements are commercial and not romantic."

"They're neither, I've done nothing."

"Jack, it doesn't matter, you can do what you want. If you want something with me, let's talk about it."

"I love you."

There was a long pause. Should he have said that? He hadn't planned to. Then why YLJ at the end of the text? The L was loving, he'd committed himself already.

"So, I can assume that YLJ was your loving Jack, can I?"

"Yes."

"Well, for the aforementioned reasons, I'm not going to take that seriously yet. At some point, on the Saturday morning after you get back, I hope we'll lie in bed and discuss these things, but I'm not going to take you seriously until your cock is soft and your balls are completely empty, and it won't take just one attempt to do that. You won't have any residual stripes to spur you on, I'm not having the conversation confused by jealousies, but I do hope you'll be able to rouse yourself to give me a sound spanking the evening before, nonetheless…"

"I now have one stiff little friend who's enjoying this conversation."

"Jack, let's leave the love talk until you get back. Right now, in my mind, I'm lying across your lap and you're pulling my panties down. Tell me what you want to do to me. Make it brutal but keep holding me, I'm playing with myself already thinking about it…"

* * *

MDJ,

Thank you for the wonderful conversation, and for what it led to. Coming is a glorious way to start the day!

I hope you'll understand why I am so cautious about making any plans. I don't mean to doubt your intentions, but I am sensitive to what protracted absence can do to one's perceptions. I do feel confident, though, that we'll find some way of dealing with each other, and maybe that can be a little more than we have recently re-established. So, I would like to think I can see you as soon as you're back, that I can get that spanking, and, if I promise to be gone by lunchtime, that I can have that cuddly Saturday morning.

YLL

PS Didn't you have a device in Singapore? If it was a bench, then I should tell you I enjoyed something similar immensely in New York.

PPS I hope that makes you jealous enough to deal with me properly when you get back!

He read the email when he picked up his phone in the morning, and he smiled. That was quite clever, he thought, she had reawoken his jealousies a little, enough to make sure she would get a severe spanking when they were next together. But, in truth, he knew it was the Saturday morning he was looking forward to the most.

Chapter 29

Tania had worried about how Peter would be. She'd had conversations with Claudia and Will in the previous week that made her fear the meeting with Greg would go badly, but the Peter who strode into her office was the Peter she'd always known, he glowed like no-one else she'd ever met.

"My darling Tania, I hope I can escape modern censure when I tell you that you are looking absolutely wonderful," and he hugged her warmly.

"Just this once, you're forgiven. Peter…"

"This is Greg, of course," and Greg, who'd stood, had his fist pumped vigorously, "I am so delighted to meet you. I've heard a very great deal about you and your business, and I've been very impressed."

"I've heard a lot about Dickinson, sir, even before I met Tania and Andy," Greg seemed entirely relaxed with this imposing presence whose aura seemed to take up most of the room.

"Well, we try to keep a low profile around that name, so I'm impressed you've heard of us. But you're a major Molloy fan, I gather, it's the business names that are so much more important, they're the brands, like Molloy, or like Radius, so they're the names we need to be known by. Anyway, madam CEO, how were you planning this meeting?"

"I thought we'd sit over here," she pointed to the sofas. She was smiling, Peter was projecting his suave, relaxed dilettante persona but he'd grilled her for more than an hour the previous day on every detail that would be important to her — he'd even wanted to know the exact Molloy speaker type Greg had in his office. "Would you mind giving a brief overview of Dickinson history and Dickinson future, and I'll warn you, Greg was concerned about the sale of Personal Care last year."

Peter had positioned himself in the armchair opposite Greg, leaving Tania on the sofa between them. "I'm not going to deny that the prompt was given by my divorce, but we'd been thinking some time about the Group and the need to give it more focus. Oh, where's Will, by the way, isn't he joining us?"

"Greg's having lunch with him and they're meeting afterwards."

"That's a smart move, who wanted it that way?"

"Greg."

Peter laughed loudly and beamed at Greg, "You're a clever man. That's the sort of thing I used to do. What ground will you cover?"

Greg, for the first time, looked slightly edgy, "I wanted to know more details about how Dickinson is put together financially and then a lot more about how we'd structure this deal."

Peter was nodding, "OK, that's good. Anyway, I

have to sing for my supper…" and even Tania was captivated by the stories of how things had come together, the strange mix of design and serendipity, the peculiar philosophy of how the Group, in particular, had been created — 'but I accept that we're too big now to be so personal, and Tania and Will are rightly emphasising the need to be strategic and forward-thinking'. She was interested in how he spoke about property and resorts, with the major push into the new area — everything she'd heard from Claudia had made her think that was dead. But all together, it was almost dazzling, speaking freely about mistakes made and treating every question, and there were many from Greg, with utmost respect.

When it was Greg's turn to talk about his business, Tania was surprised, although she told herself she shouldn't have been, about how detailed Peter's questions were, and about how much knowledge he'd acquired about the business and the industry. Greg responded with avidity and enthusiasm. There seemed to be so much more still to discuss when Will appeared at the door.

"Ah, Will, am I overrunning? Come and meet Greg."

Will smiled, "We met before you arrived this morning."

Peter shook his head, smiling, "You young people and your early starts," he turned to Greg, "it's even worse on the west coast, isn't it?"

"It is, sir, but we can't let the east get too far ahead of us every day."

"Well. I suspect I've eaten into your lunch appointment…"

"You have," said Will politely, but firmly.

"I'm afraid I could talk for hours, Greg, I love what you're doing. I hope you'll see a way to joining us, but I know you've got plenty thinking to do. If you need anything more from me, I'm available any time but I can promise you that Tania and Will have full authority to structure any deal as the three of you best see fit."

"Thank you, sir, I appreciate that. I'll admit I'd have been put off if there'd been too many steps. I'll get my finance man involved more closely tomorrow if we can make some progress this afternoon."

"Excellent. Well, it's been wonderful meeting you, Greg. We'll let you two…" he stopped himself, "I nearly did it Will."

Greg looked puzzled.

Will smiled and turned to Greg, "He has to pay me a hundred dollars every time he calls me boy. It would be lucrative if it weren't all going to charity. Anyway, let's go, we've a lot to get through."

After they'd left, Peter sat down again, "Did you want to go out for lunch, my dear?"

"No thank you, I've ordered some sandwiches, they should be here by now, and I thought we'd be better off talking privately."

He looked serious suddenly, "That's undoubtedly true. There's a lot to discuss."

"Beyond this deal?"

He nodded, "Yes, beyond this deal. Can you guess what else?"

"Isn't this where I refuse to let you trick me into saying something?"

He laughed, "Ha, you're too close to Claudia," but then quickly looked serious again, "but you can use it as an opportunity to show great insight — and to ask about anything that's troubling you."

"Then I'll start with something that I thought was troubling you. You spoke just now about the resort programme as if it was going ahead. That wasn't the impression I had from conversations with Will and Claudia."

He looked taken aback, "That wasn't where I expected you to start."

"But I did. Has your thinking moved on?"

"Not yet, but it might, and I want us to look dynamic rather than indecisive. After all, I can decisively change my mind later, but, for now, I've at least become a don't know. What have you heard about the resort programme?"

"Not enough to have a view but enough to be curious about how it's being handled. Two of the people I admire the most are, independently, giving me a similar message. They're both saying it's ambitious and it's too early to make a big move, but I'm getting a feeling from both of them that they're unhappy. What's going on?"

"Well, you're right, it's one and a half billion behind a programme we haven't proven yet. Good enough reason to be cautious, I think."

"I'll take bullshit as an answer because it's not my business, but I'm going to be talking to my father soon about buying out a bit of his business to add it to Radius to make a different approach to logistics and service management, then I'm going to talk to Jack Stephens about getting Collins to let us manage all their logistics as a first global customer. If you have any hidden agendas in that set-up, I'd appreciate dealing with them openly."

"Woah, you're leaping several hurdles at once. If they all have to fall into place for this proposition to work, then my agenda is quite open. It's not going to fly." He was looking very serious, but she was comfortable about that. She knew there must be something in the background on resorts, but this wasn't the way she'd experienced Peter doing business. There were many pitfalls he could have objected to in Andy's Japan acquisition, but he'd seemed to stay calm and steadfast through all of them. But, without either of them explaining why, Will and Claudia were clearly unhappy about how resorts were being handled.

"No, I wouldn't do that anyway. Radius makes sense on its own. It will gain Molloy as a customer straightaway and I'm confident it will have a link with Giddings, it will improve efficiencies there. It could just do more if we could pull out the IT department and integrate it into Radius, but that's not a necessary step."

"And Collins, why them?"

She wondered whether this would expose an

emotional link. It hadn't caused a problem to sell Personal Care to them because that was a one-time decision, but this would be a link to a Jack Stephens-run business, would he worry about old relationships here? "We would get momentum from managing logistics in North America for a global company. They would have a part share in the business, subject to appropriate Chinese walls being built, so that we could take on similar business with other big companies. Collins because there are strong links to Giddings…" she looked at him carefully.

"And?"

"We have strong links too."

"Are you suggesting that Claudia negotiates that one?" there was an edge of contempt in the question.

"Oh, no, I would do that."

He guffawed, "Oh, do forgive me, perhaps I didn't hear the story correctly, which would be a shame, because I rather enjoyed it."

"The story about my last conversation with Jack Stephens?" She had undergone embarrassment and contrition on that one, but, when the dust had settled, she knew she'd been right.

Peter, however, looked slightly on edge, "Didn't you call him a… a…"

"Cunt, yes, which is what he was, although I didn't have to let him know that. That was my mistake, but not one I feel like apologising for: hello Jack, it's Tania again, I'm sorry I called you a cunt last year, but one year

367

later, I'm still convinced it was the right way to describe how you were behaving."

"And you think he'll talk to you?"

"He's talking to Lavinia again, apparently, so something's changed. Anyway, that's the third step, and if we get that far, it's my job to talk to him. That's not a job for Claudia." She'd been very firm on that, and she wondered how he would respond. He was stroking his chin.

"The Molloy step you mentioned, that's a done deal, is it?"

"Pretty much, both sides are keen. Radius technology's something Eddie's been looking for to manage the service network better anyway. He's thrilled by the prospect."

"And Andy?"

"He's very positive."

"I mean, generally, how are you getting on with him?"

"Very well. He offered to help with Greg."

"You know he's not living with Jen any more."

"Yes, I know," and she smiled at him. *Damn you, Peter Dickinson, I will answer any question you put to me, but I am going to make you put each question to me.*

"Does that mean your relationship has been resurrected?"

"It was never a big thing in the first place, then it was nothing for a long time…"

"And now it's a small thing again?"

"That's probably a good way of putting it. He was in New York at the weekend and we saw each other."

"Had he come to see you?"

"Mostly, I think," and I can still feel it, she thought, it's Wednesday, maybe my new addiction doesn't quite match what Andy's offering, but it felt wonderful at the time, "but I'm quite clear about not committing to any exclusive relationships, and so is he, I think."

"You're very wise to be cautious."

"About not committing?"

"Well, about that too, but I was thinking you should be careful about how deep Andy's feelings might run."

She shook her head, "You do surprise me, Peter Dickinson, we've glossed over a billion and a quarter on resorts…"

"A billion and a half…"

"Sorry, old boy, but you've already spent two-fifty," she was relieved to see him smiling at her cheek, "and we're talking about over half a billion here with Radius if we can get Giddings to go along, and you're only talking about Andy's feelings."

"But those are the sorts of things that can drive or destroy businesses."

"Am I right in guessing there's a little bit of that in the background of resorts, and that's why nobody's being open with me?"

He took a long time to answer, "I'm afraid you may have a point."

"Why don't you take me to dinner tonight?"

369

"What?" he looked shocked, exactly as she'd hoped he would.

"Take me to dinner. Talk to me. I'm supposed to be having dinner with Claudia and Martha, but I think they have plenty to catch up on together. I'm guessing that you're dealing with an issue that you can't talk to your nearest and dearest about. Take me to dinner and talk."

He pondered longer than she wanted him to, maybe this had gone wrong, but slowly he nodded and smiled, "Actually, thank you, that's a wonderful idea." He pondered longer, she felt like she should wait, "I'm going to suggest we have dinner in our suite. If we're going to have a successful conversation, I suspect we shan't want to be listened to, is that OK with you?"

"That's fine with me."

"Could you be there by six? You ought to say hello to Claudia before she's off out. I think you were meeting at seven, is that right?"

"And are we talking my business tonight as well? I need your support on Radius."

"Oh, that's a done deal," he said, almost dismissively, "I like the business, I like the man, and I like what you aim to do with it."

"Thank you," she said, almost too gleefully.

He raised a warning forefinger but, still smiling, he added, "That's not a green light for steps two and three. If there's a chance, I would like to meet your father before you commit to that link-up."

"That would be a huge help actually. He's very

impressed by your business and he'd love to meet you. Would you and Claudia come to stay? They'd love to see her again."

He looked a little thoughtful, "I'd love that to work, I really would, but you'll have to make sure the light's almost green before we could come. I wouldn't want any embarrassments there."

"And if that works and then I get past Jack Stephens?"

He smiled slowly, "Then I shall meet Oscar," and here his grin turned a little wicked, "but in New York. He won't be averse to that, I don't think."

Here she was a little uncertain, "I'm not sure the New York connection is quite so strong as it was."

"We'll see. You did a wonderful job with your Uncle Rodney, my dear, and I am deeply grateful, I'm sure he operates a little more ethically these days. But talking to him occasionally, which is a necessity but very far from a pleasure, leads me to think that the addictions he feeds are not cured, but he does exploit them less. He wouldn't dare talk about your parties, for example," and she coloured as the wicked grin reappeared, "but I'll share some confessions of mine over dinner," and now she got a saucy wink from him.

"I am very much looking forward to that."

"Then I shall see you at six," and he stood up and wrapped his arms around her when she stood next to him.

When he'd left, she called Claudia, "I think he's given a green light to Radius, he had a good meeting with

Greg, they got on well. He warned me that he wasn't saying yes to the Giddings and Collins steps but he also, when he was talking about Enterprises, said we were going ahead with the resort programme..." Claudia didn't respond, "Are you there?"

"Yes, I'm listening, and I am surprised."

"So was I. I had the impression from you and Will that he was against it. You both gave me the same reason and I didn't believe either of you. Anyway, I challenged him on it, and he gave me a story about wanting to make the place look dynamic as a selling feature for Greg. I told him I thought that was bullshit, but I moved on to my own business. So, what gives?"

"I'm mystified."

"Well, I asked him to have dinner with me tonight. I hope you don't mind, I thought maybe you and Martha wouldn't mind some time on your own," she waited for an affirmative murmur, but none came. "Peter wanted to talk to me anyway about Andy, and I want to see what I can find out about resorts. Are you going to give me any help?"

It took a long time for Claudia to respond, "You're right, there is some other background that came out. It surprised me. It didn't seem to me to be relevant, but Peter is questioning why Alphonse is so keen on the sector."

"Are you going to tell me about it?"

"You might be best attacking it with your usual bull-at-a-gate subtlety..."

"Thanks!" Tania felt miffed.

"I'm sorry, there was a compliment in there. You're more ebullient than Will, but you both have a way of being so disarmingly open about things, it makes it very easy to work with you — and be friends with you, I don't know if that's something you want to hear?"

"Of course it is," Tania felt herself curiously moved.

"But an additional piece of information is that Alphonse and I used to be close. It was more than just the party encounters, I should say."

"But isn't he... I'm sorry, I don't know what you're saying."

"I don't know if I'm giving you too much information. Alphonse is more gay than anything else, you're quite right, but he enjoys occasional relationships with women, and I enjoyed his company."

"You slept with him?"

"Well done, Tania, I didn't particularly want to spell that out, but if you're going to help, I suppose you have to know. Anyway, it was just a very occasional thing, but we stopped when Peter and I got together but it still seems to rankle with Peter and I don't know to what extent that's disturbing his decision-making, but he hasn't been his old self for a while."

"He was perfect this afternoon. I've never known someone display such effortless command. It was like Tokyo again, he seems to have every fact available but uses the most relevant few to make his points succinctly."

"I know, he's still got it somewhere, but he seems to

get thrown by, well, who knows what. I mean, I think I can make a good guess, but, good luck, see what you can find out. Where are you going?"

"Your suite. He said it would be a very private conversation, but that I should come at six so the three of us can have a drink before you go out."

"OK, I'll see you then."

"Boss, are you OK? It doesn't sound like it."

"I'm probably not, but it's not your fault. Should we extend our meeting tomorrow into dinner, we've probably got a lot of ground to cover. You owe me some information on Andy as well, young woman."

Tania laughed, "I'd love an extended conversation, but I'll see you at six tonight, Bye."

Claudia looked wonderful when Tania arrived, "Now I know what was so important at three this afternoon, you look stunning!"

"Thank you, but I thought I was competing with you. Still, it's not wasted. Martha's organised this dinner, I can't let her down."

But Tania felt a little shabby, still in office clothes. She'd been reluctant to go home and change. She was sure her motives would not be questioned, by either Peter or Claudia, but it would be best to avoid sowing any seeds. Nevertheless, when she caught herself in the mirror side by side with Claudia, she wished she'd made a little more effort. But where would she have found time? It had been a good debrief with Will on his meeting with Greg, but it left them with lots of work to make the acquisition happen. She'd been left rushing to be punctual and here she was, next to a gorgeous woman, who almost looked like she was in love. It seemed such a silly thought when it struck her, but, as she looked at Peter, pouring champagne — he had obviously showered and changed, and looked, as ever, suave, elegant and infinitely in command — then maybe the thought wasn't so silly, but that wouldn't be consistent with Claudia's accounts of the difficult recent meetings. Oh, well, that would make tomorrow interesting. Tonight, it was Peter she must try to understand.

He handed them their glasses and raised his own, "To my absolute favouritest ladies," they clinked and sipped, "I think Claudia will confirm that I fear only one person on the earth, so what possessed me to agree to have dinner with her, I cannot remotely imagine," the wide, disarming smile did not speak of terror, but she was aware that she could sometimes disturb his composure.

He'd existed at the fringes of her life for five years now, a little more maybe, and he'd been something like a moon, something large, mysterious and unchanging, even as the magnification increased, the details were added but nothing surprised. She'd been closer to him in Japan but had somehow expected him to be always masterful.

She'd been aware, when she first responded to him on his offer of the group position, that she had the capacity to unnerve him, but when the calm reflection came the next day, she felt she had the right to be pleased with herself. He was in no way diminished, he'd almost grown by showing that he could treat other people as equals, if they earned it.

But neither Will nor Claudia was discussing him in their usual terms in the past two weeks. To them, it seemed, the Sea of Tranquillity, which should be the dominant feature, was now, somehow, storm-tossed.

When Claudia left them after a perfunctory peck on the cheek, he turned to Tania and said, "I do love that woman!"

She could see that in him but, as Claudia had left, she wasn't seeing it in her. She couldn't see why he felt it necessary to tell her either, did he think she was going to come on to him? Even he, she thought, might be no more than a mere man. Nevertheless, it opened an opportunity, "When did you first know that?"

"There was something the first time I met her. Has she told you about that?"

"Only that it was at one of your parties. They were a little scandalous, weren't they?"

He smiled, "Not much different from your New York affairs, I shouldn't think."

"But you don't host them anymore. Why not?"

"I think that's largely to do with Claudia."

"Does she disapprove?"

He laughed, "Do you know, I've never asked her," now he seemed to hesitate, "has she said anything to you about them?"

"In general terms, yes, and you're right, they don't

sound much different from what I sometimes see here, but she's been very coy about herself and I haven't pushed to know," she smiled, "although she did warn me about Andy."

"Are you coping?"

"Physically, or emotionally?"

He laughed again, "Well, I suppose I mean emotionally, but I must admit it was sometimes entertaining to watch some ladies trying to cope. I've known a number of men who would have loved to try but Andy's not orientated that way."

"Well, he does have some preferences that are challenging, so I can answer your question about coping physically quite easily; just about, is the answer, but it seems to have become a favourite of mine," and they were relaxed enough to smile at each other. "On the other question though, I think I'm doing better than he is. We both got a little emotionally tied before he went back to Jen and that hurt a bit. I suppose I felt more for him than I'd felt for anyone, but it wasn't disabling when he went back, does that make sense?"

He suddenly looked very thoughtful, "I'm afraid it does. Shall I order some food?"

"Only if you promise that when the entrées are on the table and the wine has been served that you will pick that thread at exactly that point."

"You are where you are because I have the profoundest admiration for you, and it wouldn't occur to me for a millisecond that I could escape your scrutiny."

She smiled, "Then you may order. You can also have a thank you for the compliment. Do you know, the first one I ever had that I really valued, was from Claudia." He raised his eyebrows , "I'd found things pretty easy until then, at school and as a student, and then at work I was always," she hesitated, "not mistrustful exactly, but, when your father is chairman and principal shareholder, you always wonder where people are coming from, but she didn't know who I was, and it meant so much that she singled me out."

"She's a brilliant reader of people."

"She says the same about you…"

"I'll order food, but the implied but at the end of your sentence is another point we'll come back to."

She laughed, "OK, and I'd prefer light and fishy, please."

* * *

"So, have you spoken much to Andy lately?" she asked as soon as the butler left, having been reassured by Peter that they would manage everything themselves.

"Ha, I suppose I would have been disappointed if we'd not restarted the conversation at exactly the same position. *Zum wohl*," he raised his glass. She smiled and drank too. "I have, because he and Jen have worried me for some time. I'd always seen them as somewhat precarious, partly because she's so confused sexually. They do better when they accept it and relax."

"You know I'm going to ask you about Alphonse

378

later, don't you?"

He looked serious and shook his head slowly, "I suppose I knew I wouldn't be able to avoid that. I haven't committed to being open about everything, you know."

"I know that," she began eating and gestured to him to do the same, he seemed to hesitate, "but I'm staying here until I get answers, or until Claudia gets back," she smiled at him, "and then you'll have two of us to answer to." He groaned theatrically.

"We were talking about Andy and Jen," he said, she nodded while she ate, "their best times were when she had occasional lady partners. Andy has always been a little, shall we say, available, but, until he began seeing you, I'd not known him to get romantically afflicted."

"That's an interesting choice of word."

"I'm afraid it applies to two phases of my life and I suspect it's why we're sitting here this evening."

She paused, put down her fork and rubbed his hand lightly, "Well, I made that assumption too. And Andy and I are a foothill on this one, we'll get to the Himalayas later."

"I'm a Himalaya?"

"Of course you are! But first, Andy and I have to work together. I love being with him. But I don't want him unbalancing my life again. I know he's not with Jen, but I don't know truly if that's permanent."

"And if it were?"

"I have another relationship that's almost as important…"

379

"And less demanding?"

She smiled, "Exactly, and non-restrictive, so I just hope Andy's happy with what we have now."

"Is he aware of how you feel?"

"Of course."

He guffawed, "You know, you're probably the only person I know who can live like that. Well, you're the only person I can believe when you say something like that. Claudia always aspired to full openness, but I think that was a mistaken defensiveness."

"But now she has secrets?"

He stopped, and she couldn't tell if he was asking himself the question or deciding what to reveal. "Secrets are better than lies," he said slowly.

"I suppose I try to avoid both. Well, in personal relationships, but even I can see that a certain amount of discretion is sometimes necessary in business."

He laughed gently, the remark seemed to pull him out of the thoughts that had plainly preoccupied him, "Anyway, if you've found a stable equilibrium with Andy, I'll be delighted."

"What are the chances?"

"Over a year or two very good, I would have thought. Certainly, long enough for you to get my group into shape," he said jocularly.

"I never kidded myself it was about anything else."

Now he put his hand on hers, "You're far too wise already to crave simplicity or certainty. We fashion our lives out of unruly clay. I worry now that I'm feeling more threatened by the uncertainties, rather than being able to rejoice in them."

She held on to his hand as he attempted to withdraw it, "Is that what love's doing to you?"

"Well, it is one of the biggest uncertainties, isn't it? And we think it shouldn't be, you think that someone is there to catch you, then you worry they might not be."

"Are we in the Himalayas now? Are we talking about you, and maybe Alphonse? Tell me about his story, please. He's a man I barely know, and I'm glad I was warned. I could imagine a girl being silly. But then," she paused and squeezed his hand, "that must have happened many times with you."

He laughed, "Oh, fewer than you'd think," he stopped himself, pondered, and laughed again, "there's no way of commenting on that without sounding fearfully arrogant. False modesty's the best I can do. But you're quite right about him, quite a few do make that mistake, and he's interested enough to play along. But he had a relationship that was poisoned by lies."

"Like yours? Your first big love?"

"I'm fighting against drawing those parallels."

"Why?"

"Avoid facile explanations. They're always seductive, always deceptive. Look at every situation on its own merits."

She looked at him steadily, "That's not what you're doing, is it?"

"What do you mean?"

"Are you looking at the resort programme on its own merits?"

"I'm considering all the relevant factors," he seemed slightly indignant.

"Are you sure you're giving them all the appropriate weight. Why don't you worry that I'm just here trying to independently emulate my father," she paused, "actually, maybe I am at some subconscious level, but I'm feeling driven by the excitement of the thing in itself. If you asked me to go and work for Alphonse and help build that resort empire, I'd jump at it. It would be so exciting, and I assume, without knowing him, that that's how he feels," now she smiled teasingly at his troubled face, "It would be so… Dickinson."

He seemed to crumple into a large, smiling lump. "You, Tania Gunter," he was shaking his head, "are an absolute minx!"

She laughed, "I've never known what that word meant, but from now on I'm seeing it as a massive compliment."

"Which is exactly what you should do."

* * *

Claudia sat in front of her desk, looking more poised and relaxed than she had done for a long time, "I know we've got work to do, but what on earth did you say to him last night? Quick summary, please."

"I didn't have that big an impact, I'm sure."

"Oh, my dear, all cuddles and apologies and talk of just looking at the thing in itself. I wasn't feeling at my most coherent, Martha and I had a wonderful evening and may have…"

"A two-bottle evening?"

"Oh, and grappa. But anyway, he was buzzing when I got back, talking about wanting to move forward, apologising and, inevitably, eulogising about you. I could get quite suspicious…"

"Well, I'd rather keep a secret than tell a lie."

Claudia paused, then seemed suddenly captivated by that thought before, equally suddenly, bringing her attention back to Tania, "Well, we'll get back to it later, but he seems a changed man and he went off this morning with his old glow. So, thank you."

"I don't know what I've done, but you're very welcome. But, the Group, let me fill you in. I'm going to need your help on some next steps."

"Which ones?" Claudia looked puzzled.

"It will become clear when I've laid out the whole picture, but I may need help with my father. Frankly, he's embarrassing. I'm very happy having you as a friend. I absolutely do not want you as a step-mother," now Claudia laughed. "It's a seriously good proposition but he might need a little nudge, and who better…"

"I'd be very happy to help but you shouldn't worry about your other concern. I already know that his wife is utterly charming and the most beautiful woman in the South, and besides, who would take on those dreadful daughters?"

"Well, he's the easy bit…"

"Are we going to be talking Collins? Is that where this is headed?"

"Just listen to the whole pitch, then we can talk about whether you need to play an active role, but I will need to know more about Jack Stephens."

Claudia laughed again, "You don't even know whether he'll forgive you."

Tania paused and looked hard at her, "He's a bigger man than that, isn't he?"

Claudia nodded, "Yes, he's a bigger man than that."

Chapter 30

They'd agreed on no words when she arrived. He'd left the door unlatched and she'd turned up, as he expected, five minutes late. He stood when she came in and his arms welcomed her into a long embrace. One kiss was to be allowed, that was her proposal. But it was long and passionate and their whole bodies began responding. He knew he was growing, and her belly was plainly enjoying feeling the swelling. When his hands moved down to her ass, however, she eased herself away and nodded towards the sofa but then she caught sight of the bench, erected in the corner. He got an approving smile from her. But she was soon pulling his hand to guide him to the sofa. She casually reviewed the items on the coffee table, lifting the large dildo and looking quizzically at him. He lifted the tube of lube and smiled wickedly at her. She closed her eyes, smiled and nodded, but then lifted the large plug and turned to him again in mock consternation. He allowed himself a chuckle, but she looked at him sharply, as if he'd broken a rule, she waved an admonitory finger, but smiled and began removing her skirt.

He sat down to enjoy the slow striptease. It was a warm June day, but she'd still chosen to come wearing garter belt and stockings. He loved the view as she turned, and then made an exaggerated bend to drape the skirt over the arm of the chair.

Normally she would slip the panties down and kick them away but today, with her back to him, she lowered them all the way to her ankles and took them around each shoe in turn, making sure that he could see everything.

Now she turned towards him and curled her forefinger at him. He was puzzled. Now she lifted both hands; he stood up. She knelt down in front of him and began unbuckling his belt. He moved to stop her, she slapped his hand, he let her carry on, almost overbalancing as she took his pants from around his feet, his hands moved to her shoulders to steady himself. When his cock was free it was already half-erect — and it rapidly became stiff when it disappeared into her mouth.

But he knew she wouldn't tease him for too long. Soon she leaned back, gave him a wicked smile and pointed to the sofa behind him. He sat down and she draped herself across him — how he'd missed that. He stroked his hand across the gorgeous white flesh, sometimes squeezing to feel its supple firmness. It was an altogether perfect ass, he thought. Soon he had to slap it lightly on each side. She wiggled but made no noise. He slid his hands across her skin, down on to the thighs and then let a finger slide down into her crack. She tried to wriggle away. He slapped her very hard twice on the ass and then pushed the inside of one thigh to make her open her legs. He moved to get his knee on her mound, now she seemed to understand, and he felt the warm, soft, wet sensation of her clit rubbing herself on to him. He might not manage to come more than twice but he'd not encountered her limits before — and if she came six times before she reached the bench, she would still get a severe caning. Now he touched her briefly, lifted his fingers to his lips and licked them and began stroking her ass again, but now, slowly, he delivered more intense slaps and her cheeks began to glow. After twenty, with his hand stinging, he reached to the table to pick up plug and lube. She reached back and pulled her cheeks wide open. He stopped, stunned, he couldn't remember a more erotic gesture. He ran a finger lightly round her rim, she wiggled slightly and moaned. Now he squirted lube directly on to the anus, when he began rimming again, one finger slid easily in. She pushed her ass up to welcome him. He squirted more lube around his finger and pushed another finger easily in. It felt comfortably tight. He let his pinkie brush her clit. She wiggled more and in the moan this time there was an audible 'no, no, no'. He left her clit but pushed his fingers deeper. It was thrilling, feeling deep inside her, and more would be wonderful, so he withdrew slightly, squirted more lube and pushed in a third finger, now he was stretching, now she was gasping — but still pushing back. Should he try more? Some other time, and he had the momentary distraction of knowing he would want more; more times, more experiments. And the plug now was an experiment, for them anyway. He squirted lube on the tip. She seemed to squirm in anticipation and pulled her cheeks wide apart again. She gave a deep, deep sigh as he pushed it slowly in, she tensed slightly as the widest part pushed past the sphincter but then exhaled deeply with a satisfied groan when it was lodged inside her.

Now, almost languidly, he slapped her half a dozen more times and then reached for the paddle. He could feel her, expectant, as she now pushed her mound on to his knee. But he allowed himself a long, sensuous fondle of her cheeks again before he began to slap, slowly, rhythmically and listened to those familiar, satisfied moans after each strike.

He reached twenty, with the intensity rising, but found his target moving beneath him, she was gyrating her hips to make her clit grind on to his knee. He smiled, no need for his fingers, he began to apply the hardest of slaps and felt her, heard her, falling into an extreme of ecstasy, shouting, gasping, moving almost violently. He threw the paddle down, focused on making his knee stay in place for her and fondled her beautiful ass as she went through her peak and then slumped on to him, breathing very heavily.

* * *

"I don't know when we're allowed to speak…"

"Are you going to take that thing out of me?"

"I take it we're back into verbal," he said. She sighed. "That thing isn't coming out yet. It's there for me

388

too. I plan to enjoy that tight feeling of us both having you together. Now we know you're a naughty slut, you'll probably enjoy it."

She turned and looked up at him, smiled and then settled back down, ass uppermost. "I'll probably tell you more about my naughtiness. It seemed to earn me a very good caning last time. But if I let you come first, perhaps that won't be so good."

"That's a risk we'll all have to take. You must know by the bulge against your hip that he isn't going to wait much longer and I'm still, nominally, the dom."

"Yes," she said slowly, "but I do have a surprise for you later, if I'm staying on tomorrow."

"A surprise?"

"Yes, a surprise. Now, are you going to fuck me? Where do you want me, big boy? Doggy on the floor? Chair back?"

"Get in the bedroom, kneel on the bed!"

She got up on hands and knees, smiled at him and said, "Yes master."

* * *

"I came again," she said, as they lay naked in each other's arms, "I loved having both of you together. Are you going to take him out now? Am I allowed to take him out?"

"No, and no. I might decide to pull it just before the caning starts, we'll see if it interferes, but, right now, I'm feeling a little loved up and I don't want to move." But he did pull her gently towards him to feel her breasts squashing on to his chest. They kissed languorously again.

"Actually, I'm beginning to enjoy him being there."

"Good, because he's going to dinner like that with you tomorrow."

She pulled back and stared at him, and then laughed, "That's funny, I'm less surprised about having to go to dinner with a plug in my ass than by the fact that you've asked me."

"Oh, I haven't said *I'm* going to dinner with you. Maybe I'm sending you with some friends."

"Says Mister Loved Up!"

"You're right. I shouldn't be teasing. I do love you, you know."

"Enough to cane me later?"

"If you tell me more about your New York memories, yes, then I can cane you really hard."

"Then I'm going to want that very much, especially if I know I'm staying."

"And my surprise?"

"I don't want that threat to make you go easy on me. I got fucked twice as well as caned in New York, remember, this bad girl deserves some serious punishment."

"I agree, but what does the bad boy get tomorrow?"

"I think you're going to like it. You'll be on the bench, and I have a strap-on. I seriously want to fuck you too."

"I can't tell if you're serious, or just angling for a harder caning."

She smiled, "I think you'll find we're both sitting uncomfortably at dinner tomorrow."

Chapter 31

Claudia hoped this would be the final step in what had been an extraordinary month. It would certainly be the hardest.

She was missing Alphonse, he'd been almost all the time in the Far East since Peter had agreed to the purchase of the chain and the other sites. He'd flown back for a few days to work on the London sales and that had given them an afternoon in his apartment. She loved his tenderness.

She had no idea whether Peter knew. She thought he'd probably guessed but he'd been lovely with her since New York and she'd rediscovered her old feeling for him. And if they weren't quite really in love, it was still a lovely relationship, and they found it possible again to have fun in some of the old ways. Once the tensions and the uncertainties had subsided, she found that self again, the one Peter had helped her find. And if she had to live with a few secrets, well, she was confident enough to do that now.

But, meeting Jack again? That would be a challenge, she'd realised from her reactions when Tania had first asked her, and the answer to 'why do you need me?' — 'because he's asked to meet you', had left her even more unsettled.

Even Peter's rediscovered calm had seemed to wobble at that, but at least they were easy enough with it to take it to bed with them and solve it with words and cuddles.

Temporarily, anyway.

But, according to Tania, Jack was back with Lavinia and when Tania reassured her that that was a solid relationship, she felt relieved — but honest enough with herself to realise that it would still not be simple.

The weekend in Atlanta had been wonderful. They'd had a full business day on the Friday, with Greg there and his finance head, spending the morning convincing Arthur of the new arrangements, helped a great deal by David, who seemed to her to have grown a lot, and he and Tania seemed to be very relaxed with each other at dinner that evening. Martha had flown in to join them and the dinner was almost magical with her two favourite raconteurs in full flow. They were wonderful men, Peter and Arthur, each giving each other space for their copious stories and bringing everyone else in by turns, even coaxing contributions from David. The men had more work with Tania in the morning. "You and I would just be doubling up," was Peter's comment when she'd asked if she should join them, "I'm sure you'll have more fun with Samantha and Martha." And she had done, enormously so.

But that was three weeks ago. Now she was in DC again, being driven to Collins.

"You're nervous, aren't you?"

"Not helped by you making that comment for the fifth time."

"Oops, snappy too!" and it was impossible not to laugh with Tania.

"All right, but part of me wishes he'd just told you to fuck off, as he should have done."

"Oh, everybody forgives me!"

"Even David, apparently."

"Especially David."

"Tania, you didn't, you haven't!"

"No," she said emphatically, but then added, "but I might do."

"I think you have enough to deal with young lady."

"I have to agree you're right there. But what about you. And don't go all enigmatic on me."

Claudia settled more deeply into her seat as the familiar buildings on the airport road rolled by, "I'm staying enigmatic. I've got enough to worry about with your fucking Jack Stephens meeting."

"Intriguing though, isn't it, although I really do have to say, he seems very into Lavinia."

"And I'm very happy for both of them."

"Oh, boss, said with real feeling."

Claudia realised she'd spoken with an edge, "No, honestly, I am — and I'm feeling very content myself, thank you."

Tania laughed, "Just a little enigmatic."

Claudia smiled, "Yes, just a little enigmatic."

They arrived early. Claudia had planned that, although she'd been ambivalent about it, but she knew she'd have to meet some old faces and catch up with news. It helped that Jack was tied up in a meeting and that his corner was empty. Tania found a desk and busied herself, as she always did; away from the banter and her interesting love life, the woman worked extremely hard.

But she gathered Claudia at Sarah's desk at five to. "Sorry to interrupt, but we're on at eleven."

"Oh, don't mind me," said Sarah, "I'm just thrilled to catch up, thanks for stopping by," and she hugged Claudia and kissed her.

"Do you know who's in on this?" asked Claudia as they walked across the office.

"Davis, you know," said Tania, "then he has joint COOs and his finance man. Do you know them?"

"Davis, of course, but the COO job was Saunders and he got fired," they stood near Jack's PA. Claudia turned to her, she'd been the first person Claudia had spoken to when they arrived, "Do you know who's joining us, Sally?"

"Davis, Rick Barnard, Robert and Oliveira. They'll be ready very soon," she lowered her voice, "I think Mr Stephens quite likes the idea, it's the others who need convincing, it's a new thought for them."

Claudia smiled, "Thank you very much."

And then, suddenly there he was, standing beside them, "Hello guys, thank you so much for coming, do you want to come through?" A shake of the hand for Tania, a light peck on the cheek for Claudia, like an old friend you'd only seen last week, she thought — too hasty, concealing is revealing — and that applied to her own feelings.

The others followed in quickly and introductions were made.

"I've given the guys your paper, Tania, but, like we agreed, I think it's best you walk them through it and let them ask questions where they wish."

There would have been a time when Claudia would have been nervous, but she'd never known anyone put arguments so cogently as Tania could. She'd been convinced by the idea as she thought more about it over the preceding months and it made so much sense that, if it wasn't to be Collins, they would find another partner to begin with. Even Arthur had come on board quite quickly and she'd been expecting more resistance there.

It was now a well-honed presentation, but these were bright people, well, perhaps not Davis, she thought, but he wasn't asking much. The younger guys, the Brazilian and the Chinese, were very sharp; friendly, but picking the important propositions apart but always, it seemed, from the perspective of trying to make the idea work.

"Well, guys, we wanted to form an opinion by lunchtime and we're there now, do you want to offer a view?"

"I'll start," said Robert brightly, "because it won't affect my regions in the beginning, but I'd be looking forward to it. I like the technology and it would take layers and inefficiencies out of the system. I'd go to the next stage."

"Oliveira?" said Jack, "You're the one it hits first."

Oliveira was slower than his partner, apparently more considered, "I like the look of it. I guess I'm apprehensive. I can see the advantages, but the implementation might give us problems. Well, it would, let's face it, but that shouldn't stop us."

"Good, Rick?"

"The numbers look good in principle," he turned to Tania, "Would you mind accepting a compliment for one of the most concise presentations I've ever seen, and in the paperwork," he waved a file, "I could find the answer to almost every question I had. I think Oliveira's point is a good one, but I can't think of anyone I'd trust more to get it right quickly."

Claudia was almost blushing on Tania's behalf. She appeared to accept the remarks coolly and politely, but Claudia knew how she'd be feeling.

"Davis?"

"Well, it's an organisational problem to manage."

"Insurmountable?" asked Jack, with barely concealed impatience. That hadn't changed, thought Claudia.

Davis shook his head.

"OK, I guess we move on to the next stage. Thank you very much, guys, it looks like a big step forward. May I echo what Rick said, Tania? That was splendid, it gives me a lot of confidence."

"Thank you," she said, just managing to keep her cool.

"OK, guys, that's it, thank you," and they began packing away and leaving until Jack alone was left with them. Now his composure seemed to fray a little. "I wonder, Tania, if I could have Claudia for a moment?"

"Of course," she said, and packed her things, "I'll be at that desk when you're ready."

"Sure."

"She's brilliant," he said when she'd left. But then he seemed to struggle with what to say next. "Sit down a moment again, please," but even then, when they'd settled, he was still hesitant. "Did you ever work it out? Everything that happened to us?"

"Not really. Maybe we just didn't catch each other, Jack. We were both focussing on other things."

"Maybe it's not love, if you don't do that."

She waited, did he have any more to say? "Is that what you believe?"

He shrugged and looked... what was it? Sad? Or just thoughtful? "Nah, it was definitely love."

The surprise was that he'd said it. She knew it. "Still is, a bit, isn't it?"

Now he did look sad and shook his head, "That doesn't help anybody."

"Is that what you believe? Sorry to repeat myself."

He smiled — "Nah, I'm glad it lingers on."

"Me too." She smiled, stood up and kissed him when he stepped towards her.